NEW VOICES

A Collection of Soviet Short Stories

RADUGA
PUBLISHERS
MOSCOW

Translated from the Russian
Compiled by *Yuri Lopusov*
Foreword by *Oleg Shestinsky*
Designed by *Alexander Berdov*

ГОЛОСА МОЛОДЫХ

Рассказы и повести

молодых советских писателей

На английском языке

Printed in the Union of Soviet Socialist Republics

$\Gamma \dfrac{4\,702010200-464}{031\,(05)-85}\,009-85$

ISBN 5-05-000013-0

CONTENTS

THE PATH TO MATURITY

The prose of beginning Soviet writers develops according to its own internal aesthetic laws as a complex phenomenon within the realm of art. This prose is born of the talent of young people who are active participants in the dynamic life of their country and who are attempting to comprehend the social and moral spirit of their people. As writers, they are trying to analyse the main current of the march of time. Therefore, we have good reason to say that this prose reflects the life of society, for it outlines the psychological and moral parameters of the contemporary individual, presenting the thoughtful reader with profound questions of our social development.

Each new generation wants first of all to have the possibility of examining reality from the perspective of its own times, based on its own emotional and moral experience. And there is always something novel and interesting about such a vision of life. A new concrete view of history emerges, and this view, along with the aesthetic comprehension of life allows the young artist to create works possessing features which have not appeared earlier in literature. Therefore, the writing of these young authors always attracts the serious attention of our society, for it enables the reader to see the world through the eyes of the new generation in whose works are signs of the social renewal of life.

In speaking of prose by young Soviet writers, we mean those authors who will constitute the main body of Soviet national literatures at the end of the 1980s and beginning of the 90s. We must keep clearly in mind the reality which will confront those writers 10 or 15 years from now. This will be a time of further technological progress, of solving ecological problems, of increased moral demands to be placed upon art in general. And given the richness and intensity of social life, art—literature in particular—will have the right to exist only to the extent that it is commensurate with the other powerful manifestations of the human spirit.

In examining the features of prose by young Soviet writers, we must take heart in the fruitful tendencies which have appeared in recent years.

What are these tendencies? Briefly, they may be characterised as follows: beginning writers treat ever more persistently and profoundly themes of immense social significance and the basic problems which confront our society. They are more analytic and are increasingly interested in moral issues.

The pieces included in the present collection are extraordinarily varied in style, vision of the world, and scope of phenomena dealt with. But they have one feature that unites them, and that is the common civic and moral position expounded by each of the authors. This is felt first and foremost in the seriousness with which these young writers treat art and life, and in their rejection of triviality and art for art's sake.

An awareness of the past, present, and future of their homeland, and the way historical traditions have become interwoven with the new, socialist way of life; the spiritual maturing of contemporary man; the complex interrelations between the city and the countryside, between the world of nature and urban civilisation—these are but a few of the major themes dealt with by our young writers in whose works are combined the resolution of social conflicts and a profound attention to the inner world of the individual.

From purely autobiographical sequences by people with limited life experience to the recognition of the endless variety of human characters and fates and the comprehension of the profoundest aspects of the lives of their people—this is the path along which young Soviet prose develops today.

We must emphasise the multinational character of the prose by young Soviet writers. It is sufficient to mention the fact that Soviet literature is presently published in 78 languages of the peoples of the USSR. Prominent among the national literatures are those of the Ukrainian, Byelorussian, Georgian, Armenian, Estonian, Kazakh, Tatar, and Karelian peoples. However, none of these ethnic literatures are isolated from one another or from the mainstream of Soviet literature as a whole. Quite the contrary: their constant dialectical interaction results in a synthesis of the best, most forward-looking trends which exist in every culture found in our country. Young writers are also making their contribution to the development of Soviet multinational literature, bringing to it the particular mode of thinking of their own peoples and unique blends of local colouring provided by the customs and traditions of their respective ethnic groups.

This collection should not only give foreign readers an idea of the writing of the new literary generation in the Soviet Union but also acquaint them with present-day life in our society, providing the readers with a fuller understanding of the spiritual and moral essence of our people and the world of their cares and aspirations.

Oleg Shestinsky

Nikolai Gladyshev

COLD AUTUMN

Nikolai Gladyshev was born in
1949 in Ryazan Region in
Central Russia. He worked as a
carpenter, a loader, a Young
Pioneer leader at a school, on the
staff of the regional newspaper,
and served in the Soviet Army.
In 1976, he graduated from the
Gorky Literary Institute. His
writings were published in the
magazine *Selskaya Molodyozh*
and in the literary miscellany
Serdtse Rodiny.

The wind was buffeting the log walls. Cold and wet, it would roll round the back of the fence girding, die down for a moment and then, with new-found fury hurl rain-drops at the windows of the cottage, breaking off twigs and lashing at the trees. There was no electricity to be had that evening, somewhere the wires must have been brought down, so now there was nothing for it but to light up the kerosene lamp.

It was all the same to old Semyon though: books were something he did not go in for and he could smoke just as well in the dark. Taking his time about it, he tore a strip from the newspaper, rolled a cigarette and drew in the smoke hungrily. Then he coughed for a long time, heaving his whole chest and cursing the tobacco he had bought at the local market. His cat had appeared from out of nowhere and now rubbed its thin ribs up against one of his boots: then it wandered slowly over to the stove, tottering as it went. "Old age has hit you hard, too," said Semyon with a wry, weary smile.

With a groan of pain he straightened his hunched back and helped the cat up on to the stove. The cat who had been rather unfriendly and mischievous in his youth, was now only too happy to respond to being stroked. He gave a contented purr and then settled down quietly. Time and time again Semyon's neighbours had told him what to do with the creature: "Why d'you still keep that old cat? Go and dump him somewhere far away, so that he can't find his way back any more!"

Semyon answered with no more than a gloomy silence: dumping the cat was easy enough, but for the

9

time being there was at least another living creature under his roof, and without him?.. For three years now he had been on his own. It was not all that long really, yet it seemed a hundred years ago that he had followed his wife's coffin to the grave.

Now he had to think things out and decide about his future, yet he kept putting it off. While he smoked, the smell of the cigarette seemed to drive away his gloomy thoughts but as soon as he had taken his last puff, his heart was once again weighed down with worries. No, it looked as if there was nowhere he could take refuge from those thoughts, nothing to hide behind.

Semyon pulled off his boots, blew out the lamp and climbed up onto the stove-ledge. He lay down on the cold bricks and let out a deep hopeless sigh. Right away all the doubts started flooding back: should he have ever set things in motion in the first place?.. For the very next day he had to go to the neighbouring village and propose to his future bride. God knows, bride seemed a stupid word—him well past sixty and all! — but what else could he do? Semyon let out a moan and clutched at his chest: as if in anticipation of disaster there was a dull pain gnawing at his heart. Yet he could not go on like this, he had to make up his mind. No two ways about it...

Everyone had come along to the hay-making as if it was a special occasion. The muzhiks' merry shouts filled the air as they walked along clanking their scythes together, while the womenfolk, their voices husky after the long ride, now again struck up little ditties to the strains of a harmonica... Meanwhile the young people were rushing down to the river to bathe.

Semyon ran on down behind them but stopped in his tracks dazzled by the whiteness of the clover and the daisies, which made his hands start to tingle in his eagerness to start work, work! He could hardly wait for the moment when he would be allotted his patch. Then he took up his scythe at just the right angle, made a wide sweep and then at one fell swoo-oo-oop the succulent blades came tumbling down on the stubble.

He went on mowing in this nimble way for a long time, relishing the feel of his muscles rippling up and down, yet by midday he was starting to feel tired all the same. Far behind him could be seen the white flecks of the men's shirts and the dashes of colour made by the women's headscarves. Semyon grinned with self-satisfaction; there was no catching up with him! He took up his scythe again and then started in surprise—in front of him a tall girl was plying her scythe. Her smooth sweeping movements looked almost lazy—yet after each one the freshly cut blades of grass fell in steep waves.

"So, she thinks she can beat me does she! " smirked Semyon scornfully and braced himself to begin mowing once more, harder than ever.

When he was near enough to see the patches of sweat on the back of her blouse and her sunburnt legs, wide apart to set off the sweep of the scythe, the girl turned round to give him a glimpse of her laughing face and after that the strokes of her scythe grew even wider and stronger.

Semyon was never one to be work-shy. When he

11

took up his scythe, it seemed to become part of him and from the side he used to look like an enormous spider quickly and nimbly spinning its web. Seeing now that unless he tried harder still he could very well end up the loser, Semyon tucked his head into his shoulders and got on with it, squatting down on half-bent legs after each stroke. The handle of the scythe creaked in the grip of his enormous hands, but each time he straightened up, that familiar back was there drawing him on. Red with shame Semyon mustered all his remaining strength and at last managed to draw even with the girl.

"You know a thing or two about mowing! " he gasped, all hot from his exertions.

"When all's said and done, it's not as if I was born in a town," she answered with proud calm. The top buttons of her blouse were unfastened and Semyon could see the drops of sweat trickling down her neck and vanishing between her breasts. The girl caught his glance, yet left the buttons as they were, merely throwing him a defiant smile.

"How did you turn up here? It's only the men who do the mowing! " said Semyon in happy astonishment.

"There are six of us at home, all girls! And somebody's got to feed the cow..."

They finished the patch together. They worked along side by side, every now and then taking a sidelong glance at each other. Every time they stopped for a little rest, a shyness he had never known before came over Semyon and, trying not to look at Darya, he would grip his scythe more tightly than ever, breathing heavily.

12

In the evening fires began to blaze on the open ground to one side of the cart-track lighting up the tired faces of the collective farmers with a pale yellow glow. Ragged shadows danced in the twilight beyond the fires. The appetising smell of hot gruel mingled with the sweet scent of lungwort lingering in the air above the meadows.

Darya had just come back from the river, where she had been splashing about in the warm water for a long time. Plaiting her long hair as she walked along with her head thrown back a little, Darya sauntered past the fire by which Semyon was lying. The vitality and freshness that wafted about her was too much for Semyon, who rose to his feet and blocked her path.

"Shall we go for a stroll perhaps? It's such a wonderful night..."

Darya looked him straight in the eye but replied gently: "No, Semyon, we have to get up early tomorrow. We should start mowing while the dew's still wet."

Semyon's gaze followed her for a long time, till the night had swallowed her up in its shadows. He lay down to sleep under a hay-cart using some grass, that had barely started to wilt, for a pillow. The flames of the fires were no longer dancing and all that was left of them was the faint glow of the embers. It was as if someone had deliberately scattered glow-worms over the meadow, there were so many of them. It was warm and quiet, only the horses were munching away at their hay in determined fashion, and then far away beyond the river some men could be heard light-heartedly bickering. It became harder and harder to lie still: so he got up and wandered past the shelters of branches but once beyond the ravine, he stopped, hesitating, wondering where he was going and why.

Overhead the stars seemed almost threateningly near. Semyon gave a shiver. For some reason he had never really noticed them before. Yet now the stars were winking at him like so many juicy autumn apples. They mocked him like the eyes of someone he knew. Then Semyon suddenly realised what he was doing: he was looking for Darya! The thought made him feel all confused.

The next morning Semyon picked out a patch for Darya and himself and took up his position beside her. It was as if he had never worked with such zeal before, and he kept trying to mow more than his share so as to make her task easier. He did so unintentionally as it were, but Darya soon noticed and said: "There's no need, Semyon, I'll cope."

From that day on they were always seen together. The muzhiks and the women of the village would exchange knowing smiles, but Semyon did not mind. Whatever he was doing, he always tried to keep an eye on Darya. If they were making a haystack Semyon would start hurling aloft with his fork enough hay for two ordinary men—all for Darya! When they went bathing, he would dive from the steepest banks—just for her. He felt now that no-one, that no-one at all would ever be able to part them.

Semyon hardly seemed to have feasted his eyes on Darya and talked to her properly before the mowing was over.

Hot July with its thunder storms and lush meadow

grasses came and went, yet for Semyon everything was only just beginning. Every evening he would jauntily walk the five miles to the next village. Darya would be waiting for him at the edge of the village and together they would go over to the local club-house or down to the river. They would sit down somewhere on the bank under a spreading bird-cherry tree and watch the early stars floating on the dark surface of the water or listen to the ripe apples dropping to the ground in the near-by gardens that sloped right down to the river. For them everything about those evenings had a special secret meaning all of its own.

Semyon caught himself thinking about Darya all the time. He would stop in his tracks and, lips apart in concentration, he would recall down to the very last detail—her face, her walk, her words; he would remember it all with a happy, sheepish smile.

"What's up with you, Semyon? You're not quite yourself these days, as if someone has been hitting you over the head with a hammer! " the other villagers used to say teasingly.

He would say nothing, just go on his way. He felt he could not bear it any longer. Semyon tried to talk about it all to Darya, but she saw everything in a humorous light. So he came straight to the point: "Let's get married, shall we?.. I'm like a rooster running round a hen in circles. I can't look people in the eye anymore."

Darya had been waiting for him to come out with that for a long time, yet she felt herself blush—the words had been so direct, they had taken her by surprise.

They decided to hold the wedding in the autumn after the harvest. Then out of the blue—WAR! The first few days flashed by, seeming totally unreal: the recruiting office, the hurried preparations to leave, the train packed with soldiers... There was not even time to say goodbye to Darya properly, to tell her all that filled his aching heart.

Yet even out in the trenches, during the short breathing spaces in the fighting he used to think about Darya, he used to write her letters, and whenever he received an answer he was like a dog with two tails. He could have come to terms with it all... But then one day during an offensive Semyon was shell-shocked. He had fallen down on his own ground, but when he came round he found himself a prisoner.

Only then did he grasp what a terrible word PRISONER really was. He tried to escape, but what hope was there of getting away with dogs on your heels?

Four years later Semyon returned home. He came back with a medal, his lungs shot through. While he was happily answering his mother's endless questions, what he was really thinking about all the time was Darya. He decided to go and see her that very day, without further ado. Even when he had been paying her his very first visits, the road had never seemed as long as it did on that day. Three times he had to sit down at the roadside, listening to the bubbling and whistling going on in his chest. Then, after taking a gulp of fresh spring air, he slowly pulled himself to his feet and trudged on.

Yet the moment he caught sight of Darya's little

house, his feet seemed to grow wings. He flung the
door open with a bang—"Here I am at last! "—and
backed away. Darya was holding a baby to her breast.

"But you promised to wait! " gasped Semyon.

Darya sat there wide-eyed in astonishment, staring
at him without saying a word. At last in a frightened,
unbelieving whisper she came out with: "You're
alive?.."

"What did *you* think then?" asked Semyon bitterly.
"You've already buried me I suppose. Got a bit ahead
of yourself..."

"Alive?! " whispered Darya again, deaf to the cries
of her child, who was almost choking with sobs.
"But Andrei said he'd seen you die with his very own
eyes. In a bomb attack."

"Who the devil's this Andrei?"

"My husband."

A man with hunched shoulders appeared in the
doorway. "What's happening?" he asked in surprise.

Semyon realised that this must be Andrei. "So
you had me killed off, did you?! " shouted Semyon
and went out slamming the door loudly behind him.

He didn't remember how he got home again. While
he had been away, his mother had spread out all her
meagre reserves and called in the neighbours to celebrate her son's return. By this time they were crowding
into the tiny house, waiting for Semyon to appear.
Yet without even looking at them Semyon went to the
bedroom and collapsed on to his bed. All at once,
just as at the moment he had been shell-shocked, his
eyes clouded over and a familiar wave of nausea filled
his throat. Oh Darya, Darya! What the hell had he

struggled back those thousands of miles for, only to find this?..

His mother slipped cautiously into the room and touched his shoulder: "P'haps you'll come out, Semyon?" she asked. "Everyone's come over..."

With a great effort he took a grip on himself, rose and came out. He gave such short answers to all the questions and was so reluctant to talk to his relatives and neighbours that it made it seem like a horribly difficult chore that he resented.

The two days that followed were like a waking nightmare for Semyon: he did not know whether he was coming or going. If his mother asked him to do something he got up to see to it without saying a word, otherwise he just lay there all day staring at the ceiling. So as to try and forget himself, he set about covering the shed with straw. At first he did it grudgingly, but then, sick after all those years for work on the farm, he became absorbed in his task almost without noticing it. Then he was caught unawares by the thought of Darya as real, as if she was standing right there before him, not the Darya he had just met, careworn and thin, but the beautiful girl he had known and whose image he had carried in his heart through all the long war years. He leant on his fork, shutting his eyes, and only then did he manage to drive the vision away.

He could not stand just sitting around at home any longer: his mother and the neighbours simply would not let up with their questions about what was going to happen next. He went to the farm office and asked for a job as a carpenter, thinking to himself that if he was out and about with other people he would forget and the memories would fade.

The whole of that summer, he was putting up houses and cow-sheds with other men like himself who had just come back from the war. From morning to night his axe just seemed to dance in his hands. During breaks from work Semyon used to fall over on to the wood shavings, coughing and wheezing painfully.

"You'll do yourself in, Semyon," chided the other men gloomily. Yet all he did was just take up his axe again, trying to drive away grim thoughts.

Once on a cold September evening Semyon was sitting in his house at the table sharpening his saw: the next day they were all due to go and fetch timber for the new school building. Drops of rain were rattling against the windows, leaving long trails of water on the panes. The dry warmth of the house made him all the more aware of the miserable wet outside. Suddenly, there came a timid knock on the door. Semyon put his saw down and listened again: had he just imagined it? There was another knock. Semyon swung the door open and there on the threshold stood Darya with her baby in her arms. The water was dripping off her wet hair, and her imploring eyes were filled with hope. Semyon leant back against the wall to steady himself and looking her straight in the eye, unblinking, he waited.

"I've come, Semyon," she said struggling with her words. "Will you let me in?"

"What have you come for? To show me your pity? I don't need your pity, I tell you! " At last he came to his senses again and slammed the door in her face.

2*

As he was trying to light up his cigarette he broke half a packet of matches. He sensed that Darya was still on the porch. People do not walk five miles just for the fun of it. The wind died down for a moment and then a real downpour hurled itself at the roof. It immediately became dark in the room. Semyon pictured to himself how Darya would trudge home wearily along the water-logged road back to her village, and unable to hold back any more he opened the door.

"Come in. At least till the rain's over."

Darya came timidly into the house. She halted on the threshold, not daring to take a step further. Semyon noticed this and raised his voice: "Come in and put the baby down! I'll find you something to change into, you're soaked to the skin." He walked over to the stove and called: "Ma, Ma, have you got any clothes handy?"

The skinny old woman climbed down from the stove. Groaning and complaining as she went about the task, she brought out a new blouse and skirt from the trunk.

While Darya was changing, Semyon brought in some firewood, and his mother began to light the stove in the bedroom. They were alone then for a moment, looked at each other and then turned away. Darya sat down on the bench and whispered in a voice that was scarcely audible: "I've left him, Semyon. I can't hold out any more, after all he lied to me. He kept on saying—'Marry me, Semyon's finished!'" At that she slumped forward on to the table and began to sob.

Semyon stood there in front of her, not knowing

what he should do. Two feelings fought within him, pity and resentment: "You're crying now, but what were you doing before?"

Realising probably what he must have been thinking, Darya got up and without saying a word began to put her things together.

"Where d'you think you're off to, now that night's falling?" Semyon said so as to keep her back. "You can stay, there's room enough..."

All sorts of things happened in their life together, but there was one thing Semyon could not forgive Darya—the stranger's child. He kept trying to get his own back on Darya almost without being aware of it. Sometimes without saying a word, for a whole week, or even two, he would go off with his work-mates to do some carpentering in neighbouring villages. Darya would grow haggard from worry but would meet him without a word of complaint, as if nothing had happened. Such meekness on her part infuriated Semyon even more. If they had had children of their own then perhaps Semyon could have come to terms with it all but they did not. Once again the war had robbed him of happiness. Every day he used to trudge off to work, downcast, unable to look other people in the eye. In helpless fury he would hurl his axe at the logs. Chips of wood and drops of sweat would be flying in all directions. Before the other men had finished chopping one log, Semyon would have a whole pile ready.

Yet he still could not drive away his despair and bitterness. He would come hurtling into the house drunk, swear and break plates and dishes, and then start using his fists.

Darya put up with it all, only too well aware of her own guilt before him. Yet one day she could hold herself in check no longer: "If you start laying into me now, Semyon, I'm leaving, you can be sure of it! "

Semyon looked at her and started back in surprise: there before him stood the Darya of years gone by, the proud young woman he had almost forgotten. The fist he had brandished aloft froze still in mid air and he stepped back, dumb-founded. That was the turning-point. It was as if scales had fallen from his eyes: what was he torturing her for, what for?.. He tried to look for a way of making up to Darya for everything, but whenever he thought he would embark on something he would find that there was nothing left to do. Darya used to go about all her household tasks so quietly you did not even notice her, everywhere was clean and tidy.

Some time way back she had asked Semyon to dig out a cellar, but he had kept finding excuses. Now Semyon remembered this and brought out his spade. By the end of the day he had dug out enough earth to make a hole the size of a well and, after that, he had to take to his bed for three whole days.

Darya treated him with herbal tea and scolded him saying: "You knew you shouldn't go at it like that. Look at the state you've got yourself into..."

It was then as he lay there in bed that for the first time in three years Semyon noticed how orderly the house was, and that little Maria was the spitting image of Darya with the same fair hair and shapely build.

He noticed this and felt ashamed somehow. From that day on he always tried to bring home some little present for the girl and he began playing with her. It would have been difficult to say who felt happier about it all—Semyon himself, Darya or her daughter.

Things were very different when it came to Semyon's mother. From the very day when Darya had appeared on the threshold the old woman had not said a word to her—her lips were sealed! Whatever Darya did to appease her she would just look on gloomily, determined not to be reconciled.

Night after night Semyon's shirt would be wet from Darya's tears. "I'd find it easier if she were to shout at me," she used to complain through her sobs, "but she just sits there refusing to say anything. The food sticks in your throat."

Semyon was at a loss: he could not please both of them. He felt sorry for his mother, but for Darya, too. He tried to have things out with his mother but all she would say in a barely audible whisper was: "You ought to be ashamed of yourself—taking up with a married woman! Aren't there enough girls in the village?! "

Till the end of her days his mother refused to be reconciled. Even on her death-bed, when Darya sat down at her side, only for a brief second was there a sign in the old woman's face that she was ready to relent, but then it vanished as quickly and she turned her face to the wall without saying anything.

Semyon did not even notice how quickly the years flew past. Maria had long since got married and gone to live in the North, he and Darya grew old and bent and seemed to have shrunk somehow. Semyon had lost all his old cheer. He had retired a long time ago and the villagers now called him Semyon Ivanovich. His walk was now heavy as if he had to root up his feet from the earth after every step.

On warm summer days he and Darya used to sit out on their porch. If one of the neighbours dropped in Semyon liked to go in for tall stories. "Yesterday I lifted thirty sacks of potatoes from the allotment," he would declare after a pregnant pause, proudly squaring his thin shoulders.

"Well I never! " the gullible neighbour would reply.

"God is my witness! "

"Give over now!" Darya would interrupt him in midflight. "It was thirteen, not thirty."

"We-ell, perhaps I did make a slight mistake," Semyon would admit blushing, and then when they were alone again he would grumble at her all out of sorts: "Darya! Don't let me down in front of other people. I won't have it."

Darya knew that he would start reproaching her now and so she would always hurriedly suggest: "Never mind Semyon. Let's talk about something else and read Maria's letter."

She would bring out the envelope and after fixing her spectacles on her nose she would begin to read. Darya by then had changed beyond recognition: her nose looked longer, and her cheeks were like grey parchment and all sunken. She had begun to look like an owl.

Yet none of that would have really mattered if it had not been for the fact that Semyon had recently begun to notice how Darya seemed to be fading away before his very eyes. She would lie down more often and would groan in the night.

"What's aching?" Semyon would ask, climbing down from the stove.

"Everything," Darya would gasp mournfully.

She did not want to go to hospital. "Forget it, I feel better at home anyway." One night she called her husband over to her bedside, and then in a very ordinary matter-of-fact tone she said: "It's all over, Semyon, I'm dying. Write to Maria and tell her to come, and now give me a drink of water."

When he came back with the water Darya was lying there with her mouth open, clutching at the blanket with one of her bony hands.

The next morning he sent Maria a telegram and waited for three days but for some reason no-one came down from the North...

The sky had been covered with grey clouds since dawn and squalls of rain were coming down. The road that had not had a chance to dry out for days was now awash and overflowing its sides like a river its banks, beyond the fences and over into the ditches and allotments. Men from the village carried Darya's coffin with careful concentration, trying not to miss their footing and to keep in step with each other. Old women dressed in black kept on coming out to join the procession, following after the coffin with the stern expression on their faces that the occasion demanded.

His wife's death seemed to make Semyon take even deeper root in the earth. His cheeks sagged, and his head seemed unsteady as if too big for the neck that carried it. His friends and neighbours looked at him with pity. He kept his gaze doggedly to the ground and his eyes were dry and bloodshot.

At the cemetery Semyon gave his wife a farewell kiss on her cold forehead and quickly stepped back from the coffin. He still could not believe that she had gone away for ever.

At home, while there were still people bustling about, Darya's absence did not make itself so keenly felt. Everyone seemed to be sharing in the tragedy. Yet when the wake was over and the house gradually emptied, Semyon's eye was caught by the mirror hung with a black shawl and the clock with hands that were not moving any more. It was only now that he grasped it: he was quite alone! His very own house had turned into something hateful. Feeling like a stranger in his own home, he slumped forward against the door-post and burst into tears. Then he made his way out into the street and staggered over to the neighbours.

Silent and with a face like stone, he sat in their house till midnight and when they started to go to bed, he got up to leave.

Without bothering to put the light on he lay all night in a heap on the stove-ledge, his eyes wide open. It was strange: his mind seemed to be empty of thoughts, there was just a heavy weight on his chest and his mouth felt dry. Yet at the break of dawn the lump came back into his throat and he went straight over to the neighbours again.

At first they felt sorry for him, but then he began to get on their nerves. They started to make fun of him openly. He noticed what they were up to at once, and looking gloomier than ever, locked himself into his cold empty house. Yet he had to find some outlet for his misery and for the first time in years Semyon turned to the bottle.

First of all he squandered all his money, then his pension proved inadequate and he started selling clothes. One day while he was going through the cupboard he came across his wife's fine fluffy woollen shawl. He picked it up, then pulled his hand back quickly and whispered through his teeth in desperation: "It's come to this! .."

After that he stopped drinking once and for all. Yet he kept on being overcome by bouts of depression. He kept on seeing Darya at night, calling him over to her, and then he would wake up groaning. He tried to drive away these dreams, yet the vision of Darya always seemed to be there before him. Then Semyon would climb down from the stove, turn on the light and roll himself a cigarette. So it went on night after night.

In the morning he would walk out into the road and wait patiently in the hope that someone would come along. So as to waylay whoever of his neighbours happened to chance by that bit longer, Semyon would ask him for a smoke, although he had a pouch full of homegrown tobacco, and would ask how life was treating him. Yet so many of the people in the village were busy; they just gave him the briefest of answers and hurried past. If anyone was prepared to stop for a chat, Semyon would pour out all his troubles and try to come out with all that had been on his mind since the day before.

He could not use the excuse of a smoke when

27

talking to the village women, but he had something up his sleeve when it came to them as well. He would thrust Maria's letter into their hand and ask: "Do read it for me, I'm getting old and can't make any of it out."

They would read it to him and, although he knew its contents by heart, he would always exclaim as if in astonishment: "Just imagine it, Maria wants me to go and live with her. It would be nice of course, but what would I want to leave here for? My mother and Darya are both buried here."

Yet he could not bear living on his own any longer. His heart was giving him trouble at night more and more often now and he had to lie down on the bench for hours on end. Each thought that came to him would be gloomier than the one before: "What if I have to take to my bed all of a sudden? There wouldn't even be anyone to bring me a mug of water..."

It was then that the idea of marrying first came to him. The thought frightened him at first: "It's mad! What on earth made me think of it!? It was only yesterday that they had carried Darya to the cemetery, there hasn't even been time for the dust on my boots to be shaken off..." Yet there did not seem to be any other solution. For a few days he drove the idea from his mind, but then began to clutch at it again...

This particular night he had to make up his mind. He did not have the strength to put it off any longer. Semyon closed his eyes and did not remember falling asleep. All at once the sun-dappled meadow was before him, radiant and colourful as he and Darya mowed the grass. Darya was walking along beside him, so near he could almost touch her. He ought to have moved further away but could not bring himself to do so.

"Move away a bit for Heaven's sake! " shouted Semyon, but Darya looked at him with a smile and turned away. It was a strange smile with a note of contempt and resentment in it.

Semyon had woken up from his own shout, then wiped the cold sweat from his forehead and lay there for a long time without moving, trying to work out what all this might mean. The dawn light was streaming in through the windows, scattering strange shiny patches over the dirty floor. The wind was still moaning and rattling the wires overhead and hurling wet leaves at the window. "What will be, will be," decided Semyon accepting his fate, and he began to dress.

He had a good long way to go and without any further ado Semyon went out of the house. When he had been buying tobacco at the market not long before, Semyon had learnt there was a widow by the name of Polina living in the next village who was not against marrying again. That was where he set off to now.

Autumn had turned out cold and wet that year. For over two weeks now the rain had been pouring down and everything was swathed in white mist. While following the rutted road across the fields Semyon looked at the black ploughed earth, at the straw stacks, trying to drive gloomy thoughts from his mind. Yet as soon as he entered the village each step brought with it a gnawing pain in his heart as if he was voluntarily setting out to meet his shaming or execution.

"But what will Maria think? How shall I explain it all to her?" he wondered all of a sudden and even stopped for a moment feeling quite at a loss. He wanted to turn round and run back home as fast as his legs would carry him. He forced himself to trudge stubbornly on, however, flushed with shame, yet knowing that if he were to turn back now, nothing on earth would make him retrace his steps to this village again. So as to justify his actions, Semyon lifted his head and whispered: "Maria, Maria... She's not my real daughter, just adopted. Let her think what she pleases."

No sooner had he said that though, than Semyon felt ashamed of his words and lowered his gaze once more.

Polina turned out to be a sturdy-looking woman with plenty of life in her yet. When she heard why Semyon had come over, she blushed right up to her ears and after a short pause replied: "Let's give it a try then and see how we get along together. I'm tired of sitting around here on my own, too."

"So you really mean you'll come?" said Semyon in surprise, pleased that everything had proved so simple. "When shall I expect you?"

"Tomorrow, if you like."

While he was hurrying home, doubts started creeping into his mind: what if she were not to come? "Well," he thought, "she's her own master..."

Polina did come though. Semyon looked her up and down warily, thinking to himself: "She looks all right, but not half as good as Darya! " Polina took off her coat unhurriedly and then said: "Hullo there, Semyon. It's me."

"Yes, yes," Semyon responded nervously. "Sorry

I haven't even got the stove alight yet." Then he fell silent, not knowing what else he could say.

"Never mind," said Polina with a laugh. "I haven't come to be entertained. We'll get it alight in no time."

The merry peals of her laughter seemed to fill every corner and all of a sudden Semyon felt there was not enough room for them in one and the same house.

Polina was a merry soul and a hard worker. She quickly scrubbed the wooden floor spotlessly clean, singing some little song under her breath; then she brought in water from the well and began to cook lunch. Semyon looked at her from out of the corner of his eye, yet he could not help but feel uneasy: "She does everything right—she keeps house properly! Yet why does she pour so much water on the floor-boards? You'd think she wants them to rot..." He had never in all his born days been mean, yet now for some reason he felt sorry for his property.

They sat down to eat, but Semyon soon pushed his plate away: the cabbage soup seemed too salty. He got up from the table, and as he caught Polina's perplexed gaze, he muttered huskily: "I'm going to call the neighbours round. We'll throw a party."

He invited the neighbours to a wedding party, but no-one took the word "wedding" seriously and the only people who came over were those who had been invited out of politeness rather than because Semyon really wanted to see them: the local accordion-player Simka Kutyakov and his friend skinny, long-legged Mitya Flyagin who was only too happy to drink at other people's expense.

Simka, drunk since morning, had brought over his

accordion, and after pulling out the bellows he started bawling out in a stupid voice: "Give her a kiss, Semyon old fellow, or give me a kiss! Ha-ha-ha! .."

Mitya realised at once what the lie of the land was and he tried to stop Simka, yet by this time any atmosphere of genuine celebration had been spoilt. However hard Semyon tried, there was nothing else to be heard by now than drunken compliments and congratulations. Malice began to fill his heart and his eyes already had a look of wistful sadness about them. For the time being he was holding himself in check, feeling though that he could not keep it up for much longer.

When the vodka was finished he turned his visitors out of the house and sat down wearily on the bench. Polina went over to him and said quietly in a very homely way: "Well, Semyon, we're man and wife now. All we have left to do is going to sign the register."

"Really?" he inquired in an absent-minded sort of way, and, without adding another word, he turned away.

Four days went by. Polina tried as hard as she could to please Semyon, but sometimes, when he seemed quite oblivious to her, she lost heart and came over all quiet.

On one occasion when she was sitting watching television she put Darya's fluffy shawl round her shoulders. Stamping across the room, Semyon came up to her and asked: "What did you go and do that for?"

"What?"

"The shawl, why did you go and put that on?"

"But it was cold, Semyon. What's so special about it? You don't mind me wearing the shawl do you?

After all I am your wife."

"To hell with it all... You're not my wife! " he shouted heatedly in a high-pitched voice. "What kind of wife are you for me? The very idea! "

"What's got into you, Semyon?" Polina started to get up from the chair, bewildered. "What are you making all this fuss for?"

"Fuss!? You just get all your belongings together and move out. Out of here... for Heaven's sake."

She collected her things slowly, still hesitating as to whether she should make the move and kept glancing at Semyon, wondering whether he might have changed his mind. When all her things were packed Polina moved over to the door with small steps and then murmured quietly: "So you want me to be on my way, Semyon?"

"Yes, on your way! What are you pulling at my heartstrings for?! " he shouted.

It was only after the door had finally slammed shut that Semyon began cursing—he was so sick at heart after the whole depressing business. He lay face downwards on the bench till evening, and then with difficulty he pulled himself to his feet and made his way over to the village churchyard.

The wind had died down but it was still cold and damp. There were puddles of water on the paths between the graves and yellow leaves floating on them.

Semyon knew that Darya was buried close by. What was all this though? Wherever he stepped there were neglected crosses covered in moss, and wet grave stones. He slowed down feeling all bewildered: surely he had not lost his bearings?.. Here it was, at the edge of the cemetery, the place he was looking for. Yet try as he would to strain his eyes down at the grey clay, he could not find the grave. The black earth of the ploughed fields stretched far away into the distance beyond the railings that had caved in long ago. The pungent odour of rye straw filled the air. Suddenly Semyon caught at the crossbar of the railings with his stiff fingers and yelled out: "Darya! "

A few ravens flew out of the trees overhead, scared by his shout and traced a circle over the cemetery cawing away hoarsely as they went. Semyon did not turn his eyes aloft but instead let go of the railings and trudged back the way he had come. It was then that he caught sight of Darya's grave at last. The autumn rains had thoroughly soaked the little mound with water and the fresh earth on the top of the grave had subsided. Semyon felt his throat go dry.

"Darya! " he wanted to shout out once more, yet all that came out this time was a hoarse whisper. Grabbing at the cross and scratching his hands over its tarred surface, Semyon knelt down on the withered grass and began to sob.

It was the first time he had cried so desperately and inconsolably since the death of his wife, yet the tears did not bring him the relief he longed for and the unbearable pain of his loss weighed heavier than ever.

Semyon could not remember later how long he lay there. When he raised his head slowly, he saw Polina looking down at him. Her face wore a stern expression.

"Don't scold me for it, Semyon, I couldn't go back. Get up, you're not a child now, are you?! Just look how damp the ground is..."

Denis Bulyakov

THE WHITE HUTS OF MY VILLAGE

Denis Bulyakov was born in 1944 in the village of Arslanovo in the Bashkirian Autonomous Republic. After finishing high school he worked as a tractor and combine driver and subsequently as a machinist on the local collective farm. In 1964, he graduated from an agricultural technical school with a degree in mechanisation and electrification. Some time later, he went to work for the regional newspaper *Znamya pobedy*. He served in the Soviet Army from 1965 to 1968 and entered the Gorky Literary Institute after demobilisation. He returned to Bashkiria to work on the central newspaper of the republic and became a department head there. He transferred to the magazine *Agidel,* and is presently chief editor of the magazine *Pioner*.

The author of nine prose works, member of the USSR Writers' Union, and winner of the Galimov Komsomol Prize of Bashkiria, Bulyakov treats rural themes as a rule.

It was very early when we drove up to the landing-stage. The sky was only just beginning to turn grey.

"There's nothing better than a boat trip when you're on holiday. Especially when it's such beautiful summer weather outside! " commented the amazingly chatty taxi-driver, as he took my case out of the boot.

"The boat you need will be leaving in about an hour's time, I think. The ticket-office is over there."

After getting back in, the driver pointed to one of the doors and then, after pushing back his peaked cap over one ear, he drove off quietly.

"Indeed, what's the point of getting shaken about in a hot bus?" I thought to myself as I walked over to the door the taxi-driver had pointed out to me. "As it is, I had to spend the whole of last year's holiday in the town amongst the asphalt and hot stone houses. This way I'll be able to watch the Agidel River to my heart's content."

Remembering the taxi-driver's smile, I repeated out loud the words of the song: *"Along the sweet banks of the glistening Agidel..."*

In the passengers' waiting-room people were trying to nap. I walked over to the ticket-office, yet despite the early hour there was a notice up to say that there were no tickets left: someone had even drawn a curtain across the little window.

There was nothing for it but, after marking time for a bit by the ticket-office, to be on my way. I looked at the sleeping people and thought to myself: these folks don't need telling twice the best way to travel in summer. But you're going to have to go for the bus as usual. Thoughts like this made me determined to get on the steamer come what may.

Nothing venture, nothing win... Deciding to try my luck I knocked at the little window. The curtain swayed and rose a little at one edge: through the gap I caught sight of a young girl's head. Obvious annoyance showed on her swollen face: surely you can read what's written up there—it seemed to say!

"All I need is one ticket to Tashmurun..."

"They're sold out," the girl replied in a tight-lipped refusal. Yet the expression of disappointment on my face obviously had some effect because she added in a more understanding tone: "If you'd come just a little earlier..." She looked at me sympathetically now.

"Just this once I'd decided to take the steamer and then I have to go and make a mess of it..."

Before I had had time to move away from the ticket-office the girl called me back: "Where did you say you were going?"

"Tashmurun... I am going back to my home village to spend my leave there—Tashmurun."

"Tashmurun, Ta-ashmurun... Just wait a moment... I'll be right back! " Throwing a scarf across her shoulders she hurried out of the ticket booth.

Quite some time passed before the girl reappeared. This time she came straight up to me. In a confiding tone she announced with a happy smile: "You can go and see the man on duty, he's waiting for you! " From her face I could see how pleased she was at this chance to do someone a good turn.

Shrugging my shoulders despite myself—I still could not be certain what would come out of this whole enterprise—I walked over to the door. "How wrong first impressions can be," I thought to myself, remembering the girl's kindness gratefully.

The man on duty was past his prime. Ignoring me, he continued tearing someone off a strip on the telephone. After he had put down the receiver at last he stood motionless for a time and then unhurriedly brought out his handkerchief, wiped his forehead, loosened the corner of his checked shirt—it was hot in his office—and finally walked over to the table. Each time he stepped on to his right foot I could hear the creak of an artificial limb. I took a closer look at his face... His nose was slightly arched, his hair had gone quite grey and there were marked wrinkles on his wide forehead. His skin was weather-beaten with some dark blotches on it, his eyes were pensive and stern... I had the feeling that life had not treated him kindly.

The man took a sideways look at me and then asked drily: "So you're going to Tashmurun are you?"

"Yes, only I couldn't get hold of a ticket... I haven't been back home for a long time." I was standing in the doorway of the room and looking expectantly at the man before me.

"So going to Tashmurun will be going back home for you..."

All of a sudden the lilt in his voice and the face appeared familiar. With another unhurried gesture he took out a pair of spectacles from his breast pocket, put them on and then began to look me up and down without saying anything.

"Wait a moment..." His voice shook. He quickly moved over to me, limping badly as he came, and then gripped my hand. "It's Farit isn't it?

"And you must be Uncle Gaizulla?! " I shouted before I could stop myself.

"Well I never! Farit, from back home! " He turned round to look at the young cashier from the ticket-office who had just come back into the room. "Fancy that, meeting after all this time! .."

Still gripping each other by the hand, we walked over to the side of the room and sat down on a sofa. The girl sat down next to us, her face wearing a happy smile. She looked as if she had known this was bound to happen all along.

"Just imagine... It's amazing... It was me who re-cognised you first, don't you forget that! " said Gaizulla beaming, tripping over his words as they came gushing forth. Yet he did not look me straight in the eye—he obviously still felt guilty towards me after all this time... Then he asked: "How many years is it since we last saw each other?"

"It must be a good fifteen..."

"You're right... How time flies! " He paused for a moment and gave a deep sigh. The dark blotches on his face stood out more clearly now. "Life's just like the river out there, it goes on and on flowing by and there's no stopping it... And before you know it," once again he looked me up and down, "Farit is a grown man! How long is it since you last rode your hobby-horse... There's life for you! "

Gaizulla rose to his feet and walked up and down the room limping as he did so. He sighed again: he seemed to be recalling something pleasant this time, his eyes creased in a smile for a moment... Yet it vanished as quickly as it had come. Once more Gaizulla gave a deep sigh and then, as if there had not been anyone else in the office he sunk into his reverie again.

There was one question I longed to ask him. In the end I could not hold it back any longer: "Gaizulla, tell me, d'you know where my brother's wife, Makhmuza, is?"

I had the impression that Gaizulla even started on hearing that name. He looked at me with a long searching gaze. It became so silent in the room that we could hear how a fly kept banging into the dusty window-pane in a vain attempt to get out. "Why did I have to go and ask that stupid question?" I thought to myself angrily. "Who was I to him after all? Perhaps I'd touched on a sore spot... Perhaps he just takes every day as it comes and doesn't worry himself about the past any more..."

I do not know how long we might have stood there in silence, if the door had not opened to let in a man wearing high rubber boots.

He inquired in a loud voice: "Gaizulla, the barge has come in, where should they unload it?"

The face of my fellow-villager came over all angry and with slow weary steps he walked to the door. He gave the loud-voiced man in the rubber boots an irritable shove on the shoulder and complained: "You see, Farit, they won't even give us the chance to have a chat. Off we go then... You wait for the time being, Farit, I'll see you off later. Don't worry about the ticket. We'll sort all that out..."

I sat there on the sofa for a bit, but the girl from the ticket-office had gone away too, and I was getting bored, so I went out into the little garden near the landing-stage. The morning air was so incredibly fresh and clean, of the kind one only associates with home and childhood. In the leafy tops of our local squat poplars some birds were flapping about, and when they took wing noisily, a shower of dewdrops fell on me. I strode across the damp, soft sand of the garden, still very much under the impression of the unexpected meeting. I could not forget the question which I had put to Gaizulla. Where was Makhmuza? Why had he seemed so upset on hearing her name?

Life, although so short, can sometimes be so rich in experiences! Some of us are granted straight, smooth paths, others have to follow winding ones full of stones and pitfalls. What suits one person will be disaster for another. For someone those very same stone paths might add that all-important spice to life. Then, after mooring in a peaceful harbour, when it is almost all over, they may live happily through their memories and in those very same memories they may find happiness and consolation...

As I thought about Gaizulla, I could not help thinking about Makhmuza, too. I could see her before me as if I had only said goodbye to her yesterday: her face with its first traces of wrinkles, eyes which managed to remain calm, even though a fiery nature burned within her, her tight-pressed lips and mannish hands—calloused and with veins swollen from hard work... Yes, the war had left its mark on them all... It was only her figure that reminded all who saw her that Makhmuza was a woman of no more than thirty. Moreover it was only at first glance that Makhmuza's face seemed tired and indifferent. As soon as you came to know her better and talked to her you realised she was a very different kind of person.

I remembered an episode which had made an indelible impression on me although I had only been a boy at the time.

In our parts it was the custom for people to whitewash their houses as soon as spring came. After that the village looked like a grove of flowering bird-cherry trees. They would all set off to fetch white clay from the Alatau Mountains. Several families would team up together, then they would harness their horses to long narrow carts and set off along the roads across the steppes that were beginning to dry out. The custom had taken such firm root that for the people of my village it had become something in the way of a special occasion. Digging out the clay, bringing it home and then decking out the village huts—all this work was usually rounded off with a party for one and all, when the various families would pay each other visits from house to house.

I remember that it was Makhmuza's turn to go and fetch the clay. At that time she was already a widow and Gaizulla who lived a few houses away had offered to help her.

The neighbours had commented: "He may be a cripple but he's still a man!" And they nodded their heads approvingly.

Gaizulla had come back from the war with a leg missing. I had heard that before the war he had been studying at medical school, and then from August '41 onwards he had worked as a medical orderly. Anyone would have felt at a loss after losing a leg and then into the bargain suffering from shell-shock. When Gaizulla had come back to his native village he had started drinking and moped about silent and gloomy. The children used to be frightened of him.

"Gaizulla's smiled, so the sun's bound to shine to-day," someone was heard to joke in the village. Yet most of the villagers pitied him. Pity was all very well but it did not make Gaizulla's lot any easier. Gradually he cut himself off from other people more and more and used to wander about the village, a wretched figure reminiscent of an eagle with clipped wings.

When she set off to fetch white clay Makhmuza took me along too. They decided to take two carts so as to be able to bring home all the more clay.

"Come along, little brother-in-law, you'll have a day out and you'll see what it's all about: then when you grow up and become a horseman as good as the rest of them, we'll send you off on your own," said Makhmuza, giving me a friendly pat on the back. I knew that she was fond of me. I understood why as well: I was remarkably like my elder brother Karamat who had been killed in the war. "The spitting image, like two peas in a pod! " our mother used to say.

It is always a bitter blow to lose a loved one, and twice as bitter when the person managed to survive right through to the end of the war only to be killed in the last few weeks. Even in our part of the country, hundreds of miles from the fighting, you could feel at the time that the war was almost over: we started guessing when Victory day would come, imagined what it would be like, anticipating the welcome home we would give all the sons, fathers and husbands on their return...

The notification about my brother's death came at the beginning of May.

Makhmuza had been made a widow...

She did not marry again (now that years and years have passed and I come to look back at those times through the eyes of a grown man, I can say with confidence that she had had several chances to do so) and did not ever talk about the possibility. Yet from that time on she showed an even greater fondness for me and would give me a kiss and a hug every now and then. At such moments her eyes would fill with tears, then she would quietly withdraw into the house and start sorting through the yellowing papers that she kept in a big trunk. I knew that those were the letters my elder brother had written her...

That first year after the war it was obvious that if you managed to get hold of a horse you would find there was no collar to go with it, if you managed to get hold of a collar then the cart would be broken. By the time we had scrounged all we needed from the neighbours it was already midday and it was getting on for dusk when we reached the Alatau Mountains. We dug the clay we needed but by then it was dark. We decided not to go back home, but to spend the night where we were. Gaizulla made a fire, while Makhmuza washed out one of the buckets and hung it up to boil water in. I kept on running round to collect brushwood while they just went on sitting there talking quietly about this and that. Every time I heard Makhmuza laughing, I felt a little pang of jealousy.

The night was a warm one. Stars were twinkling in the sky and in a nearby thicket the rippling song of nightingale could be heard... Not far away a hooting owl lent a more ominous note to the darkness.

After we had drunk our fill of tea we all lay down in the carts to sleep: Gaizulla and I in one cart and Makhmuza in the other on her own. I did not sleep for very long. I woke up from the cold. Then I saw that the place next to me was empty... In the hazy light of the moon everything round about was easy to distinguish. I looked over towards the second cart. On waking I had thought straightaway that someone was talking over there. I had not been wrong: again I caught Makhmuza's angry whispering and then Gaizulla, who had turned up there out of nowhere, suddenly flew out of the cart and landed on the ground with a thud.

"Shame on you!" hissed Makhmuza furiously, sitting up in the cart. Her hair hung loose about her shoulders. "How could you!"

"D'you know what kind of a man I am!" Gaizulla countered defiantly. "I've been through fire and water!"

"You might think of Karamat... Have you no shame?!"

"I left a leg at the front ... for the sake of your happiness!" went on Gaizulla relentlessly, holding back a groan. He must have really hurt himself as he fell. You could sense the shame, the man's injured pride and the hurt in his voice. "You just don't understand!"

For a time neither of them said anything.

Suddenly Makhmuza got down from the cart and went over to Gaizulla. Quite unexpectedly for me she put her hand on his shoulder. "You ought to snap out of it, you silly fellow! Find some work you can enjoy... Then you'll feel a proper man again."

Gaizulla seemed to have slumped over again, once more the hunched pathetic figure.

"It's misery that makes me give in, Makhmuza... Misery that makes me turn to the bottle!" he suddenly cried out shaking his fist in mid-air. "What do you know about it? Both your legs are all right! But mine... I can't settle down to work. I just can't! What's the point of trying, no woman's ever going to understand what suffering really is..."

Makhmuza turned away from him and quietly walked over to me. On seeing that I was awake she put her arms round my neck and began to cry.

"What a tragedy—he's got one leg missing ... and can't get over it... And my Karamat ... He's dead! One leg missing... He ought to be grateful that he's still alive. A leg..."

Makhmuza's warm tears were dripping on to my cheek: "Surely you don't think it's easy to be left a widow at an age when you should be living life to the full... Just think of it, people don't understand what a hard time he's having, poor fellow."

"No, you never will understand!" Gaizulla shouted out, forgetting himself. It was as if at that very moment he had chosen to seek revenge for all the torments and the suffering that he had been put through and which had forced him, without a murmur, quietly to drink tears of blood. He was seeking revenge for the bitterness and the burning pain in his heart. Makhmuza was to be the scapegoat for it all. "A magpie won't ever fly high enough to get to an eagle's nest. That's all old wives' tales. Real suffering's out there! " Gaizulla shouted pointing into the darkness with his crutch. "In the eagle's nest, at the front! "

Makhmuza covered her face with her hands and rose to her feet. She threw back her hair that had been hanging loose over her shoulders, and ran into the bushes near to which our horses were grazing. Gaizulla and I both stood rooted to the spot. A few minutes later, minutes without end—something was bound to happen—a cart thundered past us. Makhmuza was standing erect in it, shaking the reins as hard as she could, driving the horses forward for all she was worth.

"Makhmuza, Makhmuza! " Gaizulla's plea echoed through the night air.

Stretching out his arms he tried to lever himself up from the earth, but failed and flopped back on to his side with a groan of pain and a shower of curses. By this time the cart had disappeared into the night. For a time the rattling of the wheels could still be heard deep out in the steppe, but then that too faded away.

It was then that for the first time in my life I felt hate well up within me. There was an angry lump in my throat and what loathing I felt for this man who had offended my very own, very special Makhmuza!

I got up. The one remaining horse was pawing at the ground impatiently—he too obviously felt left behind and abandoned as I did. The moon which had been like a gleaming red-hot plate before was now wreathed in clouds—she too wished to turn her face from my grief. The clouds seemed to be relishing it though and whispering: "You've got what you deserved, serves you right! "

I hurried over to the horse. Then it suddenly flashed through my mind: I should go and catch up with her. Then Makhmuza and I could ride on together leaving Gaizulla out here on his own...

Without giving it all a second thought I saddled the horse and set off after Makhmuza. After galloping a short way I reined in the horse—Gaizulla, I thought to myself, has only got one leg and how is he going to get home? For Makhmuza was too proud to come back for him...

Angry at my own thoughtlessness and feeling sorry for Gaizulla and myself, I started crying. I turned back. As I rode up Gaizulla was standing there supporting himself on his crutches.

"So you didn't catch up with her?"

"No..."

We lay down to sleep again. There was only one cart now so we had to share it. I tried to lie as far away as I could from Gaizulla but he moved over to me and gave me a cautious pat on the head. He was clearly trying to say sorry for all he had said to Makhmuza.

The next morning we loaded the cart with clay and set off home, our legs dangling over the sides. Every now and then Gaizulla gave a groan. It turned out that the wound above his knee had opened up again and he kept gently pressing the sore place. Sometimes he shifted his whole body round to face my side of the cart, pulled his leg up on top of the clay and rolled himself a cigarette. He said nothing as we went along but sat greedily drawing in the smoke as if his life depended on it. Then out of the blue he suddenly came out with: "I love her."

At first I did not grasp what he was talking about, and when it dawned on me I was at a loss for words—just imagine—he had been thinking about her all the time. It was only then, when I took a closer look at him, that I saw how his eyes had changed—I could hardly believe it—they seemed to have lost all their colour, as if he was in desperate pain.

"All we've got is one life, little fellow... It doesn't look as if I'm going to get the chance to live mine like other people though."

Gaizulla looked at me trying to find out whether I had understood anything of all that he had said. Then he went on, just as if he was talking to another adult: "You just think about it little fellow and ask yourself, if a bat can ever catch up with a bird flying up in the sky?" Then he answered his own question and said: "No. Well I'm like that bat, while your sister-in-law..."

He paused for a moment and then started up again: "Makhmuza's like a coal a-glow in a stove. She's already been lit, and keeps alight in her heart your brother Karamat's caresses... What about me? I'm a cripple. I haven't even got a proper nest. I'm an old fool to want to take that glowing coal into my arms..."

I understood little of what Gaizulla was trying to

50

tell me. Yet the pain this man felt, his tragedy and his sorrow made my heart bleed...

The clay we had brought home was soon unloaded and shared out. The new white walls made our village look more cheerful and festive right away. Each one seemed to shine. There was only one hut that looked like a neglected orphan without its new coat of white. That was Gaizulla's.

After that memorable drive into the mountains Gaizulla took to the bottle again. At first people felt sorry for him, but when his drinking bouts became more and more regular they began to ignore him.

One day a neighbour of ours dropped in and among other pieces of news announced: "Poor old Gaizulla, he's really going downhill. Got drunk again. His eyes are all blood-shot and swollen and his face is the colour of ashes: he's going to come to a sorry end. Mark my words! "

Makhmuza said nothing while she busied herself about the house, but just listened: afterwards she put on her jacket and went out.

As I was to discover later on, she went to see Gaizulla. As time went by she used to visit the abandoned, orphaned hut more and more often. Sometimes it was not until late in the evening that she came back, and strange as it might seem, from that day on no-one ever saw Gaizulla drunk. When one fine day Makhmuza whitewashed his hut the whole village gasped in surprise.

Various rumours began to spread. Some people said that Makhmuza was in the family way and when her time began to grow near she had gone to see Gaizulla of her own accord; others that the Evil Spirit had got into her, and sometimes it was even suggested that while waiting and pining for Karamat she had gone out of her mind... There was no end to the rumours you could hear.

Not long afterwards Gaizulla disappeared from the village. "He'll be back soon, don't you worry! " people would say with a wry shrug of their shoulders. "He's done for. He'll roam around for a bit and come back." Later, without saying anything to any of us Makhmuza, my sister-in-law went off as well. Everyone assumed that she had gone to Gaizulla. Yet, where they were and how they were getting on, nobody knew for sure...

I had been very fond of Makhmuza and missed her badly. Tears used to come to my eyes when I remembered how she used to stroke my hair and give me a pat on the back. Yet waiting for her and asking her in my thoughts to return was no use, she never came back. Later there was a rumour that Makhmuza had settled somewhere near Tashkent and that Gaizulla had died. Then all of a sudden this meeting, out of the blue...

I wandered around the garden for a long time thinking of the past. It was as if there was no end to those memories that had suddenly surged up from the past. Incidents that had faded with the years, or vanished from mind altogether, had come to life again and so vividly that it took my breath away... Yet I could not get that one question out of my mind that would give me no peace: where was Makhmuza and what had become of her?

The time for the steamer's departure was drawing near. I went down to the landing-stage but there was still no sign of Gaizulla. At that early hour, when the sun was not yet up and the moon was hanging like a tapering icicle in the light sky, the surface of the Agidel was still swathed in milky mist. That in its turn brought back memories of the white huts in my village sparkling in the sun, as if the river itself had been given a coat of white clay brought down from the Alatau Mountains...

There was Gaizulla at last. Falling forward on to his right leg with each step he walked over to me. His face was sad. My memories of him went back fifteen years and so this present face of his looked old to me.

"The steamer's late," he said breathing with effort. "Come along, let's take a walk along the bank."

We walked along, our feet scraping the pebbles, breathing in the damp air. Both of us remained silent.

"Gaizulla, why don't you come home to our village for a visit?! " I blurted out, unable to hold myself in check any longer. "You ought to come and see everyone back home..."

"Farit, old friend, I too would give so much to go and see Tashmurun again. Yet that path's barred to me forever... I can't." All of a sudden his voice grew livelier as he suggested: "Let's sit down and rest here for a bit."

We sat down on the bank there and then, near the quiet waters of the Agidel. A gentle breeze started up, a ripple went through the mist and it began to lift. The water became pale blue, the colour of the sky.

"Greet the white huts of our village from me," said Gaizulla in a pensive voice. "They mean more to me than life itself. Yet I can't go... Not without Makhmuza..."

"But where is she?" I interrupted, unable to control my curiosity any longer.

Gaizulla gave me a long thoughtful look and then spoke: "From the time we first left, we lived in this town. We made out all right. I found work and we brought up our two sons. Then ... last year ... I lost her, Makhmuza, who brought me back to life, who opened my eyes to everything." Holding back a sigh, he turned away.

The mist had almost completely vanished by now. In the distance could be heard the siren of the steamer that had not yet come into view.

"I'm nothing but a lonely old man now. Yet my heart still beats for the two of us." Gaizulla hesitated, picked up a smooth pebble from the ground, and stroked it cautiously. "Make sure you give everyone back home our best wishes."

Soon after that the steamer arrived. We said goodbye. Gaizulla, standing there all alone on the bank, kept waving his cap till the steamer was out of sight round the bend in the river. Soon he disappeared from view and all there was to be seen were the bustling seagulls circling over the river and filling the air with their mournful cries.

Victor Suglobov

REGARDLESS OF
CIRCUMSTANCES

Victor Suglobov was born in 1948 in the town of Kemerovo. He used to work at the Carbolite factory there, and then the Novosibirsk Agricultural Machinery factory as a fitter. After graduating from the journalism faculty of Irkutsk State University he worked in magazines and newspapers for young readers and in the central publishing houses. He graduated subsequently from the Gorky Literary Institute as well.

His writings have appeared in the journals *Sibirskiye ogni* and *Smena* and the literary miscellany *Istoki*. Suglobov's first book of stories, *Lessons of Suffering*, was awarded a prize in the Maxim Gorky All-Union Competition for the best first book by a young author.

1

At half-past one they brought the band over at last—five elderly, scruffy men. It was hard to imagine at first glance that they were musicians. Pershin looked at them from the window of his office in the Workers' Committee headquarters and he did not know how to put up with his depressing sense of irritation at everything and everybody, that came over him in waves.

Pavel Petrovich looked in to see Pershin, asking: "Why are you just sitting there? It's time to go!"

He was already in his rubber boots and a jacket of fashionable cut: that meant he was intending to help carry the coffin. The rain had poured down that morning and had made everything very muddy. He always was among the bearers if anyone from the state farm, who had really done their bit, was being buried. People liked it that way. The farm's Party organiser Grigori Pechonkin came out too. He was a local celebrity having outlived four farm directors in his current post. Pavel Petrovich was the fifth.

It was a ten-minute walk to the Prokhorovs' house, so they decided to send the musicians on ahead and, themselves, go on foot. It looked less ostentatious on this occasion and, more important, it meant that they would arrive virtually at the moment when the coffin would need to be carried out. Then they would have to waste less time listening to all sorts of meaningless chatter, irritatingly stupid arguments between the old women about various details of funeral ritual, which no-one was really sure about and all that people could resort to so as to prove that they were right were comparisons with other ordinary, badly organised funerals.

The Prokhorovs' large yard with its gates flung wide open was full of people and in front of the gates a sizeable crowd was gathering and spilling right across the street. The musicians in the thick of it all made up a separate little group of their own. Holding their well-used brass instruments under their arms, they stood waiting around, clearly not for the first time, thinking about their own concerns and probably paying very little attention to what was going on around them.

All of a sudden things started moving, there was a ripple through the crowd in the yard and loud shouting issued forth from the house. The musicians made ready to play, the leader raised his trumpet to his lips and nodded—then a clear, mournful tune started up and hovered above the hushed village, the kind of tune which makes people's hearts miss a beat and their breath come in gasps. The musicians were all at once transformed, especially the percussionist; he pulled himself together, straightened up as if he was trying to soar aloft when, after each crash of the cymbals, he lifted his arms up and out, keeping a stern solemn look of concentration on his face the while.

For the whole of the rest of that day till late at night, Pershin kept seeing that picture in his mind's eye.

Ivan's body was left in a closed coffin, just as it had first been brought home, because he had been badly burned in the lorry before it had eventually been put out. Perhaps as a result of the fact that no-one had actually seen him dead—and there was an enormous number of people present—the wake proved to be a very lively affair like those meals out in the field canteen, when workers turn up in groups from neighbouring fields and after quickly "stoking up" make way for the next shift. Or perhaps Pershin just had that impression because of his dreary mood.

What Pershin wanted more than anything was solitude, but the working day was not yet over, and out of pure habit he went back to the office. Although it was quiet there, like on a ship abandoned by its crew, he tried to get into his office without being heard, fearing lest there might be someone behind the door who had got tired of all the quiet emptiness and would start trying to engage him in conversation.

He sat down at the table but its habitual look with various papers shoved untidily under the glass top made him feel gloomier than ever. He turned away from it and looked out of the window, that had a view over Khoroshilov Wood, which rose in tiers up the slope from the river—bright green undergrowth and darker higher up. Low down there were aspen-trees and birches and higher up dark green pines with a brownish tinge to them. When White Guards had been running wild in that wood they had killed two Khoroshilov brothers. They had appeared not wearing any epaulettes and sporting red ribbons on their caps, as the partisans used to. Tricks like that had been heard about in those parts before and many people had thought it strange that no-one from this detachment seemed to know anyone at all in the district. The brothers however were impetuous and reckless; they were taken in by the ruse and asked if they could join the newcomers. The Whites agreed, but as soon as they were on the other side of the river, they tied them up behind the first bushes they came to. Then they pushed them off the cart once inside the wood and hacked them to pieces with their sabres. When still a small boy, years back, Pershin had not been able to think about that incident without tears coming to his eyes: it was heart-rending to imagine them at sabre-point, defenceless and clumsy like birds with their wings clipped. How could they possibly have known as they climbed into the cart that their life would be brought to such a sudden, horrific end?..

Then again, how could Ivan Prokhorov have known that that fatal journey was to be his last? Could anyone at all know in advance that they were about to die unless they were fatally ill or sentenced to death... Then what was the purpose behind it all? It was a banal question. From a philosophical point of view there was no purpose to be found at all. And from the historian's point of view? After all Nikolai Pershin was a history graduate. As a historian he knew only one genuine purpose in life—leaving behind you something that would be of value for future generations.

The Khoroshilov brothers may not have had time to accomplish anything but they had left in their wake a hatred for dastardly murderers which would live on while there was anyone left on this earth who remembered them. Yet if anything were to happen to *him* the next day what would *he* be leaving behind him?

Pershin got up and walked about the room looking at his watch: there were still forty minutes till the end of the working day. If Ivan Savelievich was on the spot he could talk to him about the meeting scheduled for tomorrow. That was when he would have to go to the district trade-union office. Pershin sat down and pulled the telephone over towards him. Your word was something you had to keep ... particularly in his position: if he were to get the push, heaven knows where and how he might be able to pick up the pieces again afterwards... "I've caught the same disease that people working in administration always catch. There was a time when I used to think to myself: 'What the hell! If they throw me out of here it's not as if I'm going to be unable to keep body and soul together! ' "

He dialled the number, and began: "Good morning, Ivan Savelievich! It's Pershin here from the Path of Truth state farm."

"Oh, yes, how are you?" came the answer down the line, sounding energetic and happy. "What can I do for you?"

That response was a pleasant surprise and cheered Pershin up. After all, they had not met very often, yet Ivan Savelievich had remembered his name, and his voice sounded very amiable.

"Ivan Savelievich, could I possibly drop in to see you tomorrow ... about a very important matter?"

"Do. What time do you want to come? I'm busy in the morning unfortunately. Why don't we meet straight after lunch? Does that suit you? Fine. But can't you give me some idea of what you want to discuss. Then I could give it some thought in advance."

"He's probably in the picture already," Pershin thought to himself after that. "There's no point in beating about the bush, I've got to make a clean breast of it sooner or later. It will, there's no getting away from it, give him some time to assess the situation and perhaps come up with some answers."

"The problem is, Ivan Savelievich, that I've just graduated from the Institute of Education, with an external degree, and I'm not working in my specialist field..."

"That's how it is, is it? I see. That's all that's worrying you. I've only got one question to add at this stage: what's your subject? History, probably. I thought so. With regard to historians, we have quite a good supply of those at the moment."

"So, I don't need to come along then?" asked Pershin in alarm.

"When I say quite a good, it's all relative, if you look at our situation as a whole. After all that's not the most important of the problems facing you, as I see it... The rest we'll leave till tomorrow, shall we?"

In the corridor old Evdokia started clanking round with buckets: she was the cleaning woman who in her youth had been known as Dusya. She had not had a husband but had not gone short of children: two sons and last of all a daughter Lena who had matured very early and who had been the first girl towards whom Pershin entertained unchildish feelings, back in his teens. A good deal of water had passed under the bridge since then. Lena had spent some years in the town after getting married but had kept her looks regardless. As for old Evdokia, she always made the most of any opportunity to speak to Pershin about her daughter. So he would have to wait till she went away so as to be able to slip out unnoticed.

He managed: he slipped out of the doors and straight round the corner and then crossed a piece of waste ground at the back of the allotments which ran down to the river slope. He finally reached his house after walking a little further down that slope.

2

His father had not come home yet from work and his mother was still wearing the grey overall, faded from constant washing, that she wore when working with the calves: she was feeding the cawing geese that were trying to grab the potatoes mashed up with flour straight from her bucket.

"Calm down, you'll have me falling over," she cried and then looked up at her son. "Will you have something to eat now or d'you want to wait till your father gets in?" she asked.

"I'll wait," said Pershin.

His father turned up and then spent a long time washing out in the yard at the outside tap, rubbing dry his oil-stained fingers one by one and then looking them over. He put on a clean flannel shirt, a brown one with orange stripes, which had been Pershin's favourite among the new garments he had bought when he arrived home after his military service. For some time now his father had stopped bothering to buy shirts because his son worried about what was in fashion and used to bring piles home from the town, more than he himself could possibly wear.

They sat down to eat in the summer kitchen. Pershin's mother put the frying pan with hot buttery pancakes in it down on the table, and a bowl of cold curd dumplings left over from lunch, with milk and sour cream to garnish them.

"What else shall I put out? Some salted cucumbers perhaps? After all everything out here on the table is from the dairy, you haven't got any meat or vegetables! "

The head of the family sat there, looking tired, leaning with his full weight on the table. In an irritated voice he replied: "I don't need any cucumbers..." Then he looked over at his son and asked: "Well, have they buried Ivan then?"

"No, they just left him to rot," said Mother throwing up her hands, irritated by her husband's remark. "What on earth makes you ask? What nonsense! "

"They've buried him," Pershin confirmed in a gloomy tone.

"Yes, that was a pretty mess..." said Father with a deep sigh. "It was money all over again! They say he didn't even really want to go! After all on Saturday he'd spent eighteen hours at the wheel already—he was moving the barley the combine-harvesters had brought in. Those wretched women are all the same: 'Off you go, it's overtime—double rates.' "

Mother shook her head with a desolate air. "What rubbish you're talking. People'll say anything."

"And what about you, trade-union boss, why

weren't you keeping an eye on things? It was a violation of regulations—questions may well get asked."

"It was harvest-time," answered Pershin limply.

"You just think back," said Mother chipping in again. "Remember how you used to work in the collective farm, before it became a state farm: what attention did we pay to work regulations then? You'd get up at the crack of dawn and return to find that the cow is mooing out in the yard, not yet milked."

"All right," said Father, cutting her short, "that was a long time ago, things are different now. Another thing I want to know, boss, what on earth's happening with all the machinery. In the old days when the combines were half-wooden they used to last for years. Some of them I remember even dated back to before the war. Now we get issued these new ones, all shining colours and sparkle, like some golden toy, and after a season they're finished, falling to pieces, coming apart, the metal rips as easily as an old shirt. You just don't know what to do with them! Welding doesn't help, the patches have to be riveted on."

"Get them riveted then," said Mother in an irritated voice. "After all that's what the repair shop staff are for."

They finished their supper and then went out into the cool air. The kitchen was small, with a low ceiling, and it was hot inside even though they kept the door open: if they shut it there was no air left to breathe after a mere ten minutes. Father brought out his cigarettes—he would never smoke any other brand but Sailor's Delight—wiped the sweat from his forehead and said jokingly: "Eating makes you sweat and work has you shivering! " Then he paused, took a puff at his cigarette and said: "You've hardly touched food, son. Had your fill at the wake?"

"Yes, that must have been it..." agreed Pershin in an absent-minded kind of way.

"But he didn't eat a thing there," came Mother's voice from the kitchen. "Why have you got so worked up about it all? It's not as if he was one of the family. There are plenty of people to mourn for him."

"Were you there, then?" asked Pershin in surprise.

"The women were talking. They said you had a drink and that was all. They saw that you were very upset, that you were as white as a sheet."

Father shook his head and coughed scornfully. "They don't miss a thing, those women! " he said.

Mother was not having any of that and countered: "You men, you get everything served up to you on a plate but when a fishing net needs setting up to catch some carp there's always some excuse. It's not as if it takes long to get a motor-bike out and pop down to the lake: some people come from miles away."

There was no denying that: people did cover large distances to get there, some just for a day out in the country sitting in their rubber boats with their little rods and with their feet hanging over the edge trailing in the cool water, or sitting on the bank that was also pleasant even though the midges might be lying in wait. Others came down with all possible equipment: extra salt, large plastic canisters or enormous poly-thene sacks that had had fertilizer in and which would take a man inside and still leave room to spare.

"I was planning to get some firewood sawed up

today," mumbled Pershin's father in an uncertain voice, and he cast a disgruntled glance at the heap of birch-logs of all different shapes and sizes that had been dropped, just as they came, by the hay-shed, and which he had been counting on sawing up right away.

"As if there won't be another chance!" Mother insisted. "Nothing's going to happen to them here in the yard now, is it?!"

"Well, what's it going to be, Nikolai? Perhaps you'd go over to the lake and I'll have a look at the saw and check out the motor?!"

Pershin changed his clothes, and swapped his shoes for rubber boots. Then he went into the lean-to where all kinds of household equipment were kept including two inflatable rubber boats and two tents. In the same place, ever at the ready, was the heavy Ural motor-bike with its side-car, and right at the back in the furthest corner was the home-made circular saw with its small petrol-driven motor. After he had stacked into the side-car everything he needed, Pershin pushed the bike out into the yard. While he was shutting the door behind him, who should appear out of the blue but Olga from next door.

"Nikolai, are you going to the lake? Do give me a ride over there, I promise I won't get in your way."

Then she turned round towards her house and called out: "Mamma! Is it all right if I pop down to the lake?"

No answer came but in a split second the latch rattled and Polina, Olga's mother, came out through the gate.

"Why not!" she said spinning her words out as if

she half sang them, and giving a knowing little laugh. "You just be careful, neighbour, not to hurt my beauty! "

Olga's two sisters, Nina and Vera, aged thirteen and eleven, also scampered out of the gate to have a look, and last but not least, five-year old Misha, the long-awaited boy of the family. He squealed: "Me too! Me too! " and they all rushed over to the motor-cycle.

"I'm not just off for a joy-ride! " shouted Pershin, losing his temper once and for all and then, feeling ashamed of himself, he added guiltily: "There's been that terrible rain and we're bound to get stuck in the mud somewhere."

"Come on, back home with you all! " ordered Polina, shouting at the children who had all run out. They came to an obedient halt, although they did not hurry home after that. "But you two go and have a ride—just the two of you'll get through all right."

"So they've got no faith in the colonel suitor..." thóught Pershin to himself bitterly. "You just wait I'll show you: I'll see you're lumped with a whole family of big bosses! " That thought made him feel calmer right away and almost cheerful. One kick was all that was needed to get the obliging engine to start, he revved it up noisily and then after he had settled back into the seat, he said quietly so that only Olga could hear: "Remember I've never used a pistol so I don't intend to fight any duel with the colonel."

Olga burst into carefree laughter and almost fell on to the ground when Pershin got off to rather a jerky start. That made Polina burst into rippling laughter too as she watched them move away from behind. The sound for some reason reminded Pershin of the time when as a first-year schoolboy he had been picked out to present a bunch of flowers to Polina when the last bell of the school-year went. Each fresher had been told in advance which of the school-leavers he was to present flowers to, and he had made straight for Polina, holding in front of him a large bunch of flowers in two hands. Polina waited for him to reach her and had then suddenly bent down and kissed Pershin on the nose, like some little kitten. That had been at the end of May and in December of that same year she had married Ilya Pochinkin, who had returned from his military service only a year before. Most of Polina's relatives had been of Ukrainian extraction, and so the bride had worn a wreath of flowers in her hair with long ribbons flowing from it that reached as far as her waist. The young couple had ridden round the village in a light carriage drawn by two of the farm's best horses, and personally invited the numerous relatives on both sides of the family. The wedding had been a generous, raucous feast, with Ukrainian and Russian songs ringing out, yet there were plenty of ups and downs before the young couple settled down together properly. Ilya was hot-tempered, and Polina proud and obstinate. Yet this did not seem to dampen their passion, rather the opposite. After a quarrel Polina walked about looking as happy as could be, singing songs and declaring loud and clear for every one to hear: "If my Ilya doesn't shout at me for a week, it has me all worried."

The road had dried out well and the surface was reliable, especially on higher ground, but in the dips there was still water. Pershin had been driving motor-bikes since he was twelve and so was able deftly, and almost without thinking, to avoid the wet places by using the edge of the road or slopes to the side of it so that the side-car was sometimes thrown up into the air and it seemed that they would turn over any minute. Olga put up patiently with these bends and did not even cry out, but Pershin was anxious to shake her about as much as possible so that she did not ask him to take her out again.

He knew one road to the lake that would take them across low willow-bushes. Beyond the bushes was a small patch of open high bank, bordered on all sides by osiers, wild-cherry bushes, small aspen-trees and at the very bottom of the slope in the middle of the small path leading down to the water there grew a large spreading birch-tree which made a useful land-mark for anyone who wanted to find the place again: the tree also provided shelter from light rain and vital shade for a motor-bike on a hot sunny day.

While Pershin was blowing up the inflatable boat, Olga was standing right by the water, looking at the shining mirror of the lake and driving away the mos-quitoes with a birch twig. Then she took off her sandals and walked a little way into the water.

"The water's so warm and like an idiot I forgot my bathing-suit! Should I swim in my dress, p'rhaps?"

"If you go and do that," muttered Pershin crossly,

"you'll drive home in wet clothes and catch a chill."

"It's so tempting..." said Olga again wistfully.

Pershin did not bother to reply to her last remark. Once he had finished pumping up the boat, he threw it onto the water right by the bank, then brought along the oars and cast off. First of all, he found his pegs in the nearby reeds, arranged them along the edge of his boat, took hold of the twine to which they were attached so that they did not slip down and slowly, with one oar, he moved the boat along the shore, looking for a suitable place as he went.

He had only had time to stick the peg in place and tie the end of the twine to it, when the pure ring of a familiar voice floated over the water to him, interrupted every now and then by short gasps for breath. It was Olga, evidently some way from the bank by now, who was floating on her back and singing rather out of tune:

> *Karelia I shall never forget*
> *But shall dream of ever more...*
> *Its lakes like sparkling blue eyes set*
> *In tall firs round the shore.*

"She couldn't resist it!" said Pershin in a loud disgruntled voice.

When he reached the bank, Olga, already dressed, was standing underneath the birch-tree and rubbing away hard to get her hair dry. Then she shook her head, swishing her hair from side to side to get it dry quicker.

"Is that it then? Are we going now?" she asked sadly.

Pershin climbed out of the boat and stood there for a moment thinking. The sun had already floated out of sight beyond the horizon, but the sky had cleared: it was bright and cloudless and promised to be a long, calm evening, when the fish would not stay at the bottom but would play and frolic till late into the night. If he were to wait an hour or so, he might well catch something for breakfast.

Olga went off to look for some currants, although the bushes were probably bare by now, while Pershin broke off a birch twig to drive away the mosquitoes and sat down on the bank. He looked at the water, at the distant wood on the opposite shore: above the wood the silhouettes of some seagulls stood out against the sky as they hovered low, circling as if they were competing with one another; now and then a stupid fish jumped up to the surface, chasing after some insect skimming across it... "Poor Ivan Prokhorov, though, lies motionless, buried in the earth forever. How ridiculous it all was, how terrible, defying all understanding! " thought Pershin to himself bitterly and out of the blue he started thinking of Lida.

They had met shortly after he entered the institute, during the exam period. They had been sitting next to each other in a trolley-bus and alighted at the same stop. It had been after midnight and the hostel was about to shut, but Pershin, while sitting in the trolley-bus, had decided that if they should get out together then he would try to start up a conversation. He had to carry out his plan, otherwise he would be ashamed of his cowardice. In a hoarse, rather jerky voice, Pershin burbled something about the late hour and insisted on seeing her home. Lida agreed with a wry smile and when they reached her house Pershin, worried that she might just walk off, began to tell her about himself. In the end she gave him her telephone number and said he could ring between four and five in the afternoon: she was a day student at the university and she usually was home by four and her parents used to get home between five and six.

Pershin used that telephone number, they went out together to the cinema, to the theatre, and he grew more and more agitated; his days in the town were numbered, then he would have to leave and all it would have meant to her would be an amusing interlude with a country bumpkin who had even been bold enough to hope for something more. He had spent a long time afterwards composing letters to her: he mostly wrote about his work, his efforts to organise leisure activities for young people in the village and to encourage amateur music and theatricals. She sent him replies but not very regularly and for the most part she too wrote about her leisure activities, about the plays she went to, about the concerts given by visiting stars and other such things. Everything she included in her letters seemed to underline the fact that city life was infinitely superior to the one he knew in the village, and her tone was such as if she were making sure that he would have no cause to reproach her if she suddenly announced that she was getting married.

They met almost a year later as Pershin was not given time off to take exams in the autumn because of the harvest, and this, strange though it might seem, made Lida respect him more. She seemed really happy to meet him again and behaved very differently the second time, she was less aloof and formal. They went to an ice-cream café complete with disco. They sat in comfortable seats, drank iced cocktails through straws and watched sophisticated young people living it up—smart girls hardly out of school and boys as yet unaware of what military service was all about. Pershin looked at them with a sense of resentment and envy, worried by the fact that he could neither dance nor conduct himself the way they did... Yet Lida belittled all those goings on so sincerely that Pershin felt happier right away. He felt she must like something about him and that was wonderful. The reticent way she behaved was quite understandable; she was a respectable girl who wanted to have guarantees as to where she stood... But what guarantee could he give her? It was clear as daylight from what she said and wrote in her letters that she would never join him in the country. Then, if he was to contemplate "moving in" with her, he had not even got so far as meeting her parents: he had no idea what kind of people they were and what they would think about their son-in-law who had popped up out of nowhere. He was not going to ask her to introduce him or go out of his way to assume that role.

After the café they went back to his hostel. For the time being Pershin had a room of his own there because he had turned up before the others for obvious reasons. They almost forgot themselves ... but Lida stood firm: she obviously had her sights set on some smart lad who gave her all the guarantees she needed.

It was over a year before he saw Lida again: one day during the next exam period fate brought them together again at the trolley-bus stop. Pershin did not recognise her at first as she had changed so much: she no longer held herself proud and straight and had aged ten years... It hurt him to look at her: her scrawny shoulders, skinny legs and the lifeless expression in her eyes. She had experienced all possible disillusionment in the intervening year or more and no longer expected anything worthwhile out of life. She asked then with a pathetic smile whether she had offended him. Pershin shrugged his shoulders as if to say he had no reason at all to feel offended. A shadow of faint hope flickered over her face at that reply and her eyes shone for a moment.

They began to go out together. Pershin was more confident now, but Lida did not resist his advances any more. Shyly she even tried to appear passionate, but he could sense that she found everything disgusting. Pershin's pleasure was ruined as a result.

Nothing went right for them—he couldn't forget. It was as if his predecessor was standing over them all the time, smirking, and Pershin felt bitter at the thought of one comparison that he could not get out of his head: how resolute she had been when resisting him, Pershin, because she could not see any practical solution of their relationship, and how easily, perhaps even hastily she had succumbed to the city boy in a luxury flat all his own. So, perhaps if Pershin had told her, for instance, that his parents and brothers would have no trouble in helping him collect money together for a co-operative flat—which was indeed the case—everything might have turned out differently?! How could he have possibly said that though, for it would have looked as if he was buying her...

Coming back down to earth again, Pershin gave himself a furious slap on the neck, hoping to finish off a persistent fly. Olga's laughter rang out behind him: she had walked up behind Pershin without him hearing her and, squatting down, she was tickling his neck with a blade of grass.

"Well, what next then?" she asked cheerfully. "You've waited long enough now, perhaps the fish have carried off all the tackle with them."

"They could not carry all of it off," muttered Pershin and with that he walked over to the boat.

Olga hurried after him. "Can I come, too?" she asked.

They set off in the boat together. Olga sat in the front facing Pershin, touching the water-lily leaves that were peacefully lying on the water: pensively she gazed at the water streaming through her fingers.

The catch was not bad: nineteen carp, all a good size.

"All we would need would be one more to make it twenty! " announced Olga, all disappointed. "Even so, they'll fill a big frying-pan and easily make fish soup."

"I'll have to get married sooner or later," thought Pershin to himself, "there's no getting away from it. A man's duty must be done, so to speak. Here people have already begun to look sideways at me and drop hints. Once I start working as a teacher, they'll start

keeping tabs on me. If I put a foot wrong I'll be report-
ed and then they'll start asking why he was allowed
to work with children and so on and so forth."

"Olga, how'd you like to marry me?" asked Pershin,
taking himself by surprise.

Olga frowned, lowered her head and looked at him
sideways before answering: "Are you taking me for
a ride?"

Pershin said nothing for a moment, cursing himself as he thought: she'll go and tell her mother now,
then she'll tell mine and I'll get it in the neck from
both of them.

"Why d'you just stand there? Why don't you go on
with your questions: am I a virgin, and if not when,
who with and how often?" blurted out Olga in such
an unfamiliar tone that Pershin was taken aback and
almost dropped his oar. "She's no fool," he thought to
himself in surprise, "just pretends to be more stupid
than she really is."

"D'you think you're an incredible catch—the big
boss and all that?" Olga went on in a malicious
voice. "If one's going to marry for money, then a
better bet would be the colonel, Victor Ivanovich:
he's got rank, he's a somebody, he has a flat and a
car. Then I'd have city life—theatres, cinemas, restau-
rants. I'm not going to marry just anybody! " These
last words she uttered in a caustic tone; then, looking
almost cheerful, she turned away with a sudden jerk
to face front, almost upsetting the shaky boat.

There was no point in answering back and there was
very little he could ‘ say anyway; all she had said
was perfectly true. He felt so ashamed of himself.

"A fine husband I'd make and all! " admitted Pershin to himself. "You'd better look out... Who on earth needs you anyway?! What you should do is to sit tight and belt up, mind your own business and in general just think about other things! "

They came back to the bank in silence and still without saying anything climbed out onto the bank. Pershin brought with him a polythene bag, collected the fish in it, pushed the boat into the bushes, so as not to have the bother of pumping it up the next day, knowing quite well that no-one would find it during the night. Then they set off home. Olga was no longer sitting pillion, but in the side-car that was now empty, and kept on looking Pershin up and down with a guilty expression on her face. Pershin was oblivious to this: he was watching the road, the woods lining it, the fields of ripening wheat or the harvested barley lying in sheaves. He took it all in, letting it seep into the very depths of his being, as he thought to himself how inexplicably beautiful the world was after all, how important it was to feel oneself a part of that world and to cling to that awareness come what may, not to run around in circles and go in for idle talk, but to get on with one's work and be oneself. It was difficult and would not always be possible but there was no other way open to him after all he had experienced and pondered over during the last few days...

A mist was starting to float over the river: long wisps of it stretched down the main channel, getting caught up in the bushes along the banks, and when Olga and Pershin came down to the bridge the chilly still air enveloped them, invigorating and cool.

When he had stopped in front of Olga's gate for her to get out, Pershin handed her the fish saying he did not need any that day and tomorrow he would be catching some more anyway. Olga stood firm.

"Take it, I tell you! " ordered Pershin. "Don't eat any yourself if you don't want, but the kids'll enjoy it."

4

The chairman of the Workers' Committee did not yet have an official car of his own, but the director never refused him one if he needed to get to the district trade-union office or somewhere else near by in a hurry, and the party organiser was still less likely to do so. Pershin seldom had to request one, for more often than not he would be called out at the same time as one or the other of them to party meetings, to the party office or executive committee headquarters, and they were even hauled over the coals more often than not altogether.

"Do use it," agreed Grigori Ivanovich willingly, when Pershin turned to him with the request in the morning, and with a strange, slightly condescending smile he said: "You'll have one of your own soon, get used to it."

"Why, are you getting a new one?" asked Pershin in surprise.

Grigori Ivanovich gave him a searching look as if he wanted to say something, but then changed his mind, shrugged his shoulders, as if to say: "Don't disturb me," and then buried himself in his papers.

A week before Pershin might have been glad to be given such a hint because the director had long since promised him a car as soon as he got issued a new one. This could not have come at a worst moment though: people would start saying: "They even issued him a car, yet he went and..." As luck would have it: when you need something, you can't get hold of it and when you don't want anything at all then they come and offer it to you on a plate!

The nearer Pershin came to the district centre, the more worried he felt. How difficult it was to make a fresh start, everything was designed to make you keep a low profile...

Pershin, on arrival, sat down on a bench in the dusty little garden near the district education office and, like just another of the many petitioners, he began patiently waiting for Ivan Savelievich to get back from lunch. Pershin had probably walked or driven past the two-storey building hundreds of times by now: he had known the man in charge all of seven years but had never once been inside.

At five to two the squeak and clatter of an artificial leg announced Ivan Savelievich's approach and Pershin, after emerging from his ambush, met him in front of the entrance. He had done that specially so as not to keep bobbing up and down in front of him or to provoke superfluous questions.

"His smile is friendly, the handshake's firm and sincere," Pershin noted. They went up to the first floor by way of a squeaking staircase and they had hardly got into the door of his office before Ivan Savelievich announced in a resolute tone: "I've found just the job for you, director of a school on a state farm for fattening livestock. Listen and don't interrupt," he warned. "You can ask questions later. It's a 7 to 15 school. The building's new, purpose-built, complete with gym and workshops. There's no second shift but the best thing of all there's a wonderful craft teacher who the boys worship! We all know that boys are the biggest problem in schools, but at the same time they can be our best trump card for future success. Who usually holds back a school's achievement record, causes all the panics and so on? Boys! Teachers, on the other hand, are usually women, and women by their very nature are not so community-orientated as men. While they're young, things are all right, but once they get married and start having children, then at work they only pay attention to rules and procedure and can't see any further than that... During a craft lesson one of the boys got hurt, cut his hand. That was that! The director wanted to put a stop to those lessons so as to avoid any further such incidents. But, after all, a child can just as well have accidents at home, with a fork at table, for instance, or what could be far worse, with an axe in the back-yard, but that would be at home and would not concern the school... Are you with me?! "

"Yes, I think so," replied Pershin cautiously.

"So there you have it," Ivan Savelievich went on. "I took the teacher's part. Then the director applied for a transfer maintaining she could not work under one and the same roof as that teacher. Of course that move was made with her counting on the teacher being transferred instead. Yet she's going to be the one who gets transferred with all due respects paid and to a post in keeping with her service record—here to the district centre as director of studies in Secondary School No. 2. And you are going to replace her."

It was pleasant and flattering, yet at the same time totally unexpected and somewhat alarming.

"But I know nothing about running a school..."

"No-one does when they're first given a director's post. You, on the other hand, have got wide experience in dealing with people as well as your teacher's training. Where there's a will there's a way. Is the will there?"

"Yes," confirmed Pershin.

"That's all that matters! " said Ivan Savelievich and then he went over to the table and picked up his cigarettes and matches. "D'you smoke?" he asked. On hearing Pershin's "No" he was pleasantly surprised and went on: "That's good. Before the war I never touched one but ever since I've been unable to break the habit."

He sat down at the desk and pulled the ash-tray over towards him. Then he pointed out: "Your job now is to leave your present post without any official reprimand. D'you understand? I'd take you even with one, but ... you understand, I'm sure, without being told?"

"I understand," replied Pershin with a sigh.

"There's no need to worry about anything! " said Ivan Savelievich with a smile, trying to sound encouraging. "I'm glad you've agreed... Lots of people take up teaching reluctantly; unfortunately, not everyone appreciates the crucial importance of work in schools. One can't gear everything to industry." He lit a cigarette and blew out a match. "They say that it was the school-teacher who welded Germany together as a nation, and it may well be true. A school can plant any kind of seeds, good or bad, it all depends on who's doing the sowing... What kind of generation did Hitler mould? I saw those youths with their bazookas... Yet not long ago I was in the GDR and we were told there that the first thing that the East German communists did was to send their finest manpower into the schools. Many of them left teaching later—to become writers, scientists or to take up prominent posts in industry—but at the crucial hour they devoted part of their lives to bringing up that new, post-war generation. So you see how important it is. Oh, there's one last thing, I almost forgot, are you still unmarried?"

"Here we go," snorted Pershin to himself. "I might have known." He asked gloomily: "What about those German communists, who went out into the schools, were they all married?"

Ivan Savelievich burst into loud laughter: "No-o... Or rather I don't know one way or the other. It's just that it'll make things a bit awkward for you. You live with your mother now and she cooks and washes for you. And anyway at your age it looks a little strange not to be married, wouldn't you agree? But it won't, I repeat, stop you getting the job. Perhaps you're a woman-hater—if that's the case, never mind, only make sure you behave in a respectable fashion where women are concerned, or else we'll start getting letters of complaint. Some people make a regular habit of writing them."

"I just haven't managed to bring it off so far," muttered Pershin.

"It happens," agreed Ivan Savelievich. "That's everything then, is it all settled?"

After he had got up to leave and was almost out of the door, Pershin remembered the most vital thing of all, which for some reason they had not touched on. "Until the internal Party elections are over they're not going to release me even with a strict reprimand—that goes without saying."

"You get them to accept the idea in general. For a month or two the school's not going to fall apart if it has no director: the director of studies'll cope."

"Well now," thought Pershin to himself on the way home, "I'll have to make an official application about my resignation saying I don't want to stay on the job, or better still I'll make it less official, less abrupt ... talking about dreams, long-cherished hopes, the reason for my studying in the first place. I must get down to things straightaway though, so that they have time to find a replacement. I'll tell the parents straightaway today. I wonder, how they'll react?"

5

At half past three Pershin was already back at work. Grigori Ivanovich was not in his office, but the door was not locked which meant he could not be far away.

When he opened his door he heard voices from the waiting-room: one was Olga's and the other belonged to Victor Ivanovich or the "bridegroom" as he was known locally.

"One has just to get some fresh air," Victor Ivanovich was saying. "You can't run round in circles all the time. The days fly by and before you have time to look round, it's time, as they say, to bid goodbye to this earth."

"Don't be silly," said Olga in mock surprise. "It's far too early for you to be talking like that."

"Thank you, Olga! " said Victor Ivanovich with heartfelt gratitude. "But life really is like that ... you rush around and bustle about like someone's wound you up. The only pleasant relief from it all, Olga, is finding time to come out here to you—to have a bit of fishing and to get a breath of fresh air, to have a look at you, Olga, and watch you smile..."

"Come now," protested Olga chirpily, not quite knowing what to say in her embarrassment. "What's so special about looking at me when you've got all those city girls?"

"D'you envy them?"

"What's so surprising about that? Of course I do. You've got everything you need in the town—theatres, shops..."

"Come away to the town then! "

"What would I do there?"

"Don't you worry about that, Olga—there's no need really." (Pershin could tell that Victor Ivanovich was getting really excited—quite carried away.) "You come over some time—just for a short time! I'll show you

round the town, show you everything there is to see...
I can get you into any theatre, no trouble at all ... to
see plays or musicals, and the very best seats, too."

"Some theatre people came out to our village, too,"
said Olga, lowering her voice. "They're going to come
here on a regular basis. They're in Pavel Petrovich's
office now."

"Sure to bring some trash, just to fulfil their quota
once a year perhaps."

"He's besieging her," thought Pershin to himself
bitterly, "in keeping with all the rules of military
tactics. Soon the final assault will take place." Then he
stopped himself in full flight. "And what about me?
Eavesdropping like some malicious old gossip." He
quickly strode into his office and shut the door tightly
behind him. He stood for a moment by the table and
decided then that he should go to see the director:
first of all he had to show himself and secondly he was
still the chairman of the Workers' Committee, without
whom important questions could not be decided.

In the waiting-room he gave Victor Ivanovich the
briefest of nods and asked Olga whether Pavel Petrovich was in his office. He addressed her in a strictly
formal voice and only because it would have been bad
manners to ignore her completely. "Yes, he's here," replied Olga happily. "He said he wanted to see you as soon
as you got in. Some people from the theatre have come."

In the spacious office they were all sitting near the
window round a small coffee-table—Pavel Petrovich,
Grigori Ivanovich, an elderly man with the face of a
crafty but tired man on the make, whom Pershin immediately recognised as the manager of the regional

theatre, and a woman, no longer in her first youth, dressed in flashy clothes. Cognac and sweets had been put out on the table.

"Meet Nikolai Pershin in charge of our trade-union committee! " cried Pavel Petrovich, obviously all excited by now. "And this is Comrade Buzuev, the chief manager of the theatre, and Nina Volchkova, the theatre's leading actress and head of their trade-union committee."

"Why make it all so official?" said Nina Volchkova, pretending to be embarrassed by it all.

Buzuev nodded to Pershin in greeting and asked: "We've met before, haven't we? You came to see me three years ago to arrange for a play to be put on here at the end of the harvest or on some such occasion, but the season had only just begun and we couldn't fix anything up."

"That's some memory you've got! " exclaimed Pershin in genuine astonishment. "It's not surprising that I remember you, but that you should..."

Buzuev spread his hands, saying with a sigh: "A rogue lives by his wits and I by my memory: I have to remember everybody and everything..."

All of a sudden Nina Volchkova interrupted him, saying: "We must be going now. Thank you for the welcome you gave us, I shall set great store by our friendship in future! "

They all rose to their feet and went to see the visitors off. On the way out Pavel Petrovich was taken by surprise on seeing Victor Ivanovich and went up to him to shake hands. "Olga, why didn't you tell me he was here?"

Victor Ivanovich came to the rescue, saying: "But I've only been here ten minutes."

"You didn't telephone or let me know! "

"I hadn't really planned on coming, but then I managed to make the time."

"I'll be with you in a moment—we're just going to see off these visitors."

Buzuev, as he shook hands to take his leave, frowned and repeated: "Everything's fine. Everything's going smoothly." Yet, his thoughts were clearly miles away by now. As he got into the car he raised his gaze skywards and muttered guiltily: "Sorry! "

The car started up and the three men waved after it before going back into the office. Without addressing anyone in particular, Grigori Ivanovich muttered: "You've got to be on your guard or he'll really take you for a ride."

"Yes," agreed Pavel Petrovich, nodding to him with a wry smile. "There's no flies on him. What d'you expect—the modern version of the smart businessman."

"You can't get much more modern than that! " grunted Grigori Ivanovich disparagingly.

Pavel Petrovich laughed again, turned to Pershin and put a hand on his shoulder. "I need to have a chat with you, Nikolai, but an important visitor's just turned up. I'll set aside some ten minutes for him and then you pop in—all right?"

Pershin nodded. Then he thanked Grigori Ivanovich for the car and asked just in case: "You don't know what it's about, do you?"

Grigori Ivanovich laughed and shrugged his shoulders.

He merely commented: "God moves in a mysterious way! .. And thoughts still more so."

Pershin thought to himself: "He wants to surprise me with a car, it can't be anything else. If that's the case, I'll have to tell him straightaway... He's convinced he's doing me a big favour and when he finds out that isn't the case, he'll be really hurt. Perhaps now's not the right time, perhaps another day..." He started getting cold feet and remembered: "I haven't even told the parents yet." After waiting the prescribed ten minutes in his office he got up, still without having made any firm decision.

The important visitor was already leaving to fix himself up with a hotel room and Pavel Petrovich reminded him as he set off: "Come back here afterwards, I'll still be in my office, and then we'll go back to my house for supper, if that's all right with you?"

When the visitor shut the door behind him Pavel Petrovich heaved a deep sigh and laughed as he watched him go, "D'you know why he has taken to visiting us?"

"Everyone knows the answer to that one," replied Pershin in a matter-of-fact voice.

"She's a lucky lass, don't you think?" Pavel Petrovich gave him a knowing wink and burst out laughing.

"Is that what you wanted me to come and see you about?"

"Of course not! " exclaimed Pavel Petrovich, brushing the idea aside. "But it is time you got married, old chap! It'll hold you back if you don't! "

"Hold me back, how?"

"It'll hold you back, I tell you. It's been suggested, for example, that you should be made Secretary of the Party Committee and that, as you know only too well, is a very serious step! Running round after that like just another young bachelor somehow wouldn't seem right."

Pershin could feel a wave of anger welling up inside him and knew he couldn't control himself much longer. He tried to keep his feelings down but they got the better of him. As he looked at Pavel Petrovich he thought to himself: "There he sits self-satisfied, revelling in his power—the wielder of destinies—and yet he's only three years older than I am. That's what power does to people! "

"And who's been suggesting it?" he asked in a deadpan voice.

"I for one, and certain other highly placed Party officials."

"I see," replied Pershin far from enthusiastically. "Where's Grigori Ivanovich going to go then?"

"He's retiring."

"Was that his own idea or other people's?"

"His own, don't worry. He, by the way, thinks you'd be the best possible candidate for the post."

"But surely there are plenty of good candidates among the Party members?"

"But who? You know quite well it's the best solution, and the simplest too! You know people round here well, you'll be working with the same people as before, and the work will be more or less the same. You'll just be moving out of one office here into another—that's all there is to it! "

Pershin paused for a moment and then gave a deep sigh.

"And what if I don't want to?"

Pavel Petrovich looked at him again, as if he was taking aim.

"Why on earth?"

"We-ell... perhaps I've got other plans."

"What kind?"

"I graduated not so long ago," Pershin answered, choosing his words carefully, "from a teacher's training institute, you know."

"You're going to go and be a teacher?"

"Perhaps... It's a possibility."

Pavel Petrovich started. "You have picked your moment! .. He's been made a really good offer... Posts like that don't grow on trees, d'you hear? It's not something you joke about! What on earth put that idea into your head? I've never heard you say anything about it before..."

Pershin shrugged his shoulders and looked Pavel Petrovich straight in the eye. "I want to live my life honestly. That's my one modest goal! "

Pavel Petrovich's astonished, arrogant stare bored into him, as he asked: "So you think working for the Party would make that difficult?"

"That's not quite how it is," answered Pershin in a firm, calm voice. "It's just that if I took this post I should have to work for a long time with the present director, find a common language with him and in general feel obliged to him for all the blessings he bestows on me."

That answer was not at all what Pavel Petrovich had

been expecting and must have been very painful if not downright offensive for him. He was knocked off balance at first, but soon he managed as usual to get a grip on himself. He asked: "So it's the director who doesn't suit you?"

"Yes, the director: there was a time when I was ready to do anything for him, but now I'd be very reluctant about it."

"And what is it about me that doesn't suit you?"

"A great deal."

"Be more specific. You can give me at least one reason surely."

"To be specific then, Pavel Petrovich, you see everything in terms of money," Pershin went on in his direct, firm voice. "In the old days I didn't pay much attention to it: I saw it as all tied with economic levers, material incentives and so on. Everything seemed in order and quite natural, and then one day I had a real fright, when I realised that you measured everything in terms of money. Good and evil, people's actions and how important they were—it all came down to roubles! Then all of us who worked alongside you began to slide down the same slope. We no longer notice how we base all our relationships and our conclusions on your principles."

"Stop! " Pavel Petrovich interrupted. "I too should like to clarify a few important points. First of all, who was it who called for self-financing work-teams louder than anyone, maintaining that they were in keeping with the principle of material incentives and made workers responsible for their own work and the results achieved? Was it you, or wasn't it?"

"Well, and so what?"

"Wait a moment: why did we refuse to introduce double shifts and introduced two-cycle milking? It was because it would perhaps have meant a drop in the milkmaids' salaries in the situation as it stood then—am I right?"

"Yes..."

"Who tried the hardest to convince our experienced Grigori Ivanovich that there was no law which laid down that cows had to be milked three times rather than, say, two or four?"

"It was me," agreed Pershin, undaunted.

"Then I don't understand what you're on about. You said that you would regret supporting me now."

"We can't go on talking about advantages and profits all the time. That's all you hear about nowadays. Everything's a question of roubles, roubles and more roubles! "

"How noble it all sounds. What happens if it's a question of profit for the state?! "

"It makes no difference."

"Come now, Nikolai. That's going too far."

Pershin interrupted him to say: "When those theatre people were here, they could have told you that most theatres don't bring in any profit for the state and are kept going on subsidies. They don't bring in the roubles! Why are they kept going? What for? There must be some other advantage?! "

"How does that apply to me, to the director of a state farm?"

"Just as it does in the other case."

"What d'you mean by that?! " shouted Pavel Petrovich, losing his temper. "Give me examples! Let me see what you mean, feel it for myself."

Pershin laughed a wry laugh and went on: "You can't feel something like that... All I know is that, if you ignore the other side to things, people start going downhill."

"Are you just generalising, or is it already happening?"

"It's already happening."

"What, our people? On our state farm?"

"Yes."

"So that's it..." Pavel Petrovich said thoughtfully, drawing out his words. "Let's ask them here and now..." He solemnly stretched out his hand to the bell on his desk and rang it hard—once, twice, but no Olga appeared. "Where can she have got to?! " He got up impatiently, went over to the door and opened it. Then he called out: "Ivan Stepanych ... come in a moment! Vera Filippovna, you too." Pavel Petrovich showed in a stocky bailiff and the middle-aged woman who managed the dairy-farm, and shut the door after them himself. "In you come, sit down."

They sat down, looking expectantly at the strangely excited director. "Tell me, Ivan Stepanych," he asked, "the self-financing work-teams—are they a good idea? Not for you necessarily, as one of the bailiffs, but for the workers, the men growing the corn?"

"Why not? They're a good idea," answered Ivan Stepanych, not clear what all these questions were for.

"And following on from that," Pavel Petrovich went on relentlessly, "the new system of payment based on the year's results—these immediate material

94

incentives—are they bad for people or not? What d'you think about it?"

"No," was Ivan Stepanych's blunt reply. "They're not bad for people! The opposite! Back in the old days when I was still working in the fields I used to rush around in the fields watching other people sowing and ploughing. If someone has even a bit of conscience things aren't too bad: if you tell him to plough thirty centimetres deep, he'll at least do twenty-five, but if someone's got no conscience at all, then as soon as you leave he'll raise the ploughshares and roar away in fifth gear—just to make sure the blades get dirty: he's paid by the hectare, not according to the depth of his furrows. If a man does not care about those who are going to sow and harvest in that field, he won't really worry about it... In a work-team it's a very different picture: you reap what you sow and can earn up to 400 roubles a month, or hardly manage enough to cover your mid-month advance. There's no time for people to be led astray. If we were, it would make life more difficult for us, ourselves."

"There you are!" announced Pavel Petrovich, very pleased with himself. "Now what about you, Vera Filippovna. Tell me, why did we drop the two-shift system and introduce the two-cycle milking in our dairy-farms?"

"That's clear for anyone to see."

"You still tell me why you think so."

Vera Filippovna smiled: "As if I were at an exam."

"That's right."

"As I see it, we're not ready for the two-shift system yet either from the economic or technological angle. We need more milkmaids, and that would mean bringing wages down, or putting cost prices up. Then again we'd have people unable to do a full working day—you can't just pay out good money for nothing."

"So it's only a good idea from the money angle?" asked Pavel Petrovich to make sure. "The main thing is that no-one should lose out where money's concerned."

"That goes without saying," agreed Vera Filippovna. "Other things are worthwhile too, it depends who you listen to. Work's got easier, more fun and more interesting..."

Pavel Petrovich gave a satisfied grunt and nodded to Pershin as if to say: "D'you hear that? Well?"

Pershin did not say anything and asked himself whether there was any point in carrying on this argument. This was not what he had wanted to talk about and this was not what Ivan Savelievich had encouraged him to do. All that could be done to spoil relations had been done, though, and there was nothing more to lose.

"I also want to ask something," Pershin said in a slow, subdued voice. "What d'you think, Vera Filippovna and you, Ivan Stepanovich, over the last fifteen to twenty years have people got worse or better?"

Vera Filippovna looked cautiously first at Pershin and then at Pavel Petrovich, trying to understand what lay behind their questions.

"People are better dressed," she forced out by way of a timid reply, "and take more care about how they look..."

"They know a lot more..." proffered Ivan Stepanovich in a hesitant voice to give her moral support.

"That's not really what I'm getting at. Something quite different in fact! " Pershin repeated, all worked up by this time. "I'm talking about individual men and women and their characteristics. I remember for instance how in the old days people used to come out here from the towns to help at harvest time, for a month or even two. People took them in as lodgers and they lived like members of the family or relatives, eating and drinking with the rest of us and no-one thought about money. How interesting it all was! They talked away in the evenings about where they came from and what they had seen; we children often used to stay awake very late, listening to them. And nowadays? Students come out here and we count up what they owe us for food down to the last kopeck... There's no comparison."

Pershin paused, and silence set in. It did not last long though. Vera Filippovna shook her head sadly and said in a quiet voice: "That's very true, Nikolai, we've begun to get too particular about things."

"What d'you mean begun?! " roared Ivan Stepanovich angrily, quite red in the face. "All people care about nowadays is money! " But then he remembered where he was, lowered his voice a little and explained sheepishly: "Yesterday evening a lorry was on its way to us from the village store, and it broke down by the bridge outside the village. I found Petya Anikin and said: 'Start up the tractor and go to help.' By way of an answer I heard: 'If you fill in a duty sheet for a whole day's work then I'll go, otherwise you can set off yourself.' "

"That's what I mean! " cried Pershin enthusiastically. "And why d'you think Petya Anikin's turning into such a selfish grabber? It's because we're always waving roubles in front of his very nose. We say, Petya, for this you'll get so much, for this a little more, and so it goes on. Money means more to him than everything else."

"Well then," shouted Pavel Petrovich angrily, "do you think people shouldn't be paid for the work they do?! "

"They should, and paid well for good work. But that should happen automatically, be the natural order of things. But waving roubles under people's noses, that's all wrong! No good will come of that! It's obvious... Poor old Ivan Prokhorov's out there in the cold earth now and nothing makes any difference to him any more ... even if we put a million on top of his grave! "

After that Pershin got up, waited a moment, and then went slowly over towards the door. Pavel Petrovich made no attempt to hold him back.

Victor Ivanovich was sitting in the waiting-room, looking dejectedly at the floor. When he raised his head and met a hostile gaze, he came over all embarrassed and turned his eyes away. Pershin had almost walked past him when, to his own surprise, he stopped and turned to address the "important visitor".

"I apologise but I don't know how I ought to address you, use your rank or just your name... Aren't you ashamed of yourself?"

"Yes," replied Victor Ivanovich openly and without making any excuses.

Pershin had not expected such a direct answer and he lost his bearings somewhat. Then he asked: "When all's said and done, is that the way to behave?"

"You're right, quite right! " Victor Ivanovich hastened to admit. "I'd like to wait for her and say I'm sorry... Then I'll leave at once, and I'm damned if I set foot here again." He laid a hand on his chest to emphasise his vow. "You too must forgive me! It's up to you, of course, but I'd like you to understand what led up to it all. I live alone ... and have done for a long time. I married while still a student at the academy. It all happened very quickly and it didn't work out. Then things got more and more difficult as I got older. Then I came out here one day, saw Olga and lost my head. I can't do anything about it, I've fallen in love at my time of life, to hell with it! " He paused for a moment and then said sadly: "I have offended Olga, of course. I must apologise. I'll do that and leave. Heaven knows how long I've still got... It's just that I don't want to leave any hard feelings here." He stopped, turned to the window and stayed in that position for some time, frowning with a look of intense concentration on his face.

Pershin felt really awkward by this time. He thought to himself: "I've only been doing all this out of jealousy."

"I'm sorry," he said, sounding rather guilty.

Victor Ivanovich nodded mechanically by way of reply.

For supper at home they were eating the carp coated in flour and fried in rows in the big frying-pan. Father chose one whose head was sticking out further than the others, hooked it out with a finger and carefully released it from the serried ranks.

"I'm probably going to leave my job," Pershin announced.

His mother and father looked at each other. Mother opened her mouth to say something but Father made a sign to her to stop her from interrupting at this stage.

"And where are you going then?" asked his father in a calm, even voice as if he was talking about some perfectly ordinary matter.

"I'm going to work in a school, if they'll take me on."

"Might they refuse you?"

"It depends how I leave this job: if that all goes smoothly they'll take me, if there's trouble this end..."

"Why on earth d'you want to move! " cried Pershin's mother, unable to control herself any longer. "What's wrong with your life here? It's not a hard life and people respect you."

"Hold your horses, Mother! " cried Father in a temper, trying to silence her. "You don't understand anything! Where he works people don't ask whether the job they're assigned to is good or bad."

"No, that's not it," said Pershin. "You've got the wrong end of the stick: no one's throwing me out."

"What's up then?"

"I just want to move."

"What d'you want with all those little whipper-snappers! " squealed his mother, quite frantic by this time. "Dealing with them plays havoc with your nerves. You're responsible for them all regardless. They're real little devils and nowadays they don't listen to anyone." She shook her head sadly and was on the verge of tears. "What's wrong with life here? You're in the public eye and people respect you..."

"Give over, Mother, that's enough! " said Pershin, interrupting her sternly. "That's enough. The discussion's over." He realised they would not understand: his father might, at least part of the way—he would speak to him later—but his mother never would. There was nothing he could do about it. He got up from the table. "Come on, Papa, let's go and saw up some logs."

When they had sawed up a good half of them, Pavel Petrovich suddenly appeared in their yard from out of the blue. Neither of them had heard him open the gate, come in, stand and wait till the next block of wood fell to the ground and the circular saw quietened down for a bit, before he started up loud and clear: "Hallo! Happy sawing! "

Pershin's mother looked out of the summer kitchen and called out in surprise: "Pavel Petrovich! Hallo! Come along in."

"God helps those who help themselves," replied Pershin's father, sounding like a model of unruffled calm. He had been about to bend over the next trunk, but immediately straightened up, looking expectantly at the uninvited guest: he had not just come to pass the time of day, he was bound to have come to take Nikolai off somewhere.

"I've just popped in, for no special reason," explained Pavel Petrovich, noticing the hesitation in their welcome. "Have you got a lot more work to do out here?"

"An hour's worth, not more," replied Pershin's father.

Pavel Petrovich stood there wondering what he should do next, then he peered down at his trousers, shirt. Deciding not to worry about them, after all, he said: "Off you go and rest, Uncle Yegor, and I'll stand in for you."

"Heaven forbid!" cried Mother in horror. "You'll get all oily and tear your clothes."

"It won't be the end of the world," said Pavel Petrovich to calm her down. He picked out the largest trunk he could find, walked over to its butt-end and nodded to Pershin, saying: "Let's go!"

Soon the work was under way again, but at a livelier pace this time. Pavel Petrovich was soon caught up in the rhythm of the work and almost got carried away, so the motor began to hiccough from the strain till Pershin's father could bear it no longer.

"Where are you racing to? You'll jam the engine!"

"A real treasure and all," murmured Pavel Petrovich.

"This one'll do us fine!" protested the father.

In less than an hour all the work was finished. Pavel Petrovich rubbed his hands clean one against the other and then looked round for somewhere to wash his hands.

"Just a moment—over here ... this way" pattered

Mother after running out of the house with a clean towel. "Then please have a cup of tea with us out on the verandah. I've put everything out, it's all waiting, ready, and the kettle's on."

"A cup of tea would be nice... I'd like one," said Pavel Petrovich, accepting the offer. After washing his hands he willingly walked up to the verandah. "Now, now! " he cried, protesting for all to hear. "How on earth are we going to eat all this?"

On a big round table covered with a clean cloth stood two frying-pans, one containing fish and the other fried eggs; round them were clustered plates and little bowls with bread, boiled potatoes and mushrooms, slightly salted cucumbers, smoked bacon fat, three kinds of fruit preserve—wild strawberry, black currant and rowan-berry from the previous year. There was also a big jug of cold milk, and next to that a jar of sour-cream.

"What can I offer you... We weren't expecting visitors, I'm afraid," lamented Mother.

Pavel Petrovich sat down and surveyed the table once more: "Really, well, there's no end to what you keep hidden in your emergency store then, Aunt Maria! "

Mother beamed with pleasure and added: "This isn't all of it! "

"If no one minds?" Pavel Petrovich looked at Pershin and then at his father. "I'd like a glass, now that I'm off duty and someone else is in charge."

No-one, as it turned out, did mind: of late Pershin's father had got into the habit of having a small tot of vodka to help him get to sleep but did not often get the chance, and Pershin himself was simply tired after the long day, tired physically and emotionally, so that he too felt he could do with a glass.

Pavel Petrovich said nothing, was obviously deep in thought about something and it was clear that he had really had a reason for calling. So the father, after downing his hundred grams, left the young people to it and led his wife into another room to watch television. Silence reigned at the table for a long time even after they had gone.

"Why didn't you say anything to anyone about all this before?" asked Pavel Petrovich at last, carrying on the conversation they had started in the office. "Did you think you would just slip away unnoticed?"

"I thought I might," nodded Pershin. "What else could I do? I couldn't count on you appreciating my point of view, but who else could I go and see to discuss it all? They'd all say, 'What on earth are you after? You're working with a splendid director—energetic, competent, ready to learn about all that is new and progressive. You're both young well-educated people. Surely you can come to terms on the question of material and non-material incentives?' They'd just pat me on the shoulder and see me off with good wishes for success in the future. No-one would take me seriously."

"All right then. But what made you go over the top?"

"Ivan..."

"So you did decide to blame me for his death?! "

"I was partly to blame, too," admitted Pershin bitterly. "There's more to it than that, though. When people of your age die, especially when it's such a futile unexpected death like that one, you remember that you too are mortal and can't help notching your own achievements or lack of them... It's frightening, not death itself but looking at the way you're leading your own life."

"What's wrong with ours?"

"I told you before... you're obviously not going to understand me."

Pavel Petrovich banged the palm of his hand down on the table, making everything on it rattle, and Pershin's mother, even though she was the wrong side of two closed doors, shivered on her settee in front of the television: she wanted to jump up and go and find out what had happened but her husband kept her back. "Sit still," he insisted.

Then Pavel Petrovich thundered out: "You should try sitting it out in my place—just for a couple of years at least! Then I'd watch how far you'd get with your non-material incentives and your high level of political awareness! What do you know about it all?! I brought people back to the soil, back to production. They stopped pining for the city lights. You try tempting them with the advantages of town life—it won't hold water any more. They realise now that there's no point in setting off somewhere far away to look for what you can find close at hand, as long as you're prepared to make good use of your brain and to work hard." Pavel Petrovich's voice boomed out in the enclosed space of the verandah and was so deafening that Pershin frowned as if in pain. "They've begun to think! Worry about how best to sow their crops and harvest them, how to take proper care of the machines and economise on fuel. It's made their lives more interesting. It's crucial that they should think! All of them! A field of wheat is not a crater: it's not just a question of dig deeper and you'll find more! Then a cow is a lot more than just an apparatus for producing milk, that needs fuelling with hay and water! "

"And is all that just in honour of Tsar Rouble? Just for the sake of profit?" again feeling anger well up inside him, asked Pershin. "Perhaps just for love of the soil and the work which their fathers, grandfathers and great-grandfathers carried out in the past?"

"Even if it is for the wrong reasons for the moment, never mind. It'll be for the right reasons in the end, I have no fears on that account. As for love of the land, that will come of itself later. As the gypsies say: Marry me and in a year you'll love me. We've got to marry off the farmers and the land: enough of this bachelor life! "

"A marriage for money?"

"Incidentally experience shows that marriages for money are often more lasting than love matches. Love at first sight can soon fade. But enough of all that..." Pavel Petrovich had again adopted that confident tone and was sitting as he always did in his office, with his head thrown back and his left eye screwed up, as if he was taking aim. "I know quite well what you think about me: all he cares about is high target figures at any price, that is success, and he wants nothing else, that's the only thing he's interested in. I've got it right, haven't I?"

"Yes," Pershin admitted.

"You see," said Pavel Petrovich, sounding almost

happy. "There's no denying you're a great fellow, really honest, I've always admired that in you. Well, I shall tell you in all honesty what matters to me other than money, what kind of dreams I have. I've got to let things take their course for the time being but what I dream about is putting communism into practice here on our state farm. There's no need to look so surprised ... the food in our canteen is virtually free of charge already, the prices are a formality, no more. No charges are made for the cinema and we'll be bringing the theatre out here, all expenses paid by the farm. Then just think about the living standards people enjoy nowadays. There's no end to the consumer goods an average family can afford. Then again, people have got so much money in their pockets that if a hundred or two hundred cars of any make or price range were to be brought to the village shop, they'd be sold out straight away."

"What you call communism is just a high standard of living," said Pershin in a rather patronising tone, "a high *material* standard, what's more! You're mixing up the end and the means, or rather you're putting the means before the end. Surely you realise that?"

"I'm providing the material base: 'conditions of life determine consciousness' and all that! "

"Tell that to a Rockefeller or a Rothschild ... Their living conditions are very high in your sense of the word." Pershin snorted and shook his head. Then he went on: "So you're building the base. We must ask how and for what, surely that's crucially important. Let's turn back in history for a moment, seeing we're on this subject and talking straight, man to man. D'you think our Russian capitalists and kulaks, if they had come to power after the February revolution, would not have started working all out again to prosper financially, to build factories and set up highly productive farms on American lines? But again the question crops up—to what end? It's crucially important! That's why the Bolsheviks went one stage further and implemented their Revolution, fought the Civil War through to the bitter end and made so many sacrifices. Then, all of a sudden, a mere two generations later we have a champion of pure economics and unadulterated material incentives. He's decided to build communism on his own state farm, communism in which Petya Anikin refuses to go and help a lorry driver from the local provision centre to get his vehicle back on the road until he's paid and can smell a rouble or two."

Pershin and Pavel Petrovich sat together talking long past midnight. At last they went outside to get some fresh air, wiped the sweat from their flushed faces as if they had just emerged from the bath-house. Pavel Petrovich lifted his head to look at the sky studded with large August stars, and said: "Look how it's clearing up there. The weather's settling, we'll be able to get the crops in, won't we. The barley's already in." He paused for a moment and looked over towards Pershin. "Perhaps, you'll have another think? We've had things out now, and once the air's cleared, it's always easier to make decisions... What would you suggest in general? Let's suppose I'm wrong, what should I do about it, if I were to take a different course?

What about some practical suggestions?"

Pershin shrugged his shoulders. "I don't know what to suggest just off the cuff like that. You yourself say that we've all got to think. The most important thing is not to lose sight of the overall goal, to remember what life is all about..."

"All right then," said Pavel Petrovich. "Perhaps you'll reconsider, after all. We'll quarrel and fight, I know, but that doesn't matter. Sensibly of course, to avoid differences in public... That's something we're duty-bound to avoid."

"And what about Ivan Savelievich? I virtually gave him my word. Even if I say I would not be released from my present post and therefore he can't take me on it's going to be difficult, it's not as if I'm known as some kind of empty-headed windbag. I've got to be consistent, shortly."

"I'll let you go without an official reprimand. I'll see to things. You can depend on it. You know me well enough to be sure of that. But do think it over again, please. I've been perfectly straight with you..."

Pershin went half-way home with Pavel Petrovich and then sat out on the porch for a long time after that. He looked up into the boundless sky and listened to the sounds of the night. He knew he would not get to sleep that night and would probably not go to bed at all. He would probably just sit there, sit there till morning, watching and listening.

Anna Kozlovskaya

MOTHER-IN-LAW

Anna Kozlovskaya was born in Moscow. After graduating from the philology faculty of Moscow State University and the All-Russia Studio for the Performing Arts she worked as an actress for the Moscow Theatrical Agency.

She also wrote short stories which were published in the weekly newspapers *Literaturnaya Rossiya* and *Nedelya,* and in the magazines *Ogonyok* and *Smena.* In a competition organised by Moscow's evening paper *Vechernyaya Moskva* she won a prize with her short story entitled "The High Point". She has also won another literary prize for a translation from Greek into Russian.

Ever since old Pelageya had left her native village and moved to Moscow she had been referred to as Granny Pelageya. She lived almost right in the very centre of the city in a single-storeyed house which by some miracle had been left untouched in a quiet little street. The house was an old wooden one with carved shutters and in the not-too-distant future a sad fate was in store for it — demolition. Yet Granny Pelageya made it quite clear to the house committee: "I'm not going, I'm not going anywhere." She left the residents' meeting feeling all worked up. She had not originally intended to leave her village although her son and daughter-in-law had been urging her to do so in their letters: "Do come and live with us, Mother: what will people think?" She had been in no hurry to leave. It seemed unthinkable to leave behind her all the places she had grown up in, the land of her fathers which in that hungry spring of '46 the women had had to plough all on their own with no help from the men... The little house where she had known all her happiness and cried all her tears, where her whole life had been spent and where on that black day they had brought her the notification saying her husband had been killed... Grigory was wrong to write: "What makes you want to live there all on your own?" She had not been on her own at all, she was surrounded by all the people she knew and loved. Together they had set up the collective farm, they had all helped her bring up her son without a father and sent him to town for proper schooling.

Yet news came of her younger sister's incurable illness. This bitter blow uprooted Granny Pelageya from her native village and brought her to town to nurse her sister who had been working there for twenty years. It was with a heavy heart that she set off on her way. "Lord, what a calamity! Her illness has got a name so long you can't remember half of it. If only our Zinaida had stayed back home. Illnesses like that haven't even been heard of out here." The journey was a grim one.

The city welcomed Granny Pelageya as all cities welcome people from the country—with hustle and bustle and unaccustomed noise: however she quickly grew used to both.

For eight months she nursed her sick sister and to her surprise became quite attached to her new home as she did so. She came to enjoy the quiet little Moscow street and her sister's large, light room which in some ways reminded her of the bedroom in a village house. Beneath her window there grew an eglantine bush. The house even had a little garden in which other tenants had planted dahlias. So it came about that after her sister's death Granny Pelageya decided to stay on. She was reluctant to uproot herself again. Anyway who then would tend her sister's grave? Her son was out at work all day. Her daughter-in-law was always running round in circles, she was so busy. Last but not least, Granny Pelageya used to pay a visit every week to the Grave of the Unknown Soldier.

Granny Pelageya enjoyed a peaceful life and was perfectly content with her lot.

"Why should I complain to the Almighty?" she used to say to her neighbour, a thin unmarried woman who worked as a cashier in one of the street kiosks selling theatre tickets and then at weekends battered away at a typewriter to earn extra money. "I've got everything I could possibly wish for, Lyuba. A son who's got as far as his Master of Science degree, then my grandson Vadim whose school marks are always the best you could wish for. God has seen fit to keep me healthy as well. The woman in Flat 2 was complaining she couldn't sleep properly. Yet she's younger than I am—no more than 68 or so. And me?! I sleep like a log and have pleasant dreams what's more. So that's how it is, Lyuba."

Yet the fateful meeting of the house committee almost shattered her contentment.

Meanwhile her son kept urging her to move in with them: "We can't have you living on your own again, Mother! The house is going to be taken down soon anyway. You should move in with us." His wife was positively offended: "Have I done anything to upset you, Mother? What will people say?"

And Granny Pelageya finally agreed. She took the icons down from the wall and wrapped them up carefully. She folded her best black shawl, the towels with red cocks embroidered on them and moved in with her son. She had not gone for good, but just for a stay as it were.

Ten days later she was back, telling the neighbour in a stern voice: "Don't look at me like that, Lyuba; no-one's offended me. I've just got used to this place. I don't like their polished floor. I'm like a skating cow when I try and walk on it..." She praised her daughter-in-law who had really impressed her: "She's so pretty and she works hard. She looks after Vadim properly, doesn't let him out of her sight. She does everything round the house all on her own. She's a real gem..."

"Why didn't you manage to get along then?" asked her neighbour suspiciously.

"I told you that, didn't I! I'm used to things here. Here I can clear up and wash my dishes as I please... I'm not just another piece of furniture, but real live flesh and blood! Whatever I start doing in that flat all I hear is: 'You have a rest now, Mamma.' She may be right—I could break their expensive china... And Natalia recently bought a chandelier of real cut glass. It sparkles away..."

"How do the two of them get on between themselves?" the neighbour persisted.

"You're an empty-headed one, Lyuba, to be sure: you don't seem ever to listen to anything I say. He lives in clover, that he does. She's a daughter-in-law in a million! You should see the mushroom pies she cooks! I wanted to bake some myself. She wouldn't hear of it! 'You have a nice rest, Mamma.' She didn't want me to leave either."

"You see, that's how mothers-in-law always get treated! " said the neighbour while digging the eyes out of a newly peeled potato with extreme care.

"You're a fine one, Lyuba! " said Granny Pelageya with a sigh, feeling so annoyed that she stopped in the middle of kneading her dough to object: "You haven't heard me complain about anything. I told you, she's a daughter-in-law in a million! It's just that I'm getting old... and I get in their way..."

"What d'you mean get in their way?" protested the neighbour angrily, banging a saucepan lid.

"But of course, Lyuba! " sighed Granny Pelageya. "The other day, for instance ... they were expecting people... Natalia said to me: 'Mamma would you take the icons down for a little while. Then when the visitors have gone—do put them back.' I'm too old to start taking icons on and off the walls..."

The last frosts of winter were already a thing of the past and in the quiet little street cheery streams of water were bubbling along. Warm bright days had set in and each brought with it a quiet sense of joy. Then the neighbour came out with a truly wonderful piece of news: they were putting off the demolition.

The bush under the window began to show green, when its time came round. Every morning on waking up Granny Pelageya used to look at its young leaves and think to herself happily: "A blessing from Heaven! Spring's in the air again. How God looks after us! "

Then it happened—like a bolt from the blue. One Saturday, Granny Pelageya was waiting for her son to come and visit her as usual, and in keeping with her country habits had got up at six o'clock in the morning. She was just taking a cake out of the oven and priding herself on the golden crust, when the telephone rang, shattering the morning peace. "Who can that be so early?" Granny Pelageya wondered to herself and she toddled along to answer it. She did not grasp at first who was ringing, for her daughter-in-law was sobbing all the time as she spoke.

"Wait a bit now! Wait! " exclaimed Granny Pelageya in alarm. "Go back to the beginning, step by step and tell me everything... What's been happening?"

She could not believe her ears when Natalia spelled it all out.

"What d'you mean gone? Where to? Wait a moment, Natalia, don't cry so loudly. I'll be round straightaway. I'll take a taxi. You just wait there." She lost her bearings, wondering to herself: "How could that be?— 'Has gone away'? Where to? Curse it all! .. So he went off yesterday... Surely not! "

A tear-stained daughter-in-law opened the door to her. By this time though she had stopped sobbing. She just peered at her mother-in-law with a sad reproachful look on her face. To begin with, Granny Pelageya felt the urge to rush in, but then she hesitated, not quite sure what to do. On the floor a new fluffy carpet was gleaming in colours quite out of this world. She felt frightened to step on it.

"You'll find slippers under the coat-rack," suggested the daughter-in-law, and Granny Pelageya moaning and groaning began to pull off her lace-up shoes. Once she was in, she immediately noticed a large cut-glass ash-tray, or rather what was left of it. Pieces of it lay in the middle of the table, carefully reassembled.

"I sent Vadim out for some glue specially for cut glass. Grigory hurled it onto the floor, Mother, deliberately! The same thing nearly happened to that expensive vase over there."

Granny Pelageya perched on the edge of a chair and crossed herself.

"He ought to be taken in for vandalism," sniffed Natalia.

"Tell me now, Natalia, how did things come to this pretty pass? Our Grigory's such a quiet sober fellow..."

"He may be sober, but..." Natalia broke into tears again. "But why does he have to break vases and call me a Philistine?! I've known for a long time that there's someone else..."

At that horrible thought Granny Pelageya reeled as if someone had struck her. "Wait a minute, Natalia, take it easy... Perhaps he's been staying over at a friend's?"

The daughter-in-law stopped crying and from the pocket of her pink silk housecoat she brought out a crumpled piece of paper. "Friend you say?! He didn't even intend to cover up! He's lost all sense of shame. Look! He even left her telephone number—*his* new number! 'Call me if you should need me,' he writes. Just fancy! 'If you should need me'! " Once more she broke into sobs. "Go and ring him, Mother. Please, ring him! Perhaps you can convince him! What will people say?! I've given him my best years..."

When Granny Pelageya went out into the street, her legs went weak and she had to stop. A small schoolgirl with plaits tied with white ribbons came up to her and asked: "Granny, shall I see you across the road?"

The question brought her back down to earth again and handing the girl the note which she had been clutching all the time, Granny Pelageya asked: "Perhaps your young eyes could help me. Where's the nearest telephone round here?"

The girl pointed out the nearest booth, read out the

numbers and standing on tip-toe helped her dial. There was no answer.

When she reached home at last Granny Pelageya had to lie down and stayed in bed till the evening. Alarmed by the quiet in her room, the neighbour gave a gentle knock at the door.

"Come in, Lyuba," said Granny Pelageya in a faint voice. "I don't feel up to much today. Put the light on. Don't pay any attention to the mess, I haven't tidied things up today."

"Perhaps you need a doctor?" inquired the neighbour anxiously.

"I don't need a doctor."

"Perhaps I should ring Grigory? He didn't come over today..."

"There's a cake out in the kitchen. Help yourself, Lyuba."

"I'll leave the door open," said the neighbour, still feeling worried. "If you need anything, just call out."

Lyuba went back to her room and started hammering away at her typewriter. The familiar sound which now floated into Granny Pelageya's room through the open door seemed to calm her down. She got up from the bed, tidied up the room a little and toddled off to the kitchen.

The next day, just as soon as Lyuba went out to the market, Granny Pelageya dialled the horrible number.

"Hallo," answered a hoarse man's voice.

"I want to speak to Grigory Nikolaevich, please," she asked.

"They're not in," barked the hoarse voice. "Don't ring back till this evening! " After which he hung up.

Granny Pelageya began to fear the worst. "Lord in Heaven! Holy Mary, Mother of God... Who on earth was that? Not her husband surely?"

She waited, constantly looking out of the window, to see if it was getting dark. When it was evening she telephoned again. This time her son answered the telephone. He started making excuses right from the start: "Mamma! I didn't have time to warn you... It all happened so quickly. I'll come and see you ... and explain everything."

"Don't come and see me," shouted Granny Pelageya. "It's home you should be going, to your own family! You ought to be ashamed of yourself! "

At that moment the unsuspecting neighbour came in and was taken completely unawares. Yet Granny Pelageya could not stop in the middle of what she was saying.

"It's a crying shame! " she shouted at the top of her voice. "Shame on you! Sowing wild oats now your hair's going grey! At your age your father died like a hero for his country. And what are *you* up to! " By this time Granny Pelageya was getting out of breath and she stopped in her tracks, but then she took fright at the silence floating back to her through the receiver, and in worried tones called: "Hallo?! "

"I'm here, I'm listening," came her son's calm reply.

"So you're listening are you?" shouted Granny Pelageya, starting up again. "I'm glad to hear it! And where's this am I ringing?"

"It's me you're ringing, Mamma."

"No, you just tell me now, where is this I'm ringing?" she persisted.

"You're ringing me at home," came Grigory's reply, sounding impatient by this time.

"So that's it, is it!?" countered Granny Pelageya in a high-pitched squeal. "At home!! Your home, you good-for-nothing, is in a different place! You've got a wife and a son at the top of his class! You should be down on your knees now, begging to be forgiven!"

"That's as much as I can take!" snapped Grigory. "First there was Natalia threatening me. And now it's you... Get on with it then ... gang up together!"

"I shall, too!" Granny Pelageya shouted back.

There was no peace of mind for her after that conversation, not even the green bush under the window could cheer her up. She knew that sooner or later her son would come round and she would have the chance to talk to him... She waited impatiently for the encounter, yet was scared, too.

A week later Grigory turned up, and he was not alone.

"Hallo, Mamma," he said in a serious voice. "That is Tanya, I should have introduced you months ago".

The small young woman with her hair cut short and a bewildered smile on her pale, thin little face stood hesitating in the doorway, trying to pluck up courage to come into the room.

"In you come, seeing you're here," muttered Granny Pelageya, without taking a closer look at her.

Tanya came in, still too timid to know what to do next.

"Sit down, seeing you're here," muttered Granny Pelageya again and threw a disapproving glance in her son's direction. Then she pattered off into the kitchen to put the kettle on. When she came back again, she launched straight into the attack, asking: "How's Vadim? What marks has he been getting at school? How's Natalia?"

"Vadim's doing fine," answered her son calmly. "He's got top marks in everything except geography. Natalia's all right, too, she's well. She's bought another chandelier for the kitchen. It's a little smaller than the one in the sitting-room but still quite nice."

"What an early spring we've had this year," said Granny Pelageya.

"Yes," agreed Tanya, "very early."

"Without much rain either," Granny Pelageya went on with a sigh.

"Yes, there's hardly been any at all," Tanya echoed meekly.

"There probably won't be any mushrooms this year," commented Granny Pelageya.

"Blow the mushrooms," said Grigory.

Granny Pelageya could not think of anything to say after that. She just took a closer look at Tanya. "Lord, Thy will be done! She's all skin and bone. At the side of her, Natalia is a real princess! "

The visitors did not stay long.

A month later Grigory came round to say goodbye. "Tanya and I are going away, Mamma," he explained. "We're off to Siberia."

"To Siberia?" Granny Pelageya said with a gasp of horror.

"What's the matter, Mamma, there's no need to worry! In Akademgorodok in Novosibirsk we'll be

123

working together, Tanya's a physicist too, you see."

"It never rains, but it pours," was all she could think of by way of a reply.

One dull uneventful day followed another after that. Granny Pelageya woke with a heavy heart in the mornings. She did not bake any more cakes on Saturdays: her son was a long way away. She missed her grandson but she was not feeling brave enough to telephone: she felt ashamed because of her son. Then she had a sudden urge one day to go back to her village. "I'll go to Zinaida's grave to bid her farewell for the last time. I'll say goodbye. Then I'll come back again next spring to plant some flowers."

So she began to pack her things, and before she had finished who should turn up but a jovial Siberian with a beard, on the eve of her departure: "How are you getting along, Mother Pelageya?" he asked.

Granny Pelageya was taken aback by being addressed in this unfamiliar way. What was more, the beard and long hair made the stranger look very like a priest. She was just about to ask who he was and why he had come to see her, when the stranger himself explained everything: "First of all, there's this money your son has sent you. You look after it now, or I might go and spend it on drink. Now tell me how life has been treating you... Out with it all now, as if you were at confession. Grigory said I was to find out everything."

Granny Pelageya came over all excited, clapped her hands, started bustling about; soon the plates were chinking away... When her visitor had drunk two cups of tea, then they really got talking.

"Have you been out there long in Siberia?" asked Granny Pelageya in a voice that showed how sorry she felt for him.

"Not what you could really call long," replied the visitor with a smile, his moustache and beard moving up and down as he spoke.

Granny Pelageya gave a deep sigh, at which the visitor started smiling again.

"Out there in our scientific centre, Akademgorodok—it's a real paradise on earth, and here you are sighing pitifully...The birds are singing, the scientists scamper about and the leaves rustle in the forest. The most important thing is that nobody disturbs you while you're trying to think. Grigory's chosen a really difficult research project and it's going well. He's a fine fellow, your son, Mother Pelageya."

"So everything's fine?" inquired Granny Pelageya distrustfully, giving her visitor a sideways look.

"Well, how shall I put it?"

This immediately put the old woman on her guard: "Is he really well in himself? It is Siberia, when all's said and done."

"Well, that's what I think you and I should start discussing now."

The visitor came over all serious, and Granny Pelageya held her breath.

"Grigory's not well at the moment," admitted the visitor stroking his thick beard in a thoughtful kind of way. "He did tell me to mention that only in passing, though, without making it sound specially important..."

"Lord save us!" groaned Granny Pelageya.

"Mother Pelageya," began the visitor again in solemn tones, "I give you my word that nothing terrible has happened. But there is something wrong with his heart all the same. He's been told he must stay in bed for another two weeks. If he does as he's told, he should be all right. Don't worry."

Granny Pelageya began to wipe her eyes with the corner of her head-scarf.

"Now, now..." said the visitor awkwardly, "I told you, Mother Pelageya, that there's nothing terrible the matter. Do I look like someone who would lie to you?"

The stranger did indeed look honest, but when he had left, Granny Pelageya grew really agitated. At night she was plagued by all sorts of bad dreams. There was her Grigory with a fever, raving and ranting ... and there was Tanya, that wicked home-breaker, who had brought her son to this sorrowful state, running around with all those academicians...

So Granny Pelageya began to gather together her belongings. First of all she packed her felt boots. It was Siberia she was going to after all. Then she brought out her thick three-quarter length coat of black plush and took down the icons from their corner. She ended up with quite a large bundle, after packing in some pots of home-made jam, but the load did not worry her, she would manage...

She hardly spoke a word during the journey, absorbed in her sad thoughts. That was probably what made her feel the train was going slowly. Yet it was keeping to its proper speed after all, and on the third day martial music started up in the carriage and there was an announcement over the loud-speaker to warn the passengers that they were coming into the town of Novosibirsk. Granny Pelageya thought at first she ought to put her thick coat on, but everyone else was wearing summer clothes and friendly light from the autumn sun was streaming in through the window. She clambered out of the train with the rest of the passengers and just stood where she had landed. Everyone else was rushing around, bustling to and fro, hugging each other in greeting, while Granny Pelageya stood there beside her big bundle, looking round at everyone and wondering where she should turn for help. Soon she noticed that the crowd was melting away at an astonishing speed, and this filled her with alarm. When the platform was almost empty, she decided not to linger any longer and, grabbing tightly at the sleeve of a young man rushing past her with a rucksack, she asked in a pitiful tone: "Have you heard, son, where there's a little town for scientists?"

"That's where I'm going! " said the young man cheerfully. "Come on Granny, follow me! "

Granny Pelageya hurried after her guardian angel, but could not possibly keep up with him. The young fellow was fairly flying along the platform, but every now and then he would look round and slow down a little. In the end he grabbed hold of her heavy bundle and burst into guffaws, exclaiming: "Have you brought your whole dowry to Akademgorodok? That's quite a bundle you've got here! "

Granny Pelageya was not in a laughing mood, but she could not help liking this kind young lad who was now dragging along her heavy bundle as well as his own rucksack. She thought to herself: "They're really warm-hearted, the people out here in Siberia." The young man loaded her onto the bus, complete with her 'dowry', while he stayed behind to wait for the next one as there was no room left.

The bus moved off, and Granny Pelageya gradually started to calm down. "What a pretty town... The houses are big ones and there are trees, lovely trees and flowerbeds." When the bus went on beyond the town, what she saw really thrilled her: "Such thick woods, it's just like back home in Russia. And there are fir-trees here, too. A sight for sore eyes! "

When she reached Akademgorodok, Granny Pelageya sat down on the first bench she saw to have a rest and a look around, to listen to everything round-about.

Autumn was beginning to paint the leaves gold, and the sun was shining through the trees. The fresh air seemed filled with a quiet glow. There were none of the town noises to be heard, which Granny Pelageya had grown so used to in recent years. Her thoughts turned all at once to her bearded visitor from Siberia. "The birds are singing, just as he said; listen to them all! It's so quiet and peaceful... It's a real paradise."

She walked round the town dragging her big bundle, meting out friendly greetings to the rare passers-by in keeping with her village ways. The asphalt path was narrow, so when Granny Pelageya caught sight of a cyclist she got all agitated, trying to decide where she should step off the path, yet the polite cyclist stopped to let her past. She took advantage of the opportunity to ask him how to find her son. Then the stranger, no youngster himself, loaded her bundle onto his bicycle and accompanied her all the way to the house. He even asked her to give Grigory best wishes from a colleague. She simply did not know how to thank him.

"Put me down! D'you hear? Grigory! " cried Granny Pelageya, floundering helplessly in her son's mighty hug. When at last she could feel firm ground under her feet once more, she started scolding him without further ado: "Why did you get out of bed? What did the doctor tell you? To lie flat on your back for a couple of weeks—keeping quite still. Have you gone right out of your mind? You're not a little boy any more, don't forget that."

"I might have known," chuckled Grigory. "Valeri must have scared you out of your wits. I'm all right again now, Mamma. Just look at me! " He pulled back his forearm tight to his elbow so as to make the muscles stand out. "I'm fit to pull a plough! "

"Back to bed with you! " commanded Granny Pelageya. "D'you hear? It's you I'm talking to! "

Grigory lay down on the settee, while Tanya ran out into the kitchen and started clattering some plates.

"Tanya! Just look at her! " shouted Grigory. "A real hero of a mother! Rushing out to her son in Siberia! Like one of the Decembrists' wives! "* The very idea of it made him burst out laughing once more.

---

* After Tsar Nicholas I banished to Siberia those who had taken part in the abortive Decembrist uprising (14 December, 1825), many of the banished men's wives of their own free will followed their husbands into exile.– *Ed.*

Granny Pelageya sat down on the only chair in the room and began to look at her son more closely: "Thank goodness, he seems so happy... His eyes are shining... Only he seems thinner in the face." Then she noticed that his room was quite large. They had a settee that doubled as a bed, and there was a writing-desk piled high with papers. The lamp in the middle of the ceiling had no shade. The door leading into the second smaller room was open, and she could see that there was no furniture in it apart from a bed and two chairs. "They're living very simply," Granny Pelageya thought to herself with a sigh. Yet she was pleased to see how her son was: she had not expected to find him like this, she had been ready for a very different state of affairs.

"Food's ready," called Tanya, and they all went into the kitchen.

Granny Pelageya sat down at the small kitchen-table and surveyed the scene: "What kind of a housewife do we have here?! There's only one saucepan and that hasn't been cleaned properly. Only one frying pan, too. Not a single cupboard on the wall! Where will they put their jam and salted vegetables? Natasha, now she really knew how to run things! "

"Will you have some fried eggs?" Tanya asked.

Granny Pelageya decided not to and thought to herself: "Fancy that, giving a man fried eggs in the middle of the day! And where's the soup?"

"Will you have some of this?" Tanya suggested she try some stuffed peppers out of a tin. There was nothing for it but to accept as she was really hungry after the journey. As she chewed away at her canned lunch Granny Pelageya studied her son who was tucking into his fried eggs with great relish. "Grigory's hungry. It's terrible. She's just not feeding him properly. He's grown so thin..."

When a jar of Bulgarian jam appeared on the table after that, Granny Pelageya, carefully sipping tea from her saucer asked no-one in particular: "Don't you make any whole-fruit jam here?"

Grigory replied: "There's no need to, Mamma. There's piles of it in the shops."

"Well I never," said Granny Pelageya, this time with a sigh clearly aimed in Tanya's direction. "Grisha used to love cherry jam, without stones in it."

At that Grigory suddenly burst out laughing.

"What's up with you?" asked Granny Pelageya in surprise.

"I was imagining Tanya standing next to a pile of cherry stones that she'd been poking out of cherries for three hours."

"That'll do now," said Granny Pelageya ready to make peace with them all.

Tanya said nothing.

The next morning, almost before it was light, Granny Pelageya started to scrub down the kitchen. She introduced herself to the woman from the next-door flat and asked her where she did the shopping. Then Granny Pelageya went down to the shop, which turned out to be quite near and bought a large nickel-coated saucepan. In the same large shop she acquired a kitchen cupboard. Some kind passers-by helped her bring it home. When the young couple came home from work they found the kitchen changed beyond recognition. The new saucepan and the scoured frying-pan gleamed like knife-blades ready for the fray.

"Mamma, I don't know what to say..." Grigory just shook his head in helpless surprise. Tanya said nothing at all.

Once she had taken over this simple little household, Granny Pelageya seemed ten years younger overnight. Where did she get all that energy from? She cooked the dinners, tidied up the house and found time to go for walks in the woods... Very content she was with her new life, too.

Tanya and Grigory lived in a world of which she knew nothing, a world of happy excitement, probing secrets that were unknown to her and trying to prove things to each other in heated arguments. At first the stormy discussions used to frighten her—she was worried lest that might be quarrelling. As time went by she realised that they enjoyed arguing like that and found it fun: gradually she even grew used to such outlandish words as "atom" or "molecule".

"So here we are then," said Granny Pelageya, "in two days it will be Grigory's birthday. What pies shall we bake?"

"Perhaps we could buy a big cream cake," Tanya suggested timidly.

"Grigory used to love mushroom pies."

"He can't stand them any more! " burst out Tanya unexpectedly as she went out of the kitchen.

Granny Pelageya decided after that to bake pies with a cabbage filling. When all the preparations were over and the cabbage pies were in the middle of the birthday table giving off a delicious smell, she asked in hushed tones: "Tanya, d'you want me to take the icons down?"

"What for?" asked Tanya in surprise.

"What d'you mean 'what for'? You've got scientists among your friends and they're not believers."

"What does it matter?" said Tanya with a smile. "That's a nineteenth-century icon, and this other small one is late eighteenth-century I think. We'll have to ask Valeri. He knows all about it. I like the little one very much."

"Well I'd never have believed it!" said Granny Pelageya in surprise and toddled off to the kitchen to fetch some plates. Then she called out to Tanya: "When I was clearing things away in here I couldn't see your winter boots. What are you going to be wearing?"

"I'll be buying a pair," said Tanya.

"But you spend everything you earn," said Granny Pelageya with a sigh. "After all, Grigory has to send quite a lot back to Moscow... You make sure you put something by from your wage packet. As soon as you get it, put something to one side. Winter's round the corner."

"I'll put something by, Pelageya Vasilievna," promised Tanya.

"Mother's right," joined in Grigory sounding worried. "We don't want you catching colds!"

"It is Siberia after all..." Granny was about to go on, but at that moment the door bell rang, and she hurried off to open the door. At last the guests had arrived.

How glad she was to see him—her Moscow friend who looked like a priest with his beard and long hair. He was as full of jokes and good humour as ever. "Mother Pelageya, you're a legend here in Akademgorodok already: they say that with your cabbage soup anyone could finish off their doctorate. Grigory's lucky to have a mother like you! " he rounded off with a laugh that set his beard a-flapping.

"Let's drink to Pelageya Vasilievna first," suggested Valeri's wife Lena, as she raised her glass. Granny Pelageya had taken to her right from the start. She looked so tidy with her fair hair pulled back tightly into a bun on the nape of her neck. She had a white lace collar to her dress like a schoolgirl. She was held to be serious, yet there was a kind and cheerful gleam in her eyes.

They all stood up to clink glasses with Granny Pelageya. All she managed to reply was: "God grant you all good health! " It warmed the cockles of Granny Pelageya's heart to be surrounded by such kind guests and to be treated with such respect.

It was starting to get light by the time the visitors went. While she was washing the dishes in the kitchen, Granny Pelageya thought to herself: "It turned out such a good party, such fun. They liked the pies. Yet there was nothing from Moscow, from Vadim—nothing, not a letter, not even a greetings card. Grigory had been expecting something. Hoping so much. Perhaps Vadim will remember his father in the end? Perhaps a letter will come tomorrow?"

The letter did come... "You deserted us," wrote Vadim, "and left with that other woman. I don't want

to have anything more to do with you after that."
It was written in large childish letters. Grigory was
sitting motionless before it as it lay on the writing-
desk, his eyes were shut and he was clutching his head
in both hands. Eventually he looked up and muttered:
"It's not him ... she taught him to write like that, the
bitch! " he shouted all of a sudden at the top of
his voice.

"Don't call Natalia names," said Granny Pelageya
in a calm voice. "You'd do better to ask me, what's
it like bringing up a son without a father... It was
wartime then, but it's quite a different thing nowadays. A child needs a father and a family."

None of them said a word during supper. Tanya
hardly ate anything. Grigory told his mother to pour
him out some vodka.

"You're not meant to," warned Tanya.

"It's not your business! " he shouted all of a sudden
and in such a way that Granny Pelageya took fright.
Tanya leapt up from the table and went out into the
sitting-room.

That night Granny Pelageya simply could not get
to sleep. She just lay there on her hard settee-cum-
bed and listened to the sounds of the night. Then the
ventilation window slammed shut—the weather was
turning colder and windier. Next the water started
gurgling in the radiators. It bubbled for a bit and then
fell silent again. Then she picked out the hurried steps
of some late passer-by. Suddenly another sound mingled with those rare night noises, and although the
door to the next room was tightly closed Granny
Pelageya realised that Tanya was crying. She could

hear her bitter, muffled sobs. Then she heard her son talking in low tones. She could not make out the words, but it was obvious that an argument was going on. Yet this argument was of a very different kind, not like the ones about atoms... She began to catch some isolated words of Grigory's: "... for Vadim's sake... you don't understand... I can't... he needs me... forgive me..." Then she realised what the argument was all about.

The next morning Granny Pelageya dragged herself out of bed with great difficulty and toddled through to the kitchen. "Tanya doesn't seem to have made any breakfast at all," she said to herself. "So they went off just like that, without a bite to eat, or even a cup of tea..."

She swept the kitchen floor. Then suddenly she stopped in her tracks. She rushed into the main room and threw the door of the wardrobe wide open. So that was it! She looked round the room, searching in all the corners, on the walls, on the floor, even peeping under the table... She longed to find some tiny belonging of Tanya's, some little thing, but there was nothing there... Feeling weak at the knees, Granny Pelageya sat down on the settee and remained there till Grigory returned. He came back from work early. Then Granny Pelageya rose to her feet and went into the kitchen to heat up some of the cabbage soup left over from the day before. They began to eat their lunch, unable to look each other in the eye. Then Grigory sat down to go through his papers and stayed at his desk till late into the night. The house had a deathly hush about it.

How had she failed to notice it? It was hanging in the bathroom on a nail right in the corner—Tanya's dressing-gown; it was blue with tiny white spots on it. On top of it, on the same nail, there was a towel as well. Still holding this dressing-gown, she bumped into her son as she came out of the bathroom, was lost for words and then muttered something unintelligible. Grigory, on the other hand, carefully took the dressing-gown from her, shook out the creases and then, after taking the towel down from the nail, hung it back where it had been in the first place.

"Inscrutable are the God's ways..." Out of the blue Granny Pelageya found herself at the puppet theatre, after a call from Valeri: "Mother Pelageya, help us out! The city puppet theatre is here on tour. Lena's down with a cold and I've got too much work. Alexei's been whining that he wants to go for the last couple of hours. Would you do us a favour, otherwise the tickets are going to be wasted?"

"Willingly," she said. "Drop the boy off by the shop here."

There was a large poster displayed by the entrance to the Community Centre. That put Granny Pelageya on her guard right from the start, for it showed God sitting on a cloud with almost nothing on. He was chatting to Adam and Eve and all three looked as stupid as they come. Then, when the perfomance began, Granny Pelageya hardly knew where to look for shame. Every time the audience exploded with laughter or broke into wild applause she felt really angry. She could not wait for it all to finish. She sat it out for the child's sake. Yet the Community Centre itself really impressed her. How spacious, how beautiful it was!

"Thank you so much! We're so grateful, Mother Pelageya! " called out Valeri by way of a noisy welcome.

Lena by this time had got out of bed and was running about the flat wearing a muslin mask, "so as not to infect anyone and not to feel guilty when I sneeze". She sneezed a great deal and made it all seem very funny as every time she said: "I just can't understand it, what's the matter with me! "

Then Valeri announced in solemn tones: "So as to thank you, dear Mother Pelageya, for bringing our son home safe and sound we shall now drink tea with cream cake and drinks."

Granny Pelageya was only too happy to stay on to have tea. These people were just up her street. Although their flat was not very tidy and there were books and papers scattered about, yet it was nice and cosy and warmed the heart.

"Well Mother Pelageya, are you getting to like our Siberia now?"

"It would be hard not to," she said warming to the conversation. "It's so pretty all around here. The people are such good sorts, so full of fun. It's just like back home in my village."

"Siberia, Mother Pelageya, is something wonderful..." said Valeri, sounding serious all of a sudden. "You haven't really seen it yet, it means big construction sites, new towns, factories, iron, oil, diamonds... And an atmosphere all of its own."

"He's never tired of talking about his beloved Siberia," said Lena with a laugh. "Alexei, you'd better use a spoon for your cake! ''

"And you're right, Mother Pelageya," Valeri went on. "What makes Siberia is its people. Fine people are settling out here..."

"Right back in 1913," Lena chipped in, "the famous traveller Nansen wrote: 'How comforting it was to see at first hand that there are still many places on this earth where millions of happy homes can be built.' ''

Those words immediately reminded Granny Pelageya of her good-for-nothing son. "I've stayed here too long," she apologised. "Grigory will be waiting all on his own."

"What about Tanya?" asked Lena in surprise.

"Tanya's gone to Moscow on important business," mumbled Granny Pelageya, fidgeting nervously.

While helping her into her coat Valeri asked in a quiet voice: "What's been happening?"

Granny Pelageya was not prepared to lie a second time. She just sighed miserably. Valeri saw her home.

It was a cold windy evening, and the last leaves of autumn were rustling. The fierce Siberian winter was at hand. The streets of Akademgorodok were not brightly lit, and Granny Pelageya had difficulty in making out the path in front of her as she walked slowly along in her heavy three-quarter length coat and her black head-scarf tied peasant style. Valeri supported her carefully by one elbow.

"What's up with Grigory?" he asked.

"Perhaps he'll go back to his family," said Granny Pelageya with a sigh.

"What family?"

139

"What d'you mean... In Moscow he's got a large flat, a wife and a son when all's said and done."

"He has a son—that's true enough. Yet he never had a proper family there. Tanya is his first real family. You lived at their house in Moscow for some time, didn't you?"

"Yes, of course I did..."

"Well and what did you think of the life they led?"

"Everything seemed all right..." Then she recalled out of the blue, so to speak, "Only it was very quiet."

"Quiet?.." repeated Valeri in surprise.

"Yes, quiet. Grigory kept quiet all the time. Sometimes he'd come home from work and have nothing to say for himself. Natalia would be busy about the household more than anything... She never really had the time to talk. If she asked him something he'd reply. But then they'd clam up again."

For a while they walked on in silence, each one engrossed in his own thoughts. Then Valeri said: "So it means she bought the animals and left."

"What animals?" asked Granny Pelageya, all bewildered.

"Our institute promised the Pioneers' Palace that it would organise a Pets' Corner for them. We've been acting as their sponsors for two years now. The children had already built the cages themselves. Only our director just couldn't get hold of any extra money. Recently a whole group of children came round to us, asking: 'When will the animals come? You did promise! ' It just happened to be on pay-day. Tanya said to them: 'Come along, kids! You shall have your animals'. She went straight to the pet shop with them and spent the whole of her salary on pets. The guinea-pigs they're especially taken up with. Then there's a tortoise of rare beauty! .."

"That was instead of the fur boots she needs," sighed Granny Pelageya.

"And she's a fine physicist. Probably a better one than Grigory... She's got what you might call inspiration..."

For the first time in her life Granny Pelageya did not have a wink of sleep all night. The next morning she began to look for her black leather lace-up shoes. Her bundle was small and light this time—her warm coat she would have to wear for the journey and the felt boots she decided to leave behind... Yet even so, collecting her things together, was a long laborious process...

"What's going on around here?" asked her son in surprise when he came back from work.

"I've stayed on longer than I should have done, Grigory. I need to get home. It's months now since I've tended Zinaida's grave. Then there's your fierce Siberian winter round the corner. I'm too old to cope with frosts like that, my arms and legs aren't up to it. Then the house in Moscow has had no-one to look after it all this time... But in the spring I'll be back."

"Perhaps you might change your mind and stay, after all?" he asked one last time at the station.

"No, Grigory, I can't," said Granny Pelageya quite determined by now. "I need to be off now."

"Perhaps I'll be in Moscow soon, too," muttered Grigory.

Granny Pelageya let that pass without comment. It

merely made her feel restless and she rushed headlong for her carriage.

There was no getting away from it—she was a real Muscovite by now! When the suburbs of the capital came into sight as she looked out of the train window, she felt happy and light of heart. When the taxi raced her through the Moscow streets she felt she was coming home. There was the quiet little street and the house with the tiny garden. Thank goodness, she was back again. How was Lyuba getting on? Was she in? She was probably at that typewriter of hers, bang, bang, bang... She would be glad. She would not have been expecting her to come back...

It took some time before Lyuba came to answer the door and there was nothing particularly happy about the expression on her face. The opposite! The neighbour said hallo in an off-hand kind of way, as if Granny Pelageya had not been away in Siberia, but had just been round the corner to the baker's.

"I've got a bad back," said Lyuba, explaining the state she was in. She moved away from the door with slow steps, like those of an old woman: her shoulders were hunched and she was clutching at the small of her back with both hands.

"Oh, what a to-do," cried Pelageya in a troubled voice. "How did all this happen, Lyuba dear?"

"I don't know," said Lyuba walking on down the corridor with difficulty.

"We should rub your back with turpentine! It'll help right away." And with that Granny Pelageya dropped her luggage by the door and started pattering down the corridor behind her neighbour, anxious to help her without delay.

"What d'you mean turpentine?" asked Lyuba angrily. "Someone got hold of some poisonous Indian ointment for me, but it didn't help. And here you come and suggest turpentine..."

"We'll put a warm iron on the bad place as well," said Granny Pelageya undeterred.

The neighbour threw Pelageya an angry glance from the doorway of her room and shut the door tightly behind her.

So there was nothing left for Granny Pelageya to do but unpack her things and start tidying the kitchen which had been badly neglected. When evening came, she knocked at her neighbour's door despite what had happened earlier, and asked: "Tell me Lyuba, what would you like me to bring you? You can't go on like this! You've got to eat. That'll help you get over your bad back quicker."

Suddenly the neighbour started crying like a child and through her sobs she said: "Don't go away again like that, Granny Pelageya. They've got everything they need anyway... Do stay here, with me..."

Granny Pelageya had a great respect for documents and did not like throwing out papers. She carefully stored in her clothes cupboard old letters, rent receipts, an invitation to a meeting of the house committee, her grandson's essay with the heading "My dear Granny" and a good deal else besides. It was here that she had kept the scrap of paper with Tanya's telephone number on it, that Natalia had given her all those months back.

143

Granny Pelageya tried the number again and again until it was well into the evening, when at last she heard that familiar hoarse voice.

"Speaking."

"Good evening," said Granny Pelageya. "Can I speak to Tanya?"

"She's not in yet. She hasn't come back from work. Who is it?"

"Forgive me for troubling you," said Granny Pelageya plucking up all the courage she could muster. "May I ask who it is on the telephone?"

"I'm just a neighbour in the flat," came the hoarse voice, angry this time into the bargain. "What message d'you want to leave?"

"Tell her that Pelageya Vasilievna rang."

The next morning Granny Pelageya rang again.

"She's already gone," answered the neighbour, and then added in an unexpectedly polite tone: "She gives lessons now in the mornings, private coaching."

"Be so kind," asked Granny Pelageya, anxious to make the most of his good mood, "would you give me her address?"

The neighbour dictated the address, explaining how to get there, and he even apologised for not having given Tanya the message the evening before on account of his having gone to bed early as he was ill.

"Don't worry," said Granny Pelageya in a reassuring tone. "I can come round to see her now I've got the address."

People always said—"Ask and you'll find your way! " and Granny Pelageya was hoping this would work, when she set off to find Tanya's house. It proved no easy task however to find the right house in one of those new districts, and then the right block. After all that looking and asking she was quite exhausted.

The neighbour she talked to on the phone opened the door—a sullen-looking elderly man in striped pyjamas. It was clear that he was out of sorts again that day.

"Good evening," said Granny Pelageya bowing by way of greeting. "Is Tanya at home?"

The man coughed, and without responding to her greeting he looked Granny Pelageya up and down so disparagingly that she wished the floor would swallow her up.

"She's not here! If you want to you can wait. Hers is the second door on the left. It's not locked." Then he shuffled away down the corridor.

"It is because he's not well," thought Granny Pelageya to herself, "and he gets up on his high horse so easily." She was alone in the corridor now and suddenly came over terribly tired. Noticing a stool at the end of it she dragged herself that far and sat down without taking her coat off. She sat there like that in the dimly-lit corridor for a long time until at last she heard a key scrape in the lock.

Tanya came in, put the light on and, when she saw Granny Pelageya in front of her, she stopped in her tracks quite taken aback.

"Pelageya Vasilievna, it's you?! "

"Yes, Tanya, it's me. Who else would it be?"

"What are you sitting there for? My door isn't locked."

"Never mind, don't you worry. I'm fine."

Tanya helped her to pull off her thick coat, hung it up on the coat-rack in the corridor and then led her through into the room. With a bit of a struggle Granny Pelageya lowered herself on to the settee and while her new daughter-in-law bustled about to heat up some water, she took a close look at how the room was fitted out. So this was where Grigory had been taking refuge from his cut-glass palace!

Tanya brought in a kettle of boiling water. They drank their tea in silence and then Tanya broke the ice: "So you've come back?"

"Yes, I'm back," replied Granny Pelageya, "and when are you planning to go back to Siberia?"

Tanya looked down at her plate without saying anything. Without waiting for an answer, Granny Pelageya remarked reproachfully: "My Grigory's there waiting for you."

Tanya went on staring into her plate. The conversation did not really get off the ground. Soon Granny Pelageya made ready to take her leave.

"I'll be on my way now. Back home Lyuba's ill. Tomorrow what time d'you get back from work?"

"The same as today," said Tanya warily.

"I'll be round to see you at the same time then. If you'll have me."

"But of course, do come, Pelageya Vasilievna! "

The next day Granny Pelageya appeared at the appointed time, bringing with her some tasty titbits. They sat down at the table, and Granny Pelageya began the conversation in a vague, roundabout kind of way...

"What air they've got out there, so fresh and clean...

146

The wind rustling in those tree-tops... All those forests stretching as far as the eye can see... And birds singing."

"It's quite a place," agreed Tanya meekly.

"And then there's the people! So kind and such fun. Valeri and his wife Lena send you their love, your friends..."

"Thank you," said Tanya in a distant kind of voice.

Neither of them could think what to say next, and then Granny Pelageya sighed: "Grigory's stayed behind on his own. I only hope he doesn't fall sick again, God forbid! "

"Why did you go and leave him?"

"It's not me that he needs. It's you," commented Granny Pelageya.

All of a sudden Tanya flared up: "But he's got a family in Moscow! " casting a stern, almost vengeful look in Granny Pelageya's direction.

"You're his family now, Tanya," said Granny Pelageya gently.

The next time Granny Pelageya turned up was two days later.

"Are you still here?" she inquired from the threshold.

"Where else should I be?" asked Tanya hesitantly.

"What d'you mean where? With your husband, in his house. Where he is—there you should be."

"Look here, Pelageya Vasilievna," burst out Tanya angrily. "You're putting me in an awkward position. Grigory hasn't phoned once, or written me a single letter."

"Go and ring him up yourself. Tear him off a strip. You tell him what's what. Ask him what he's playing at?"

Tanya turned away to hide the tears she could not hold back. Then Granny Pelageya decided that God would forgive her a little white lie, and she said: "You complain he hasn't written to you. Yet some time back now he sent me money telling me to buy you a ticket and tell you to go back to him."

At that Tanya immediately turned her tear-stained face round to Granny Pelageya and asked: "When did he send it?"

"I don't remember... Some time back..."

"Really?!"asked Tanya, like a helpless child.

"Come now, get going, see to your things. Pack all your warm clothes. You've got a coat thank Goodness, and a fur hat. I left my felt boots there for you..."

"Yes, all right..." mumbled Tanya, perplexed.

When she arrived home the neighbour was singing a nursery rhyme about Prince Charming on his noble steed. Granny Pelageya heard the song as she walked up the stairs, then she opened the door into the apartment cautiously and had another listen. Once she was sure the song was a happy one, she boldly went to knock on her neighbour's door.

"Thank Heavens for that," she said. "You ought to have listened to me ages ago, Lyuba! If you'd put turpentine on when I first told you, you'd have been singing songs weeks ago."

"Next time I'll put some on straightaway," promised Lyuba. "Where have you been going off to every evening?"

"Just out for some fresh air," replied Granny Pelageya evasively. "Lyuba, there's something I'd like to ask you... Forgive me, my dear, but...."

"Ask anything you like. I'm ready to do anyone a favour today! "

"A long time ago you got me tickets for the circus... Are there tickets like that to be had from your work?"

"But of course! "

"Bring me a couple for Sunday would you?"

"Who are you planning to go with?" asked the neighbour enviously.

"With my grandson. I'm going to go with Vadim," came the answer to satisfy the neighbour's curiosity.

The next day Lyuba had hardly got in the door when Granny Pelageya came running out to meet her.

"Calm down now. I'm just going to have a bite to eat and then I'll go and fetch the tickets."

"You could have a quick plate of my soup, Lyuba. Why bother to go and start cooking from scratch..."

"All right then, I'll have some soup," agreed Lyuba.

Granny Pelageya dialled the number several times, but each time she put down the receiver before it rang. In the end she plucked up enough courage. It was Vadim who answered the telephone.

"Hallo, Vadim," said Granny Pelageya happily. "Well my love, have you been forgetting your old Granny? Why haven't you rung up the old lady, to find out if she's still in one piece or perhaps already taken to her bed?"

"I've had ever such a lot of school work," answered Vadim, apologetically.

"They really pile it on nowadays, don't they! " she said sympathetically.

"Then there's music on top of that," said Vadim with a sigh.

"Studying's all very well, but you need some time off as well. What d'you feel about the circus?"

"The circus! " cried Vadim in a much livelier tone.

"A friend's promised to get hold of some tickets for me. I'm frightened to go on my own. They say they've got some big animals there like tigers."

"That's nothing, Granny! Don't you worry! If they bring on the lions or the tigers, then they put up great big nets like fences."

"Perhaps we could go together, and then you could explain it all to me when we get there?"

"When?" asked the boy overjoyed.

"This Sunday. Is Mamma at home? You go and ask her."

Vadim put the receiver down and Granny Pelageya waited on tenterhooks.

"It's all right," said Vadim when he came back at last.

Granny Pelageya was as happy as he was: "Well then, my love, you be ready for me on Sunday morning. I'll come and fetch you. Give Mamma my regards, too."

"Fine," said the little boy merrily. "I'll be waiting."

"To him that hath shall be given, and to him that hath not shall be taken away even that which he hath," thought Granny Pelageya to herself. Then she booked a long-distance call to Novosibirsk.

She sat by the telephone until the long-distance pips at last rang out.

"Grigory," called Granny Pelageya, as if she thought

she could cover the distance from Moscow to Akadem-gorodok by raising her voice. "D'you hear me, son? Tanya's leaving for Siberia the day after tomorrow. Make sure you meet her and remember flowers! You can expect a nice letter from Vadim soon, too. Depend upon it. You're bound to get the kind of letter you've been waiting for..."

Valeri Khairyuzov

THE GUARDIAN

Valeri Khairyuzov was born in Irkutsk in 1944. He graduated from a flying school and is now crew commander of a plane that is on scheduled service along the route of the Baikal-Amur Railway.

The main subject of Khairyuzov's stories is the life of young people in the harsh conditions of the North on the building projects of Siberia. That Khairyuzov sets his characters in difficult surroundings allows him to portray strong-willed people with open minds who seek a high goal in life.

Khairyuzov's collection of stories, *Forced Landing,* was awarded a prize in the Maxim Gorky All-Union Competition for the best first book by a young author. He is also a winner of the Lenin Komsomol Prize.

Valeri Khairyuzov is a member of the USSR Writers' Union.

In the middle of January, returning by an off-schedule flight from Zhigansk, we landed in Vitim to spend the night there. The short winter day had reached its close. I was making the bed when Alexei Dobretsov, the crew commander, entered the room and handed me a wireless message. It read: *"Second pilot Osintsev immediately return to base..."*

At first I could not grasp the meaning of the message; I read it a second time and suddenly the writing seemed blurred and the letters began jumping—my mother had died.

I looked at the silent Dobretsov in bewilderment. There was a lump in my throat, a pricking sensation I had not known for years.

I did not sleep all night, I sat by the window waiting for morning to come. In the morning twilight the grey silhouette of the airport building showed through the frost-bound window, and in the distance, on a hillock, the yellowish outlines of the aeroplane came into view.

I felt I could wait no longer and walked out of the hotel. The low sky did not promise anything good. The crew commander returned from the weather-station and by his frowning look I could tell that we were not allowed to fly that day.

We spent three days in Vitim; there was no flying weather and the airports did not function. On the fourth day we only got as far as Ust-Orda; we were not given permission to land in Irkutsk, and the only thing I could do was get there on my own, hitchhiking a car going in the same direction. We reached the city towards evening. I got out in the centre and took the

155

bus to the railway station. There were hardly any people in the streets. The driver braked carefully at every bus stop, letting in a few late passengers, and drove on. I arrived on time. The local train I needed was leaving in several minutes. I bought a ticket and began watching the people rushing past me along the platform. There were many elderly women among them. And then I suddenly realised that I was unconsciously looking for my mother's face. The grief that had been suppressed by the long journey gushed forth and filled my entire being.

"Why do all misfortunes in the world happen to our family? What have we done wrong? First Father died and now Mother... My brother and my two little sisters are left orphans."

The local train arrived, the doors banged open and people began getting in. Half an hour later the train pulled in at a small station called Relka. I got off and decided to walk to the village rather than wait for a car. The path took me across a field with clumps of bushes scattered here and there. The grey sky hung low overhead; in the distance it was a denser colour and it was impossible to distinguish the horizon. The snow crunched under my feet. Ahead of me I could see an even row of lights like the signalling lamps on the runway.

The path turned off to one side. Not wishing to take a roundabout route, I went across the untrodden snow, choosing the places where the ice crust was thick enough. Closer to the village the snow began to yield underfoot. It was getting dark. The grey heads of yarrow stuck out of the snow, their stalks leaning towards the houses. It seemed that they had dried up and had been covered with snow and ice just as they had been running to where there was human habitation. I suddenly felt a constriction in my chest. I found it difficult breathing.

"I'm home at last. Just a few more steps..." But I felt paralysed with fear. I last saw my mother in autumn when I was flying to the North. She got several hours off at work and ran home to see me to the airport. I noticed then that Mother's fluffy woollen shawl was well-worn and shabby. "She tried to give us what she could and never had money to buy anything for herself."

I did not meet a soul in the street. The snow-covered wooden houses were as alike as twins, with stacks of thick pine firewood by each fence and narrow paths leading from the gates. Yellow strips of light fell on the road through the chinks in the shutters.

I walked on and could soon see our house from the top of a hillock. In the twilight it looked like an old woman wearing a white shawl on her head. The windows were frozen over. At the gate I pushed my hand behind a plank and lifted the latch, as I had done so many times before.

I hesitated, afraid to enter the house. On the porch I felt for the door-handle and having found it, pulled the door open. Frozen from the outside, the door creaked loudly and a gust of cold air swept into the room. I was aware of the smell of home and warmth, so familiar to me since childhood.

"Stepan's arrived," somebody's voice said with relief.

It was Aunt Nadya, my mother's sister. She was very much like my mother—the same kind grey eyes, the same open countenance.

"Where's mother?"

"We buried her yesterday." With her handkerchief, Aunt Nadya wiped her eyes that were red from weeping.

"What do you mean 'yesterday'! Didn't I say I'd come?"

"When we got the telegram it was already too late," Aunt Nadya said apologetically. "Don't be angry."

I took off my pilot jacket, hung it on a nail and went into the room. Vera, Kostya and Natasha were sitting quietly on a bench. They were tired out with crying, but the moment they saw me, they burst into tears again. I took little Natasha in my arms, and she stopped weeping and cuddled up to me. I stroked her hair tenderly, lowering my head so that the children would not see my face. Vera and Kostya jumped up from the bench and clung to me.

"Did any of the relatives come to the funeral?" I asked a little later.

"They did, all of them came," Aunt Nadya answered quickly. "Didn't you meet them on the way? They went to the bus stop, Efim and Frosya are seeing them off."

"No I didn't. I came from the direction of the railway station."

"What do I think I'm doing, sitting around when you must be hungry after the journey?" Aunt Nadya began bustling about. She ran out into the kitchen and started clattering some plates. Then she quickly set the table.

"Drink to your mother's memory," she said handing me a glass. I emptied it in one gulp, not noticing the smell of liquor.

The children sat down at the table.

I looked at the familiar faces and my eyes clouded with tears. Only just recently our whole family gathered at table, and I couldn't believe this would never happen again.

"Aunt Galya was here, but Vladimir couldn't come," Aunt Nadya continued. "He sent a telegram saying he was ill. We did everything properly. Our neighbours, you know, they're like members of the family. They helped us a lot. And the factory people took care of the funeral. Director Kutin is a very good man. And mother was held in such respect there, you know. The director had a tombstone made and an iron railing, and he allowed us to use the factory car. He also came to the funeral. Your teacher, Irina Vasilievna, came too."

Aunt Nadya fell silent, brushing away her tears.

"While Mother was ill, she kept waiting for you all the time. She would listen every time someone knocked, and she kept looking at the door. When she saw it wasn't you, she wouldn't say anything: she'd just lie there quietly. She was taken bad during her last days. She would tell the children to sit in a circle around her and check their notebooks. Kostya is weak in arithmetic and she tried to help him, but she couldn't. Vera acted as head of the family—she kept house, cooked dinner and did the laundry. When I came visiting, she would show me your letters. She is so proud of you."

"If it hadn't been for the weather, I'd have come on time. At first there was this beastly fog..."

I clenched my teeth trying to swallow the tears that choked me. My emotions got out of control. It was as if I had been carrying a glass of boiling-hot water, patiently enduring the pain, but the moment I put it down, the pain became agonising.

"Cry a bit, you'll feel better if you do," Aunt Nadya said. She looked at me, and I saw tears rolling down her cheeks.

"I don't know what we'd do if it weren't for Yefim."

"How is he?"

"He and Frosya are planning to live here. They only have one small room, and the children can't live here with nobody to take care of them."

"I've brought some money," I said to Aunt Nadya. "You must've spent all you had."

"No, you'll need the money yourself," Aunt Nadya objected.

Soon after, my uncle Yefim returned. I could tell by the stamping of feet on the porch that he was trying to shake the snow off his felt boots.

"My, how you've grown up," Uncle Yefim said as he entered the room. He had changed a lot, had put on weight and seemed to have become shorter somehow.

"How long are you going to stay?" he asked.

I didn't have time to reply. Yefim's wife Frosya saw me from the threshold and began wailing at the top of her voice.

"You poor orphans! She's gone, she's left you all alone in the world! "

"Cut that out! " Uncle Yefim raised his voice. "It's bad enough without that noise."

Blowing her nose and wiping away her tears Frosya walked across the room and sat down next to Aunt Nadya.

"I loved her so much, the poor dear. It's such a terrible loss! " Frosya began lamenting again. "How many times I told her to take better care of herself! 'Don't forget you have children,' I said. And what will they do with themselves now that she's gone?"

"Stop it, Frosya," Aunt Nadya cut her short. "Stepan's just arrived, he's tired and can't get over what's happened, and here you are, whining. And besides the children are listening."

Frosya bit her tongue; she was somewhat afraid of Aunt Nadya.

"What's the matter with us? Food is ready. Why don't we talk at table?" said Aunt Nadya.

"That would be a good idea," Uncle Yefim supported her.

Aunt Nadya brought several more glasses. Yefim poured out the vodka.

"Let's drink to her memory, Stepan," he said.

We emptied the glasses, had a bit to eat and drank another one. Uncle Yefim began telling us how he and his wife saw off our relatives.

"We have to decide what to do about the children," Frosya cut in.

"Yes, yes, she's right," Uncle Yefim said hurriedly. "The Kutins were asking me if we wouldn't let them adopt little Natasha. You know for yourself, God didn't grant them children, and what sort of a life is it without children? They wanted to take one from a children's home, but why take someone they don't know when Natasha is like a daughter to them already?"

Uncle Yefim stood up, scooped up some water from a pail and gulped it down greedily. Frosya kept silent and studied the expression on my face. The look in her eyes reminded me of a cat keeping watch over a mouse.

Aunt Nadya, softened, was wiping away her tears. Then she raised her head all of a sudden and banged her fist on the table.

"Listen to what I'll tell you, kind folk: they have relatives, don't they? Can we leave them in trouble? What will people say if we do?"

"You're absolutely right. We have to decide," Uncle Yefim said. "We don't have a big enough flat, otherwise I'd have taken the children to live with us and that would've been that."

"Of course, Yefim, of course!" Frosya chimed in.

"We were so close, Anna and I," Yefim went on, glancing once in a while at Aunt Nadya. "I was always ready to help—I'd bring her coal or firewood to heat the stove. I knew she had a hard time with the children on her hands. Last year I managed to get five rolls of roofing felt for her!"

That's how it always was. He'd bring us some white-wash and mother would coat the walls in her own room and in his too. Frosya couldn't manage it for some reason. Mother always apologised for him later: "Don't be angry, sonny," she would say. "Yefim is a good man, it's just that Frosya can twist him round her little finger."

For as long as I remember him, Uncle Yefim had been constantly changing jobs; he always wanted more money than he had. They never bothered with the kitchen garden or anything.

"I'm working as a store-keeper now," I heard Uncle Yefim speaking. "It's a very responsible job, I have to account for the goods entrusted to me, you know."

I felt a growing hostility towards Uncle Yefim. Afraid to lose my temper I rose from the table and went outside. The frosty damp air got into my lungs and my eyes filled with tears. The roofs of the neighbouring houses left open a patch of starlit sky that reminded me of an aeroplane instrument board. There was a deathly stillness around. A dog ran out from behind the porch and began circling round my feet, wagging its tail.

"Polkan, old friend, where were you?"

The door creaked and Uncle Yefim came out of the house. Holding on to the wall, he came up to me.

"Why did you dash away?" he breathed out behind my back. "Wanted to be alone for a while, eh?"

Polkan flattened his ears, growling menacingly. Uncle Yefim stepped back a pace or two.

"I talked to the school headmaster yesterday," he said, suppressing a yawn. "He promised he'd send the necessary papers to the children's home. All you have to do is submit an application."

It was as if a spring had snapped inside me—I grabbed Yefim by the shirt and pulled hard.

"Why didn't you ask me first?"

"Are you crazy or what?" Uncle Yefim tried to free himself from my grip.

Polkan attacked him from the side and seized him by his trouser leg. Uncle Yefim kicked, but the dog held on tight.

"Take that dog away! Take him away or I'll kill him."

"Polkan! " I called. "Get off with you! "

"Why did you have to bury mother without me? So you got her five rolls of roofing felt? Aren't you a benefactor! "

Uncle Yefim stood breathing heavily.

"What are you doing out there? Go inside or else you'll catch cold! " shouted Frosya from the porch.

"Shut up! " Uncle Yefim waved his hand. "We're talking about serious matters here."

"You're just like your father. Just as hot-tempered," said my uncle, recovering his breath. "Why don't you want to understand me, Stepan? I can't take them to live with us, we've got two children of our own. And Frosya is no help, you know that. She is so sickly, spends most of the time in hospitals. She may follow your mother into the grave any day."

A hot wave of shame and pity I had never experienced before swept over me.

"I'm sorry for what I said, Uncle Yefim."

"It's all right. It's the grief in you."

We both went back into the house and sat down at the table. I put my arms around the children. I felt ashamed and disgusted with myself.

"Why don't you say anything, Stepan?" Aunt

Nadya asked. "You're the eldest in the family now. It's for you to decide."

"The children will stay with me," I said firmly.

"You're too young, they'll be such a burden on you," said Frosya with a sigh. "Today you put on a brave face, but we'll see what you say tomorrow."

"Keep quiet, Frosya," Uncle Yefim cut her short. "You're just like your father. But you've got to think twice before you decide a thing like that, my boy. You're a pilot; who will look after the children when you're away? Perhaps we should send them..." Uncle Yefim did not finish the sentence and cast a wary glance at me.

"...to a boarding school," Frosya helped him out.

"That's it. They'll be looked after and provided for there," Uncle Yefim supported her readily.

"That won't do. I've made up my mind. I have a room in town, and then we'll see; perhaps the director of the airport will give me a new flat."

"Kostya's such a mischievous child! You'll have problems with him! " Frosya said. "Think twice, Stepan."

"We're not forcing our opinion on you. All of us just wish you good," Aunt Nadya joined in suddenly. "I'll take Natasha, she's only a child. She can live with us for the time being. Where there's room for five, there's room for six. And if you'll decide to take her back later, it's up to you."

"That's fine, Nadya, and Vera will stay with us, we'll manage somehow." Frosya had finally made up her mind.

"She'll live with you and wash your floors the way mother did," I thought angrily.

Uncle Yefim heaved a heavy sigh, looked around, examining the ceiling and the walls, then tapped his foot on the floorboards.

"What are you planning to do with the house, Stepan?"

"It'll have to be sold."

"It's an old house. It's only good enough for firewood. You won't get more than two hundred rubles for it."

"Why, after repairs it can still be lived in."

"You're right of course," Uncle Yefim admitted, "but the people who buy it will have to spend a lot of money on repairs. Don't you remember how much that house cost your family?"

I nodded without saying anything.

...There was a log-built hay shed right by the house. When I did something wrong I always used to hide there so that Mother wouldn't find me. I would cling to the wall of the shed, which was always warm and dry. Greyish whiskers of hay stuck out between the logs, and mice would be darting about somewhere down below.

Once I made myself a toy gun and stuffed it with matches. I was afraid the noise might wake up the children so I went behind the shed. I stuck some cotton wool into the muzzle, aimed at the wall and fired. It caught fire and bluish smoke trailed along. I grabbed a stick, trying to beat out the tiny tongues of flame, but the hay was on fire and my feeble attempts to put it out had no effect whatsoever. I rushed to the house, picked up a pail of water and ran back. By then the whole shed was enveloped in smoke and the fire had spread to the house.

The children were asleep, so I hurried inside and woke up Vera. The two of us ran out into the street. The roof of our house was burning, and people scurrying to and fro. They pulled Vera and me further away from the fire. "Where is Kostya?" I thought in terror. By then the whole house was in flames and the logs were crackling loudly.

Mother came running. Not knowing what she was doing she rushed into the burning house, but somebody held her back in time. One of the neighbours poured some water over himself and ran inside. At that moment they brought Kostya. He had been hiding in the raspberry bushes.

It was a hot windy day. The whole village would have burned down if it hadn't been for the soldiers from a military unit stationed in the vicinity. The alarm was raised; they came to the village at once and put out the fire.

Wood for new walls was brought from the Angara River. Soon after, the soldiers finished putting up the log frame and laying the floors. Father and Uncle Yefim made rafters for the roof and covered it. But before long the house was too small for us and father decided to build a new one. At that time he was working in a logging camp and he brought a lorry-load of logs for the new house. But he never built it... Soon after he was killed in an accident.

"Stepan, what if we stay here for the time being?" Uncle Yefim asked me.

"Of course you can stay."

"So it's settled," Frosya said happily. "We'll do the necessary repairs ourselves and you'll come visiting. After all, it's the house your parents lived in."

"And Vera will be with us," Uncle Yefim added.

"I think I should start back," Aunt Nadya said. "When I received the telegram I left many things half-done and came here, leaving the children with my neighbours."

Aunt Nadya embraced Kostya and Vera and burst into tears.

"Be sure to come and see me next summer. You'll drink all the milk you want. Be friends and don't fight."

Aunt Nadya helped Natasha to put on her overcoat and warm boots. Natasha couldn't understand what was going on and looked around in confusion: when they were half-way out of the house she began crying. On seeing this, Vera and Kostya cried too. I could barely hold back my tears. I lifted little Natasha on my shoulders, and the three of us went to see her and Aunt Nadya off to the bus stop.

* * *

I lay near the wall and felt the cold seeping through the chinks between the logs. Kostya lay asleep next to me, making a sucking sound with his lips. I could see shimmering reddish shadows dancing on the kitchen wall. "The firewood will burn out soon, I must close the flue, or else it'll be completely cold here by morning," I thought to myself.

All was quiet in the house except for the monotonous ticking of the clock on the wall. The fire was out and the shadows disappeared. I got out of bed and went barefoot into the kitchen, stepping on the cold cracked floor. I closed the flue to keep some of the warmth inside. Then I heard Vera tossing and turning in her sleep. I came up to her, adjusted the blanket and sat on the edge of her bed. She sat up at once and put her arms around me.

"Why aren't you sleeping?" I asked.

"I heard a knock and thought you'd gone somewhere."

"I was only closing the flue."

"Don't leave us, Stepan, please don't. I can do everything around the house. I can cook and do the washing. When mother was ill I did it all myself."

"Don't worry, calm down and go to sleep. I'm not going to leave you. I'll try and find your papers right now and I'll go to the district executive committee tomorrow."

I went up to the cupboard and opened one of the drawers. I knew Mother kept family documents, papers and letters there. On top lay our family album. It began with a large photograph showing all six of us—Father, Mother, and four children, clinging to them. Next there were several old yellowed photos: Mother and Father, still very young; Father in an old-fashioned blouse and Mother with a short hair-cut, the kind girls wear nowadays. On a separate page lay Father's war-time pictures. One showed Father, in a rumpled wadded jacket and dirt-spattered boots, standing next to a Studebaker. There was also another, post-war photograph of Father. He is shown sitting by the house, holding me in his lap. His crutches have been leaned against the wall. I am wearing a field-service cap on my head. Father had just been discharged from hospital and he came into the yard on crutches. A nurse walked by his side, helping him along. Father was in such a hurry to reach the porch that the crutches slipped in the mud. Awkwardly waving his hands about, he lost his balance and fell on his side. The nurse rushed to help him to his feet but he pushed her out of the way and crawled up the stairs, supporting himself with his arms. Mother ran wailing out on to the porch.

"Don't cry, that's enough! Thank God I'm alive," Father said, trying to sound cheerful.

A minute later he was patting me on the head with his calloused hand, smiling through his tears. In his other hand he held some sticky chocolates which he had brought for me.

We went through hard times. Father couldn't work as a driver now, so he began mending shoes and fixing heels. Soon the whole house reeked of shoe-makers' wax. When Father got well and could use his legs again, he felt an urge to return to the garage where he had worked before the war. He was given a badly battered old car. He started bringing bolts and nuts into the house and his clothes began to smell of gasoline. His wartime friends often dropped in. They recalled the war and sometimes had a drink or two. After that Father would have a bad hangover. At such moments I watched him with fear. Later, Father went to work for a logging enterprise, bringing timber from the taiga to the railway station. He often took me along with him and then I felt I was the happiest person on earth. My family was convinced that I would follow in my father's footsteps and become a driver like him...

It seemed to me now that I was looking into my childhood from aboard an aeroplane. I could see much of it distinctly as if it were somewhere near, as though I were flying only several metres above the ground. But when I wanted to take a closer look, I could not see anything, because the early years of my childhood were hidden behind clouds, and all I could remember was what my mother told me.

I was a weak, sickly child, and before I had time to recover after one illness, another was already waiting for me. Mother was tired out and was about to lose heart but still she managed somehow to pull me through my illnesses. I grew up to be a strong, healthy lad, but the consequences of Mother's exertions were quick in coming. Mother was always so busy taking care of us that she never had time to think of herself...

I looked at Vera's photograph. She was such a quiet child that I did not even notice how she grew up. She would tuck away in the corner and play with her dolls all day long. I would bar the way with chairs and benches so she couldn't get out of the house and then run to the river with the other kids. When I came back she would be sleeping in the corner, curled up in a ball.

I remembered Kostya ever since that first day when they brought him from the maternity home. He cried day and night. My parents were busy, so I had to rock the baby to sleep. He began bossing me around as soon as he learned to talk. He would lie down in his cot, squint his roguish eyes and demand: "Rock me! " When he was five he was up to all sorts of mischief and his favourite pastime was going for a ride on the neighbour's goat. My father doted on him and spoiled him. "He's a madcap, just like me," he would often say.

For most people, childhood passes gradually, but for me it ended abruptly, on the day my father was crushed to death by a tree in the logging camp. That year Vera went to school and little Natasha was born. Mother began receiving a pension for my father, but there was still not enough money. I decided I should help her.

"I'm ashamed to be a burden to you, Mother," I said. "I'll get myself a job and finish my tenth year at night school."

"You've got to study, Stepan. You're all brawn and no brains! " Mother replied. "You'll have all the work you want later on."

...I found the children's birth certificates and put them on the cupboard. Kostya was muttering something in his sleep, but as soon as I got into bed he clung to me and quietened down.

* * *

I was awakened in the morning by the merry crackling of firewood in the stove. Vera had already made her bed, and from the kitchen came the tempting smell of fried potatoes. Vera looked in and, seeing that I had woken up, brought me a freshly ironed shirt.

"I washed it while you were sleeping and had to iron it while it was still wet."

I felt somewhat embarrassed because I hadn't changed my shirt for several days.

"Wake up Kostya, or else we'll be late for school," Vera said.

I shook my brother by the shoulder; he snuffled, made a face, and jerked the blanket over his head.

"It's the same old story," Vera said with a sigh. "Mother always had problems getting him out of bed."

"So you say," drawled Kostya in an offended voice. "I did it on purpose, just to annoy you. If that's what you want I'll get up earlier from today on."

We had a quick breakfast. Vera cleared the table and brought the satchels to the kitchen. Then she carefully wrapped a scarf round her brother's neck.

We went out into the street together. Every now and again we heard the banging of gates as people hurried out of their homes and walked down the road. Some of them were pulling sledges with children muffled up in heavy coats and warm scarves. It was freezing cold. The piercing whistle of an electric locomotive came from somewhere behind the village. Mother used to take me to school along that same road, and then she would walk downhill towards the Angara River, where the animal feed factory stood.

"When will we go to the cemetery?" Vera asked.

"I'm going to the district executive committee right now, and then to the cemetery."

Near the school building Vera and Kostya disappeared into the crowd of children. The first person

I saw in the committee waiting-room was Galina Stepanovna, the mother of a schoolmate of mine. She worked as a secretary there. When I came in Galina Stepanovna was typing. A lit cigarette lay in an ash-tray next to the typewriter.

"Come in, Osintsev," she said amiably. "You are certainly an early visitor."

She picked up her cigarette, inhaled, and deep dimples appeared on her cheeks.

"I've come to legalise my guardianship. I want to take Vera and Kostya to live with me."

"Poor Anna, she was still such a young woman," Galina Stepanovna said, putting the cigarette in the ash-tray. "It's so unfair to her... How old was she? Not yet forty?"

"She'd have been forty in autumn."

"You know, the papers are already at the children's home," Galina Stepanovna said and looked at me with sympathy. "I saw the signed resolution with my own eyes."

"I wonder who could have been in such a hurry to do it?" I didn't mean to ask that question but I felt so hurt I couldn't help it.

"Yefim and his wife. They came to an executive committee meeting."

"Nobody wants other people's children! The easiest thing of course is to get rid of them and send them to a children's home. Let the state take care of them! "

"I understand how you feel about it, Stepan. People are all different, and your uncle isn't the best sort I've seen. But you're too young; they might object to your guardianship."

"What am I to do? Tell me, Galina Stepanovna."

"You'll need a reference from your place of work. The airport administration should support your claim. There will be a committee meeting next week. You must try to get all the necessary papers by then, and I'll do my best to help you. Are you planning to get married?" she asked in a serious tone. She treated me as a full-grown man.

"There's no one I could marry."

That was the truth. I really didn't have a girlfriend.

"You know what my son told me recently? 'I'm getting married', he said, 'it's high time I hitched up! ' What he really wants is to live without his mother."

Galina Stepanovna looked at me, sizing me up.

"You should get married if you want to be a guardian. You won't manage without a woman."

I said goodbye and left.

Day was breaking. The snow-covered roofs of the houses were dimly visible against the pale grey sky. The gloom of night was gradually receding to merge finally with the waters of the Angara. The opposite bank seemed to be growing out of nothingness. The wooded mountain in the distance looked like a green woolen hat; the foothills were hidden behind a scarf of grey mist. The contrast between the temperature inside and out made me feel chilly. I tightened the belt round my jacket, turned up my collar and headed for the children's home.

In summer, there was a small stretch of marshy land which was crossed by a foot-bridge—several boards nailed to half-rotted piles. But now, in winter, the path went over the ice. The top layer had been scraped off by the bridge where the children tramped across, forming a narrow tongue-shaped bluish run in the ice. I gave in to temptation, dashed forward and slid across. From the bridge the road seemed narrow like the strap of a parachute, and the snow-covered hawthorn bushes growing next to it reminded me of white canopies. A greyish crust of snow covered the earth all the way to the children's home.

... When I was a boy I used to play basketball with the children who lived there. I wasn't really very fond of the game, but still I would often come to the court. Their best player was Tanya Grebenozhko, a thin, angular girl. She would speed across the court like an imp, and get into the very midst of the crowd. She gave us more trouble than any of the other kids in their team. When she sent the ball into the basket she had a funny habit of pushing out her lower lip and then she would vigorously blow the hair off her forehead.

The captain of our team was Alka Serikov. He would clutch his head in despair and shout at us:

"D'you realise we're losing, boys? Stepan, hold that witch! "

Some time later, Tanya disappeared. The children told us that her father had turned up and she went with him to Izmail. I stopped going to the court because without her the game lost all interest for me. She returned half a year later—either she didn't get along with her father or maybe she felt she couldn't live without her old friends.

As before, she often came to the basketball court

with her girlfriends, but she did not play now; she stood and watched the game. Tanya had changed a lot; she had cut off her braids and no longer looked angular.

We arranged to meet the day before I left to train at the flying school.

I was on my way to the children's home when Alka Serikov intercepted me and took me to his house. Several of my other friends were already waiting for us there. One of them went to get some wine. After all, it doesn't happen every day that someone leaves the village to go and study at a flying school! I tried to explain that I had to see Tanya, but they wouldn't listen.

"Never mind, she can wait," chattered Alka. "A farewell party with friends is sacred, she'll have to forgive you! "

When my pals went to see me off it was already evening. We weren't allowed into the children's home because we came so late. We climbed over the fence and banged on the door of the building where Tanya lived. Children looked down at us from their windows, and the next thing we saw was the woman doorkeeper running from the gate and shouting at the top of her voice.

"That's Tanya's steady, come to see her," a big-headed boy explained to somebody. The director appeared. He heard me out without saying a word and called Tanya.

"Go away. And don't write to me, there's no need," Tanya said quietly.

"Well, as you say," I replied, with a strained laugh

and went off. I understood deep inside that something irreparable had happened...

The territory of the children's home was surrounded with poplars and the trees were now white with hoar frost, as if wrapped in woollen yarn.

In the centre stood a two-storey wooden building with carved shutters and cornice. It was surrounded by a number of smaller houses, perched like sparrows round a birdbox. The front porch was covered with untrodden snow, so I found another entrance at the back of the house. A narrow path cleaned of snow led to it. It was warm inside, the stove droned with a hollow sound. A stoker, squatting by the stove, was brushing bits of coal into a dustpan.

"Where can I find the director?" I asked.

"He's not here, the office is closed," the stoker replied in a husky voice, straightening his back. "If you've come to the birthday party, it's not today, it's tomorrow."

A freckled boy peeped from behind the door, looked around and shouted:

"Kids, look who's here! It's a pilot! " And a flock of children came pouring into the room, like chicks out of a hen-coop. They surrounded me.

Hearing all this noise, their teacher came out of the room. I looked at her agape—it was Tanya Grebenozhko. She had hardly changed at all.

I was surprised to find her here, and I suddenly felt hot as if the stoker had opened all the furnace doors.

"Hail to the team of the children's home," I said jokingly and raised my hand in salute.

She wrinkled her forehead and arched her eyebrows in surprise.

"How come you're here? The director gave orders that strangers should not be admitted," Tanya said in an embarrassed voice.

"So you work here?" I asked, not knowing how to start the conversation.

"I've been here for half a year already. I took a primary-school teachers' course and asked to be sent here."

"Honestly, I thought I'd never see you again."

Tanya laughed and walked up to the window. A little girl of about eight ran up to her and clasped her by the hand.

"Go back into the classroom, children," Tanya said.

They withdrew reluctantly. The most curious of them continued peeping out and banging the door. The sun appeared from behind the white poplars and its bright rays lit the passageway.

"Where can I find the director?" I asked.

"Pavel Grigorievich has gone to see some people at the neighbouring factory. We are going to have a birthday party tomorrow." Tanya turned and gave me a close look. "So you don't want to leave your brother and sister with us?"

"How do you know?"

"I lead the school chorus and Vera sings in it. She told me."

Tanya stood with her back to the window, her earlobes looked almost transparent in the blazing sun and her hair glowed and shone from within. It seemed that her whole body could catch fire any minute now and burn up without a trace.

"Come to our birthday party," Tanya suggested. "You'll meet Pavel Grigorievich there, too. He won't be back until late tonight anyway, he's buying presents for the children."

"All right, I'll come."

It was warmer outside now, the snow crunched softly under my feet. When I was a short distance away from the village, I came to the main road. To its left another road went uphill to the local cemetery. From the rise the cemetery resembled a sheet of half-melted ice. There were snow-covered trees higher up the slope, and down below I could see the blue strip of the cemetery railings. The cemetery ground was well visible from the village... I quickly walked uphill. On top, the road divided into narrow winding paths which went around the trees and railings and broke off abruptly here and there. The snow was dazzling white, and bluish specks of ice glittered in the air. Hard as I tried to prepare myself for it, I stopped with a start when I came across a fresh mound of earth. I felt I couldn't walk another step. I pulled at the iron gate in the railing. It creaked gratingly and the wreathes came alive with a metallic whisper, shaking off the hoarfrost.

My mother's eyes were looking at me from a photograph. Yellow and black patches of fresh clay and frozen earth showed through the trampled snow. By some miracle, right by the railing there remained a narrow ribbon of untouched snow. I sat on my haunches and scooped up a handful. A strange emptiness engulfed me. My ears were ringing, but it never occurred to me that it was because of the deathly silence around. The only thing I felt was the violent throbbing of my heart.

My fingers were stiff and white with the cold. I brushed the water from my palm, thrust my hand into my jacket pocket and rose to my feet. I stood there a little longer, and then I walked out through the iron gate and looked down at the village. From high up it resembled a butterfly: the tiny grey houses, huddled together, formed its body and the vegetable patches at both sides looked like wings.

* * *

Kostya was in no hurry to go home. There was a wooden slide in the school courtyard and the children were going down it, seated on their satchels. The bravest ones slid down on their feet. I didn't recognise my brother at first: his coat was covered with snow, his fur hat was ruffled and shapeless, his cheeks were black with dirt. When I called him, he ran up to me and clasped my hand.

"Let's try and go down together, Stepan. I can't make it alone."

We climbed to the top of the slide. Kostya looked down at the children.

"Hey you, down there! Get out of the way! "

I held him by the shoulders and we slid down. The children ran to the slide and the whole dishevelled gang began crawling up the steps, wriggling and kicking their feet.

181

"Osintsev, Stepan," I heard a familiar voice.

I looked back. In the school doorway stood Irina Vasilievna who had been our form mistress while I was at school. She was a tall stately woman, and only her hair, now completely white, betrayed her age. She was over fifty and had been living in the village for many years now. When in the course of conversation the subject of school cropped up, everyone would inevitably think of Irina Vasilievna because most of the people in the village had been her pupils at one time or another.

"You've grown into a fine lad," she said smiling warmly as she looked me over. "Did you come to see me?"

"No, I came for my brother. We've been invited to the children's home tonight."

"Are you planning to leave the children there?"

"No, I want to take them to town with me, but I don't seem to be able to get the necessary papers. I've been to the district executive committee today. They say I need a reference, but I can't go all the way back to town for it."

"Don't worry, Stepan, I'll write you a reference."

"How can you when it's been four years since I finished school! "

"I saw you grow up. Who knows you better than I? Let's not waste words, come along."

She took me to the teachers' common room which I used to avoid as a boy because this is where we were summoned when we misbehaved.

Irina Vasilievna wrote the reference and put a seal on it.

"Take it. You've chosen a difficult path. The children will grow up, of course, but it depends on you what kind of people they turn out to be."

Kostya was still playing on the slide. I came up to him and took him by the sleeve.

"I want to play some more," he whimpered.

"It's time to go."

He obeyed unwillingly.

We had to wait for the bus. It finally came round the corner, emitting gasoline fumes. The driver braked abruptly, and the back wheels removed the top layer of snow as if with emery-cloth.

Tanya met us at the gates of the children's home.

"You've forgotten to say good day," I said, giving Kostya a slight push in the back. He mumbled his greetings and stepped aside.

"I've been waiting for you. I thought you weren't coming," Tanya said quickly. "You must be terribly cold."

She was glad we had come and didn't hide it.

"We had a long wait for the bus."

"Well, polite young man, let's go to the dining-room," Tanya said to Kostya. "We're having a birthday party today. Go pull the boys by the ears and then you can taste our birthday pies."

He eagerly agreed. She put her arms around his shoulders and they went off.

"Wait for us in the club house," she said to me.

One of the buildings was occupied by the dining-room and the club. The door leading into the hall was ajar. I could see the children were busy with something on the stage. I sat on a bench and the children stopped whatever they were doing, looked in my direction and began whispering among themselves.

One of them, a freckled little boy, smiled at me as if I were an old acquaintance. The palms of his hands were covered with small pink blotches. As I looked at him I recalled where I had seen him.

...At the end of November our plane landed in Bakalei, a tiny village in the middle of the taiga. We were expected there. The landing-field was near the village. From up high it looked like a large sheet of white paper. The plane left three ski-tracks in the untrodden snow—two broad ones and a narrow one in between. White houses stood in a row along the road. Soft tendrils of smoke were rising above the roofs. A horse harnessed to a sledge was moving jerkily towards the plane, sinking belly-deep into the snow. I got out of the plane and went up to the sledge. In it sat a boy in a sheepskin coat. His arms were bandaged.

"Too bad we don't have stretchers," said the doctor's assistant. "His arms and chest are badly burnt."

I took the boy in my arms and carried him to the plane. Alyosha Dobretsov helped carry him inside and laid him on a cover with his head towards the cockpit. A dog jumped into the plane after the boy and lay down by his side.

"What's that! Get out of here! "

"She saved the boy: she dragged him out of the fire," said the doctor's assistant. "They didn't manage to save the mother," she added with a sigh. "The boy's pure gold! You should have seen him play the accordion! When he gets better we'll arrange for him to go to a children's home.''

"So that's where you landed up," I thought with warmth. "Who could've thought we'd ever meet again."

It turned out today was the boy's birthday. He was wearing a white shirt which had come out of his trousers at the back but he was too engrossed in his work to notice.

Tanya soon came.

"Kostya has already made friends with the children," she said. "Good for him. A lad like that will be at home anywhere."

"You're right."

The freckled boy ran up to us, scratched the back of his head and gave me a quick glance.

"Tatyana Vasilievna, we are going to begin soon," he said.

"I am going to sing for the children today, and this is Sanya, our first musician," Tanya explained.

She tidied his shirt and buttoned it up on top. The boy smiled at her and snuffled.

"Too bad we don't have a good enough accordion and you can't see me at my best! "

Kostya stole up to me from behind. His face was aglow with satisfaction and his cheeks were covered with pastry crumbs. The pockets of his jacket were bulging suspiciously and he tried to prevent me from seeing what was inside.

"Who do you take after, I wonder?" And unable to control myself, I flicked him on the nose.

Kostya jumped aside, his eyes wide with anger.

"Don't you hit me again! If you do I'll go away from here."

The concert began. The first to come on stage were the amateur dancers and singers from the neighbouring factory. They were followed by the children. Sanya played a musical accompaniment on the accordion. He tried very hard, and it wasn't his fault that the instrument needed tuning. Then Tanya came out in an embroidered *sarafan* and sang several children's songs. She didn't have a very strong voice but even so everyone could hear her well. It was unusually quiet in the hall.

We got ready to leave. Tanya took me to see the director. He listened to me without saying a word, opened a drawer and handed me the papers.

"It's not so easy to be admitted to our home, but if you wish to bring up the children yourself, you're welcome."

* * *

During the days that followed I had a lot to do. I dealt with the pension and guardianship papers and registered the house in Uncle Yefim's name. I had to collect certificates, submit an application, rake through the archives and last but not least, visit a notary. In short, I did a great number of things about which I didn't have the faintest idea before.

Before entering the chairman's reception-room, I halted for a moment by the mirror. I looked at my reflection and passed my hand over my cheek. I would have wanted to look older and more impressive on that occassion. The reception-room was filled with people, some of whom I had known ever since I was a boy, others whom I had met recently when I legalised the children's pension papers. I was glad to find Irina Vasilievna among them. I felt she would help me if need be.

The chairman, a bald-headed, tall and lean man who was nicknamed Beanstalk in the village, read out my application in a husky voice, put it aside and looked at Irina Vasilievna questioningly. A young woman who sat next to her asked me:

"How do you plan to bring up the children? You must surely realise that your work won't give you a chance. You're a pilot and you won't be at home often."

The men and women sitting round the table began to speak all at once, without listening to one another. Irina Vasilievna stood up and asked for the floor.

"I know that many of you have children of your own. You love them and do not propose to send them away to be brought up, because you realise that a children's home is a sad necessity. As for me, I'll vouch for Stepan."

Everyone fell silent. For an instant they felt they were children again and she was their school teacher, as she had been years before.

"You're a teacher, Irina Vasilievna. You must surely understand that bringing up a child and flying a plane are two different things," someone objected meekly.

The chairman tapped his pencil on the desk and looked at me.

"Let's hear Stepan out. After all, he is the one who's going to live with the children, not us."

When I was going to the executive committee meeting, I realised that I would have to convince them. Now I knew that much depended on my answer.

"I shall manage. I'll bring them up," I said in a quiet voice.

Those present silently exchanged glances.

"All right. Go and wait for our decision. We'll call you," the chairman said.

Some time passed before they called me back. The chairman gave me three sheets of paper. The forms had been typed out beforehand and only the names were inked in. There were three separate forms—for Vera, Kostya and Natasha.

After the meeting I went to the department store and bought two suitcases, children's underwear, soap and toothbrushes. Kostya and Vera were waiting for me. Vera put her school uniform into the suitcase and went off to say goodbye to her girl-friends. Kostya stayed with me to examine the purchases. To begin with he brushed the dust off the suitcase with his sleeve, then he spent a long time toying with the locks and turning the little key this way and that. After he had made sure that everything was in order, he brought his playthings—a toy gun, a broken clasp-knife and a ball of brass wire. But he didn't think that enough, and ran to the store-room, bringing along an old pea-jacket and a pair of worn shoes with their tongues cut off. "Must have cut them off to make a catapult, the little devil," I thought. I wrapped the shoes in the pea-jacket and shoved both under the bed.

"What are you doing! " screamed Kostya. He fell on his knees and crawled after the pea-jacket with the agility of a lizard. "It's not yours, is it? Mother made it for me out of Father's old greatcoat."

Borya, Uncle Yefim's son, a small boy as round as a samovar, ran past us into the next room, looking for something. Uncle Yefim had already moved in. Boxes and huge bundles were piled up in the corner, taking up half the room. This was no longer the house I knew.

During the lunch break Frosya came over.

"I just saw Yefim," she chattered happily. "He's already made arrangements about a car. When are you planning to leave?"

I didn't feel like answering.

She unbuttoned her fur coat and took off her shawl.

"I promised to make Vera a new dress, but I see you've already packed your things. Make sure you lock the suitcases properly. You never know who'll be riding next to you on the train."

Borya was hanging around; there was obviously something on his mind. He finally came up to me and asked:

"Are you taking the accordion with you?"

...Father had brought the accordion with him from the front. He was a good player and he was always a welcome guest at every party or family occassion. I had made up my mind to leave Uncle Yefim everything that belonged to my mother, but I was reluctant to part with the accordion.

"What are you badgering him for?" Frosya shouted at her son. "What does it have to do with you, whether he takes it or not?"

"Aunt Anya promised to give it to me," Borya whimpered.

"So what if she did?"

"Perhaps Kostya will learn to play when he grows up a little," I put in.

Borya began to turn the knob of the radio set, peering inside.

"Are you taking that along too?"

"You can take it apart if you want."

"Oh, it's high time I leave," Frosya gasped in feigned horror. "I ought to be back at work." She stood up, looked around the room searchingly and went out.

Kostya ran to the store-room to fetch some frozen bilberries. Polkan followed him inside. Kostya peeped into the room stealthily to see if I had noticed the dog.

"Send him away! " I shouted.

Kostya took a piece of bread from the table and gave it to the dog. Polkan ate the bread and walked to the door, wagging his tail. Kostya opened the door for him and let him out into the street.

Polkan was a member of the family. In their letters to me the children always mentioned him.

Borya brought a chair from the other room and sat down next to my brother.

"Try and guess how to divide three oranges between two fathers and two sons?"

"Enough of your tricks! If you want to try the bilberries, just say so, I'm not stingy. As for your puzzle, it's for our Natasha. The answer's clear—everyone gets one orange."

"Good for you, Kostya," I thought approvingly. "You solved the puzzle so fast it makes me wonder why you keep getting bad marks in arithmetic?"

Borya fidgeted, looking insulted. The chair creaked maliciously under him.

"Your brother must've come with loads of money. Look at all the stuff he bought in the store! "

Borya was obviously repeating what he heard his father say.

"What does it have to do with you?"

"Does he fly some rickety old plane?"

"How silly! What makes you think so? He flies the latest model."

"So what?" Borya drawled out. "Mother told me he'll send you to a boarding-school in town anyway."

"No he won't, " Kostya said quietly and fell silent.

"I won't, Kostya, I won't," I repeated the words to myself like an incantation. "They trust me and the main thing now is to stand firm, not to trip up. There is no one to back me, I'm their only hope."

"Stepan, I'll go and play outside," said Kostya, looking into the room.

His face was smeared with bilberry juice. After his conversation with Borya, he had decided to behave himself.

"Wipe the juice off your lips and then you can go."

Kostya pulled his coat off the rack and pushed the door open with his shoulder. Borya ran out after him. I heard them arguing about something under the window. Then Kostya returned to the porch and I heard the pail clattering.

I opened the wardrobe and rummaged through it,

trying to figure out what else I should take along.

"Stepan, Kostya's fallen into the well! " hollered Borya as he rushed into the house.

I ran outside. My shirt instantly froze as hard as iron and it seared my body.

Through a thin mist I saw my brother's head sticking out of the well. His coat had got caught and he was propped up in the middle of the well like a bottle cork. The sides of the well were frozen over and covered with a thick crust of ice. In bitter frosts it was sometimes difficult to get the pail through the hole. I sank to my knees and put one arm around the wooden frame. My hands were trembling. Kostya moved his head and his fur hat slipped down over his eyes.

"Hold on," I cried. "If you don't you'll slip inside the well! "

I tried to reach him but couldn't. I jumped up and ran to and fro looking for a loose stake in the fence. Suddenly I remembered that we had a long pole with a hook somewhere, which was used to get out the pail when the rope fastened to it broke. The pole was now like an enormous icicle. I lowered it into the well and hitched Kostya's coat on the hook, but as I pulled I ripped the material.

Kostya screamed, I had probably scratched him with the hook. Borya was standing near the well, wailing with fear. I caught Kostya in my arms and carried him into the house. Then I sat him by the stove so he would warm up.

Towards evening he had a high fever. He moaned and complained that he had a bad pain in the arm.

As soon as Vera came home I sent her to the hospital to bring a doctor.

I sat on the edge of Kostya's bed and put my hand on his forehead. It was hot. Kostya looked at me wearily. Suddenly the gate creaked and old Chernikha entered the house.

"Show me the boy," she demanded.

"How did she find out, I wonder," the thought rushed through my head. "She lives so far down the street."

The old woman went into the room and touched Kostya's forehead with her withered fingers. Then she came back into the kitchen, took something wrapped in paper out of her sheepskin jacket and peered at me with her dark eyes.

"Bring some potatoes and put them in a pot to boil."

I climbed down into the cellar. It was cool and damp there. I struck a match, but it burned my fingers and went out at once. I put the match-box back into my pocket and groped for the potatoes in the dark. I could hear the old woman tramping up and down the room and muttering something to herself.

Everyone who lived on our street knew Chernikha. There were always bunches of herbs hanging down from the ceiling in her room and on the porch. People often came to her when they did not feel well. She never refused to help but would not take any money for it.

When I got out of the cellar I saw Chernikha feeling Kostya's arm. He was frowning and moaning with pain. Then she suddenly gave it a tug. Kostya squealed like a puppy and instantly stopped crying.

"It was out of joint, now it's all right," the old woman muttered sulkily without turning to look at me. "When the potatoes are ready put them on his elbow while they're still hot and then give him some raspberries with tea. The berries are wrapped in paper, over there," she indicated the packet on the table with her eyes. "Vera scared me to death, she came running like mad."

"Now you tell me, midge, how did you fall into the well?" she asked Kostya.

"I slipped on the ice when I was playing with Borya," Kostya said, his teeth chattering.

"That's not true. It was Borya who pushed you down," Chernikha said with conviction. "That's what my heart tells me, 'cause I know his ways. He got into my orchard last autumn. I have a wonderful apple-tree there, you know. I would've brought him a chair so he would pick as many as he wanted. But no, he climbed over the fence like a thief. Broke many branches. And when I caught him, he kicked me, the rascal, and jumped over the fence. His father was no better when he was a boy. Yours was different, he was hard-working and knew how to behave himself. Yefim was always up to mischief, he smeared gates with chalk and threw stones on the roofs. Like father, like son."

The old woman set her lips together firmly and crossed herself looking at the empty corner.

"Are you leaving today?" she asked.

"How could I? The boy's in a fever."

"You're right. Wait till he gets better. There's no hurry."

Vera brought Tanya along. They took off their coats, talking in a whisper. Vera as the hostess showed her guest where to hang her coat. Meanwhile, I did what I could to clean up the mess in the room.

"I'll be going. My family will be back from work soon," Chernikha said with a yawn. "Don't forget to put mustard plasters on his feet tonight."

"We've called the doctor," Vera announced. "He'll soon be here."

Chernikha put her hands on the small of her back, rose with difficulty and limped to the coat-rack.

Tanya helped her on with her coat.

I watched the old woman with deep gratitude as she went out.

Tanya came up to my brother.

"How could it have happened, Kostya?" she asked patting him on the head. "Yes, I almost forgot... Sanya gave me some stamps for you."

I called Vera into the kitchen and whispered in her ear:

"Peel the potatoes and bring some bilberries, and I'll go buy something in the shop. There's not a thing to eat in the house."

"All right." Vera took a pot out of the sideboard.

I pulled on my jacket and rushed out into the street. A bus stopped near the house, blinding me with its headlights. Uncle Yefim came out and walked up to me.

"So you aren't going," he said. "I met Chernikha and she told me what happened."

"We'll have to stay for a while. I couldn't go with the boy in such a state."

"You'll see, I'll give Borya a good hiding. He's got completely out of hand," Uncle Yefim said. "He's doing badly at school. And I'm too busy, don't have enough time for him. I wasted half a day in my boss's office begging him to let me use the factory car. I doubt that he'll let me have it another time." Not knowing what else to say, he turned to look at the bus-driver. "I have to be going now, I'll drop in tomorrow morning to see how Kostya is."

There was a long queue in the shop. When it was finally my turn at the counter someone clapped me on the shoulder. I looked back and saw Serikov. Of all people! Mother had written to me that Alik had gone to live in Leningrad and was serving on a sea liner.

"You don't seem to recognise old friends! " Alka said laughing. "I saw you in the street and wondered: 'Who might that be marching through the village like that?' You look like a real astronaut in your pilot jacket! "

"Don't be silly," I said with a smile. "How's life?"

"I work as a driver. Didn't people tell you?"

"Mother wrote that you applied for a navigation school."

"They turned me down, said I wasn't tall enough," Alka said angrily. "I spent two months in Leningrad and I didn't like it at all. It rains there all the time. Nothing but rain and slush. So I came back here. Got myself a job as a driver."

There was a disappointed expression on his face, one I knew so well from childhood. That was the way he looked when he lost a game.

Our conversation flared up and died like a burning

twist of paper. I felt sorry for having broached the subject, and my joy and excitement were gone. Each of us now had his own troubles and cares.

"You know, Kostya fell into the well. He's lying in bed now with a high fever," I said changing the subject.

"Burn some sugar with vodka. They say it helps a lot," Alik suggested readily. "I heard your mother had died. Bad luck! Mine is still a strong woman. But hang it all, I'll go away somewhere," he said with sudden fury. "I'm sick and tired of being tied to her apron strings."

"Are you by any chance planning to get married?" I asked cautiously.

Alik turned away and a crooked smile appeared on his face.

"I'm not, but she wants me to. She's already found me a girl. A nice girl, she says, has a university degree and all that. Does she think I can't choose a girl for myself?"

"You should understand that she wishes you well."

"A mother's love is truly blind." Alik was silent for a moment and then he nodded, pointing to my fur boots. "Can you get me a pair like that? I heard they sell them in town."

"I will," I promised. "Would you like to drop in? Tanya's come. Do you remember her? She used to play basketball with us."

"Of course I do." Alik squinted slyly. "She asked about you many times when you were away."

"Come and see me before you leave. I'll ask my boss to let me use a bus to take you to the station," Serikov said in parting. "He often remembers your father. They were at the front together."

"I'll write down my address for you," I said.

Alik thrust the scrap of paper with my address in his pocket without looking at it and hastened to the exit.

I walked home, loaded with parcels. It was very warm in the house. The firewood crackled merrily in the stove, the potatoes sizzled in the frying-pan and the open furnace door glowed red. Tanya was almost through washing the kitchen floor.

"Men never seem to know how to do things properly," Tanya said as she brushed away a strand of hair that had fallen over her forehead. "Couldn't you take a bag along instead of stuffing all those things into your pockets?"

"Why do you look so cross?" she asked suddenly, raising her head.

"Stepan, we forgot to pack my satchel," said Kostya. "I just remembered about it."

"And where was it?"

"It was under the bed, I found it when I was sweeping the floor," Tanya said with a smile.

Vera shot a quick glance at me and shook her head sadly, just the way Mother did.

"He's quite a handful. It's the third time he's lost his satchel. The first time he went for a drive in a lorry and left it there in the back, the second time he lost it in the forest."

Kostya fidgeted uneasily in his bed.

Some other time he would not have forgiven her such treachery, but he thought it better to keep quiet now. He just looked sideways at the chair stand-

198

ing next to his bed. On it were bottles of medicine and several prescriptions.

"Has the doctor been?" I asked.

"He has. He praised old Chernikha, said she had set the bone very well. He doesn't think it's serious, but he says the boy ought to stay in bed for two or three days," Tanya explained.

I took Kostya's satchel and looked inside. It reeked of tobacco. I thrust my hand inside—and there they were, tiny shreds of tobacco. Especially in the corners.

"Have you been smoking?"

"We were playing cops and robbers," said Kosya, averting his eyes. "I sprinkled tobacco around so that Polkan couldn't track us down."

"He's lying," I thought to myself as I got Kostya's exercise book from the satchel.

Kostya moved restlessly in his bed and looked worriedly at his sister.

"Let Stepan see how you are doing at school," said Vera.

It was an exercise book in arithmetic. As I leafed through it I discovered that my brother mostly got bad marks in the subject. On the last page I found drawings of tanks and destroyers. Two fighter planes with red stars on their wings were diving steeply into the attack.

"Is that the way to draw a plane?" I exclaimed, unable to control myself. "The tail looks more like a boot and the wings are like sleeves sewn on crookedly."

"It didn't come out well, you're right," Kostya admitted. "I've got better ones in my Russian language exercise book. I drew Gagarin and Titov sitting in their rockets."

"What?! " I finally recovered myself.

"All his exercise books are covered with drawings," said Vera, adding fuel to the flames.

Kostya clasped his arm suddenly and began rocking back and forth in his bed and groaning.

"You're like an actor from a third-rate theatre," Vera said mockingly.

Tanya sat smiling on the edge of Kostya's bed.

"Let's sit down and eat. Everything'll be getting cold," Vera invited us to the table.

After supper Tanya helped my sister wash the dishes and then she got ready to leave.

"Leaving already?" Kostya drawled out disappointedly. "But you promised to tell me a story about Mowgli."

"It's too late already and I have a long walk home."

"You can spend the night with us," Kostya suddenly suggested. "You could sleep together with Vera."

Tanya was obviously embarrassed and she muttered:

"Some other time. I still have some work to do at home for tomorrow."

She rose, put on her shawl and buttoned up her coat.

"Stepan, take the accordion to Sanya," Kostya asked me. "He plays so well..."

I took out the accordion and wiped off the dust. Its mother-of-pearl coating gleamed in the light and the white keys glistened merrily.

"You shouldn't do that. I could ask Pavel Grigorievich to buy a new one, he wouldn't refuse," said Tanya in a bewildered voice.

"Indeed! "

We came out onto the road. Tanya walked in front and the high heels of her boots were digging into the snow. I followed with the accordion. The path wound between the snow-bound hummocks and, high in the sky as if accompanying us, the moon danced along over the tree-tops.

"Let me help you." Tanya stopped, blocking my way. "It's heavy."

"Step aside! " I said jokingly, pretending I was about to push her aside.

"Nothing doing! You'd better tell me why you looked so gloomy when you came back after shopping?"

"No particular reason..."

"Are you cross because I came over?"

"How can you say that, Tanya! The children are so fond of you! "

"And what about you?" she asked quietly, almost in a whisper.

And suddenly I forgot the words which were in my thoughts for such a long time and which I needed so badly at that particular moment. I was silent.

Dogs were barking somewhere to the side of the village and their melancholy howling made me feel uneasy, as if I had rushed past the house of a person dear to me and felt that with every passing minute it was more and more impossible for me to turn back.

We could already see the black outlines of the children's home fence behind the bushes, and the moon looked down at me accusingly from above the fence. Tanya hid her face in her shawl, shivering all over with cold.

"Let's move on. It's cold standing."

I lifted the accordion. I wanted to say something kind to her, but instead I walked after her, cursing my stupidity.

"What sort of a man am I? Why do I have to spoil everything?"

We walked past the gatekeeper's office and stopped next to the house where Tanya lived. She climbed up the stairs to the porch and took out the key. The door clicked open.

Her room was small and quiet, with hardly any furniture in it except for a table by the window, a bed with a book-shelf above it and a small bedside table with a mirror in the corner.

Tanya took off her coat, walked over to the stove and pressed her back against its warm side. I didn't know where to place the accordion. Tanya came to my rescue, putting away the exercise books that lay on the table.

Sheets of paper with drawings on them slipped out of one of the exercise books and scattered on the floor. I picked them up and looked at the drawings. Most of them were signed in a child's painstaking hand: *"To Tatyana Vasilievna on her birthday."*

I now recalled how the children came up to Tanya after the concert and handed her their drawings, smiling with embarrassment.

"Why didn't you tell me it was your birthday?"

"I didn't want to. I was happy as it was."

Tanya picked up a sheet of paper that had landed under the table and gave it to me.

"Have a look, that's Sanya's drawing."

Sanya drew a picture of Bakalei, his native village.

"And Natasha Gorina—remember the girl who said her father was a pilot?—drew an aeroplane. She's an orphan, so she invented a father for herself," Tanya said.

Then she looked at me with a sad smile.

"I did the same when I was a girl."

Her lips quivered and she blinked a tear away but managed to control herself.

"Now you know what they're like. They gave me the whole world as a present," Tanya said smiling.

And then it suddenly dawned on me that these children were everything to her, that the children's home and the things she did here day after day gave her life purpose. This was why they loved her so and followed her every step.

* * *

Kostya was on the mend soon, and I went to the station to buy us tickets. When I came back in the evening I found Tanya there. She was reading to the children. Kostya sat on the bed munching away at an apple. He was wearing a striped blue pullover which I hadn't seen before. Vera came out of the kitchen.

"Just look what Tanya brought us! " she said to me in a merry voice.

She ran up to the table and unwrapped a big parcel.

Tanya rose quickly and said with an embarrassed smile:

"Pavel Grigorievich asked me to give you these two coats—one for Vera and the other for Kostya."

The children were pleased, I could tell it by the look in their eyes.

"Thank you for taking the trouble! "

The coats would be of use to us, especially the one for Kostya. I had ripped his old one badly with the pole and it looked terrible.

Kostya sprang out of bed and came running to the table.

"Don't you run around barefoot! Get back into bed! " Vera shouted.

Kostya quickly went back on tiptoe and jumped into bed.

"I only wanted to show you the felt boots," he said sounding offended.

"We repacked the suitcases and ironed everything. There's plenty of room inside now," Vera said.

Towards evening Chernikha came. She looked us over in silence, as if to make sure that all of us were there. Then she took off her coat unhurriedly, produced a sock, a ball of wool and knitting-needles from her pocket, and came up to my brother.

"Here Kostya, let's try it on."

Kostya stuck his leg out from under the blanket and she pulled the sock on.

"Seems they'll be the right size. I was in such a hurry. I feared you'd leave before I was through. I need a little more time to finish the second one."

I went to the kitchen, put on the kettle and added a little more firewood on the stove. The wood was damp and wouldn't burn properly.

"Watch me knitting," I heard Chernikha speaking to Tanya. "It'll come of use when you get married."

"It's too early to think of that," Tanya said laughing.

"Just the right time! I wasn't yet sixteen when my father married me off."

"It was different in those days."

"Nothing of the sort. Why? You have a good job and he isn't a spoiled lad. And his parents were nice people, God bless their souls in heaven. And I can see you love the children..."

I waited for Tanya's reply, but she didn't say anything.

"Of course, she's young and pretty, she can easily find herself a good husband," I thought to myself. "And if she married me she'd have three children on her hands. No, she's right."

Next morning we were leaving. Uncle Yefim got a few hours off from work to help us load our belongings. Frosya and old Chernikha stood a short distance away. Borya was also there, getting in the way. I expected Tanya to come, but she didn't for some reason.

When we had finished loading, I looked around the room for the last time, trying to keep everything in my memory. But deep inside I realised that as soon as we left the invisible thread tying us to our home would break.

"Well, it's time to go. The train leaves in half an hour," Uncle Yefim said.

Kostya halted by the fence. Frosya had put Polkan on a chain and the dog was barking furiously and trying to break away. Kostya gave him some bread but Polkan wouldn't even look at it. He yelped shrilly, snapped at the hem of Kostya's coat and licked his hands.

"Kostya," I shouted, "hurry up, we'll be late for the train! "

He bent over, kissed the dog's cold nose and ran to the bus. There were tears in his eyes. I turned away. I couldn't bear the sight of it all and longed to leave as soon as possible. Kostya begged me to take the dog with us. I didn't agree then, but now my heart gave a shudder—I also loved Polkan.

* * *

The room I rented was in a two-storey wooden house. Next to it stood several low-built cottages made of thick logs. They looked like hunters' cabins. This island of wooden houses was surrounded by modern multi-storied prefabricated buildings. While I was working in Siberia the island grew visibly smaller and moved further away from the centre of town.

We took a taxi from the railway station. The driver stopped some distance away from the house.

"They're digging a trench up the street. The car won't get through there," he said looking round at me.

"Please wait for a while, I have to talk things over with my landlady."

I hesitated, not knowing what else to say. I doubted that she would react calmly to the fact that I had brought the children along; she would definitely object. I felt it would be better if I went without them.

I climbed into the yard through a hole in the fence and walked past the outhouses with heavy round padlocks. It was then I saw the landlady. She had been shopping and was carrying a bag. She noticed me and stopped.

"So you've come," she said breathing heavily. "If you were a decent man you'd have warned me in advance that you were leaving. Is that the way to treat people? You just disappeared without saying a word! "

"But I couldn't let you know! You weren't at home when I left."

"You could've rung me up."

"Did she get out of bed on the wrong side?" I wondered.

"Don't be angry with me," the landlady said when we entered the house. "I let your room to somebody else, you don't really live here anyway. You can stay in the small room and I won't charge you as much."

Without turning to look at me she began unpacking her bag and putting the food on the shelves. My landlady had always been a big eater. She was a stout woman with ruddy shining cheeks...

"Your suitcase is over there. You can move to the other room right away."

"Zinaida Mironovna, I have brought my brother and sister along. Could you, perhaps, let me keep the bigger room. I'll pay in advance."

The landlady turned to face me abruptly and flung up her arms.

"You come along without warning, without asking permission ... and here you are, like a bolt out of the blue! Wh am I supposed to do now? My niece came to stay with me and she's living in your room."

"Our mother just died and the children don't have anybody but me now," I blurted out and fell silent.

The door slammed and the driver came in carrying our suitcases. He was followed by Vera and Kostya.

"What a character! He just goes off leaving the children out in the cold," he grumbled.

"Come on in, children, and sit down," the landlady said in a faltering voice. Then she offered them two buns.

"No, thank you," said Vera declining the offer. Kostya took the bun.

"You'll have to stay in the smaller room for the meantime and then we'll see. It's a warm room and the ceiling's a high one."

I went to take a look at the room. There was a sofa in it and an old wardrobe. A children's sledge and a wash-board hung on the wall. The place obviously used to serve as a store-room.

"I could live here if I were alone, but there is certainly not enough place in it for me and the children," I thought.

"I can take the wardrobe away, then there'll be more room. Will you stay?" the landlady asked.

"No, we'd be too cramped for space."

"Well, as you say. You're your own master," she sighed looking disappointed.

"The children need a desk to do their lessons."

"They could do them in the kitchen."

The landlady studied the children closely.

"One of my neighbours has a room to let, a large room on the sunny side. Do you want to take a look?"

By the time we started for the neighbour's house it was already dark. It was windy outside and there was a smell of smoke in the air. Snow fell on the road from the roof-tops.

The landlady picked her way carefully, afraid she might slip on the ice. When we finally reached the house she banged on the closed shutters for a long time. A dog barked loudly near by, rattling its chain.

"Who's there?" a voice inquired from behind the window.

"Open up, Mikhailovna, it's me," the landlady shouted. "I have business with you."

It took quite a while before the woman appeared on the porch. The landlady signed to me to wait and walked with mincing steps towards her. I heard them whispering.

"I've already let it," the neighbour said, looking me over.

"Well, we'll just have to grin and bear it," Zinaida Mironovna said.

We went down the narrow street and crossed to the other side. The landlady knocked at another window.

"If a man comes out, they'll let us a room here." I thought to myself.

"Who d'you want?" a man's voice asked.

"Semyon, I heard the students who rented a room from you have gone."

"Good riddance!" the man said moodily and spat.

His hair was tousled and he had an untidy look about him as if he had just got out of bed.

"Let's go." I pulled Zinaida Mironovna by the sleeve.

"What was it you wanted?" the man shouted when we were already some distance away.

The landlady waved the question aside. We turned to another street. Obviously she hadn't lost hope of finding us a room.

"I'm afraid I'll have to go back to the children. They're all alone there."

"Go back and I'll see another neighbour. Perhaps I'll have better luck this time."

The landlady returned quite some time after.

"It takes all sorts to make a world," she said with a sigh. "They said they'd let you in if you were alone but not with the children... Stay with me. The more, the merrier."

The children cheered up. Vera asked the landlady for a basin and poured some water in it.

"It's a nice enough room," she said wringing out the wet rag when she had finished washing the floor.

"We'll see," Kostya said, clearly imitating old Chernikha. He sat on the edge of the sofa sorting out our things on the window-sill. The window-sill was high and it was difficult for him to reach it.

"I'll take you to school tomorrow morning," I said.

"Kostya needs a haircut badly," Vera said in alarm. "Just look at him! I felt ashamed for him when we went to the old school but he couldn't possibly go to a new school looking the way he does! "

"Never mind! " Kostya chuckled. "It'll do."

"Let me cut it for you, it really looks awful this way," Vera said getting angry.

She took a pair of scissors out of the bag, wrapped a towel around his neck and began cutting his hair. To tell the truth, she was making a mess of the job. Kostya jerked and looked at his reflection in the mirror with a martyred air.

"Sit still! " Vera said sharply and brushed the hair off the towel.

Suddenly, Kostya cried out in pain. He covered his ear with his hand and darted to the window. Then he saw there was blood on his palm and he began crying loudly. The landlady looked out of her room.

"What's the matter?" she asked.

"I snipped his ear," Vera replied through her tears.

I examined Kostya's ear. There was nothing much wrong with it.

"Let me trim your hair properly," I suggested. Kostya sat down obediently and showed Vera a clenched fist. "Why do they have to quarrel all the time? If only they didn't, at least not here," I thought.

We went to bed late that evening. Kostya and I slept on the sofa and Vera on a folding bed. The children fell asleep at once and I lay awake, tossing and turning in bed for a long time. The weather had changed for the worse. The windows rattled angrily in the wind and I lay there watching the lamp swaying to and fro on its post.

* * *

Vera and Kostya got up early next morning. They were on tenterhooks because this was going to be their first day in a new school. It had been snowing all night and lop-sided snow-drifts barred the way. A gusty wind was blowing and it pressed the columns of smoke rising from the chimneys closer to the ground. The school was in a two-storey house not far from where we lived. Without wasting words, the school director took the children's papers and sent Vera and Kostya to their class-rooms. I waited for the lessons to begin and went home. The children came back at lunch time.

"I got an 'excellent' mark in arithmetic," Kostya announced from the threshold, beaming with pride. "We did sums like that with Tanya."

"And what about you, Vera?"

"Nothing to boast about. They made me share a desk with a boy." She quickly took off her school uniform and began setting the table.

After lunch my brother and I went to a furniture shop to buy a bed and I sent Vera to the grocery.

Nice couches were on sale in the furniture shop but we couldn't afford to pay such a high price. Near the cash-desk I came across Valentina, my landlady's niece.

"I've bought a couch," she said. "I felt it was high time I got myself some decent furniture."

Then she turned away to look at her reflection in a chest of drawers' mirror. She was obviously pleased with herself. She was wearing a fashionable coat, its sleeves trimmed with sable, and deerskin boots embroidered with beads.

"Please excuse me for taking up your room, Stepan," Valentina said. "You were away for over a month and in the meantime my things arrived. I couldn't very well leave them in the street, could I?"

"It's all right. The only problem is that we need another bed."

"Why don't you buy yourself a couch. Everybody buys them now, they're in fashion." She spoke with an air of an expert.

"I'm looking for a bed."

"Of course, the couch can wait. When you've earned enough money you'll buy yourself some decent furniture."

Valentina shot a glance at Kostya. She suddenly frowned and her face took on a business-like expression.

"The shop manager who works here is an acquaintance of mine. I'll talk to her."

"That would be nice of you."

They gave me a bed right from the store-house. After I had paid for it, I still had enough money to buy a writing-desk.

"We bought a new bed," Kostya said happily when we entered the house. "Give us a hand, Vera. You can hold the door open while we carry it in."

But the feeling that now everything would go swimmingly vanished as soon as I saw the landlady entering the room.

"The housing manager was here," she said looking gloomily out of the window. "He's strictly forbidden me to take in tenants. He said our house was to be demolished soon. I tried to put him in the picture but he wouldn't even listen. 'Let them find another room and that's that.' "

The room swam before my eyes! I wanted to lean against the wall but almost fell down. I suddenly had a feeling as if I were a tight-rope-walker with no support around me. But my momentary dismay soon passed.

"Do you want us to leave right away?" I asked.

"I'm not rushing you. I just wanted to warn you," the landlady muttered.

I couldn't get to sleep that night. Unhappy thoughts filled my mind and I couldn't get them out of my head, couldn't escape from them. I no longer felt angry with my landlady. What could I blame her for? Who was I to her? Just a tenant. I ought to be grateful that she was letting me stay with the children and wasn't throwing us out at once. The person I couldn't bring myself to understand was the housing manager. He gave me permission to stay in the autumn when I didn't need it half as badly, and now he was threatening to evict me from the house. Where could I go with the children? Deep inside I understood that it was thoughtless of me to have brought the children here. But what else could I have done?

"Stepan, if the housing manager comes again we'll latch the door," said Kostya trying to comfort me. "And after I bring Polkan here he won't even dare enter the room."

"A dog won't help here," I thought as I embraced my brother. "I must go and see Sorokin."

* * *

Next morning I drove to the airport to see the air-unit commander. I went up the wooden stairs attached to the side of the building. Sorokin's office was on the third floor. He was there, talking on the phone. When he saw me he indicated a chair with his eyes. My crew commander Alexei Dobretsov came in soon after.

"On Monday morning Dobretsov and you will have to fly to Cold Springs," he said, covering the mouthpiece with the palm of his hand.

"I can't."

Sorokin put down the receiver and looked at me without saying anything. He was a broad-shouldered, burly man. His thick black eyebrows and small deepset eyes gave his face a morose and unfriendly look.

"Why can't you?"

"I brought my brother and sister with me."

"What do you mean 'with you'? Where are they?" Sorokin asked half-rising from his chair.

"They're staying with my landlady now. I've been trying to find another room but haven't managed so far."

Sorokin fell silent and sat frowning for a while, drumming on the table with his fingers.

"Why do you need another room? Is your landlady turning you out?"

"It's not her. The housing manager's threatened to evict us. The house is going to be pulled down."

Sorokin opened a drawer and took out a blue folder. He leafed through it, running his eyes over the papers quickly.

"Didn't you apply for a flat?"

"No, I didn't."

"Write one now." He handed me a sheet of paper. "We have thirty six people on the waiting list. The builders will finish a new house for us in autumn. We'll try to think of something then; meanwhile you'll have to stay at your landlady's. You may just as well ask her to look after the children while you're away," said Sorokin.

He lifted his head and glanced at me. "What shall we do about you? There's no other work we could give you. You won't get many flying hours if you stay on the base. And we were planning to make you crew commander in autumn so you'll need more flying time now. I'd have been glad to send somebody else to Cold Springs, but I can't. Most of the pilots have used up the air hours allowed by the regulations. I'm flying myself today."

"And what am I to do with the children?"

"Arrange for them to go to boarding-school and you can take them to Cold Springs in the summer with you. There's a nice lake there. They'll swim and lie in the sun," intervened Dobretsov.

"When you have children of your own, you can bathe them in cold water all you want," I said resentfully.

Sorokin took an envelope out of his desk. He played with it for a while and held it out to me.

"The pilots collected some money for you and the trade-union committee also added some. Take it."

"I'll manage without it somehow," I said gruffly, rising to my feet.

"Sit down. What do you think you are, a millionaire? It's not for you, it's for the children. I was orphaned as a child myself, so I know better whether you need the money or not. By the way, do you have all modern conveniences in your apartment?" Sorokin asked, thinking of something else.

"No, it's an old house."

"What do you use for heating?"

"Firewood."

"Wood burns up fast, coal is much better," Sorokin said with conviction. "I know it from experience. There's some coal near the parking area, we use it to heat the mechanics' house. Give me your address, I'll ask the boys to bring you a lorry-load tomorrow morning. I don't think your landlady will have any objections."

I felt better after talking with Sorokin, as if he had taken half the weight of my cares off my shoulders.

As I came out of Sorokin's office, I saw second pilot Igor Bumazhkin in the other end of the corridor. We had been at flying school together.

I met him at the preliminary medical check-up. We became close friends. We went to the skating-rink together and played hockey. Our beds were next to one another in the dormitory. We were so close that though Igor was assigned for work in Byelorussia upon graduation, he asked the commission to send him to Irkutsk.

"Come here," Igor said, waving his hand. "We're playing hockey with the mechanics tomorrow."

He held out his big hand to me. His face was red.

217

The sun wasn't yet bright, but at an altitude it was hot enough to burn his skin through the cockpit window. Igor is much taller than me and the overalls he wears would have been an excellent fit for an elephant. That was a joke the pilots often made.

"I can't come," I said with a sigh. "I haven't got the time."

"What do you tell me you can't! We'll be sure to lose without you."

"I've brought the children with me. I have to be with them."

Igor opened his briefcase and brought out a paper parcel full of Baikal mullet.

"Take it for the children. I'll drop over in the evening."

I shook his hand and looked reproachfully at Dobretsov who was standing next to us. Sensing my unvoiced disapproval he said he wanted to come with me to my place.

We found Vera and Kostya sitting huddled together in the dark room. They didn't even turn the light on. I had the impression that they had been sitting like this, without moving, all the time I had been away at the airport.

Dobretsov followed me into the room and switched on the light. The children looked at him in fright but when they noticed he was wearing a cap with a pilot's badge on it, they instantly cheered up.

"Have you eaten anything?" I asked, taking off my jacket.

"No, we decided to wait for you," Vera replied. She rose, straightened her dress hurriedly and slipped out of the room. We heard pots and pans clattering in the kitchen.

"Now, how can I leave them alone?" I thought with bitterness. "They'll just sit here and wait, clinging to the wall... Why are they like that? They won't ask for anything even if they're terribly hungry. Now Borya, he'll be all right, no matter what. If they don't give him what he asks for, he'll just go and take it himself."

"Come here, Stepan," Zinaida Mironovna called me from her room. "I want to tell you something..."

A minute later the smiling landlady appeared on the threshold, but stopped in her tracks upon noticing Dobretsov. Kostya brought up a stool for her but she wouldn't sit down. She stood their casting quick glances at me and Alexei.

"Well, what did they tell you at the airport?" she finally said.

Her face stiffened and tensed up in anticipation of my reply, though I had the feeling she knew all along that I hadn't been given a flat and was asking only to make sure she had guessed rightly.

"They promised me something in the autumn when a new house is finished."

Zinaida Mironovna looked pleased with my answer.

"It's no easy thing to get a flat. Everybody seems to want one nowadays. They're building all those apartment houses and yet there never seem to be enough..."

The landlady looked inquiringly at Dobretsov, not quite sure what to do next. He understood and knitted his brows importantly.

"I'm Stepan's commander. I came to see how you've fixed him up."

"Take a look around then." The landlady beckoned me to follow her to the kitchen.

"She didn't want to start the unpleasant conversation in front of a stranger," I thought to myself. "Now I should do my best to come to an understanding with her."

"Zinaida Mironovna, I'm prepared to pay more for the room," I said, without waiting for her to speak. "We couldn't possibly leave before summer. The children have started school, you must surely understand that..."

"Wait a sec! What are you jabbering away for?" the landlady stopped me and whispered in a confidential tone, "It's my niece's birthday today. She wanted you to come over. You can take your friend along too. Oh, I almost forgot, old fool that I am! It went clean out of my mind! " she reproached herself as she thrust a little box into my hand. "Valentina bought this toy car for Kostya. She felt embarrassed to give it to you herself so she asked me to do it. Take it, you shouldn't refuse a gift."

The landlady made me take the box and smiled, pleased with herself.

"What did she want you for?" Kostya asked when I was back in the room. "Is she throwing us out?"

"No. She's just invited me to her niece's birthday."

"Whose birthday?" Dobretsov, who was sitting in the corner with a bored expression on his face, looked up eagerly. "Is her niece young?"

"Weren't we planning to go to the housing manager?" I tried to object.

"We can do that first thing tomorrow morning.

Never do today what you can put off till tomorrow," said Dobretsov laughing.

I suddenly remembered that the next day was a Sunday and it was no use going to the housing manager anyway. The worst part of it was that on Monday morning I had to leave for Cold Springs.

There was a knock on the door.

"It's only me," said Igor Bumazhkin. "I've brought you something," he added as he held out the packages to the children. "Stepan is flying the day after tomorrow. If you have no objections, I'll stay with you." And he winked at Kostya slyly.

* * *

It was Vera who got my things ready for the flight. She sewed on a missing button to my jacket, pressed my shirts and put them carefully into the suitcase. My shaver, toothbrush and soap were already packed. She and Kostya saw me off as far as the bus stop. I allowed Kostya to carry my small suitcase and he marched along, looking proudly about him.

"Behave yourself and do what Vera tells you," I said. I put my arms around his shoulders. Even through the coat I could feel his shoulder-blades. "Don't let me down. Igor will be staying with you."

"Don't worry, Stepan, everything will be all right."

The bus was almost there, when my sister tugged me by the sleeve.

"I need some money, Stepan."

I gave her a surprised look. Before leaving I had

arranged with the landlady that she would do the cooking for the children. So I figured Vera had spotted something in the shop which she liked.

"I saw a nice dress and a pair of felt boots Natasha's size in the shop. I think we ought to send them to Aunt Nadya."

I took out the money and gave it to Vera.

"When we get a flat, I'll bring Natasha to live together with us."

"Won't that be nice! If only you could do it soon," Vera said with hope in her voice.

"I'll need a room all to myself," Kostya warned me. "I'll bring Polkan to live with me."

"You don't even tidy up your own things, how can you take care of a dog?" Vera said looking mockingly at her brother.

I always left for duty with my heart at ease, but this time I felt worried. "What if something happens... How will they manage without me?"

* * *

It has been a week already since we came to Cold Springs. The local airport stands on a wide tongue of land projecting into the lake. We fly on assignment at the break of dawn every day. We take passengers and mail, and bring in the sick from remote villages in the taiga.

By lunch-time the airport had usually acquired a deserted look. If there were no passengers waiting the mechanic would cover the plane with tarpaulin and we would go to the hotel.

Our replacement was to arrive in several days, and then we could go back to town. I counted the days, anxious to leave, and went to the head of the airport in the evenings to telephone to town and inquire about the children.

Igor Bumazhkin had kept his promise to stay with them after I left.

On Saturday, while we were sitting in the control tower waiting for the evening passengers, the head of the airport dropped round and beckoned me.

"They've just put through a call from town," he told me. "Your brother went off to school in the morning and didn't come back."

"When was that?"

"I think she said it was today," Yeliseyev replied wrinkling his forehead. "It was your landlady calling, but I couldn't make out what she said—the line was bad."

"Perhaps he went some place for a walk," I muttered, trying to hide my anxiety.

"He must be wandering around town," I thought to myself. Things like that had happened before. I was beginning to feel angry with Kostya and decided I'd give him a good hiding when I got back home.

An hour later a radio message came from Sorokin: "Crew fly to base as passengers. Leave plane in Cold Springs."

"So it must be something serious," said Dobretsov. "We shall have to fly to town."

We went to the hotel, packed our things and returned to wait for the regular aeroplane. While we were waiting, a radio signal came from Far Muya. Someone

223

there urgently needed medical treatment.

"Good God! It had to be at such an hour," Dobretsov exclaimed indignantly. He looked at his watch and peered out of the window. The glass was frozen over and through the intricate pattern of ice we could see the parking area. The mechanic was covering up our plane. There was a little over an hour till sunset.

"It's late to fly now, and besides the weather is getting worse." Dobretsov pointed a finger in the direction of the window.

The clouds hovering over the airport had become denser and darkened, and it was hailing. It became quite dark on the control tower. The settlement on the hill slope, which had been clearly visible half an hour before, had vanished from sight behind the heavy curtain of snow.

"I'm not flying. Let them bring their patients by road," Dobretsov said.

I too did not want to fly in such weather. In my thoughts I was already back home. "But what if somebody there is seriously ill? They're expecting us, hoping we'll come." I knew that it could take them hours to cover the hundred-kilometre road from Far Muya by car. The road was a difficult one; it went round the gulfs, along narrow stretches of high land.

"Please don't refuse to go, I'll ask the pilots to wait till you're back," the head of the airport said imploringly. He realised that everything depended on what the crew commander decided: it would soon be quite dark and the weather was unfit for flying.

"We've got to fly there, Alexei," I said to

Dobretsov in a low voice. "It's only fifteen minutes there and fifteen back anyway."

"You should be looking for your brother and here you are, planning to fly somewhere." Dobretsov gave me a perplexed glance.

"But we must fly."

"All right then," Dobretsov said frowning.

We took off and tried to keep closer to the shore of the lake. The erratic black line of the shore stretched northwards and somewhere far beyond the blanket of snow lay Far Muya. We tried to follow all the bends in the shore. Though this made the journey longer, it was the only way we could find the settlement. The snow falling from the sky at an angle beat wildly against the nose of the plane and stuck to the windscreens, obstructing the view.

Dobretsov kept casting worried glances at the wings. The braces and the leading edges were gradually icing up.

The dark silhouettes of snow-swept houses flashed by underneath.

"That's Far Muya," I said with relief.

They were already waiting for us there. Huge lorries for carrying timber stood by the landing-strip. Men crowded near the stretchers, and the muffled sobs of women could be heard. A lorry bringing school-children to the settlement had overturned on the road. Five children were injured and the driver had fractures in both legs.

"What if Kostya was run over by a car?" I thought with horror. "Why did I have to leave them?" I couldn't get rid of this new feeling of alarm.

While they were putting the children on the stretchers, the sky became even more overcast. Now the lower edge of the clouds seemed to meet with earth.

Dobretsov was chipping ice off the wings with a stick; he seemed very jumpy.

No sooner had we taken off than a heavy snowfall began. The wings soon iced over and the plane started losing speed. All we could see ahead of us through the windscreen was snow and more snow. The snow seemed to have erased the shore line and the outlines of the forest below. I tried tuning into the radio landing beacon at Cold Springs, but all I could hear in my earphones was rustling and crackling noises—everything except the familiar bleeping of the radio beacon's signals.

It became still darker in the cockpit. We now went in circles. We had lost our bearings. The coating of ice on the plane grew even thicker.

"We should land," said Dobretsov.

And then suddenly I discerned an uneven black patch down below. It turned out to be a hollow partly covered with snow.

"The ground! I can see the ground! " I shouted.

Dobretsov turned the control wheel sharply and began a diving descent. The plane corkscrewed down into the narrow clearance. A minute later we heard the crunching of ice-covered bushes under the landing skis and then the plane came to a stop in front of a clump of trees.

"So we've landed?" the injured driver asked half-rising from the stretcher.

"Stay where you are. The airport in Cold Springs is

closed down because of the weather," Dobretsov answered gloomily. Then he closed the door and whispered to me: "Out of the frying-pan and into the fire! What do we do now?"

"I'll go and take a look around. I'll see if there are any houses round here. If I don't find any, we'll light bonfires. We have to do everything to save the children."

"They'll freeze to death." My commander looked in front of him miserably.

Something we couldn't have foreseen had happened. We had made an emergency landing and didn't know our whereabouts. Air-to-ground communications were out of order.

I got out of the cockpit and stepped carefully over the children lying on stretchers on the floor of the cabin. They looked at me with fear and anxiety, but there was no way I could reassure them.

Sinking waist-deep into the snow I went down along the river. There were times I lost it in the dense growth of bushes along the banks. In some places its polished ice-bound surface expanded, moving the banks wide apart. Trees rustled near by and lumps of snow fell noiselessly to the ground.

Some three hundred metres away I noticed that the hollow was getting wider. In front of me was the white carpet of the artificial lake. To the left I could discern the black outline of the shore, winding steeply upwards.

"That looks like Birch Ridge," I thought as I peered into the dark. "It's about twenty-five kilometres from here to Cold Springs. With snow like that we'll hardly be able to make it on foot by morning. And that's the closest settlement there is around here."

And then it suddenly occurred to me that we could try and taxi the plane across the ice of the lake. Then we'd be in Cold Springs in no more than twenty minutes! At any other time I would have laughed in the face of anyone who'd suggest such an idea, but now I was like a drowning man clutching at a straw.

Dobretsov listened to me enthusiastically, and then he asked:

"Aren't you afraid we might bend the air-screw?"

"There's a track along the riverside that hasn't been used in a long time. The bushes there are lower than in other places and are covered with snow."

"Well, we don't have any choice." He glanced at me and added in a whisper, "Our starter batteries are pretty weak, we'll have to use the starting-handle."

Dobretsov went to the cockpit. I felt about the front wall for the starting-handle, fitted it into the starting-ratchet, and began turning it steadily. The starter came to life and began building up speed with a loud metallic noise. But the engine spat several times and was dead. We waited a while and tried again. This time, it misfired. We seemed to have no luck that day!

"Let me try now," Dobretsov said, climbing out of the cockpit. We changed places. He managed to drive the starter up to speed, I engaged the transmission and opened the throttle a little way. The air-screw blades turned slowly and stopped.

"No luck! " Dobretsov said angrily. "We must have poured in too much fuel." He took off his fur hat and wiped the sweat from his forehead.

I got out and went to the nose of the plane. Then I climbed under the lower blade and tried to push it back a little. It cut into my shoulder. It was too heavy for one person. During training, at the flying school several people used to turn it together but here there was no one to give me a hand.

"Turn the handle again and I'll help you with the starter batteries," Dobretsov said, leaning out of the ventilation window.

After we cranked up the engine, Dobretsov engaged the clutch. The plane gave a jerk and I felt the floor shaking vigorously under my feet. The vibrating roar of the engine filled the cockpit.

"Don't stop, please don't! Get moving," I begged, gulping down the cold air.

The plane began moving cautiously. It went downhill to the riverside and glided along the hollow, illuminating the dark abandoned road with its headlights and edging round trees and bushes. In one place it lost its balance and began to slip sideways into the river. Dobretsov revved up the engine to take-off power, and the tail of the plane passed safely an inch away from the cliff.

"That was a close shave!" flashed through my mind.

Soon after, the plane was taxiing along the surface of the lake. It was now moving ahead smoothly, rocking slightly on the snowdrifts.

I saw that Dobretsov had relaxed and was in a better mood now. He turned to face the cabin and shouted:

"It'll soon be over now. We'll be in the settlement in no time! "

And then, ahead of us, I distinguished the blurred shape of some object. In the light of our headlamps we saw a launch trapped in the ice. We had reached the bay through which boats approached the settlement in summer. We taxied a little to the right, climbed a hillock and rolled on to the parking area past the fir trees which served as direction posts at the airport. Yeliseyev, the head of the airport, came running over to us. He looked frightened.

"How did you make it here? The radio beacon wasn't working. There was no electricity. We thought you decided to spend the night in Far Muya. Then I looked out and saw the plane taxiing along the runway."

Dobretsov was silent, hungrily pulling on a cigarette.

"Was there a call for me from town?" I asked Yeliseyev.

"No, there wasn't."

Soon an ambulance came from the settlement. We helped carry the accident victims to the car, covered the plane with tarpaulin and went to the hotel.

Some time passed before I managed to fall asleep. In the dark I could see the curtains in the windows, they were snow-white, like doctors' coats. Somewhere behind the wall droned the Diesel engine that supplied the airport with electric power. It was this monotonous sound that lulled me to sleep. I had a terrible nightmare. I dreamed that the engine of our plane had stalled, and though Dobretsov tried to control the flow of petrol vapour and I used the hand-pump, there was nothing we could do about it. The plane lowered its nose reluctantly and dived steeply. It was so quiet all around that I could hear the air whistling past the headlights. Fences, roads and multi-storied buildings flashed by underneath. Somehow I knew it before it actually happened—we were going to crash into the yard of the motor depot.

"No, no, that can't be! " I shouted in my sleep. "I have to find my brother! "

I never learned how it all ended. I was awakened by the loud creaking of the door. In came Seryozha, Yeliseyev's son. Holding up his hat to stop it falling down over his eyes, he shouted:

"There's a call for you from town! "

I jumped out of bed, ran up to the chair and hastily pulled on my overalls. My hands suddenly felt weak; my heart missed a beat and began throbbing wildly.

Dobretsov began tossing and turning in his bed. His sleepy face appeared from under the blanket.

"What's happened?"

"There's a telephone call for Osintsev," Seryozha explained, snuffling, but trying to sound like a grown-up.

"If you'd sent them to a children's home as I told you, you'd have no worries now."

Dobretsov fell silent and a look of concern appeared on his face. Then he quickly recovered his composure.

"Keep quiet about our yesterday's flight, will you," he said in a hoarse whisper. "When we get back to town, I'll report it myself. I hope everything will be alright."

231

It was a foggy morning. The orange sun hung low over the roof of the air terminal.

"It's bad flying weather again," I thought looking around.

Seryozha was mincing along in front of me. He was trying to go fast, though his legs were as thin as knitting needles and he had difficulty walking through the snow in his father's felt boots. He pushed hard at the gate but it barely moved. Then he lifted it a bit and gave another push—the gate opened, leaving a half-circle in the snow.

The telephone receiver was lying on a chair. I grabbed it and pressed it to my ear.

"Why aren't you leaving?" I heard Sorokin's muffled voice.

"There's a heavy fog, blast it! " I shouted. "It settled in shortly before dawn."

"It's all right. It should clear off by midday," said Sorokin. "Tell me, do any of your relatives live in the village?"

"My uncle does."

I broke out in a sweat and felt the receiver sticking to my palm.

"Some of our pilots saw Kostya getting on a bus that goes to the railway station. Could he have gone to the village?"

I didn't know what to say.

"Take off as soon as the fog clears. If I learn something new about your brother I'll ring you." Sorokin hung up.

I wiped the sweat off my forehead with a sleeve and sat down.

Yeliseyev came in. His face was as red as beetroot.

"Ah, you're here! " the head of the airport nodded to me affably. "The mechanic and I've been busy with the plane; we've tuned the engine up. It's a good thing you brought the accident victims here so fast. The driver and two of the children have already been operated on. Now let's have breakfast. You might not have the time later. You've been working round the clock." Yeliseyev got a loaf of bread and some fatback from the cupboard. At that moment, Seryozha peeped round at us from behind the door. We had made friends during the week I was there. He was the first person to meet us on the landing-strip after touchdown. He liked sitting in the pilot's seat, and would touch the control column cautiously. When I watched him I couldn't help thinking about Kostya. I was sorry he wasn't with me here.

Yeliseyev brushed the crumbs off the table-cloth.

"They're always making such a mess, the little devils. It's quite a job to look after them. Never mind, I'll bring their mother here soon and she'll take care of things. Sit down now and let's have a snack."

Just then Dobretsov burst into the room.

"I see you're in no hurry to get home," he said. "The plane will be leaving soon, the fog's almost cleared. Let's go."

The fog was indeed clearing up. The houses in the settlement and the dark silhouette of the hill behind it were now clearly visible from where I stood. Next to the plane an airfield heater was smoking away, its canvas hose inserted into the cowling. Dobretsov climbed inside after me. There was barely enough room for the two of us in the cockpit, but it seemed warmer.

Seryozha came running towards the plane across the deep snow just when we had taxied towards the runway. He was waving the fur boots I had bought for Alik Serikov. I got out and took them from him. The aeroplane broke ground smoothly, cutting into the cold stream of air as if it were a sheet of tarpaulin, and headed for Irkutsk. Down below lay the snow-clad taiga; a cold winter sun hung low above the horizon.

Sorokin was waiting for us in the parking area. Next to him stood Zinaida Mironovna, my landlady. I looked at them through the window, trying to figure out what news they had for me. The air-screw was still revolving when Sorokin came up to the plane and beckoned me out.

"Go to the village right away. The boy's there," he said to me as soon as I joined him. "Give me a ring after you find him. I'll have to be off now—I have an emergency mission."

Sorokin checked the time by his watch and walked heavily towards the plane standing next to ours. A minute later I saw it taxiing to the runway.

"Off you go! " Zinaida Mironovna said to me quickly. "Don't worry, I'll look after Vera. She's at school now. She was so alarmed she didn't have a wink of sleep all night."

Before long I was in the village. I had a feeling I had never left it. The snow had somewhat darkened and the drifts along the embankment had partly thawed in the sun. Huge icicles hung down from the roof-tops. A narrow string of birch-trees glimmered vaguely beyond the houses and, further back, haw-thorn-bushes were scattered here and there across the field in dark, twisted clumps. It seemed they too were looking for someone. The air was fresh and crisp, the sky soft and cloudless. Though it was quite cold outside, you could tell that spring was near.

There was no bus in sight, but I saw a tip-up lorry near the station house. Several workers were loading it. Suddenly, Alik Serikov got out of the driver's cab.

"Hullo, Stepan. So you're back again?"

"That's it."

"I bet you forgot to buy the fur boots I asked for."

"No I didn't. I brought you a pair," I said in a voice that didn't sound particularly cheerful.

"Really? How nice of you! I didn't expect you'd remember about it! "

"Where are you driving now?"

"To the river channel. I can give you a lift to the village first, if you want me to."

Alik opened the door for me and put away a toy gun that had been lying on the seat.

"Did you by any chance meet Kostya here?"

"No, I didn't," said Serikov, stealing a quick glance at me. "Is anything wrong with him?"

"He got lost. I was told he went to the village."

"I haven't seen him, unfortunately."

"Drop me off at the children's home. Perhaps he's staying with Tanya."

Deep inside, I was hoping against hope that my brother was with her. We rode out onto the road and drove fast in the direction of the children's home.

The wind beat frantically against the windscreen.

"Have you heard the latest news?" Alik asked turning to face me. "They're moving the children's home to town. The premises are to be used for a health centre."

The first person I saw when we arrived at the children's home was Sanya. I asked him about my brother.

"I haven't seen him since he left for town with you," he said, drawling out the words. "And Tatyana Vasilievna is away on leave. They are going to move us soon."

"Let me drop you off at your place," Serikov offered. "Then I'll drive to the garage and ask my boss if he'll allow me to stay away from work for the rest of the day. If we drive, the two of us will definitely find your brother faster."

He stopped the lorry near our house. I noticed already at a distance that my uncle was not wasting his time—there were new double gates in the fence instead of the old ones. And gates are a sign of the owner's well-being in a village.

I got out of the lorry. Frosya came out of the house, accompanied by Galina Stepanovna.

"Where is Kostya?" I shouted.

"At Chernikha's," Frosya replied.

This took a load off my mind—I had traced my brother and he was alive and well. Nothing else mattered now.

"I vouched for you, Stepan, and look what happened! What kind of a guardian are you?" Galina Stepanovna looked at me accusingly.

I didn't say anything and ran to Chernikha's house.

I dashed across the yard so fast that I didn't even give the dog a chance to begin barking. I groped for the door-handle in the dark porch for a long time, bumping into bunches of dry herbs hanging from the ceiling. A yoke fell to the floor with a crash.

"Oh, so it's you? I was wondering who was making all that noise," Chernikha said as she opened the door for me. "Come on in."

I bent my head so as not to hit it against the low door-frame, but tripped over the threshold that was lagged with felt. Right across the door sat Uncle Yefim. He was in his half-length coat and was crumpling his fur hat nervously. When he saw me he jumped from his seat and looked round at Chernikha.

"Where's Kostya?"

"He's in the room," Uncle Yefim said, and blinked guiltily.

I walked to the room with quick steps and saw my brother sitting on a bed, rubbing his red eyes with his knuckles. He had been crying.

"What's the matter with you, Kostya?"

"Why did they have to shoot Polkan?" he screamed in a shrill voice, his thin body shaking convulsively. "He was simply lonely without me, that's why he was howling! "

It was only then that I noticed a dog's collar in my brother's hand. It was a new one, the kind they make at factories. Our father usually made collars out of old leather belts.

"I'll tell you how it was," Uncle Yefim rattled away with a note of uneasiness. "I had to shoot the dog because it howled all the time after you had left.

237

As if it could feel another death in the house! We just couldn't stand it any longer! "

Everything fell in its place. Kostya had gone off to fetch Polkan without knowing the way properly. But it was too late when he arrived...

I heard the screeching of brakes outside. Tanya came running into the house, followed by Alik Serikov. A minute later Frosya came. She went into the room without taking her coat off and sat down next to Uncle Yefim.

"Don't cry, Kostya, please don't," said Tanya, doing her best to comfort him but unable to hold back her tears.

"I told Stepan it's going to be difficult, but he wouldn't listen to me," Frosya said with a sigh.

"Why pick on the lad? He didn't do anything wrong! " Chernikha interfered. "It's true he has a hard time looking after the children alone. But he'll make a success of it in the end, you'll see."

I couldn't look at my uncle without revulsion.

"What am I doing, dawdling the time away! " Chernikha said. "Won't you sit down at table? You're welcome to it, such as it is."

She seated me and Tanya together. I realised she had done it on purpose.

Tanya gave me an embarrassed look and turned to whisper something to Kostya. He smiled faintly and nodded in agreement.

I felt that from now on something was going to change in my life.

Pyotr Krasnov

Pyotr Krasnov was born in 1950 in the village of Ratchino, in the Sharlinsky District of the Orenburg Region. He is a graduate from the Agricultural Institute in agronomy. He worked as a head agronomist in Mari Autonomous Republic, then as an engineer in the Regional Office of Grain Production in Orenburg. For several years he made contributions of literary work to the factory newspaper of the Orenburg Gas Factory Complex. He is now a professional writer.

Pyotr Krasnov has published three books of which *Sashka's Field* was awarded First Prize in the Maxim Gorky All-Union Competition for the best first book by a young author. He is a member of the USSR Writers' Union.

Little Grishook had already been kept at home for two days running. The day before yesterday he'd been attacked and bitten by stray dogs on his way home from school. They'd given him quite a going over. The bites were healing slowly, and now he just felt ashamed that, of all people, it should have happened to him.

He had been in the habit of going to school through the big meadow. Who'd go from their end of the village along the street when it was only half as far through the meadow? And he'd been walking there the day before yesterday, head down as usual, staring at the ground because he hadn't got anything better to do, now and then hooking out the "apples" of horse dung with his felt winter boots, and kicking them along in front of him. He'd been doing this very skilfully, so he'd completely failed to notice that the dogs were right in front of him. And when little Grishook raised his head, they were about fifty metres away—no further! Six big animals, representing all races and sizes of the dog world, were trotting towards the track in a disordered group, cutting across him, barking occasionally and indifferently among themselves, whining something to each other, and taking—as it seemed—no notice of little Grishook, because stray dogs have got far more important things on their minds than those which occupy the village howlers who spend their lives on the end of a chain. Grishook reckoned they were coming back from the collective farm's yards, where they scratched out a living by ratting, thieving and so on, and were now on their way home to their regular haunt in the trench for burying dead cattle, which had been bulldozed out behind the field last summer, on the site of the old clay pits.

Straightaway Grishook got scared. He stopped, waiting for the whole rabble to cross the track, and examined them carefully. Running away was out of the question, because then the dogs would definitely chase after him, if only out of curiosity. And it was crazy to think anyone could get away from them over the clean sweep of the snow-covered meadow with its occasional patches of last year's wormwood still growing in odd corners, when there were three or—more likely—four hundred metres of empty space left between him and the willows of the village street. Immediately he recognised Volna, mistress and original progenitor of the entire population of the cattle trench. She was running a little in front of the pack, still coquettishly white in spite of her long years of vagrancy, her well-shaped, clever muzzle taking in everything that passed. And then, with a sudden sinking feeling that made his legs go unpleasantly weak, he saw that, running next to her, was the skewbald dog known as Looty, the sight of whose enormous head was enough to make any domestic dog start whining invitingly and submissively, fawning up to him with its back and folding down its ears, or else put its tail between its legs and scuttle off into the nearest gateway...

Quietly, Grishook began to make a circle homeward. Tingling with terror and trying not to swing his arms, he started to walk away from the dogs without looking back, not noticing that he was going more and more quickly. He had only one thought in his head—not to start running...

He thought he had already managed to get some distance from them. His heart had stopped, painfully. Every moment he expected to hear Volna start barking, and then the whole pack, bristling, growling and barking, in their different ways, come rushing down on him.

Suddenly, he imagined so clearly how it would be (it couldn't have been any clearer) that something seemed to seize up, or rather come away, inside him. He turned round for a second, then started to run—very quickly as it seemed to him, though in reality it was only some kind of child's little gallop-slipping in the smooth-worn ruts, hardly managing to snatch enough air into his hoarse lungs.

In all this he failed to hear how the tranquil, conversational family barking behind him had ceased and how Volna had let out an alarming and playful yelp. Next time he turned round, he saw at once how the whole pack had stretched out along the track and was rolling towards him, howling and barking, with Looty, his domed head bent down and drawn in slightly, flying along with long bounds at the front, confidently and speedily pounding along the track. Grishook, gasping hopelessly, was already running in any old way he could: sideways, without the strength to stop himself from looking back at Looty's wide forehead, bouncing rhythmically closer with every pace, at the business-like eyes which seemed ready for anything, and at the fangs bared now in the thrill of the chase, and glistening with saliva...

He stumbled while he was running, and fell down

with all his might. He scrambled to his feet, not feeling any pain, or anything else. Then he saw how Looty had circled around him along the side of the track and stopped sharply, about five metres away from him, with his starved, hollow sides heaving in and out, surveying Grishook with his slanting eyes, as if waiting for something. And just at that moment, snarling gruffly, another dog took a running jump at Grishook, aiming at the arm which was lifted in defence, missed it, and rolled head over heels. Then all the rest attacked him.

Trying to shout something, crying loudly and choking for breath, Grishook started spinning and stamping around on the spot, beating and flailing among the violent and frenzied yelping of the dogs and their bared teeth. Keeping his face turned away, he managed miraculously to stay on his feet under the weight of the dogs who were now pressing and hanging on him. One bite had already appeared on his leg, though not painfully—then one on his hand, and then another on his leg. With the sound of ripping cloth, a tear opened on the back of his padded jacket. A strong jerk on his collar pulled him to the ground, and he huddled up, struggling to compress himself into a ball, covering his head in an effort to keep it from the jaws which were tearing at him, rolling him along in the melting snow, from the sticky saliva burning at his skin, and from the dirty, scrabbling claws... Within these few moments, even though they were so short, he had already managed to think with terror of what he would say to his mother when he came home all mauled and torn, and how ashamed he would feel in front of the other boys for being such an unlucky wretch. Then, suddenly, he realised that he might not come back at all. No, he would never come back now, he would never come back at all. And in the grip of this preposterous, clear and terrifying thought, but not yet quite believing it, he froze for a moment, and a second later started to shout weakly and pitifully—struggling to be heard somewhere, but where?—with a voice quivering at its limit, so that at least someone might hear him among the frenzied snarling of the attacking pack, might learn that he was there and needed help... Otherwise he really wouldn't come back home, but would die. He drove his face and his whole body into the rough damp of the chilling snow, asking it to help him too. He was growing limp, and nearly fainting.

There was a short yelp, a choked growl, then another yelp, and the dogs suddenly fell away from him one by one and backed off. That's the end, he thought, now Looty will start, that's really the end ... and he started to cry out again, tearing his head away from the snow and turning back towards the roofs and willows of the distant village street where his home was, moaning feebly:

"Mummy! Oh please! Mummy! "

Nobody answered him, but nobody attacked him either. The dogs had broken away from him and were looking at him indifferently and blankly, as at something they had already grown bored with, and one of them, in a business-like fit, was already hunting through its mangy coat for fleas. Looty was standing between Grishook and the whole pack, with Volna beside him, wagging her tail benevolently, pleased with something. He was standing with his side to the pack, making the air vibrate with his growling, and Volna was rubbing up against him as though nothing had happened, moving away and then coming back to him again and again, laying her ears back lovingly. Sometimes, as if scenting something, she waggled her clever, pretty muzzle towards Grishook. But Looty was still snarling, and he suddenly bit Volna's side as it passed in front of him. The bitch bared her teeth sharply and snarled back at him. Then they set off along the road, leading the whole pack away with them, without turning back.

With difficulty, Grishook got up from the snow, which was now churned up by hundreds of footprints, sat down by the side of the track and started to cry silently to himself. Then he got up all the same, feeling how quickly his leg was growing numb, picked up his mitten and started to limp towards the alley which led on to the village street—this time without looking back, crying all the time, and licking something salty (tears or blood?) from his lips. A sledge was already speeding out to meet him: the horse charging forward at a gallop with its tensed head turned to one side revealing a crazy white eye, and the person in the back drawn up to his full height, brandishing his whip and shouting and swearing in a high-pitched angry voice.

It was Uncle Yefim the stableman. He reined the horse in so strongly that—flapping its ears and snorting—it went clean off the track and got stuck in the snow. Still swearing, and falling over himself in the process, he started to walk—or rather stumble—half running towards Grishook, shouting out, before he'd even finished getting out of the sledge, worried and angry:

"What on earth have they done to you? Couldn't you have looked where you were going?"

Then he slowed down, screwed up his face into an expression of sympathetic annoyance, came up to Grishook and tugged lightly at his shoulder—as if to check that he was all in one piece. Then he bent down closer towards Grishook's eyes, which were looking at him silently through tears. His face grew sorry and surprised as it took in the child's torn winter coat, his felt boots snagged by the dogs' teeth, and the deep clawmark on his cheek, filled out by a thick string of frozen blood. He grunted with displeasure, squatted down on his haunches in front of Grishook, shook him by the shoulder, and said rather roughly, but sympathetically, and with an increasingly softer expression in his eyes:

"So you're still alive are you? Well thank God for that. I came rushing as fast as I could. I thought they'd finish you, those shirkers! Are you badly bitten?"

Grishook didn't answer. He wiped his eyes on his sleeve and glanced back behind him. Like links of a disconnected chain, the dogs were disappearing towards the steppe beyond the rounded crest of the trench, their tails between their legs and their bodies hunched with the sullenness that tramps have in front of everything which is settled, owned, and allowed to stay in one place.

Uncle Yefim's eyes narrowed strangely and followed them too. Unable to contain himself any longer, he swore sharply and raised his whip-handle threateningly as though he had completely forgotten Grishook's presence.

"Just you wait shirkers... We'll teach you to do that! " he shouted, turning back towards Grishook, breathing a strong and familiar smell of roasted sunflower seeds and tobacco over him.

"Where have they bitten you? Does it hurt?" He drove Grishook over to the surgery because the boy's leg had grown completely stiff. Aunty Tamara, the District Nurse, collided with them in the doorway; she didn't need to ask what had happened, but just shook her head maternally and started bustling about, preparing a syringe. Bending her white face, with its carefully washed wrinkles, down towards Grishook, she came out with her usual "Be brave young man", and gave him an injection, not too painfully, in his leg. She painted iodine generously over the staple-shaped little wound over his knee and began to bandage it; then she did the same for the other two: one each on his arm and leg. Uncle Yefim, though he had been invited to sit down, only surveyed the white chair-covers sullenly and then squatted down beside the door, leaning on the door-post and self-consciously twiddling an unlit cigarette between his fingers. The nurse cut the ends of the bandage and looked at Grishook protectively. She spoke angrily:

"What a wonderful boy... Such a nice boy... And then those dogs! I do not understand how you parents, when you've got children like these, can stand having those bandits living so close by. Call yourselves men, do you? You've got rifles and so on, and plenty of spare time... The least you could do is ask the militiaman for help. Take yourself for example; you've got a daughter. She's a fine, healthy, plump sort of girl. How do you expect me to guarantee you—or them I mean—my help, when those awful dogs go around eating all sorts of nasty things, dead animals and all kinds of rubbish. (You know what I mean, don't you?) The most insignificant bite would be enough... Yet you prefer to take no notice. I just don't know what it is you're waiting for."

The stableman, who had been silently watching the nimble movements of her hands, crumpled the cardboard filter of his cigarette in his palm, and said with obvious uneasiness:

"Well we know you're right, Tamara Pavlovna. We'll do something."

"Well you ought to. The children won't wait for you. How much longer can it go on? I've already had to bandage five people in the last two years, and administered an unscheduled vaccination programme. You must understand how dangerous it is. The children are frightened. It's just a reign of terror! By dogs! "

"Yes something will have to be done, Tamara Pavlovna, and no denying it. We've been talking it over for a long time. It's not just the children they're bothering, it's everyone. You can't put your baby geese out in the meadow any more..."

"Well do something immediately! Today or tomorrow! "

"Today or tomorrow?" Uncle Yefim said anxiously, and apparently stunned.

"That's just what they will do," thought Grishook, full of malicious joy. "They'll all get together—tomorrow maybe—and they'll really do those dogs. That'll teach 'em to jump on people! They can't be allowed to go on behaving like this. They get away with it all too easily. One day they attack someone, next they frighten someone out of their skin. They've run so wild—there's no controlling 'em." He was thinking in the way Uncle Yefim spoke. And it wasn't just that he'd been bitten by these shirkers, he'd also caught it when he got home. As soon as his mother had seen him, torn and bandaged all over, she had run to him, terribly upset—she'd even cried a bit. Then she smacked him over the back of the head, and said that if she saw him once more on that track through the meadow, so help her if she didn't skin him alive...

Grishook smiled bitterly. What? Does she think I'm going to walk along the street like a girl. No! That would be too much to ask. He would pick up a stick, and carry on going to school through the meadow—though with Victor Kuzin of course. Then let those dogs come trying it on again! He wasn't in the Infants' School any more after all. He could hit someone back when he wanted...

Yet he couldn't get his mother's words, or more especially her face—which had been both tearful and determined—out of his head. The glumness and gloominess of the thawing winter's day, and his mother's threat, and his father's forbidding him to go out, and in general everything—the dogs—all combined to upset him; and he turned away from the fragile dampness of the window-pane, which was wet and running with cold.

The front parlour of the village house where he was sitting was empty. His parents were due back from their rounds of the dairy farm for lunch very soon. His Gran was snuffling in her bed behind the stove in the kitchen, sometimes coughing slightly as she turned over. A warm, cosy atmosphere filled the room. The alarm-clock was ticking away hastily on the chest of drawers, as though hurrying or running somewhere; the old wall clock tocked along after it, following in long paces behind. The eyes of the cat whose picture was drawn on the clock-face glanced alternately at the door and at Grishook with a satisfied and slightly mysterious feline grin. Tick—the door; tock—Grishook. Maybe he should go out, he thought wistfully, looking at the cat. No, that wouldn't do. His old Gran would tell on him, and then he'd catch no end of trouble from his Mum. "Just what do you mean by it?" she'd say. "I leave you at home, keep you away from school, and you go slinking off as soon as my back's turned."

What a bore it was. Screwing his face up, more in anticipation than pain, Grishook felt the bandage on his leg. It was hurting, and had got a bit swollen. The arm was already a lot better. You could tap on it if you wanted. But the leg... The leg still let him down a bit. When Victor Kuzin—the pushy little boy everyone called "Kuzka"—had come visiting with some of the other boys from Junior Form 4B, they had all together (keeping it secret from Mum and Gran of course) unwound the bandage, which was yellow from iodine, and looked. It was getting drier, but it wasn't healing yet. The boys had nodded approvingly. They were clearly quite envious too, and they were surprised to find what a good boy Looty had turned out to be. He'd chased the other dogs off easily, and never touched a hair on Grishook's head. They talked about how he used to nick goslings from the Gavrushins in the springtime; he would appear quite calmly out of the willow thicket, while the Gavrushin woman was shouting-and-yelling from the other side of the field, pick out his gosling and then stalk off back into the undergrowth. Out of the whole pack, only he and Volna could do it quite like that. The rest were too scared, or just never touched any livestock.

"Looty's dead clever, I bet." Kuzka had blinked his bright, brave eyes with delight. "He just doesn't like people, he's got very wild. Otherwise he's just like White Fang. Don't you believe me?" He had his bony little fists clenched ready to defend what he was saying. Grishook kept silent, smiling slightly and wondering, "What would you have done if you'd seen him close up like I did", but Kuzka was set on nothing less than taming Looty, then using him in the summer to help guard the collective-farm cows.

Kuzka popped in again in the evening and told him how the men in the village were getting a beat together. Uncle Yefim had started it. Only it just wasn't clear what he wanted. One moment he said they were to kill only Volna and Looty for being the ring-leaders; next moment he would blow his top and shout, "We'll exterminate the lot and that's all there is to it! " In short, he was stirring up trouble. And

Ponyrin—that bloke who was a lieutenant during the war and gave that speech in their school about all the medals and awards he'd got—he'd already got a shotgun out, a double-barrelled one, and was telling how, about so many years ago, they'd chased the dogs all the way through the stubblefield, then on from there to the yards and blown their brains out. He said that after that you could breathe more freely straight away. The beat was due to be today or tomorrow, and as for Kuzka, he'd already fixed himself up with a club with a nail in it and nobody knew where he'd hidden it. And as to what he'd said about White Fang, he added confidently when reminded and without even hesitating, he would make a point of saving Looty, of letting him get away, then only later he would begin to tame him. They'd never get a dog like that however hard they tried, so he would still watch the shooting as much as he wanted. Ponyrin himself was saying that he hadn't fired at anything other than magpies for a long time, that he couldn't wait to get started, and would now be able to shoot to his heart's content...

"He's all lies," Grishook was thinking. "How would he be able to save him when there was a gun? They could kill Volna if they wanted to. It'd serve her right. But it was a shame about Looty. Anisin, who used to own him, had once been offered fifty roubles for him; but he hadn't even wanted to hear about it. He was a shepherd, and—without Looty—he was like a man with no right arm. He'd never felt any pity for him though; he used to beat him with whatever came to hand. So now he had neither the money nor the dog. Looty had run away to the cattle trench. It was the same with all of them. They'd gone to get away from hard times. And things were much better for them, living in a group."

Grishook was still thinking all this over, when the latch rattled in the porch, the door opened, creaking with damp, and Kuzka burst into the kitchen. His freckled face, round as an apple, was pale with triumph. He glanced quickly along the curtains and the stove. Suddenly everything was clear to Grishook. The beat had started.

"Well, what's up with you?" Kuzka shouted in a hoarse quarrelsome voice from the threshold when he saw Grishook. "You want to sleep through it, don't you? Well, you do what you want. I'm going." He pretended to move back into the porch. "Well?"

"Wait for me," Grishook begged in indignation, rushing to get his winter boots off the stove. "Can't you see? I really didn't know."

"I bet you didn't. There's already a crowd out in the meadow. Where's your pullover?" And he started helping him to dress. Grishook was no longer thinking of what his mother would say to him in the evening, but was hastily burrowing into his pile of clothes. His Gran had started stirring crossly behind the stove, and her voice came over to him, husky with sleep:

"Damn you! You little blighter! And just where would you be going to?" Without answering, Grishook darted out after Kuzka.

Once outside, Kuzka silently shoved a specially prepared stick into his hands. Though Grishook was limping, they walked through to the side street at a quick pace, skirted round the old millstone which had been dug permanently into the earth at the corner, and came out on the track which led across the flat, snow-covered meadow towards the trench.

There, at the back of the village, between the last wattle shed and the log heap, about fifteen people were standing—a mixed group of children and adults. Almost all of them had sharpened sticks. They were smoking and chatting, and glancing from time to time at the snow-blotched crest of the trench, which was visible at the end of the track, about half a kilometre away. A low sky, swollen with the grey dampness of winter, stretched away across the steppe in unbroken monotony; and even the daylight, falling from above, was also rather grey and dusky, as though reaching them through grimy, unwashed window-panes. "So now what?" thought Grishook, getting annoyed with his friend when it was already too late. "They'll stay here for a bit and then break up, but I'll have all the explaining to do to Mum. It would be worth it for a real beat, but now it's just for nothing."

Vasya Kotyakh—a tall, rather skinny lad with a hook nose and a stern face—was standing in the middle of the crowd with his small-calibre rifle slung over his shoulder. This little piece of weaponry, with its shining, thickly transparent brown butt and its blue steel barrel, was staring silently downwards at the crowd's winter boots, while its owner was saying, reluctantly but firmly:

"All right. So you've got this scheme into your heads. But somehow I don't really believe they will run towards the gardens here. The bastards'll smell a plot."

"And I tell you that they will." The stableman was getting into a bad temper, and his face, which was usually so straightforward and carefree, now looked alarmed and quarrelsome, puckered up all the time as though there was something stuck in his throat and worrying him. "Don't you start telling me they won't run. They'll do whatever we tell 'em, if we give 'em just one good fright up the rear. It was exactly the same last time. Ponyrin'll vouch for me. They started trying to get away across the street into the thickets over by Krushinikha. They had no other place to go. We'll be waiting for them in the gardens all right. There's just one rule: not a peep out of anyone." He turned to Ponyrin: "You were the marksman seven years ago. How many did we kill then?"

"Christ knows. About five."

Kotyakh was still doubtful. "With a handful like this though..." He looked scornfully around at the children. "Mostly just babes in arms! "

"They'll be here, don't you worry," said Ponyrin, taking out his grubby, wooden tobacco-box. Holding the butt of his gun against his boots, he took out a pinch and poked it with his thumb into his nostrils, making them hairy for a moment with tobacco. Then he sniffed it, and without sneezing but yawning convulsively from the effect, finished what he was saying: "There'll be so many of 'em you won't get rid of 'em. Nobody comes when there's any hard work to be done, but for a bit of sport... There's never any shortage for that."

"Oh Christ," said the stableman nervously, looking with hostility at Ponyrin's bearlike, untidy shape and his meddlesome, flabby face with its indefinable grin. "Always sticking tobacco up your nose! When are you going to give up sniffing that shit?"

"When I snuff it," said Ponyrin, laughing good-humouredly. "When a worm gets up my nose, then I'll stop." And satisfied with his own answer, he shrugged his narrow, womanly shoulders arrogantly as if shaking something out of his dirty padded coat. He put the tobacco-box back into the pocket of his trousers. "What are you worried about, Yefim? You'd think you were delivering a baby. Take a leaf out of my book. I'm as sharp as a bayonet—raring to go."

"Nobody's worried, mate. So don't you go bothering yourself about it," Yefim answered discontentedly, and Grishook again noticed how he screwed his face up and tightened his jaw. "We must do what we have to. Let those shirkers do the worrying. And when we've finished them all off, then we'll start worrying."

The smile faded on Ponyrin's lips. He snorted in feigned amazement and, making his eyes round with surprise, he reached again for his tobacco-box. "Well I'm surprised at you, Yefim... A minute ago you were all for killing Looty and Volna, and now... You're chopping and changing all the time... How do you expect me to make head or tail of what you want after that?"

"Just fire and don't miss."

"Well, well my dear old friend. Just as I thought by Christ. Take a look at this pocketful of beans. As if I'd seen it all in my crystal ball," said Ponyrin, and suddenly hardening his expression even more, he looked around him arrogantly to show he'd had his fill of joking. Everyone listened silently to his next words:

"Did you think I was going to come jigging around out here for the sake of one shitty little dog. No, no, my dear old friend," he said, making the cartridges rustle by tapping on his pocket with his broad palm. "I shan't budge from this field till I've farted every one of these out, and I won't leave them dogs alone either. Maybe it's just a night out for you, mate, or maybe it isn't, but I've had a bone to pick with them for a long time, ever since they took all the chickens I had hatched out for me in the incubator, and ever since ... well, just in general." He paused to draw breath, and then said: "We had a bellyful of your talking yesterday, and we can do very well without it today, thank you. I don't give a damn how nice or nasty they are, or what made them run away from their masters. I've come here to get some shooting done, and I'll make them dance a jig for me! " Ponyrin grinned again, savouring the effect of his speech, and shook his rifle to show off his strength. "We'll have a real battle. Isn't that right, Vasya?"

Kotyakh didn't answer. He was keeping his eyes on the trench and the haystack in the middle of the field where he would soon be lying in ambush. He asked the driver Boborykin:

"Are you sure they're in the trench there?"

"Oh yes. Koska the bone-man has just taken a dead calf over there. He says the whole gang is there, all ten or maybe fifteen of them. He dumped the calf there, he says, and hardly had time to sit back down in the sledge before the whole bloody lot came down on the carcass. They made the whole steppe shake. For himself, he says, he's just thunderstruck—he doesn't know how that little Perevazov boy stood up to it the other day. He just galloped off as fast as the horse would carry him. And since that last feast they haven't stuck their noses out once. Their excellencies are taking their after-carcass nap." Boborykin, a well-built fellow with an expressive face, spread his hands jokingly as much as to say: "Well, one mustn't be too hard on their highnesses. A good rest is absolutely essential after such a banquet."

Kotyakh only snorted.

The crowd was getting bigger, though mostly it was only with children, jostling and boasting over their sticks. The grown-ups were fewer, it was hard to find people who enjoyed such things. They had split into little groups, and were now discussing their plans, arranging everything, arguing, swearing, and sometimes a ripple of excitement and a general feeling of insecurity would run across them. They would grow quiet and turn back to the field which was standing, as though ajar, in front of them. The stableman didn't join in the chatter, as though he'd actually gone off the whole plan; he just listened gloomily, screwing up his eyes sometimes, as though in judgement of human frailty. Then he walked over to one side, sat down on the wet aspen logs, and lit a cigarette. Catching sight of Grishook, he winked unhappily:

"So that's the way things are going, is it, mate?" He nodded towards the place next to him. Feeling flattered, but blushing, Grishook came over to him with Kuzka. They sat down.

"Well Grishook my lad, you've already picked out the right stick for yourself, have you?" The boy nodded. The stableman looked him up and down, grinning with his usual kindness, and then asked: "So you reckon you're better, do you?"

"Er ... not quite," said Grishook in a voice which was hoarse with worry and embarrassment, looking down at the wet snow and poking it with his stick. "It still hurts a bit. Otherwise it's not bad."

"He's limping," said Kuzka, assuming a professional, independent air and studying the boys from the senior classes and their sticks. "You got there too late. That's why he's a hobbler."

"So that's how it is," said the stableman without surprise. Kuzka was well known for being like that. "How could I have got there in time when it happened the way it did?"

"By the way..." Grishook surprised himself by asking, his voice faltering down to a whisper and so making it twice as embarrassing. "Will they do Looty in too?"

"They won't just do him in, they'll kill him," Kuzka corrected in an adult voice without even looking at them. "Of course they will. What else could they do with him? Peel onions? Look how many cartridges Uncle Ponyrin has brought with him. He'll let them have it. I'm going to have a gun when I get to the Senior School..."

"You'll have to grow up a bit first, young man," Uncle Yefim said, stern and surprised. Grishook was surprised too, and offended by Kuzka's betrayal of Looty. "When he gets to the Senior School! A killer he reckons!" muttered the stableman. "We'll have to wean you away from your Mummy first."

Kuzka went into a sulk, but he didn't dare answer back. Grasping his stick and sniffing resentfully, he hurried off towards the crowd, where there was now a constant commotion, everybody speaking at once and waving their arms about. Young Filka, the clerk from the accountant's office, whose fine, freckled features were—despite his youth—already bloated by alcohol, was speaking with annoyance in his high-pitched voice, trying to interrupt Ponyrin:

"Hold on a second! If you're let loose with your rifle, you'll... Hold on a second for Christ's sake... Let me have my say. I know you... You'll go hullabalising all over the place without realising what you're doing..."

"When did I ever go 'hullabalising'?"

"Every bloody time! Why did you kill Solovyov's Lady in the autumn? Mikita still regrets not punching you on the snout for it. Now here you are, at it again..."

"Never you mind my 'snout'... You come round talking to me about my 'snout', you money-grubbing little bastard. You aren't old enough to be talking about 'snouts'."

"Maybe not, but I'll get there one day, don't you worry. Yefim's right when he tells you it's only Volna and Looty who ought to be killed. The rest'll scatter by themselves... And what are you going to do? Wasn't the first time enough for you?"

"Your Yefim's already changed his mind. And what kind of talk is it anyway—feeling sorry for them? Everyone else knows how to behave. It's just you and

Yefim who come round screwing our minds up. If you haven't got it in you to join in like everybody else, then piss off back to your Manya and go back to bed. And here's to you, mate. Christ knows what sort of person you really are. You probably don't even kill flies at home because you feel too sorry for them... You're a bit soft in the head if you ask me." Ponyrin turned away from him in disgust, no longer interested.

"Have you no sense of right and wrong? Why are you being such bastards?"

"Keep your right and wrong out of this. You bloody do-gooder!"

Filka started to swear dirtily and intricately, and it was clear that he had already had quite a lot to drink. Everybody kept silent, and they even accepted the swearing sympathetically, for they knew that, though Ponyrin might be good company, he was utterly without pity.

"You're a load of bastards," repeated Filka, looking round at the crowd and waving his arms in bitter consternation. "Really, you mustn't be such bastards. Why don't you leave them alone. What's the big deal about them?"

"Don't keep 'bastardising' everybody, lad," Uncle Yefim joined in suddenly, and everybody turned to him. "See what a fine mess they made of this little boy. It's quite appalling."

("It's not appalling at all, he's just exaggerating," Grishook was thinking, uneasy because everyone had started to look at him.)

"We'll kill them as we've decided," continued Uncle

Yefim. "There's no point in calling a special conference about it. The thing is to think it out carefully."

"Yes," said Kotyakh, who'd been listening to the
argument with a non-committal expression. "You'd
better shut up, Filka. We haven't got together here
just to have a good cry. You've just had a good drink,
that's all."

"Why can't you understand anything," Filka shouted, bristling with anger, going so drunkenly red that
even his freckles disappeared. "Don't you understand
it's wrong to do this. You idiots. What do you..."

"Just watch it. Don't you 'idiot' us. Bugger off!"

"I will. I've never got myself involved in a shitty
business like this before, and I'm not going to start
now. Can't you get those dogs out of your heads?
Can't you? Is this your idea of entertainment, is it?
I'll even write to the newspaper if necessary—you'll
see."

"That just shows what a fool you are," the stableman said quietly and rose to his feet, wrinkling his
face up. "People have got a job to get on with, and he
comes round interrupting. Go away for God's sake,
before we teach you a lesson. Don't come muddling
our heads up. They're muddled enough already
without you."

"I will go away," Filka had raised his hand and was
shaking it in a fury. He moved out of the crowd,
backing away aggressively, his face steaming with rage
and his eyes welling with tears of anger. "I will go
away, don't you worry... Only don't you think, such
bastards as you are, that if there's a lot of you gathered
here, it makes you in any way representative. 'Toge-

ther', you reckon... You've got a handful of little boys together and you're teaching them what to do. They'll turn round and bite your heads off for you one day. Yes, I will go away."

"Yes do. Know-all! Go and blow your nose on your old woman's skirt hem. You underdeveloped little cucumber."

"We ought to give him a good thrashing really," Ponyrin said dreamily, unmoved by Filka's words. He was following the clerk with his eyes. "Then he wouldn't give us any more claptrap. Stupid useless little squirt!"

"Oh let him go to hell! There's no point in tangling with him," Boborykin said curtly. "He's enough to addle anybody's brains. He can be a lad like any other when his head's clear. But as soon as he's got a drink inside him, he starts thinking that folk are too hard on each other. The last time he got drunk like this, he started sobbing and chewing his sleeves and just tormenting himself. 'Why,' he says, 'are people always so hard on each other over little things, and all for nothing? They're tearing at their souls,' he says. 'It wouldn't matter if it was over big things, or only when there's a need for it, but no, they do it out of the nastiness of their characters,' he says. 'That's not how it was meant to be,' he says. 'Okay,' says I, 'you ain't such an angel yourself. You'll get over it.' He reads books by—what's the name of that writer?— Emily Zola and all that lot. That's why he's so miserable I suppose..."

Boborykin grew thoughtful for a moment, losing momentum, as though with surprise; then he laughed unhappily, recalling more:

" 'A person,' Filka says, 'should be pure before Mother Nature, like a horse, for example, or a pig.' Just like that he said it: 'a pig'."

"He's got nothing better to do. The snotty little brat! " said Ponyrin lazily, looking around. "Well, are there enough of us?"

"A few more'll be here in a minute." Uncle Yefim sat down on the logs again, hunching his shoulders. We need at least thirty people, otherwise we won't manage. Don't be in such a hurry. You'll make it all right."

Grishook was watching them with a sense of alarm which had been becoming stronger through the whole of the preceding conversation. He was looking at the people, who were growing quiet and dissatisfied. Like everyone around him, he felt and expected something bad. Really, why had they all got so het-up? It was a shame about the dogs of course; but even Tamara Pavlovna had said we could not go on like that any more, and it wasn't for nothing that Uncle Yefim had mustered all these people together and involved Ponyrin as well... There was some truth in what Filka had been saying too of course, but he didn't really understand. He hadn't been bitten. Still, there was something in Filka's swearing that made Grishook feel more and more sorry for the dogs, especially Looty, and—overcoming his embarrassment—he quietly asked Uncle Yefim, who was drawing grimly on his cigarette:

"Why is he like that, I wonder?"

"Who? Filka?" the stableman enquired moodily,

taking a last drag and stubbing his cigarette out under the rubber sole of his felt boots. "Better let him tell you himself. He just fools around all the time—nothing else. Lets everyone see how stupid he is."

"No," Grishook said, almost whispering, and without lifting his eyes. "How can it be just fooling around, when it really is a terrible shame?" Hearing no answer, he started to hurry through his words. "Looty's such a nice dog. He looked after Anisin's cows so nicely. It was Anisin that used to beat him. That's what made him run away."

The stableman didn't answer. Then, to Boborykin, who sat down next to him, he said:

"God knows how we live with those dogs. There's never any peace between us. Our neighbours aren't the sort for that it seems."

"Oh yes, they're good-for-nothing neighbours all right, you have to admit it," the driver agreed with him eagerly. "They hold a grudge against people, that's the worst of it. But we're no better... Take Anisin's Looty for example. How Anisin used to whip him! You won't see bruises or anything like that on a dog of course. The fur just sticks up oddly where they've been hit instead... Grass fades like that if you cut the turf under it. And he always did used to look a bit scraggy as I remember it. The year before last, Anisin once laid into him so hard in front of me at the milking... I thought he would come apart in the middle from that whipping... But no... He lay up somewhere, had some grass to eat, and came through it; and then, by God, he went back to his master, forgave him, and they carried on as they always had done, with Anisin lying around napping all day while Looty looked after the cows for the two of them; and if anything went wrong, Anisin would just reach for his whip again. Of course the dog got more and more malicious because of that, until finally he couldn't take any more. And now look: nobody's better off. It's all turned out badly in the end."

"Well, that's already the second dog that's run away from Anisin," Kotyakh confirmed with a lot of weight and importance. "They can't stand it. Life must be so hard on them."

"But that Volna—she must have some fox in her. I've never seen such a nasty bitch in all my life. That's where the rest get their endless cheekiness from: she just has to bark at someone to set the whole lot on him, while she just stands to one side like the bitch she is. She'll ruin all our children if we don't destroy her. So make sure you finish her first, Vasya; then pick off whichever you want."

"You don't have to tell me," mumbled Kotyakh. "That's enough of this chattering. Let's get to our places. I'm getting tired of it..."

The waiting had gone on a bit too long, as everyone knew, and that's why they started to hurry. Ponyrin, without any delay, picked out about ten boys to be beaters in his party, and led them off straight away through the back gardens to the Kazak gully. He reckoned to be able to get through to the rear of the cattle trench that way, and then drive the dogs back towards the street, past the haystack where Kotyakh would be ambushed. Very soon they had all disappeared into the gully, leaving the meadow empty, and there was no sign anywhere that the business was already under way. "You can tell immediately that he was in the army," Grishook was thinking about Ponyrin with respectful envy. "Nobody else would have thought of that, I reckon."

Boborykin and Uncle Yefim gathered the remainder together, assigning them to different gardens. It worked out at two or three people in each.

Grishook had never left the stableman's side, so he found himself together with him in the same garden. They stationed themselves on a piece of log near the wattle fence at the back. Uncle Yefim had the odd cigarette, or sucked in through his teeth and then spat into the snow which was already yellow from cows' urine. He looked out occasionally through the chinks in the fence, taking stock of the situation, silently keeping watch over the meadow. Grishook was sitting next to him, clenching the stick that Kuzka had given him, thinking all the time how bad it probably must be to kill the dogs, especially when Filka still remembers it and swears over it from the last time, seven years ago. Many times, he had seen for himself what it was like when they slaughter the sheep or stick the pigs; and it wasn't all that bad really... not too scary at all... Well, actually it was a bit scary, there was no point in pretending; but it was more just feeling sorry for them. But out here he didn't know what to think. Probably Filka was just fooling around because he was drunk... That was the sort of person he was. You could never tell what he'd be up to next. Take the other day for example: his wife, Aunty Manya, had been telling everyone how she was always pulling him out of some scrape or other. He was beginning to feel that there was more to it than that though... He hardly bore the dogs any grudge now—let them go to hell, those shirkers—and he had already secretly started to hope that the grown-ups' plans would fail.

Conversation in the neighbouring gardens was gradually dying away, after a lot of sharp remonstrating by the adults, and was slowly replaced by outbursts of disconnected rustling, which in turn grew quieter and quieter. To Grishook though, it seemed that the real silence had not yet started; on the contrary, as the commotion of voices, excited shouts and odd bursts of laughter died away, as all this was happening in the growing, expectant silence emphasised by an occasional careless noise, an indefinable, agonisingly exciting tension began to pile up in the air, stemming from the enforced quietness of two dozen hiding people: some of them very inexperienced, waiting with an enthusiasm that had never led them to think beyond the limits of the game's conventions; others who had seen more of life, wanting now only to finish this rather unpleasant, troublesome, but nonetheless needed and beneficial business (as it was generally considered to be), to get it over and done with—and then go home and relax. They all no doubt had different ways of thinking, and lived different lives; but what had recently happened to the Perevazov boy and the news that had spread through the village afterwards (that honestly, there was no end to the cheek of those dogs, they chased everyone all over the place and something ought to be done about it before it was too late); all this had made them first gather together to have a gossip about it, to smoke and to discuss how it would all be done; and then, for one reason or another (either from shame at being thought of as doing nothing, or from a sudden desire to try and grab pitchforks—like they had seven years ago—and thick sticks, spades, forged iron reaping hooks and other kinds of implements) to take up their positions behind the nervously yawning gates and wait; and then to beat them, when they'd caught them, to thrash them in hectic excitement, to smash them and to poke them, breathing irregularly with mad rage, or with fright and terror if suddenly the dog in front of them, with its broken skull, and its blind face swollen into a fatty red mash, suddenly twitched, or even stood up, reeling half-dead, taking one, then two steps in the direction of the flinching man.

Grishook didn't know anything about all that. He was just sitting and waiting. It wasn't real silence, but only an expectant quietness which was lurking in the back yards; and feeling the essence of this all-pervasive excitement, threat, lack of confidence and malicious joy only vaguely—he at last realised that all this is what is meant by the word: 'ambush'. He didn't even know how to picture what was happening; but, from everything he had already seen and heard today, he suddenly felt that discomfort and depression you feel during a long visit to people you don't know; he wanted to go home to the warm silence, to the cat on the old wall clock, to the veterinary smell of his father's overall... But the business had already started and was taking its course. It seemed impossible to get out of it now. Together with the other people he sat and waited—hoping all the time that nothing would happen.

They had been sitting for about fifteen minutes, maybe more—nobody could say exactly; then the stableman, while taking his next look through the chink, suddenly froze, and a voice in the neighbouring garden, unable to restrain itself any longer, shouted out of the enveloping silence:

"Dogs! Look! The dogs! There! "

Grishook's heart missed a beat. Quickly he went close to the fence and pressed his face against the damp slats, trying to steady the blurred grey horizon through the chink and find the dogs which were (according to the person who'd shouted) already in view. He found the trench and realised at once that something was happening. It was as though the air itself, and the warm melting day had started to move there. He saw something flashing a couple of times along the side of the trench and behind its crest, and guessed at once that the boys had already got there and were scaring the dogs out; and as though confirming his thoughts, two gunshots reached his ears in quick succession, muffled and made indistinct by the damp air—but frightening. Getting annoyed with himself, Grishook broke off a piece of the fence in his hurry, making the chink much wider.

He saw clearly how the dogs jumped on to the white runnels of the clay mound at the trench's edge, how they bounded along without stopping in the deep crustless snow of the depression, kicking their feet high, coming towards the gardens,—towards them; white smoke swelled up immediately in that place

271

too and, clearly this time, the sound of a shot reached their ears, like a balloon bursting. The crows which had risen from the trench at the approach of people, scattered over the steppe with an alarmed cawing, nosediving towards the earth and flapping their wings.

There were about ten or twelve dogs, running in a strung out pack, exactly in the direction (or maybe slightly over to the right) of the haystack where Vasya Kotyakh was sitting. Volna was leading, moving reluctantly, stopping from time to time, turning her head back towards the trench. The others were trotting behind, each in its own individual way, without yet realising the extent of the danger—just wanting to throw off their pursuers. Grishook licked his dry lips, pressing his head closer to the fence. Looty was behind, not far from Volna, running lamely on his badly set paw, his tail down and his body hunched as though waiting for a blow across the back. The other dogs had their tails down, and their heads bent guiltily and morosely too; but when Looty—strong, clever Looty who was always so self-confident— did it, it was like a warning, lending everything a sense of special and threatening importance.

The boys came pouring out into the meadow from around the left side of the trench, and their shouts, whistles, hoots and feeble discordant voices could be heard quite clearly. Ponyrin emerged on the summit, holding his shotgun at arm's length, twisting his head round in all directions. Then he hastily pressed himself against the ground. The smoke puffed, and arrived in the garden as sound. Falling shot spattered out a line across the snow, not far from one black dappled dog.

It seemed odd, but Ponyrin must have hit him. The dog made an attempt to rush forward as though it was being driven from behind; then it suddenly lagged behind its companions, running heavily and unevenly with an unnatural, diseased hop, swerving to the left. An odd, triumphant shout rang out from behind the shed on Grishook's right, and an infuriated Yefim, swearing like a trooper, dashed over to the dividing fence where the "bloody shouters" were...

Over by the mound, Ponyrin fired again. Bam! Then again. But still he couldn't hit the trailing dog. He got up at last, dusting himself, and began to move again, waddling heavily through the snow.

These shots, and the unexpected feebleness of their companion, struck terror into the pack, but still they didn't increase their speed, as if not knowing where they could run. Looty pricked up his ears. He kept straining his domed head back towards Ponyrin, who was trudging on after them through the deep snow, apparently not yet dangerous; and he was utterly unaware that he was approaching his end, the haystack where the reserved, nervy, but deadly accurate Kotyakh was sitting with his small-calibre rifle. The sight made Grishook catch his breath. He had long ago forgotten his grudge against the pack. If only Kotyakh would miss.

The village grew completely quiet, waiting with bated breath, protecting its rear with its hedges, sheds and leaning wattle fences, slouching their way from one garden to another; the gaping mouths of doors and gateways waited dumbly and indifferently. And in this silence, in this grey day, the dogs were trotting through the snow, staggering when it gave way beneath them, running as though under a raised and implacable hand, bowing their heads: ownerless, outcast, clutched at by the grey, clumsy figure of Death, who though not dangerous in appearance, was coming closer with inevitable persistence and indifference. And they seemed to yelp in submissive fright, foreboding the worst.

At first Grishook thought that he was imagining it; but then he heard, clearly in spite of the distance, how one dog was whining intermittently as it ran, on a single note, in a puppyish defenceless way, feeling how the circle of mute unfamiliar silence and possible death was closing in on it. Suddenly another dog started to whimper, then another struck up, thinly and pitifully, stopping from time to time and lifting its face towards the sky, as if sniffing despairingly at the danger which was radiating towards it from all sides. A pulsing, nervous whining had started on the meadow, and was reaching up into the sky. So doleful and doomladen were these cries, so mournful and muffled as though coming from the earth itself, so full of despair and of a childlike fear before the surrounding Unknown and the self-righteous punishing cruelty of the people behind—and of those waiting, as they could now hear and feel, in front of them—that Grishook started to tremble, and panic, and jump about frantically behind the fence. Then without understanding why, he suddenly got up and went towards the gate.

"Stay where you are! " The stableman's voice overtook him. He stopped, feeling his feet grow instantly swollen and tired. It was as though the voice had nailed him to his place. "You! Chuck it in! Right now! Sit still and don't you budge an inch! D'you hear me! "

"I was only..."

"Sit down! " the stableman interrupted, looking at him angrily and attentively. It was clear from his face that he had understood everything, and didn't recommend fooling around. "Who the hell do you think you are? Just look at the little puppy who won't do as he's told. Get back to where you were! "

Uncle Yefim turned back to the fence, watching the dogs approaching the haystack, coming step by step into the range of Kotyakh's gun, while Grishook, dissatisfied with his own behaviour, and red with worry and fright at what the grown-up might do, went back unwillingly to where he had been before.

Uncle Yefim had already forgotten. He was getting anxious. He kept pulling back from the chink and scanning the low sky as though he wanted to fix his position by the sun. His voice was husky with impatience:

"What the hell is he up to? Why doesn't he fire for Christ's sake? Has he forgotten his cartridges or something?" And he kept turning back towards Grishook in a puzzled way as though consulting him, the stubble standing out distinctly on his pale, unshaven face.

"Perhaps he really has. Get on with it, will you? Get on with it! Shoot, you fool! "

And almost at the same instant the rifle banged, cracking out and drawing back across the field; and immediately Volna leapt clumsily and unsteadily to one side. She flopped head first into the snow, then started to crawl off, veering more and more often to one side and scrabbling frantically with her paws, leaving a dark, blurred stripe behind her in the snow. Kotyakh must have reloaded in double time. The rifle lashed out again from behind the haystack, far and fast, like a whip cracking through the air. The dog closest to the haystack jumped, stopped, and then slowly and unwillingly crumpled and lay down.

A cheer went up from inside the big shed. "About time! Get 'em Kotyakh! Shoot 'em! "

"What do you think you're doing?" the stableman hissed severely, lowering his voice. "How can you, you little brats? Not doing as you're told. Shut up! "

His body stretched out in a single bound, Looty had already broken away from the pack. Kotyakh fired in a hurry—you could see how he was shifting around on the haystack—but Looty was already tearing away as fast as ever, directly towards the sheds. For a moment it seemed that the rest had started to follow, yelping and barking occasionally, but they fell behind straight away as though they'd lost faith in their leader, and remained in the empty half-kilometre of meadow.

Volna was still floundering in the snow, still trying to raise her head, and her hoarse, terrible whine rose distinctly above the frightened yapping of the confused pack, penetrating to the soul. She was living out her last moments in agony and bewilderment, still unable to understand what had happened, but brimful of terror at the impotence which had suddenly descended on her from nowhere, just at the moment when she most needed to run, whatever it cost her—run away from the disaster overtaking her from behind. She was trying to lift her head up, to take a look, but her strong body no longer obeyed her, and was already trembling and jerking with the first spasm of muscular agony, growing weaker with each instant of pain and torture.

Ponyrin, who had taken aim several times, at last decided to fire; he squatted down, swept the barrel slowly round, and then squeezed out a tight bundle of fire and sound. Bitten all over by the pellets, one of the younger bitches began spinning around madly in one place, and snapping at the air behind with her mouth as if catching at troublesome flies. Then, as though she had calmed down, she laid her face on to her paws, not looking at anything, nor wanting anything, nor afraid of anything—just lolling her tongue out and panting. It was as though she was being gradually tied up: by laziness, snow, and an irresistible inner tiredness. Defencelessly and heavily, she raised her head a few times—then it fell back again on to her paws, in the strongest of all sleeps.

Looty was approaching the gardens in long bounds. He came towards the next garden which belonged to Kharin, a religious and morally minded man. Without taking his eyes off the dog, Uncle Yefim adjusted his hold on the pitchfork, brandished it, took aim, suppressed a cough, and prepared for action, ready to jump out at the right moment and cut off his retreat. Looty had slowed his pace, and was looking behind him as he ran. He was trailing his back legs after him (a bullet had apparently caught him in his haunches).

Then he slipped through the open gate into the garden. The stableman jumped out from behind the fence and dashed after him.

The children came rushing out from the neighbouring gardens with the adults close behind them, towards the garden where Looty was now trapped. The few dogs who had been following their leader turned back towards the steppe. Grishook was left alone. He didn't know what to do, where to go, or where to run. He felt bewildered. He didn't want to watch Looty being killed, but he couldn't really go home now either...

Unsure of himself, he went out of the gate to the back of the village. The whole meadow was stretched out in front of him: a troubled sea of bustle and shouting and strangely busy movement. More people hurried past him on to the field. Kuzka shouted something as he ran by, beckoning excitedly, and Grishook started to walk in the same direction.

Unbroken blue clouds were sagging heavily in the dusk now falling over the meadow, weighing down on the surrounding countryside. The buildings looked damp and black. There was a smell of burning where the ashes had been thrown out on to the street. Kotyakh and Ponyrin were vying to outshoot each other, and one dog after another threw itself upwards, arching its back and spreading its paws wide in agony, staining the snow with dark blood. They were dying all around now, each in its own individual way. Some quietened down immediately; others were still trying to do something, to crawl or to hide... One of the closest to Grishook was a young dog whose back was broken; (he had run in their direction when he was wounded but had not lost all his strength). He was crawling without caring where he was going, howling intermittently on one note, already exhausted by pain, his only thought to get away from the meadow, from the last dying howls of his companions, from the sharp terrifying smell of blood and trailing guts, from the flickering black figures running from behind the hillock, growing in size with every second...

The remaining dogs, with their tails down, were moving away towards the side of the field, making for the nearest hollow, and Kotyakh, shooting from a standing position, was letting fly bullet after bullet, clearly in a hurry. Also in a hurry, came the swelling puffs of dense white smoke from the double-barrelled shotgun, missing all the time from that distance, accompanied by their indistinct "bam-bam" (sounding as though it were coming through cotton wool) and the whistling rustle of shot. Ponyrin had got as far as Volna. He opened his gun, reloaded, and let her have it from two or three metres, making the fur rear up along her back...

Grishook went up to the crowd, who were standing in a circle, and squeezed his way through to the front, where the young dog was lying in the middle, occasionally raising the dirty, fluffy fur on its thin sides with its difficult breathing. He was still gawky like a puppy, and he was gazing around him, uncomprehending, at bay, baring his young teeth and laying back ears. Kuzka, who was standing very close to him, shoved his stick into the dog's face. The dog jerked forward, snarling, trying to get to his feet, slipping with his front paws, but his back, broken by the shot, only

279

convulsed with the effort and pain. He was barking and howling at the top of his voice, trying to seize the stick with his white teeth, which were now running with reddening saliva.

"What a nice little baby Volna's got," someone jeered. "Look at him! Not big enough to gnaw his own bone yet, and here he is—already jumping at people."

"Yes. He takes after his mum all right. Look at him. He's got her looks exactly, he's the spitting image—just a different colour. It's time we finished him I reckon."

The dog had stopped growling, and was now only whimpering, his eyes closed with exhaustion and fear, his ears laid back as before. He started to whine guiltily and fearfully, as though he'd done something wrong, and what made it even more frightening, was that he was just asking them not to hit him—whereas they had decided to kill him.

"What are you waiting for? Get on with it! " someone shouted out from the back. Then the hefty, slow-witted youth, Vitanya, stepped forward as though someone had pushed him from behind, and grunting with the effort, plunged the manured prongs of his pitchfork into the dog's open mouth. Grishook saw how Kuzka raised his stick too... Then he was pushed away, squeezed into the crowd, which was now flowing back, creating more space; and all he could hear were the blows, thudding into something soft, and someone's hoarse, laboured breathing.

Seized by a sudden anger Grishook pushed his way violently out of the crowd, wiping his dry eyes. Dogs were being finished off at different places around the meadow. Figures of people swayed and hurried before his eyes. The boys were running around, carrying things, shouting to each other. The crows were flying back to the trench, though in a roundabout, careful way. For no particular reason, Grishook started to walk towards the dirty, distant little hummock which— no more than half an hour ago—had been the playful and cunningly violent Volna.

People were going away from the meadow quickly now, and once, turning back before he had reached Volna, Grishook could see that, apart from the corpses of the dogs scattered about on the trampled circles in the snow, the meadow was already almost empty. Only two boys were left, hastily moving away from the wet, ruffled and blood-smeared fur of the nearest dog, turning back every few seconds, as though spellbound. One of them was dragging an enormous club. He pulled it a bit further and then abandoned it. Grishook also turned, and began to walk back towards the gardens, feeling the presence of the big, silent meadow behind him more strongly with every second. He started to hurry, and went into a snow-filled hollow up to his knees. He clambered out, leaving deep columns of winter footsteps in the snow behind him, and because it took some time, because everyone had already left the meadow, because the two boys were already some way off, because the dead dogs were lying all around with their stiffened paws stretched out in front of them and their heads pressed down into the brown snow—he began to feel suddenly a sense of terror, of something seizing up inside him, and a strong adult loneliness. The same emptiness he had felt when the dogs were rolling him and mauling him beside the track...

He got to the track at last, and began to walk towards the village side street which would take him quickly home. But something stopped him. There was a crowd gathered round Kharin's place, and it was showing no signs of breaking up. Something strange was going on there, and he realised that most probably Looty was still alive. It wasn't that he was glad about it—it just seemed that everything might turn out differently. So he went there.

Kharin had just come back from work. He was standing apart from the others with his hands thrust into the pockets of his badly-fitting padded trousers. He had a red face (like a lot of fair-haired people) and his small, piercing eyes were slowly and inevitably filling with dislike. And he was making no secret of it.

"Listen," Ponyrin was saying. "Stop getting so worked up about it. What does it matter to you how we prise him out of there." And he looked around him conspiratorially, his eyes sneering and arrogant from the recent excitement. It was as though he were bargaining. "I'll just take one shot in there. It's not going to bring the roof down. Don't you worry. There'll be no harm done, I assure you..."

"I will not allow you to fire inside my cow-house, so you may as well save your breath." Kharin turned away aloofly, hunching his shoulders as though he were cold. "I know what you're like: one inch into the garden and you'll be breaking the front door down. You blooming layabouts! Is nothing sacred to you? Haven't you got anything better to occupy your time with?"

He was getting angrier and angrier, scowling like a bull at a red rag at each of Ponyrin's patronising, off-hand comments. ("You may well be the owner mate, but it doesn't give you the right to get in the way when we're doing our public duty.")

"Come on, Kharin, just let us finish number seven off, then we'll be going," said Boborykin, slightly ingratiatingly, trying to make things up. He was puffing with satisfaction and triumph. "The first bit was the best—now it's time for the rest. So if you'd just allow us, you know..."

"Number seven?" Kharin looked a little pale. He hadn't fully understood what had been going on in the meadow. "What on earth are you... You must be..." he said after a short silence, unable to think of anything else to say or do. "Just what do you think you're up to? You barbarians! Have you no respect for anything?" he said quietly, very quietly. His face had dropped, and a puzzled expression was now fixed permanently upon it, making it seem shapeless.

"That's enough of that sort of talk," Ponyrin suddenly blurted out, grimacing as though he was going to cry. "It's not just for anyone that we're doing it you know. It's for our children. You've got three of your own, haven't you? So why the hell... Talk some sense, can't you?"

Kharin was blinking in even greater confusion. Then as though clutching at the last straw, he said:

"I won't allow you to shoot in there. My cowhouse isn't the meadow."

He was trying to make his words come out in a firm, authoritative manner, but his voice betrayed him by suddenly faltering, and he almost shouted into Ponyrin's face—already only acting his firmness:

"Just you try shooting, you bounder. Just you try."

Kharin turned round, prickling with rage, stabbing at the people with his angry, disbelieving eyes; then he started to walk towards the house, with his hands still in his pockets. He turned round at the low back porch, took one hand out of his pocket and wagged his finger at them:

"Just you try it. You murderer! You Judases! It's unpardonable."

He hesitated for a moment, surveying the crowd with an expression of burning, undisguised hatred. Then he spat, and disappeared into the doorway.

"It just shows," Ponyrin scoffed aggressively, "there's no point in mixing with kill-joys like that. They're all a bit weak in the head, but we're supposed to do as they tell us. We should never have waited for him to come home, or asked his old woman. We haven't fired a shot. Now try. Get him out of there, the bloody..."

The stableman was standing just beside him, still gazing after Kharin, and with Ponyrin's last words he took a pitchfork from the eager hands of the person standing next to him, checked its strength and started to walk, without saying anything, towards the door of the big shed where Looty had positioned himself in the far corner behind the wooden partition. The dog was well established, and the lone man's attempt to budge him with a single lunge of the fork did not go well at all. Looty miraculously escaped the forward thrust; then, moving in the darkness, he knocked the man off his feet, bit his hand through to the bone, and disappeared back into his corner.

Everyone involved had now gathered round this one shed, and they were glancing into the doorway superstitiously and curiously as though they expected something, or maybe just because they enjoyed making the show last a bit longer, and dashing about and chattering, and making all kinds of guesses and predictions. Especially now, when the dog had no means of escape.

Screwing up his eyes, Yefim peeped into the shed. He stood still for a while, accustoming his eyes to the darkness and swore incomprehensibly. The people in the garden had all bunched around the entrance, and one or two of them also tried to peep in. Somehow the chattering was dying away of its own accord. An expectant hush was settling over the crowd, and again a sense of hopelessness and expectation of pain began to clutch at Grishook's heart, as though he had been beaten and tortured and now, after a short respite, it was about to start all over again. He started to work his way through the dense crowd with his head and elbows, pushing through sideways towards the middle. Somebody cursed him for it, and one of the grownups, catching Grishook's cloth hat and pulling it, said, "That's to teach you" with a kind of tough cheerfulness and clipped him round the ear—not painfully, but very offensively. But Grishook took no notice of little things like that; he went on pushing and pushing his way through to the front. He just had to.

He reached the shed at the exact moment that Uncle Yefim was stepping into it, pausing inside, getting his eyes used to the dark, holding the pitchfork thrust forward in front of him, and Grishook heard distinctly,

with every nerve of his body, how Looty let out a
long slow growl on a deep, low note, quietly threatening from his hidden corner. Taking a better grip,
the stableman shook his pitchfork challengingly. Then
he glanced back for an instant, his eyes standing out,
startling and dark, in his pale face. And what could
almost have been a farewell grin of suffering and resignation, of sudden cornered anger against the people
outside who now seemed to have elected him and
pushed him off to do the killing, still lingered in that
face and eyes...

Suddenly everything was clear. Grishook remembered the summer before last, and a time when he and
Kuzka had been playing together in the soft, thick
grass of the garden. They had been playing with
three floppy-eared, pot-bellied puppies from the litter
of Kosmatka, Kuzka's dog. The puppies, (who were
just three weeks old and whose eyes had just opened)
were trotting funnily round the yard, running sideways, getting their fat, clumsy paws tangled up in the
grass, and always nuzzling their soft faces into everything they came across. They were squeaking with
delight in high-pitched baby-like voices, and wiggling
their velvety floppy tails from side to side. Whenever
he got angry with them, Kuzka would flick at them
with a piece of twig, and the puppies, bewildered and
upset, would start yapping in their tiny voices, and
turn round awkwardly in one spot—unafraid of the
raised hand because they did not understand what
was being done to them or who was doing it. Then
Kuzka would get more annoyed at their silliness and
hit them more painfully, sometimes quite cruelly;

but they would go on coming up to him and under him, and tumbling all around him, trying to escape from the quick, painful thing which they hadn't managed to see. And Kuzka, who was squatting, had to keep backing away from them, but they would still come running and crawling under him. Later Kuzka's father left only one puppy and drowned the rest. He just threw them from the high river bank out into the middle as unwanted. They came to the surface a couple of times like pieces of wet fur, moving indistinctly, wriggling in the water; then they disappeared into the dappled, sparkling weir. Kuzka's father was holding the livid Kuzka by the scruff of his neck and saying uncomprehendingly:

"What's up with you, you little brat? You aren't a girl, are you? You won't grow up to be a man like this, you know."

His father was even a bit frightened, seeing Kuzka struggling so wildly, swearing in such a grown-up way, and then beating him and scratching his hand. A week later Kuzka had recovered from the thrashing he'd got, and was running around as though nothing had happened; Grishook, who had run straight down to the weir, had found nothing. And now, Uncle Yefim was moving forward reluctantly to kill Looty—(But why? What for?)—and Looty was growling, no longer hiding the threat he was making, straining towards the door, ready to complete his gurgling, gutteral growl with a conclusive spring.

Grishook could already sense something in common between this hoarse growling (with the unbearable spite that radiated from it) and the expression on the stableman's face. There was a parting despair in them, now reaching its breaking point, and an inconsolable, endless hatred towards everything so immense that inside Grishook everything froze, died and fell away like scales, until all that was left was his bare soul, shivering from homelessness and weighed down by trouble—and even his soul could not take any more. He was ready for anything, he would have agreed to anything just to free himself from this hatred—like someone clambering out of a deep, deep pit.

He turned his eyes up to the people standing round him, not even ashamed of his tears. All of them were watching and waiting, with a dark, hungry, pagan interest; waiting, with their heads and bodies and eyes drawn towards the big shed; waiting, and listening to a dying song of hatred and pain as one listens to something invisible; and staring into the blackness of the doorway, into the old matted straw of the roof, and into the bitter smoky sky above it—which was Looty's last sky. And there wasn't the slightest trace of malice or spite in their eyes, or of the despair and hatred which now filled the whole world, and the whole of Grishook's life too. There was only a dark, unending curiosity about death. "But they don't understand anything, they don't understand anything." Slowly, sweating with his fear for the people around, Grishook, getting more and more terrified, began to walk towards the gaping blackness of the door, and the alert, bent back of the stableman just inside it, and the two men with pitchforks at each side of it, standing in frozen postures with unmoving eyes. "Really, they don't know what they're doing. They don't understand anything. How can it be like that? I know—and suddenly they don't. How can it be like that?"

"What's up with you then?" somebody said in a puzzled voice without even trying to stop him. (They asked it sympathetically, but also indifferently, in a way people often speak to children.) Grishook stopped, caught unawares, and clumsily, as if in a dream, he turned his head in slow motion towards Boborykin, but without recognising him. The frozen face of a man, still wearing his mask of hungry curiosity was looking at him with empty eyes which had nothing in them— not even Grishook. Grishook glanced into them only momentarily, seeing Ponyrin and Kuzka's father in them, and the hatred that was in Looty, and in himself. Then he flung himself into the shed where Looty was, and where torture and hatred had built their terrible earthly home.

Nobody even had time to say anything, let alone stop him. A belated "Oh you! " hung in the air over the crowd, while Grishook rushed past the stableman, letting out a cry which was something between a hoarse gasp and a sob. Yefim's eyes flickered in front of him in bewilderment, and his face seemed mellow and white inside the darkness. Then Grishook flew head first over the foot which had been stuck out to trip him into—or beyond—the pile of manure. The stableman breathed out an abrupt swearword, dropped the pitchfork, flung himself at Grishook, caught the hem of his coat, and tugged him back strenuously towards the door. It was only because he was bashed against the door-frame that Grishook managed to stay on his feet. Then something inside pushed him forward towards Looty again. Spreading his arms wide and wheezing out "I'll teach you", the stableman caught him again. Grishook was struggling and kicking and punching, and Uncle Yefim, keeping his face out of range, shook him so violently that the boy's coat ripped. He started to drag him towards the entrance. And at that moment, as they were staggering about, the heavy, panting body of the dog flung itself at them from behind the partition, and came down heavily on top of them. With a final thrust Yefim pushed the lad towards the doorway, and fell to the ground under the dog's weight, protecting himself with his elbows and trying to offer only his back to the hot foaming jaws. Looty recoiled for a moment, letting Yefim fall, then immediately came down on him again, his paws skidding on the man's back, seizing at his shoulder, then going higher, reaching for his neck, working silently with his fur bristling, and pressing down so heavily that the cloth of the coat started to come apart with a ripping sound under his claws. The stableman had started groaning, curling up his body with the last ounce of his strength, pressing his head down between his shoulders. He let out a short, strained scream.

At this moment Boborykin, who had suddenly come to his senses, at last managed to give a jab—not strongly, more as if he were coaxing it—to the dog which was frozen in its fury on the stableman's back. Looty broke away from him, and sprang at Boborykin, jaws bared and ears pressed down tightly on his skull. At that moment Vitanya arrived, and the two pitchforks, jingling together as they touched, penetrated the dog's stomach and chest,—going in quite smoothly with an easy push, as though into a bale of straw. Looty's body began to shudder, growling and howling with pain, and the two men, swaying unsteadily on their feet for a second and red with strain, made two or three hasty steps forward over the stableman and, grunting with anger, pressed it down into the heap of manure. The prongs were already in up to the wood, and Looty's growl had become a rattle, coming to them through the reddening foam flowing from his mouth, rocking the shafts of the forks, making it hard for the two men to hold on to them. Convulsing, he stretched out his back paws. His eye stared—glassily and angrily and fixedly—not at his undoers, but at the grey day rolling downward into the viscid dusk over their heads.

And just like that they carried him out on their pitchforks: his faded, blood-spattered body still shuddering occasionally, his big head trailing across the wet, trampled snow, leaving a streak of light red foam behind it. They carried him out to the backs of the village—in the same mindless and hasty way that ants might drag their prey—and left him there beside the track. Three people were left in the yard. Kharin was standing on the low step of the porch, looking through the open gate towards the people crowded along the track. Once, twice, the thick end of a club was visible, flying up above their heads. Then the crowd could be seen parting, and Kuzka running out of it with some other boy, bending with the effort of dragging something on the end of a wire—something which had recently been Looty—out towards the meadow and the other dogs... Grishook was sitting on the logs, with his face scratched all over. He didn't cry, he was silent. Only occasionally, he lifted his empty, tired, anxious eyes towards Uncle Yefim. The stableman was smoking, drawing the smoke in deep and often, still jerking the right shoulder of his coat clumsily up and down—it had been ripped right through to the lining—and looking around the garden like a man who had left something behind. Grishook understood that he ought really to go as far away as he could from people now, but he no longer cared. He sat like that because he'd got tired, and because his side hurt him so badly where the stableman had pushed him that it was even hard to breathe. "Go away yourselves," he was thinking. "That would be a hundred times better, a thousand times better..."

Nikolai Luginov was born in 1948 in Yakutia, a land rich not only in gold and diamonds but also in selfless men and women.

After graduating from Yakutia State University he taught mathematics in a village school for several years. Later he was selected for work in the Regional Committee of the Young Communist League of Yakutia. Ever since he was a student, Nikolai Luginov has been writing stories, short novels and sketches. His prose, poetic and rich in imagery, is characterised by vivid emotion.

Mid-April '45. An army hospital outside Minsk. Two men in white coats.

"Well, and how are things in Ward 9?"

"Not too hot. There are two hopeless cases in there."

"There's one chap in the ward who had a bullet right through his chest, isn't there? Who is he? Where's he from?"

"He's a Yakut.* They say he was famous right along the front as a sniper. He has a chestful of medals, but can't speak a word of Russian."

"How could he cope in the army then?"

"I don't know. If he fought well though, it means he must have coped not only with Russian but with German as well. Any language at the front is very different from what's spoken back home..."

"That's true. Do you think he'll pull through?"

"He's in a bad way. There's little hope."

1

For some reason it took Aigylla a very long time to wake up as if he was being pulled slowly back into the waking world from some far-away place: from the bottom of some dark deep abyss or from the top of some unscalable mountain. He was being pulled on a long, brightly decorated rein.

Here were those four snow-white walls again, two neighbours, also dressed in white, and one window looking out onto the white world.

*Yakut—a man from Yakutia in North-Eastern Siberia, with an extremely cold climate.—Ed.

"Aina! .. Aina! " that was Jan in the next bed calling out. He used to call that name day and night, without ever being heard. No-one responded. Sometimes his voice was no more than a hoarse whisper and it hurt just to listen to it: "Aina! .. Aina! "

His other neighbour Sergei was sitting up in bed and nodding his gold shock of hair at him in a friendly way, saying something, probably asking what Aigylla had been dreaming about. Then he said something else with a broad smile, slowly spinning out the words, apparently hoping that Aigylla would understand him better that way. Yet Aigylla still could not understand anything; only the sound of his voice and the expression of his face showed Aigylla that his neighbour was conveying his sympathy.

"Goot, goot, Sergei," Aigylla said by way of reply.

There were not many Russian words that Aigylla knew but among those that he had mastered, "Good" took pride of place. That word, if used carefully, could denote a good half of all the things found in the Middle World* and many of men's varied moods...

The dream he had had that night had been a good one, too. Only it was strange that even in dreams it was impossible to forget all sorts of hopes and desires and then if you tried to make some wish or other come true, you were bound to encounter obstacles. So even in dreams it turned out that one minute a man was happy, and the next wretched...

---

*In ancient times the Yakuts divided the universe into three worlds: the Upper World where the Gods live, the Middle World where men live, and the Lower World inhabited by Good and Evil Spirits.

In his dream he had been mowing tall, lush grass on the island of Boruulaakh in the middle of his beloved Lena River. The grass was thick and waist-high, and each swing of his scythe brought down a whole armful of hay at the edge of the hayfield. The work was heavy but satisfying. "Stop for a minute, love, have a breather, wet your throat ... it's so hot out here," came the soft lilting voice of his wife from behind him. Aigylla looked round and saw that Maryna was gliding towards him with smooth strides across the mown hay, holding a wooden mug in her hand. The fresh breeze from the river ruffled the hem of her dress, and tresses of her black hair were peeping out from under the thin kerchief and sticking to her moist forehead. "Why are you in such a hurry?" she asked. "Isn't it time for you to have a break for a snack?" A smile glowed on her round pink face. Aigylla took the mug from his wife's chubby hands and gulped down the kumys.* The sour yet at the same time slightly sweet drink filled him with a refreshing sense of coolness that seemed to spread through his whole body, bringing new vigour to his aching limbs. With relish Aigylla now took a deep breath and looked round at the landscape. Tiny scraps of feathery clouds, looking like wisps of hay spread out to dry, were floating across the sky. Small waves with thin crests of foam every now and then crept across the sandy shallows. Into the distance, almost as far as the eye could see, stretched the broad smooth waters of the Lena that had been an essential part of his world ever since

*Kumys—fermented mare's milk.—*Ed.*

childhood... "Home, how beautiful it is ... sweet home! " he wanted to say. Maryna, as if she was reading his thoughts and responding to them, burst into a happy laugh.

Yes, it had been a good dream... Everything was as clear and vivid as if it were real. Actually, it was even better than in reality. In the hectic rush of day-to-day life he had never really had time to admire the natural beauty of his home. He was so caught up in his work and the constant bustle that many things around him had gone unnoticed or had seemed so ordinary that he had never thought to pay them particular attention. For as long as he could remember there had always been the taiga on every side, the waters of the Lena to look at and blue sky overhead. He did not know and could not even imagine that somewhere life might be different—without those very same sunsets and sunrises, without the scent of the taiga, without his beloved Lena... At that time he had not been aware how love for all that means home could fill a man's heart and how great could be the longing for that familiar setting that might well up within the heart after so short a time...

Now the whole of his past life had taken on quite a different look: not only did it all seem more vivid, but new radiantly bright colours added shimmer and sparkle to it all...

Yet wait a minute, who was that calling so desperately, so urgently, but still without being heard? How tender and loving that plea sounded! .. Oh, it must be Jan again... Poor Jan was calling for his Aina. "Aina!.. Aina! "

The new hospital day was beginning. Light steps could be heard in the corridor, somewhere a door squeaked. Then came some more steps, only this time in the opposite direction. Those were the nurses. Then came the heavy thud of some crutches and the creak from the rubber end of an artificial leg. Some hushed men's voices could also be heard. From time to time there wafted in through the open window the hoots of distant trains or the purr of nearby passing cars.

The stern, joyless day came into its own and seemed at one fell swoop to wipe out all the fragile distant pictures of the past, a past which for the time being still lived on in men's memories, but which could disappear for good any day...

Supporting himself on his crutches Sergei went over to Jan, raised his head a little and gave him a drink. Poor Jan muttered something very quietly and gradually started to calm down a little.

Then, Nina, one of the nurses came flying into the ward. She set about her routine tasks quickly and deftly. She had gentle nimble fingers and the kindest of hearts.

Circumstances can sometimes bring close to each other people who have never met before and seem to have nothing in common.

Aigylla looked at Sergei and Nina and then turned his gaze to Jan's head that was balding at the back and felt a warm fondness for them all fill his heart. How close and dear to him they had become in those grim days that were so agonisingly long! Sergei must have noticed his gaze because his friendly face broke into a broad smile. Again he started talking about something good, about something that was bound to happen... He so badly wanted to respond to Sergei's smile with one of his own, but the thick muslin bandage pulled tightly across his face got in the way. He could only answer with his eyes...

All that Aigylla needed to do was to close his eyes for a chain of silent dark figures with new, yet somehow familiar faces to start slowly moving past him, looming up one minute and fading away the next. The faces were all different yet on closer inspection he could pick out something they all had in common. They were all filled with the same hate. Where had all that hate sprung from? Had it been building up for a long time? Who was it all for, for everyone or just for him, for Aigylla?

Aigylla shuddered at this horrible vision. He badly wanted to shake himself free of it but could not... Those looks of hate had been boring into him... They were all the people whom at one stage or another Aigylla had surveyed for a long time through his sniper's sights. They were the men whom he had first looked at and then brought down in the fatal cross wires after duly taking into account the distance, the wind, the heat or the cold.

Poor wretches! .. You had not been like that since childhood! You knew other feelings, too, I'm sure. So when and how could it have happened that all these other feelings disappeared, ousted by leaden hatred? Who had made you like that, you poor wretches? That was not what you had come into this world for!..

Aigylla had had to do a great deal of killing in his time. He had been a hunter after all. Hunting had been his main means of livelihood, and that was why he had found no difficulties in his relationship to the natural world around him. Everything was honest and fair, and he caused no real harm in his natural surroundings, his conscience on that point was quite clear.

Only one incident in the whole of his life before the war had troubled his heart, leaving sad traces behind. Once he had had to put down his old, feeble cow, who had fed them all in the difficult hungry years. Aigylla to this very day could remember how she stood there helpless before him, looking at him out of her big, so trusting eyes...

Aigylla had gone off into the taiga as a fifteen-year-old boy after his father had been killed. He had been the eldest of his brothers and cruel fate had made him the main family breadwinner at the age of fifteen.

The White Guards* had killed his father because they said he had helped the wounded chairman of the Revolutionary Committee to get away. It had been strange to find out later that his father had been betrayed by a neighbour, another equally poor hunter by the name of Okhonon: the two of them had lived side by side for many a long year sharing their joys and misfortunes. Soon Okhonon was to be brought down by a bullet in the woods of far-away Amga together with his new-found friends. The neighbour's orphaned children had lived in dire poverty after that.

*White Guards—counter-revolutionary forces in the Civil War (1918-20) in Russia. —Ed.

Hunger was a stern master, and sometimes it used to bring the poor brats over to their house. Aigylla could hardly bear to look at them—they were so pathetic—he would turn away and leave. Yet his mother used to take pity on the orphans, would give them whatever she could find to eat and would go out of her way to find an explanation for them for what their father had done. Aigylla's mother was sure that it had not been Okhonon himself who had taken such a terrible step, but some other person's wicked idea that had led him astray, all the more so because he had never had a will of his own. He had never even had any clear likes or dislikes. He had married a widow who was no longer young, not on his own initiative, but after someone else had put the idea into his head. Yet Aigylla's mother, who knew all that about Okhonon never reproached her former neighbour for anything. As a matter of fact, it made her pity him all the more. Now she transferred her pity to his poor unfortunate children... What a heart of gold she had had... How wise she had been, how much love for others had filled her heart! ..

"Aina! Aina! .." groaned Jan again. Yet again his call went unanswered.

Where are you, Aina? Hear him and come, show yourself just for a moment and soothe his aching heart... Oh Aina, Aina! If you only knew how much he loved you, it might help to ease your bitter widow's fate a little. Yet who is there to tell you, who can send on to you that last faltering call?! ..

"Aina! Aina! .." Jan had been calling that for many days now. His voice was like a stone falling into a deep bottomless abyss or an arrow shot at random to fly out into the boundless blue of the sky. His calls were swallowed up in an empty void!

Aigylla began to feel hot. How nice it would have been to drink something cold!

As soon as that thought occurred to him, Aigylla saw in his mind's eye a neatly cut hole in the ice over a river. A reassuring freshness wafted up from the dark depths beneath. Yet gradually that fresh breath of air began to fade, as if someone had caught it in mid-flight. Now only the tips of his fingers sensed the welcome touch of the frosty air current. Just one sip of that icy water to bring cool relief to his whole burning body, so that for a minute, or one brief moment at least, he might relish within him that coolness which might save him...

As soon as Aigylla had conjured up that picture of his homeland in the taiga he saw himself resting after a successful hunt under a tall larch. The wind was moaning in the tree-tops overhead, shaking their huge leafy crowns, and on the earth down below all was quiet and reassuringly cosy. And the thoughts that ran through his mind were tranquil, kindly, homely ones.

Throughout the ages, the unwritten law of the taiga had been passed down from one generation to another, the law that man should treat his fellowmen and the natural world he lived in with kindness. That law needed no explaining and was inviolable. People who had never set eyes on each other before would hail each other out in the taiga like close relatives, and any such meeting in the endless stretches of the sparsely inhabited taiga would turn into a great occasion.

Then came the WAR. Everything was disrupted, turned upside down. No-one talked about kindness now. The reign of cruelty had begun. How many dead and wounded men his eyes had had to behold! But that wasn't the worst part of it, after all war is war. Yet how many maimed and mutilated old men, women and children there had been as well! What fault was it all of theirs? Cruelty towards innocent children was something terrible that Aigylla could not begin to understand.

Just as good breeds good, so evil breeds evil in response. An unfamiliar feeling had begun to ripen in Aigylla's heart. Perhaps, it was what they called hate, or perhaps it had another name—Aigylla did not know. Yet now he knew that people, who were basing their lives not on kindness but on cruelty, ought to be stopped at all costs. "Stop them"—that had become Aigylla's main mission in life. "Stop them! " There was only one way he could stop them—that was by using his sights... Many times he had encountered them through the fatal cross wires of his sights...

Old hunters used to have a saying: if only the spent arrow could be brought back! .. If only people could foresee the consequences of an action they were about to take before they carried it out. Even if not they themselves but other people could see what had been done, they might come to recognise and admit their mistakes and then human bloodshed would have long been a thing of the past. People would meet together in the white fields of Friendship and Kindness, not in the sights, where there was no room for two people...

The window frame somehow reminded him of the black cross wires, and so as to shut out that persistent vision Aigylla turned away from the window and closed his eyes.

This time he saw himself as a handsome young rider on a milk-white thoroughbred stallion. He himself was surprised by the sight and looked at his reflection in the water for a long time... In his youth there had been nothing out of the ordinary about Aigylla, nothing to make him stand out among his peers, and certainly not that he was handsome. He had never known what it meant to arouse admiration. He was small in stature, had a round pock-marked face and, to make things worse, was rather hard of hearing, which always made the people round him rather condescending. Yet he had long since grown used to that.

And here came this dream that was more like a fairy tale...

He marvelled at his own beauty, revelled in a sense of his own strength and irresistibility, something that he had never known before. How his muscles rippled! How boldly he galloped through the flower-filled meadow on his steed, the thundering of its hooves echoing in the distance. Probably at no other time in his life had he ever been so intoxicated by the sense of freedom, so keenly aware of the sweet thrill of free flight as in that passing dream. For as long as he could remember, day in, day out, there had been the need to get up and go somewhere or do something. And now at last he was free, and moreover on this miraculous steed. His horse was led by its silver reins, from out of a fairy-tale past into a large clearing by a lake: for some reason though the whole of the clearing was ploughed up with craters. In the middle of the clearing there towered three tethering posts. They went past that for the youngest horses, then the second and stopped by the one for the finest, most valued horses. He stopped, filled with pride and happiness, admiring the intricate pattern on the tethering post which went well with the pattern on the reins.

It was a sunny but not a hot day in the middle of June. The grasses were coming into bloom, and the fragrance of the flowers mingled with the scent of the taiga made his heart miss a beat. All around him stretched his home, the land of his people... Then he saw the next clearing with a lake in the middle which showed bright, virgin green through the thin trees of the nearby copse. When it smelled the exciting scent of the grasses his steed at once felt the urge to gallop into the next clearing, giving a whinny of delight: the high sound rippled across the green taiga in a distant throbbing echo for a long time...

Aigylla looked at the reins with which his stallion was tied to the tethering post and saw that the knot had come undone by itself. Feeling it was free and intoxicated with this sense of liberty, the stallion dashed forward with lightning speed. It soon reached the copse... but then the rein which had been dragging across the grass got caught in something and pulled the stallion back. Next it stopped, stepping first to one side, then the other, but the more it tried to free the rein, the more tangled it became. It pulled at the rein, struggled with all its might, lunged forward towards the eagerly awaited goal, so near—but could not move from the spot. The fresh flowering meadow in the clearing glistened through the thin birch-trees just in front of it, and it could even see free unbridled horses like himself sweeping across it... The steed neighed again, but this time the sound was stifled, so that no-one heard it...

2

Aigylla never learnt a great deal of what a soldier was meant to know, or even an adult for that matter, things which might appear essential for anyone who was going to cope with life on this earth. There were many rules and regulations he did not know. He was not always aware for which martial feats he was awarded medals and decorations. He always viewed literate people with great respect, almost rapture: just to think of it, they had gained such wisdom! Perhaps he too might have learnt to read and write easily like many of his relatives, if he had not always lived in such poverty. From an early age his father had taken him along when he went into the taiga and had taught him the hunter's trade, but as luck would have it the school "season" fell at the same time as the hunting season.

At the front he adapted to the new conditions quite quickly. For this not much had been required of him: he needed to do what everyone else was doing immediately and with no questions asked. He was almost always the last in marching order because of being so short and this was very convenient: all he had to do was go where everyone else was going, there was no need to ask any questions. At the front line it soon emerged that there was much in common between the work of a hunter and that of a sniper. Aigylla had mastered his skilled craft to perfection. He realised that in many tasks and occupations where his sniper's sights were not needed, almost all of his fellow-soldiers would be able to put him in the shade. Yet when it was a question of tracking down, lying in wait for and then aiming at the enemy, then Aigylla had no equal, he outshone all his comrades.

Yes, there was so much Aigylla did not know, or understand properly. Perhaps, though, that was all to the good rather than a problem. Thanks to his ignorance, he was free of many of the delusions and prejudices ingrained in many other people. His was a more simple conception of human life, a more basic view of the relationship between one man and another, not complicated by advanced civilisation. There was no denying that much of the knowledge the taiga had given him, was to prove superfluous, even out of place in this new world. Aigylla had to adapt, somehow to come to terms with these new conditions of life.

Now as he lay in his white ward, he strove to but still could not fully understand the underlying reason for the cruelty which had blinded not just one odd man, but a whole people. After all the enemy soldiers were human beings, not animals, and each one of them must have had a mother, family, children. How did they let themselves be blinded? How could they, these people, let themselves sink to the level of animals?..

This was why Aigylla had such mixed feelings towards the men who were caught by him in the fatal cross wires of his sights and above whom there now stood aspen, birch or oak crosses. Aigylla understood that by stopping them he had averted many disasters and protected thousands of the defenceless and helpless from their blind hatred. So this meant he could not have acted differently. Yet all the same they were still not animals but *people,* and surely there could have been some other way of stopping them long before they reached the fatal line.

He sincerely believed that if he had met them in some other set of circumstances they could have understood each other and perhaps even have made friends...

3

Where had this brittle, glassy silence suddenly sprung from? There was something wrong, unnerving about this silence, that made a shiver run down Aigylla's spine. Why could he not hear Jan any more? What was the matter with him? Perhaps his Aina had come to see him at last? Or perhaps his torment was over?..

Sergei on waking up immediately made a clatter with his crutches. Nina came running in, and then several other people in white coats. They clustered round Jan, short phrases were exchanged, and without looking at Aigylla or Sergei they then left the ward. Immediately after that two other men carried Jan out and his bedding was removed. Only Nina stayed behind. Standing by the iron bed with its bared springs she burst into bitter sobs. An unbearable sadness seemed to flood through the ward.

Aigylla did not remember or know how long the tender-hearted nurse remained by the empty bed. When Aigylla next came out of his coma night had fallen. This time night seemed gloomy to him. Aigylla sensed more keenly than ever how near he had come to the Big Night which was relentlessly closing in on him. He imagined that night as something immense, that radiated unruffled calm. At times, Aigylla almost longed for it to draw near and lure him away mysteriously with that promise of eternal rest: rest was something he had always needed most in his life on earth, in the bustle of everyday concerns...

Soon the ward filled up with people in white coats again. First of all they went over to Sergei, poked at his leg, his hip and asked him questions about something. Then they turned their attention to Aigylla. A tall man with hunched shoulders, who looked like the one in charge, took hold of Aigylla's wrist and gazed down sadly at him out of his tired blue eyes. The others began to discuss things quietly, they seemed to be talking about the wounds in his chest and head. Then the faces of the doctors leaning over his bed turned to fragments and blurs as if he had been looking at them through a hole in the ice...

Then his mind cleared again and Aigylla once more glimpsed the blue eyes which shone out with heart-felt sympathy and deep sorrow. The doctor rose to his feet and went to the door. The others followed him out of the ward. Only Nina stayed behind. She drew a chair up to Aigylla's bed and while she wiped the cold sweat from his face with her handkerchief, she began to say something friendly, trying to smile through her tears.

Leaning on his crutches Sergei came over to Aigylla as well, sat on the edge of his bed and also started saying something that sounded concerned and friendly. Probably so as to help Aigylla to understand him, Sergei started waving his arms about, one moment screwing up his eyes and the next opening them as wide as they would go. Aigylla understood every word anyway; he could read the words from their faces, which glowed with kindness and heartfelt sympathy. How grateful he was to them! He wanted to hug those two dear people and say to them: "What kind hearts you have, my friends! May god grant you long and happy lives! May your children be obedient and as kind as you are! .. May joy and happiness enter into your house never to leave it again..."

4

Somewhere, further away than you could possibly imagine, many hundreds of miles away lay Aigylla's home, his taiga that had not merely fed and nurtured him but had taught him all he knew as well. That was where the river Vilyui flowed into the Lena, where the village of Kharypalakh stood in a clearing by the lake.

There, too, it was probably already spring—the

most beautiful season of all. The first tender green was showing through, the western slope was yellow with crocuses, and the taiga was filled with the heady smell of the pine-trees...

How many times had he returned in his thoughts to his native soil during those long war years! In his mind's eye he could see his reunion with the land he held so dear; it was all so vivid, so radiant!..

Now he was galloping along on his white steed through the wide open spaces back home. He did not hurry as he rode, holding back the fiery horse and his ardent imagination so as to savour the joy of his return. He listened happily to the familiar clatter of hooves and saw before him the meadows and copses he knew so well, where every tree, every bush was an old friend...

Now he rode up to his own tethering post, dismounted, fastened the ornamental reins and slowly perused his house. One or two things had grown shabby during his absence, others had become crooked. How happy he would have been to pick up his axe, his saw or his hammer, all with their handles worn smooth by long use! Yet first of all he had to go to the eastern edge of the clearing to his mother's grave.

Then something disrupted the even flow of Aigylla's thoughts. He found his whole body was shivering. No, it was not physical pain but something else that made his heart burn within him. For the first time in many days Aigylla groaned. Large tears welled up in his eyes...

Sergei came over straightaway to sit on his bed, and Nina came running in. Both of them began reassuring him, interrupting each other as they spoke. Again, although he did not understand the words, he knew quite well what they were saying. Touched by their concern, Aigylla longed to be able to say: "May happiness shine on you, my friends, whatever happens! May you only know what is pure and happy! May you meet nothing but kindness at every turn! We shall take away with us all that is black, all the hate and cruelty there is on this earth..."

5

His right eye was badly swollen and he could barely see anything at all. Then he lost his hearing completely. In the past Aigylla had had problems with his hearing as well, even before the war. Every now and then his hearing would improve a little, and then a bout of deafness would follow. Yet, strangely enough, even during the bad patches he made out his wife's voice easily while other voices, even if they were louder ones, failed to reach him for some reason. This gave rise to all kinds of jokes: people used to say that Aigylla and Maryna whispered to each other right through the night, that he only pretended to be hard of hearing, and in fact could hear properly when it suited him. Maryna did in fact like to whisper to him at night or speak to him very softly. He did not worry about grasping what the words meant, perhaps there was not all that much meaning in them anyway...

They were called away from the hay-making at the very beginning of July. Their call-up papers were brought to them right there, in the meadows of Borulaakh Island. There was not a moment to spare. The goodbyes to their nearest and dearest had been unnervingly hurried and hectic... He could still see before him the endless stretch of the river and the golden glow of the sunrises and sunsets over the Lena...

When the time came for them to climb up the steep slope before they set off down Mother Lena, the new recruits ran over to the river and, lying down on the stony bank, they took a long drink of the cool water. The river, like a mother seeing off her sons into the grim Unknown, caressed them with her life-giving water, washed their faces and hands and caught their parting tears...

Then a whole group of different faces began to float towards him, each one different from those that had gone before. Yet Aigylla's imagination gathered them all together and lent them all a common hate-filled stare. Actually, even in their last fatal moments they were different: some of them wore a tired or indifferent expression, others seemed pensive or dreamy, and some just smiled, relishing life.

How many young men there were among them, some mere boys! There probably must have been even some who were unaware of how handsome they were. Yet all of them, like Aigylla himself, were equally beautiful, destined as they were to bring happiness to themselves and many others...

Yet ... what was left of them? An encounter in the cross wires of his sights inevitably ended up with a graveside cross. It made little difference whether it was made of aspen, birch or oak wood—the end was the same... All that was left of those of Nazis were crosses, crosses, and more crosses...

6

Now there were just the two of them—Aigylla and the Black Eye facing him.

Nobody, nothing else was left in the whole world, everything else had gone, had been blotted out. They were the only two left: all night they had been staring each other grimly in the eye, like two snipers, each waiting for the slightest let-up on the part of his opponent. "No, you won't catch me out," thought Aigylla, clenching his teeth in his ardent longing to overcome the Enemy and survive! ..

When it grew lighter in the morning the Black Eye gave way to a pale blue transparent sheet of ice. Rippling up and down on the waves it floated along. The waves made it spin, as they rolled ahead of it or at one side, and with every hour the sheet of ice grew smaller and smaller. It floated and melted, floated and melted. As it melted and grew smaller and smaller, Aigylla began to feel better and better and life seemed to flow back into him. He could already see the waters of the great Lena again as they sparkled and shimmered, speckled with patches of bright light: above the dark blue waters, above the wide open spaces of his beloved northern homeland sailed flocks of white cranes, their cries ringing in the air.

Atageldy Karayev

MISCHIEF-MAKER

Atageldy Karayev was born in 1944 in Charjou Region (Turkmen SSR). He worked in poultry breeding on a collective farm, served in the Soviet armed forces and graduated from the History and Geography department of the Ashkhabad Teacher Training College, after which he worked as a reporter for youth periodicals. At present he studies at the Gorky Literary Institute in Moscow.

Karayev's works received a high appraisal at the 7th National Conference of Young Writers. The principal subjects of his works are the life of young people in the countryside, real and false human values, the moulding of the young person's personality, and his search for intellectual and moral guideposts.

CHAPTER ONE

My mother likes chickens very much, as do all the women in our village. I'm also fond of them, boiled or fried, and I really have a crush on chicken eggs. Yet I can't stand live chickens—when they run about near the porch climbing up on it and fouling the place I scream at them and throw stones, but they still keep at it, cackling like mad all the time and manage to foul the porch anyway. Then I always step into the stuff. To top it all, Mother, if she is in low spirits, will clout me a couple of times for not looking after those cursed hens.

Generally, I often catch it from my mother. I'm particularly annoyed by her yell "I'll do it myself!" whenever I start doing something, even if it's just lifting some hay or drawing water from the well.

To make a long story short, my mother doesn't let me lift a finger, while other parents quarrel with their children because they can't force them to help around the house.

Once my mother said to me:

"You exasperated me even when you were still in the womb, tossing this way and that, as if playing tag inside me. You even made a hash of getting born. The children in our village are born at home, almost always at night, and you were born in broad daylight in the cotton field. I didn't even have time to reach the field camp."

I liked to imagine my own birth.

There was the cotton field, the air was so hot you could hardly breathe. Everyone had finished weeding their part and had gone to another field. My mother was all alone. She still hadn't finished her part when I began to appear. She trudged off to the camp.

But my desire to take a look at the world was so strong that she failed to reach the camp. Mother peered around, saw a spot with some grass under a mulberry-tree and lay down on it. Soon my crying rent the air.

There were no people around, but plenty of donkeys and dogs. The animals had never heard such a squeaking noise before. They perked up their ears and stared in Mother's direction. I lay on the hem of mother's dress and cried.

Mother lay at home for a week, after which she went to work in the field again. She was so afraid something would happen to me that she took me with her everywhere she went. I didn't go to the kindergarten for a single day and grew up in the cotton field. I caught wasps with my bare hands like butterflies and fell asleep in the field among the cotton plants and weeds. Once I was almost run over by a cultivator. The ox pulling it stopped short when it came up to me and refused to budge despite all the driver's urgings. Finally, the man noticed me and carried me to my mother. Mother mowed grass for that ox every day afterwards.

Mother is still afraid that something will happen to me. And generally I'm tired to death of being little. I want to be grown-up as quickly as possible.

I got the idea of making wine. I knew that all grown-ups could make wine and decided that I could too. I found nothing on the subject in books. Then I went to see Mukhamed Palang. He is regarded as the best wine-maker in the village. There was a time when he distilled home-brew, but one day the retort blew up with such force that Mukhamed was almost dispatched into the heavens. It was a narrow escape, he was only thrown to the ground and lost consciousness; a deep scar was left on his right cheek after the accident.

When I arrived, Mukhamed was giving a motherless lamb milk from a bottle.

"Ah, Kuvanch, come in."

These words reassured me, accompanied as they were by a friendly smile.

"I've come on business."

"On business, you say? I thought you'd come to steal melons."

I went red in the face as if I were hit by a heat wave and stared at my scratched feet. What he said had a grain of truth. A while ago Jakhan, the daughter of the manager of the collective farm store-house Kuvanch Kossa, had fallen ill. Jakhan and I share a desk at school. And generally I like her. One *tabib** said a person could be healed by means of stolen pumpkins. The important thing was to steal the pumpkins from a miser, otherwise they would not be effective. I knew no other person in the village who was more miserly than Mukhamed. At noon I went to the melon *aryks*** along which pumpkins also grow. I had just picked an enormous pumpkin near a big yellow

---

*Tabib—a quack.
**Aryk—a small canal used to irrigate the fields in Central Asia. —*Tr.*

flower when I heard Mukhamed's voice:

"Shall I help you lift it?"

My heart sank. I didn't know where to run because I couldn't make out where the voice was coming from. But when Mukhamed said: "Take the pumpkin to my porch," I realised that he was some place behind me. I turned carefully and saw Mukhamed sitting on a mulberry-tree with a grape-vine winding round it. He held a pail filled with grapes in his hands.

Now I felt safer.

"I won't take it there," I answered calmly.

"I say you will!"

He began descending the tree awkwardly. The pail slipped out of his hand and dropped.

I ran as fast as I could. Mukhamed only had time to yell:

"Just you wait when I get my hands on you, you thieving brat."

Now, eyeing me mockingly, he said:

"O, I believe I'm mistaken. It's not the time to steal now. You steal at noon, when everyone's asleep. But you don't even know how to steal. They catch you before you reach the melon field. When the boys and I went stealing, they couldn't even catch us with wolves' traps."

I calmed down and asked:

"Did you also steal melons?"

"A child that has grown up in a village and has never stolen melons, apples or apricots is not a proper child. Of course we stole things! But I was not a thief. Only a person caught stealing is a thief. They didn't catch me a single time."

"Not once?"

"Not once! "

"Why do they call you *Palang** then?"

Mukhamed's dark face grew pale as cottage cheese and then turned bluish.

"Who told you they call me that?" he asked me in threatening tones and came towards me. The lamb minced after him. "Get away from here!" Mukhamed pushed the lamb away with his foot. "Who told you?"

"I heard it in the field when I went there with Mother."

"Did your mother say it?"

"It was not Mother."

Mukhamed seemed to relax a bit, but breathed noisily.

"The person who said that is a blabbermouth."

"A whole village of blabbermouths?" I wondered to myself.

"Well, what did you come here for? Don't stand there like a dummy," he said and kneeled to feed the lamb.

"I want to make wine."

"Wine?"

"Yes."

"Hum."

"Teach me how to do it."

"First go and wipe your nose."

I felt humiliated.

"I didn't ask you how to make home-brew, only wine."

---

*Palang—a donkey's saddle cloth.

The word home-brew hit him like a stone.

"Get out of here, you fool!" he screamed and threw the milk bottle at me. It hit the wall and broke into tiny pieces.

I darted out and caught my wind only when I reached home. The desire to make wine still remained. I would have died of grief if I were to fail.

Every person knows that a peasant has a plot of land called a *mellek*. Every *mellek* has a garden. And what is a garden without grapes? There were grapes growing in our garden too. After thinking a while I picked two pails of grapes, emptied them into a pan and crushed them thoroughly. I got all of mother's yeast and put it in the pan with the grapes. Then I covered the lot with an old sackcloth and put the pan in the sun.

A day passed. I peeked into the pan and found nothing had changed. There was no wine odour and the colour hadn't changed. On the second day I asked Jakhan for some more yeast and added it to the mixture. On the next morning, raising the sackcloth I sensed a sour smell. I checked the pan in the afternoon again. There was froth like soap-suds on the reddish liquid. A swarm of midges hovered above it. Now I thought I felt the odour of wine. I wanted to taste it, but didn't dare take the fermenting mash into my mouth. I knew that neighbour Mukhamed never was the first to taste his home-brew. First he would treat his neighbours. "O honourable neighbour of mine, my fathers and grandfathers venerated your ancestors. And the other way round. I don't know your attitude to me, but I respect you very much. Today I have prepared home-brew and request you to taste it first." After such flattering words a person would take the beautiful cup full of home-brew and drink it up. Screwing up his eyes Mukhamed would follow every gulp to determine the taste and strength of the drink.

So I also went to look for someone who would be the first to taste my wine. I was immediately lucky: I saw Mukhamed's son Yagmur walking with an empty sack.

"Hey, Yagmur, come here!" I yelled and waved a hand.

"What is it?"

"I've got a job for you."

"I've my hands full already."

"Are you going to get grass? I'll help you later."

"You won't let me down, will you?"

"A person who lets a friend down is a woman!"

"All right," he said heading towards me reluctantly. "What job do you have?"

"Don't worry, I won't put a yoke round your neck."

"The cow's hungry."

"I promised I'd help you pluck some grass, what're you afraid of?"

"What if Father finds out?" he said looking around fearfully.

"Try my wine."

"Have you got wine?"

"Yes, I made it."

Yagmur's eyes flashed.

"Where is it?"

I led him up to the pan and let him smell it.

"It's wine all right, but it's not purified."

"I didn't have time."

"Have you tasted it yourself?"

"I have," I lied resolutely.

"Then bring a cup and some food."

I brought a cup held together by a piece of tin and two tomatoes. Yagmur scooped half a cup from the pan and gulped it down. Then he frowned but did not reach for the tomatoes.

"It doesn't taste like wine: it't too bitter."

"That's because it's strong."

"No, it isn't: your head won't go round even if you drink up the whole basin."

My spirits fell. Without seeing any effect of the wine on Yagmur I grabbed the cup from his hands, scooped some wine and drank it. It was indeed unbearably bitter. But since I had never tasted wine before I comforted myself that it was supposed to be like this.

"All the Caucasian wines are bitter like this," I told Yagmur.

"How do you know?"

"I read about it."

"Let me have another taste."

"Go to hell."

"You're a miser."

"I'm not a miser, it's just that you don't know how to drink!"

"Do *you* know how to drink?"

Instead of answering I scooped a full cup, gulped it down and wiped my lips.

"That's how you drink."

"Who drinks wine like that?" said Yagmur disdainfully. "First of all, you didn't make a sour face, second, you didn't grunt, and, third, you didn't smell the tomato."

Everything Yagmur said seemed fair enough to me.

"Let's begin from the beginning," I proposed.

"Let's."

After the second cup Yagmur said:

"It's not bitter at all."

"Rather it's sweetish," I added.

"And there's no smell."

We downed one more cup each.

"My wine's Caucasian."

"It's better than Caucasian wine."

"You're my friend."

"And you're my brother."

"Let's go and get the grass!"

"What do we need the grass for?"

"You've got a sack."

"What's a sack?"

"Indeed what does a sack need grass for?"

"The cow needs grass."

"Then let's go?!"

"Where?"

"To get the grass."

"What do you need grass for?"

"For the cow."

"Did the Lord give the cow a mouth?"

"Yes."

"And legs too?"

"And legs too!"

"Then the cow can go and nibble the grass itself."

"That's true, it can."

Holding on to each other we made our way to Yagmur's house. We untied the cow and let it out on the melon fields.

Then we seated ourselves in the deep shade of the mulberry-tree.

"Why is the cow eating only melons?"

"She likes them."

"Is a melon tastier than a tomato?"

"How does an animal know what's tastier?"

"You're a miser after all, brother."

"Why?"

"If you'd given the cow a couple of cups of wine it wouldn't want the melons and would eat only tomatoes, both red and green."

"You're quite right, Yagmur, even green ones. Well, I'm off."

"Where you going?"

"To get the wine."

"Well, get it, we'll take another cupful."

"We won't drink any more."

"Why's that?"

"We'll give it to the cow."

"What for?"

"So it'd eat tomatoes."

"That's good, bring the wine."

I got up with great difficulty and was petrified.

"It's not your cow."

"Wha-at?"

"Your cow was red."

"Hm, that's right."

"This one's black."

"B-b-black?" he looked at the cow and said, "You fool."

"What did you say?"

"It's whi-ite."

"No, it's black."

"Whi-te, you fool."

"Don't curse!"

"It's whi-ite. It's not ours. How did it get here," Yagmur grabbed a stone, got up, made one step and fell. I called him for a long time but he never got up. He had fallen asleep, and I went home to bring some wine for the cow.

Just before sunset I opened my eyes. Mother was standing over me and looking at me in surprise.

"Where'd you get drunk?" she asked calmly.

My head ached, I felt sick, there was a ringing sound in my ears. I could hardly open my mouth.

At this point Mother gave vent to her feelings.

"Where'd you get fuddled? Why don't you answer?" she scolded me and pulled my ear so hard I became quite sober. "I ask you where'd you get drunk!"

"In the shade."

"Who gave you the drink?"

"I got it myself."

"Where'd you get it?"

"From the pan."

"What pan?"

"The pan."

"You wretch! Do you want to mock me? I wish the earth would swallow you!"

She pulled my ears again.

"Really, Mother, the wine's in the pan."

"Where did you say?"

"In the pan."

She let go my ears and walked towards the pan. When she bent down, the odour of wine hit her nose. Making a wry face she screamed:

"Who made it?"

"I did."

"You?"

"Yes, I did."

"O Lord, how have I sinned? Why such a punishment? He's only a pup and look what he's done! O-o-o! Get away, do you hear me?!"

I remained seated, still unable to understand anything properly.

"I said get away! Otherwise I'll strangle you!"

I remained calmly seated. Mother had threatened to kill me many times. And every time, after terrible threats and cursing, she would merely whip me a couple of times. Then I would begin to cry, and so would my mother. My younger sister would join us sometimes. And we would wail all together.

Once Mother told me to divide the remaining beans into two parts and cook one. There were about two handfuls of beans.

"What is there to divide?" thought I and put all the beans into the pot. My sister and I did not wait for the beans to be cooked properly, but filled our mouths with the hot, raw beans. Tears came sprinkling out of our eyes.

When Mother returned from work, she whipped me with a rope. Then she sat for a long time with her face in her hands. A little while later she embraced me and wept bitterly.

Mothers cry much more bitterly than their children. This time, too, I was waiting for her to beat me and to burst out crying afterwards.

"Run away!" Mother suddenly screamed in anger.

"I won't!"

Mother fell upon me.

"Take this if you don't want to run away, and this!" she whacked me a couple of times. "Cry, will you!" Mother screamed almost weeping. "Will you cry, you ass?! Why aren't you crying?"

"You never hurt me very much, Mother," I answered calmly.

She was about to pounce upon me again but suddenly patted me on the head and asked:

"Is it true I don't hurt you?"

"It is, Mother."

"But you used to cry."

"I just felt sorry for you, that's why I cried."

"And now you don't feel sorry for me, is that it?"

"I do."

"Then why aren't you crying?"

"I don't know."

"You'd better cry when I beat you."

"Why?"

"It won't hurt then."

"It doesn't hurt anyway."

"What if I get mad and beat you soundly. You'd better run away when I get angry."

"You won't be able to catch up with me."

"That's good."

"If you don't catch me you won't be able to beat me, and if you don't beat me you'll get even angrier."

"That shouldn't worry you. O Lord, everyone has normal children. They cry and run away when they're beaten, and this one sits staring at me."

Then Mother remained silent for a long time. All of a sudden she said:

"Why are you sitting around?"

"What should I do?"

"Pour out this muck and wash the pan."

I got up.

"Never do it again!" Mother shouted as I walked away.

"All right."

I poured the wine-mash out near the *aryk*. When I was washing the pan I saw our chickens. They were crowding round the place where I had poured out the wine. They were pecking at the crushed grapes with the motley cock at their head.

Along the dusty road Yagmur was driving his cow that had stuffed itself with melons. As soon as the cow slowed down Yagmur would lash it on the back.

"Chuv-chuv!" he shouted at the top of his lungs, while Mukhamed Palang was standing at the roadside with a twig in his hands and also yelling:

"Stop dragging your feet. Drive the cow faster. If the cow croaks I'll tan your hide."

Some time later Mukhamed sauntered over to our house. I was afraid of his twig and ran away, inside. Mukhamed shouted to Mother:

"Listen, woman! You should welcome a neighbour."

"A neighbour, yes."

"Your son..."

"What about my son?" Mother suddenly began shouting. "We must find out who taught him to make wine and who made him drunk. Damn your family to the seventh generation."

"Instead of feeling ashamed, you're screaming impudently!"

"Get out of here!"

"If my cow croaks..."

"I wish you'd croak with it!"

"Just wait till I get my hands on your pup..."

"Only touch him with a finger. I'll make your whole face raw. I'm only a woman, but I'll be able to cope with a sop like you..."

I was very satisfied with my mother.

Mother awakened me very early. Her dark eyes burned in the morning haze.

"What should I do with you? Now we won't have a single chicken, not one! You killed all of them!"

I decided that yesterday's anger had not subsided in Mother yet.

"Mother, I didn't touch them."

"I don't know about that, but they're *all* dead!"

"But..."

"Shut your mouth! They all croaked from your vile wine!" Clenching her fists she wanted to rush at me as usual, but suddenly grew weak, tears burst from her eyes, and she muttered through her wailing:

"You destroyed our breadwinners! Get up and help pluck them, at least the feathers won't be lost."

I entered the hen-coop and saw all the hens, twenty of them, and the cock lying legs stretched out.

I plucked the cock with particular care. He was my enemy. He had attacked me and pecked me many times. His beak was not as soft as Mother's hand.

Mother was plucking the hens and tears came rolling from her eyes.

"Why were you born like this?" she wailed. "You'll always be the way you were born. Unless a mean wife gets her hands on you and corrects you. But it's such a long wait!"

My palms grew blistered, my hands ached but I remained silent. If I were to say so much as a word Mother would hit me on the head with a hen. At this point we heard my little sister crying. Sighing sadly Mother said:

"Go and see what's wrong with her. Take a bit of *churek** in the pantry and give it to her!"

When my sister was born I looked after her as if I were her mother. Now she was not a bad sort, but when she was in diapers, what a mean girl she had been! I would rock and rock the cradle, nothing could make her go to sleep. The boys' voices came from outside. I would get angry and scream at her: she would close her eyes in fright. I would tiptoe to the door, and she'd start to squeal. I would sometimes start crying too from chagrin.

Now things had become much better! I could go anywhere I wanted to, only I had to take my sister along.

Seeing me, my sister stopped crying. I looked in the pantry and saw the piece of *churek* there. I gave

*Churek—a local kind of bread bun. —Tr.

it to my sister, and she grabbed it with both hands.

At this point Mother entered, sighed heavily and said:

"What fat hens. And the money I bought them for was so hard-earned." Tears continued to roll from her eyes.

We threw the hens in a heap at the edge of the *mellek*. Some time later, when Mother and I were getting ready to drink tea, my sister ran into the room pale as death.

"*Bechche, bechche,*"* she gasped, her hand pointing outside.

"Take a look what it is," said Mother.

I went out and was dumbfounded. Then I rushed back into the house.

"Mother, the hens."

"What hens?"

"The hens we plucked."

"What are you blabbering, silly boy."

"They've all come alive, look."

Seeing the bare chickens Mother gasped and then said:

"I told you they were purchased with honest money. Go and catch one of them and I'll fry it for you."

I ran after a hen. Then Yagmur appeared.

"Mother sends you some *matsoni*,"** he said, offering a wooden bowl.

Yagmur's mother was a kind woman.

---

*Very frightening (Turkmen). —*Ed.*
**Matsoni—a kind of sour clotted milk. —*Tr.*

"Your cow hasn't died, has it?" inquired my mother.

"No, it hasn't."

"Our chickens haven't either. You're not in a hurry?"

"No."

"Then help Kuvanch catch the chickens. In the evening I'll treat you to some fried chicken."

Mother left for work. My sister and I were alone. All children like sweets, but you need money to buy them. Mother said that money was obtained from a gazelle's horns, and it was not easy. Sometimes I imagined Mother trying to get the money from a gazelle's horns and the gazelle raising its head higher and higher. No, I wanted to grow up very much to be able to earn money to buy my sister sweets.

Taking my sister by the hand I set out for the collective farm office. The office was behind a high fence. The courtyard was very big and was divided into two parts by three tall mulberry-trees, which weren't touched even during the feeding of the silk-worm. The office staff liked to drink tea under the mulberry-trees. When the sweet berries ripened on the trees, it was a real feast for us children.

*Usta** Allaberen's forge was situated in one corner of the yard. He made sickles, spades and repaired harrows. You could often hear metal ringing there. Sometimes we stood at a distance and watched, fascinated, as he battered red-hot metal into a shape.

My sister and I began to play ball near the fence. Then I saw some of my pals and remembered that I had five kopeks in my pocket.

Usta—craftsman, master. —Ed.

"Let's play a game of kopeks," I proposed to the boys.

"Let's!" they agreed.

Each boy had a few kopeks, and we started the game. I did very well throwing coins against the wall. Soon I had forty kopeks which I needed to buy sweets with. Then I suggested that we go to _Usta_ Allaberen's forge. Allaberen looked very fierce, but actually there wasn't a milder and kinder person in the whole village. His worst curse sounded like a kind wish: "Let your house be filled with grain." Allaberen was very lean, and everyone marvelled how he managed to lift the heavy hammer. When we came to the forge, Allaberen greeted us with a friendly smile.

"Ah, the _jigits_* have come," he said, putting aside the hammer. He picked up a crooked piece of iron with pincers and threw it into the fire. Then he looked at me.

"Come here. Try to pull the rope from the bellows," he said.

I tried. The bellows hissed and the coals flared up and crackled. Sparks flew to all sides.

"Well, you'll make a good _usta_," said Allaberen grinning.

I looked at the boys haughtily and suddenly noticed my sister. She was making her way towards me. All the boys began pulling the bellows-rope in turn, and when my sister tugged at it, nothing happened. The _usta_ patted her on the head and said:

"You still have to eat a lot and grow up. And

*_Jigit_—horseman or warrior. —_Tr._

although you'll never make an *usta* anyway, you'll be a fine cotton-picker."

Very pleased with ourselves, we ran noisily out of the forge and came face to face with One-Eyed Dovli. One of his eyes was misty as if ashes were sticking to it. And generally Dovli was an unpleasant man. He had a particular dislike for me. Just seeing me made the number of wrinkles on his forehead increase. I wanted to count them but couldn't. There must have been about forty.

Dovli rolled up to me, grasped me by the shoulder and ordered:

"Come on!"

"Where?" I asked retreating a bit.

"You'll bring some water from the *aryk*."

"What am I, a water-carrier?"

"You must obey your elders without question."

My sister had already puckered her face ready to burst out crying. This forced me to comply.

"All right, I'll go." And turning to my sister I added: "I'll soon be back."

Dovli brought a pail from the office.

"Here! And make it snappy!"

I immediately invented a trick and told the boys:

"If you listen to me, I'll return you the money I won."

"Okay."

We scooped up a pail of water from the *aryk*. When we entered some tall reeds on the way back I said:

"Who wants to get his money back, pee into the pail."

338

"What for?!" The boys stared at me in astonishment.

"To teach Dovli never to ask us to bring him water again."

"But he's our elder."

"Elders should also ask properly instead of yelling and ordering us around."

"And he once pulled my ears."

"And mine too."

"Then let's do it!"

"Let's!"

"I'm first!"

"I'm second..."

. . . .

"Here's your money." I took all the change from my pocket.

"Never mind."

"You won it."

"But I promised."

"Never mind."

We decided to buy sweets for forty kopeks, give half to my sister and distribute the rest evenly among ourselves.

We left the pail on the porch and called:

"Dovli-aga!"*

He yelled fiercely from his room:

"Bring it here!"

"We're in a hurry."

"Just think, they're in a hurry!" Dovli mumbled as he came out of the office.

Aga—a respectful appellation to an older man. *—Ed.*

We moved aside and waited impatiently. Dovli scooped a full mug and gulped it down. Then, wiping his lips, he yelled in puzzlement:

"Why's the water salty?!"

One of the boys guffawed. Dovli guessed what we had been up to, threw away the mug and rushed after us. But we had already run out of the yard, shut the gate and put the chain on. There was no other way out of the yard. We were perfectly aware of this, so we jumped and yelled right in front of the gate, while Dovli screamed and cursed on the other side. Then we ran off to get the sweets, and then the sun began to set. It was time for us all to go home.

In the morning, as I was washing, Mother talked to herself:

"God forbid and stave off the misfortune!"

"What happened?" I asked.

"Oh, don't ask," she answered sighing deeply. "Everyone who was working in the office have not come home. One-eyed Dovli, and *Usta* Allaberen, and Agjagyul. They've all disappeared God knows where. Woe to their children!"

Suddenly Mother stared at me.

"What's wrong, son? You're pale as death."

"They're in the yard."

"Who's in the yard?" Mother asked in fright.

"One-eyed Dovli and the others."

"In what yard?"

"In the office yard."

"Why?"

"We locked them there."

"Who did?"

"We the boys."

Mother burst into tears. I rushed off to free *Usta*
Allaberen and Aunty Agjagyul.

* * *

Mother left for work, and my sister and I set about
eating sweet cane. Then one-eyed Dovli's wife appeared,
tall and thin. The yellow kerchief on her head was
completely faded. Staring at us with dull eyes she
asked:

"Where'd you steal the cane?"

"We didn't steal anything. This cane's from our
mellek."

"Don't lie. If your mother learns about it, she'll
tan your hides."

My sister and I exchanged glances and almost
burst into tears.

"All right, eat it. I won't tell. If you want, I can
give you some sugar-cane."

We remained silent.

"Don't you want it?"

"We do," my sister whispered sniffing.

"Then I'll give it to you. Is this cane sweet?" she
asked sitting down next to us.

"Of course it's not like sugar-cane, but it's okay," I
answered and pushed the end of a cane towards my
sister.

"It's a far cry from sugar-cane," said Dovli's wife
sighing deeply, then suddenly turned to me and asked
in an ingratiating tone: "Tell me, dear boy, did you

lock Dovli and others in the yard for the night or did they do it themselves?"

I told her in detail how we locked the gate of the office yard. She knew all about it from others, but was very amused by my account.

"You're a wonderful boy," she said pleased and then added sighing: "Did you see what Dovli does in the office?"

"He writes and clatters with the abacus."

"I know that without you. But what do they do with Agjagyul?" she whispered quickly.

"Aunty Agjagyul also writes and counts on the abacus."

"What they do when they're not writing and not counting?"

"They drink tea."

"They touch knees, don't they?"

"I didn't see it."

"You fool, when they drink tea you see it, when they rub knees you see nothing!" Then she put her hand on my shoulder and said in a conspiratorial manner: "You're the smartest boy in the village, that's why I came to you. I'll give you a bundle of sugar-cane each only remember if they were ever cuddling together."

"But I never saw it!"

"O Allah! Perhaps they were holding hands?"

Even my sister was looking at me with entreaty in her eyes. She wanted to taste the sugar-cane very much.

"I remember now: when we came to Allaberen once, they were sitting and drinking tea," I said.

"Well," Dovli's wife cried out impatiently.

"A sparrow twittering on a branch let it drop on Dovli-aga's shoulder."

"No!?"

"Yes!"

"That bum never told me a word about it. What happened then, my good boy? I'll give you two bundles of sugar-cane each."

I could tell Dovli's wife something exciting to earn four bundles of sugar-cane.

"Seeing the sparrow's dropping on Dovli-aga's shoulder Aunty Agjagyul burst out laughing."

"She did? I'd like to pull out her hair, tan her hide and fry her!"

"Then she took some paper..."

Seeing that our visitor's eyes were bulging I fell silent.

"Why've you opened your mouth as if it were a rat's hole? Go on!"

"Aunty Agjagyul took a piece of paper and wiped the sparrow's dropping from Dovli-aga's shoulder."

"The bitch! How dare she touch another woman's husband?" Tears rolled out of Dovli's wife's eyes. I was very surprised by these tears. It seemed to me that she should be glad that she had not had to wipe one-eyed Dovli's shoulder herself.

"How did she wipe it, did she stroke his shoulder?"

"I didn't notice that."

"You should notice, notice everything, miss nothing. And take the sugar-cane any time."

I realised that it was best to get the sugar-cane right away.

Dovli's wife took us to the place where her cane

grew. Some five minutes later she cried out:

"You've cut too much."

I almost choked, but my sister replied quickly:

"We cut a bundle each, aunty."

It was not difficult for me to watch one-eyed Dovli. I took my sister to Allaberen and climbed a mulberry-tree from which I could see the room where Dovli and Agjagyul worked as if it were on the palm of my hand. I sat on the tree for three hours, yet they were still not holding hands and not hugging. I grew tired of all this and was about to climb down. But a cart came through the gates with a squeaking noise bringing three sheep carcasses. Fat-Belly Allak stood on the cart urging on the oxen:

"Chuv, damned creatures!" The oxen were indeed hardly moving their legs.

The cart stopped at the doors of the store-house. The oxen gazed lazily at the ground, while Allak went to find the store-house manager. Kuvanch was not to be seen near by. Dragging his whip along the ground Fat-Belly Allak headed for the opposite end of the yard, to the forge. As soon as he disappeared from view, One-Eyed Dovli came into the yard. Looking around furtively, he crept to the cart like a fox and grabbed a pile of entrails with his hand. I saw him take the entrails to the larder, then he came out again, looked around once again and disappeared in the office.

Failing to find Kuvanch in the forge, Fat-Belly Allak headed for the office. The ware-house manager came some time later. He saw the cart and shouted:

"Allak, hey Allak, where the hell are you! How can you leave the meat in the sun?"

"What could I do if you're God knows where?" Allak grumbled, coming out of the office.

"It's none of your business."

"Then it's none of your business where I stop the cart."

The manager Kuvanch pretended that he hadn't heard these words and went to open the door. Then he asked Allak in a conciliatory tone:

"Have you got some tobacco?"

"I don't have any for you."

"God damn it, I haven't got any tobacco left. My jaws ache for a smoke, I can't find a place for myself. One-Eyed Dovli must have some, but it's easier to scrape some *mumiyo*** in the mountains than get a pinch of tobacco from him."

"I've only got a little," Fat-Belly Allak grumbled.

"Give me enough for one cigarette. I'll give it back to you later."

"It'll be a long wait," snuffled Fat-Belly Allak but took out his pouch and offered it to Kuvanch.

Rolling a cigarette Kuvanch said:

"These sheep have fine meat."

"Shaiym-aga's flock always has well-fattened animals."

"That Shaiym-aga is a good man if we believe the stories told about him. They say he shot a bandit when he worked as a militiaman. The relatives wanted to avenge themselves. Once three men came to his pasture and said: 'We've come to kill you,' and he an-

---

*Mumiyo—a rare medicinal resin-like substance found in the mountains. —*Tr.*

swered calmly: 'You can kill me but first let's dine and drink some tea.' He slaughtered a sheep and cooked some *shurpa*.* They ate and drank, and the three men changed their minds and didn't kill him."

"It must've been rich, that *shurpa*, if they did not avenge their kin."

"It was not due to the *shurpa*. They didn't kill him because he was not afraid of them."

"Look, the meat might spoil in the sun and there you stand smoking and telling me tales."

They began to carry the carcases into the warehouse, and I saw One-Eyed Dovli, his face pressed to the window-pane.

All of a sudden, Fat-Belly Allak began yelling:

"Hey, there must be another head and legs!" He climbed into the cart and looked all over it. "They're not here!"

"Could a dog have carried them away while we were talking?"

At that moment One-Eyed Dovli came out:

"Well, brothers, let's have a smoke, eh?"

"It's no time for smoking, a head and legs have disappeared."

"What head and legs?"

"A sheep's head and legs."

"Maybe the sheep was born without a head and legs."

"Cut out your jokes," Allak was angry. "I'll have to pay for these damned legs!"

"Perhaps you dropped them along the way?"

Shurpa—national dish—soup with mutton. —*Tr.*

"That can't be."

Then One-Eyed Dovli proposed:

"Kuvanch, let's say that the liver and lungs spoiled, and write them off; as to the legs, that's nothing, worms were in the legs, and that's all"

"I don't know..."

One-Eyed Dovli decided to mock Allak some more:

"You're not a very good worker, lying around in your cart like an old yoke."

"I work as much as you do, Dovli-aga," mumbled Allak.

"You're just as clever as your oxen."

One-Eyed Dovli marched with an important air to the office.

I slipped down the tree and ran after Fat-Belly Allak. He had already almost reached the gates driving the oxen with his whip.

"Hey, Allak-aga, wait!"

"Want to get on the cart?" he asked giving me a fierce look. "When you need something you always make up to me: Allak-aga, this, Allak-aga that, and behind my back I'm always Fat-Belly Allak."

"Allak-aga, I know who stole the entrails!"

"Who?"

"One-Eyed Dovli."

Allak glanced incredulously at me:

"Believe me, I even know where he hid them."

"Where'd he hide them?"

"In the larder where all the old things are kept. Really."

I brought him to the larder, and we began the search. Soon Fat-Belly Allak cried out:

"There they are, I've found them. What a blind ass I am!"

The head lay on the bottom of an old crate together with the legs and some entrails.

"You know what," Allak said suddenly eyeing me. "All this has been written off already, and it's not a sin to steal from a thief. Let's divide it equally between us."

I hesitated.

"Take it, your mother will be glad," said Allak.

When I came home and showed my sister the sheep legs she clapped her hands. We skinned them as best we could and began to cook the meat so Mother would have less to do.

However, when Mother came home from work and learned how I had gotten the legs, she became terribly cross:

"Go and throw away the stolen meat! I don't want to see any stolen things in my house. What did I say?" Mother advanced towards me holding a rolling-pin in her hand. "I'll make mincemeat of you."

Taking the pan-holder I went to the hearth...

Mother didn't eat or drink anything that night. She put us to bed and after a while, thinking that I had fallen asleep, buried her face in the pillow and wept. Her shoulders shook as she wept. I couldn't restrain myself and let out a sob.

Mother raised her head right away.

"What's wrong?"

"Nothing."

"Then sleep."

She got up quietly, sat down next to me and put

her hand on my forehead. It was wonderful to feel the warmth of her hand, gentle and caressing.

I fell asleep very quickly.

* * *

The boys and I had assembled at *Usta* Allaberen's again to work the bellows. The bellows hissed, the coals flared up and sparks flew. *Usta* Allaberen put his heavy hand on my shoulder.

"You're a good boy and you're growing fast."

I understood what he wanted to say and could not restrain my joy.

"Do you want to be my assistant? You'll make a fine blacksmith."

I saw the boys' eyes glowing in envy.

"I do! I do!" I exclaimed.

"Then try."

Allaberen put a red-hot piece of iron on the anvil, fastened it in the vice and told me to hold the clamps tightly.

I tried as hard as I could.

"Relax, Kuvanch. I'll beat it with a small hammer."

Showers of sparks flew at every blow. My sister, who was standing there, cried out loudly every time:

"Look at the fire scattering!" She watched me in admiration and looked at the other boys with pride for her brother.

When we got ready to go home, Allaberen gave me a little penknife as a present.

"I made it for you a long time ago," he said.

I showed Mother the penknife and said that I would work as an apprentice in the forge. Then it started:

"I won't let you work there!"

"Mother, I'm a big boy. All my friends are working."

"Let them work."

"I'll work too."

"I know better what you'll do."

"Ma, please, let him work," my sister pleaded.

"Be still, or I'll slap your lips," said Mother tearfully.

The next day I went to Allaberen to tell him about Mother's refusal. Kuvanch and he were having tea. Offering me a seat, *Usta* Allaberen gave me a cup with strong tea. After making a gulp I refused to have any more:

"It's too bitter."

"Ah, you don't know the good things of life," said Kuvanch and took my cup.

"Excellent tea!"

"The tea's good all right, but tell me when we'll take this *iner** into our caravan," Allaberen nodded in my direction and smoothed his beard.

"Yes, it's time for him to join the caravan, it's time to work," Kuvanch agreed. "All the boys of his age are working. Listen, namesake, would you like to work in the cotton field?"

"That won't do!" Allaberen said abruptly.

"Why not?" asked Kuvanch.

"I'll take him as an apprentice!"

"Why should everything be as you want it?! In a few days I'll give up my damned ware-house and be-

Iner—camel leader.

350

come a team-leader in the cotton fields. Maybe my namesake would like to join my team, eh?"

They were talking as if I were not there at all.

"Mother won't allow me to work," I interrupted their conversation.

"It seems we've removed our trousers before seeing the river," mumbled Allaberen.

"Well, anyway, let's try to find a way out. Namesake, have you heard that Abdulla is holding a *toi*?"*

"I have."

"Well, don't make any hasty decisions before the *toi*."

Unable to understand how the *toi* was linked to my work, I was perplexed. Kuvanch understood my state:

"You exercise. Show your mother that you're quite grown-up. And it's good to work in the field, you can ask Jakhan," Kuvanch winked at me, and I grew red in the face.

"What a cunning man you are!" Allaberen threw up his hands.

CHAPTER TWO

Yagmur and I were seated under a mulberry-tree drinking tea. Branches from the tree had been cut off to feed the silkworm, and now the shadow from the tree resembled a goat without horns. Fledglings peeped in the hollow of the big bare trunk because of the heat.

Yagmur had one foot dangling in the *aryk*; suddenly

**Toi—feast, celebration.

he noticed the approaching team-leader, Kuvanch. The man was short, and had a limp. He had no beard, just a thin little moustache. They said that his leg had become shorter after he was wounded. He always had a mulberry twig with him. If he stood idly he always whipped his shorter leg with the twig as if he were urging it to grow. Even now Kuvanch was whipping the leg.

We had in front of us an iron *kumgan** with a broken lid and two cups. A piece of *churek* and two bits of sugar lay on a kerchief. Yagmur quickly took his lump of sugar and dropped it in his cup, then he pushed me with his elbow and said:

"Quick, here comes Kuvanch tripping on his beard."

Then I also dropped my sugar in the tea.

However, the team-leader suddenly turned, stepped over the *aryk* and looked at the plot we had directed water into. He whipped his short leg twice and shouted:

"Hey you, brats, come here!" He threw away the twig, grabbed the spade and began throwing earth.

We exchanged worried glances.

"Are your asses weighed down with stones or what?!"

We jumped up as if we were bitten and ran to Kuvanch.

"How many times do I have to tell you that you must water the cotton through a hose? Next time I see anything like it, I'll tan your hides!"

Picking up the spade I mumbled:

"Kuvanch-aga, we were watering it with a hose, but the dam was washed away."

*Kumgan—pot. —Ed.

"Blast you! You, waterers, are here to see that the dam is not carried away. Don't just stand there like a scarecrow, take the spade and work! " he raved at Yagmur.

Kuvanch began to toss intertwined reed roots into the washed away place, and Yagmur and I cemented the dam with soft red clay. We had to muster all our strength to lift one spadeful of clay. In the time it took us to do that, the water would wash away the clay we had just piled on. The gap gradually grew wider. Kuvanch threw everything he could get his hands on into it. He became hot. He removed his jacket and waded into the *aryk* in his boots. There he stood in the waterway and bid us throw clay faster. I was so bewildered and clumsy I hit Kuvanch with the liquid clay.

"God damn you! When we secure the dam, I'll tan both your hides!" Splattered with clay he was not at all frightening with his threats. I wanted to help him wash but he barked: "Get away!"

Yagmur and I walked along the distributing *aryk* to check the side drains, and when we returned Kuvanch had already washed and was waiting for us.

"Did you check everything?"

"Yes, we did."

"Then come here and let's have some tea."

Yagmur warned me that it was not for nothing that the team-leader was now talking in such a friendly tone. We whispered with each other hesitantly and went to the *aryk* to wash the dirt from our trousers.

"Waterers should always have their trousers rolled up to their knees! " shouted Kuvanch.

We began to roll up our trousers, and then sat down with the team-leader under the tree.

Kuvanch sipped the tea and made a sour face.

"Your tea is sweet. Drink first, I'll have it after you. Oh yes," he slapped his short leg, "I almost forgot that I left my lunch basket by the *aryk*. Bring it here, *jigits*!"

In a flash Yagmur ran off to get the basket. Kuvanch-aga opened it and produced a loaf of bread, a cup and some slightly melted fruit-drops.

"Well *jigits*, this is for you." He gave us the fruit-drops. Yagmur and I exchanged glances and blushed.

"You must find the work hard. I'll send you some helpers tomorrow."

I was worried. Kuvanch had already sent up help, the young woman Bagdagyul who was big and fat. Yagmur and I taken together would hardly make up half of her. She had waddled up to us, thrown aside the *ketmen*,* sat down in the shade and said in a drawl:

"I'm to help you."

"We'll do the watering, and you build a dam," I said shyly.

"What a nice little boy with a voice like a young cock's. Speak some more, and I'll listen to you." We were dumbfounded by her cheek. "Women are the flowers of life," continued Bagdagyul, "and you want me to work in such heat. I'll wither away before your very eyes."

We felt like mice in a cat's claws.

"We're only responsible for the water," said Yagmur.

*Ketmen—a tool like a hoe used in Central Asia to work the soil. —Tr.

But he sounded helpless, like a boy who had peed in his pants and was excusing himself before his mother.

"If you're responsible for the water, then boil some for tea." Bagdagyul produced a *kumgan*, black from soot, and handed it to Yagmur with a smile. "Well, my good children, how long will you torment me without tea?"

Yagmur took the *kumgan* and went to get the water.

"Kuvanch, dear, go and gather some brushwood. Women and girls don't like stubborn boys," she said stretching luxuriously. "I'll lie down for a while because your Allak-aga didn't let me sleep last night."

Yagmur returned with a full *kumgan*. I collected some brushwood. We made tea. Bagdagyul slept soundly. We tried to wake her but she only mumbled:

"I'll sleep a little bit more, my children."

We built a dam ourselves and let in the water. Bagdagyul was still sleeping. From far away she looked like an inflatable mattress ready to burst.

Looking at her Yagmur suddenly said: "I wish we grew up soon. If we were *jigits*, she wouldn't dare lie around like that."

I suggested that we pour water over her.

"Let's not disturb the wasp's nest," answered Yagmur. "She'll scream her head off, and it'll be even worse for us."

"Do you want us to drive the flies away from her too?!"

When Bagdagyul finally opened her eyes, the sun was low.

"Those damned flies won't let one sleep," she said yawning. "Now we'll have some tea."

We boiled water again. She drank her fill and made us mow some grass and load it on the donkey.

"And now, my dear children, I'd better ride home," she said in a kind voice and asked Yagmur to hold the donkey by the neck and me to help her mount it. I could hardly restrain myself from biting her fat leg.

I decided to pay her back for everything, broke off a twig with thorns and went after the donkey, but Yagmur stopped me.

"What do you want to do? Are you in your right mind? If you stick that thorn under the donkey's tail, it'll throw Bagdagyul off. All that'll be left of her after that is a wet spot like from a *vakharman*.* Then we'll be held responsible. As the saying goes: 'Ransom yourself from a woman and run as far away from her as you can.'"

"'Ransom yourself from what's bad,'" I corrected Yagmur and threw away the thorn.

Having recalled that instance, I told the team-leader resolutely:

"We don't need any helpers, Kuvanch-aga."

"No, my namesake, it'll be a bit difficult for you without any help. Tomorrow, Jakhan and Bostan will come," he said pouring some tea.

Yagmur glanced at me. I became red and Yagmur's face was also blazing.

I got up and went to the *aryk* to wash the cup. Having calmed down a bit I returned to my place.

"Good boys! You've made fine tea," Kuvanch praised us. "I feel much stronger now. Have some tea too,

---

Vakharman—a species of melon.

356

jigits. It quenches thirst very well.''

"We've had enough already."

"In his youth a man does not appreciate the taste of tea, but once he's over forty he begins to respect tea like he does a friend and companion. And you'll soon become grown-up *jigits*. Well, anyway go and sleep for a couple of hours and I'll watch the water."

"No, we don't want to sleep, we're quite all right."

"Don't show off. There's still thirty hectares to water. You'll need a lot of strength for it. And you're growing slowly, like lambs without mother's milk. Go and have a nap!"

The wrinkles on the team-leader's face became more prominent, a vertical groove appeared between the eyebrows.

"Look alive, don't sit there like hens!" Kuvanch shouted, putting a bun from his basket into ours.

I was both alarmed and glad that Jakhan and her friend Bostan would come tomorrow. I was embarrassed in advance. I remembered the letter... My schoolmate Begli wrote letters to a girl. And I served as their postman. Begli always showed me his letters, which he wrote in verse. I was amazed how he could write such fine poetry. All of a sudden, I wanted to write Jakhan a letter and also in verse. I was afraid someone would do it before me. I couldn't write poetry, so I turned to Begli for help.

"It's easy as pie to write poetry," he said. "Come back in an hour and it'll be ready."

In an hour he gave me a piece of paper with some verses and advised me to rewrite them in my own hand.

"If you don't rewrite it, she'll guess you didn't write the poem."

I was ready to rewrite it a dozen times, if only Jakhan would be pleased. Putting the letter into a book, I went to her house.

"Oh, it's Kuvanch," said Jakhan's mother, coming out on the porch.

"I brought Jakhan a book."

"All right, my boy. I'll give it to her."

"No, no," I objected and hid the book behind my back. "I'll give it to her myself."

"Then come in."

I entered the house, put the book into Jakhan's hand and immediately rushed out.

Jakhan and I had not seen each other since then, but my heart beat faster at every recollection of her.

"Be bolder when Jakhan comes," said Yagmur screwing up his eyes. "I was also shy when I first met Bostan. Why do you think it's so easy to write 'I love' in a letter and quite impossible to say it—as if your tongue is tied up?"

In the morning I kept looking at the road from where Jakhan and Bostan were to appear. So as not to think about the girls I took a spade and said:

"I'll go and look at the dam," and set out for the big *aryk* from which our irrigating *aryk* branched off. I walked reluctantly, looking around at every step. The earth was like a flaming ball. There was not the slightest breeze in the air.

At the dam I saw Allak, Bagdagyul's husband. He was about to cut off the water.

"What're you cutting off the water for?"

"I have my reason."

"Did you think about us?"

"If you need water, go ahead, take it. I don't need water. I need fish."

"Don't you dare cut off the water."

"Don't shout, you'll frighten the fish away! I'll only cut it off for half an hour. Do you know how much fish we'll catch in that time. Half is yours. Let's shake hands, right?" With a forced smile he put out his hand; he was so angry his hand shook.

"No!"

"Then I'll be going."

He took his wicket basket and spade and went off. At every step his stout body shook like jelly and the protruding stomach seemed to be about to tear away and fall to the ground. One trouser leg was rolled up, while the other hung freely. It was said that Allak was fat in his childhood too. In order to protect him from the evil eye his mother hung a talisman on his neck in the shape of a coloured string. Bagdagyul took off the talisman when they got married.

"Perhaps the evil eye would get hold of your stomach and you would become trim," she said.

However, Bagdagyul's hopes did not come true. Allak remained as fat as he ever was.

One could tell countless stories about Allak. He was even a teacher at our school for a short while. It all started with goats.

One day the school principal bought a goat from Aunty Orazgyul, Allak's mother. The goat proved to be so fertile that soon the principal had a herd of ten goats.

The villagers have a custom: never to repay evil with evil but to repay kindness with kindness. The principal offered Allak the post of teacher at his school.

Occasionally, the job of grazing the principal's goats fell to the lot of pupils who had misbehaved.

"You won't be a scientist," said the principal in such cases, "but you must be useful to society. First learn at least how to graze goats. Who knows, perhaps you'll become a shepherd."

The principal's goats were the very devils. Once they had scattered, you couldn't get them together again. It even happened that they got into the cotton field. Then you would have to chase them bare-footed over the thorns!

Once I had to graze the goats. But I found a way: I peeled some bast, tied the goats' legs and went swimming in the Jensi *aryk*. When I returned, the goats were standing in the same place. People even made up a saying: 'still as principal Bairam's goats'. After that the principal did not trust anyone to graze his goats.

We had lessons in the afternoon, but Allak arrived at school early in the morning to avoid doing household chores. He would move several desks together in the centre of the classroom, lie down on them and catch up on his sleep. The monitor was supposed to wake him before lessons began. Allak would be very angry when he was awakened and would even curse.

We tolerated such goings on for a long time, but then became angry and decided not to wake Allak and spend the lessons running about the corridor. The noise in the school was unimaginable. We chased each other and screamed as loud as we could.

At the very height of the fun a girl noticed two strangers in the school. They watched the rumpus goggle-eyed.

"Where's your teacher?"

"He's asleep."

"What?!"

"He's sleeping."

"Where?"

"In the classroom."

"Since when?"

"Since morning."

"Does your teacher always sleep during classes?"

"No, only when the principal's away."

The men headed for the classroom from where Allak's mighty snoring was coming. We all became still.

"How do you wake up your teacher?" the men asked.

"We squeeze his nose shut. When he opens his mouth we hold his mouth too. Then he opens his eyes."

Soon we had a new principal and a new teacher.

Recalling these events, I walked along a path through some thick undergrowth. My feet were scratched by thorns, but I paid no attention. Only one thought occupied me: had the girls come or not. Finally, I couldn't stand the suspense any longer, turned back, got a good running start and jumped over the *aryk*. Yagmur was seated under the mulberry-tree with a book in his hands, all alone. Had Kuvanch deceived us? Or maybe Jakhan was angry with me?

"Yagmur, haven't the helpers come yet?"

He lifted his head from the book and answered smiling:

"They've come. They're digging an *aryk* near Bilgir's."

"And who came?"

"Bostan and Jakhan. Don't stand there like an image! Sit down."

"What are you reading?"

"*Shukura bakhshi.*"

"Where'd you get the book?"

"Jakhan gave it to me to read."

I grabbed the book from Yagmur's hands. It was the book I had put the letter in. Leafing through it quickly, I found nothing.

"What are you looking for in the book?"

"Nothing."

Yagmur went back to read the book, and I sat and threw some pebbles into the muddy water. All of a sudden, the water began to flow back in the big *aryk*.

"Block the outlet!" shouted Yagmur. "The water with nitrogen mustn't flow back. What could've happened?"

"Allak probably closed the distributor."

"What would he do that for?"

"To catch fish."

"Why should he close the distributor? He fishes with a rod."

"He wants to use a net," I said. "When the gate of the distributor is closed the fish swim towards it. Didn't you know that?" I rushed in the direction of the distributor.

As I had expected, Allak was standing up to the waist in the water with a net in his hands. Sheat-fish and carps were thrashing on the bank opening their mouths. I threw them back into the water.

Crazy with anger, Allak jumped out of the water, grabbed the spade and rushed after me stark naked. Seeing Allak's bloodshot eyes, I fled but he was hot on my heels. With the back of my head I could feel his hissing breath. It was difficult to believe that such a stout man could run so fast. I reached the field where the farm-workers were resting after weeding. Naked Allak was right behind me. Women and girls buried their faces in their hands and dropped to the ground screaming. Only Kuvanch and Aunty Orazgyul watched us.

Suddenly the loud breathing behind me ceased and I turned round. Something round and white, like a fodder pumpkin, was rolling back across the cotton field.

"Who was chasing you?"

"I don't know."

"Didn't you see his face?"

"I did. It was all hairy. Maybe it was a jinni?"

"Where'd he come from?"

"Why, from the water of course!"

The women wailed in fear:

"O Lord, protect us!"

"You must be to blame for it," said Orazgyul wiping her lips with parched hands. "You probably hid his clothes, and that's why he was running after you naked. My Allak's a meek man, he wouldn't harm a fly."

I saw that Orazgyul had recognised her son. I didn't want to humiliate him before everyone. It was fortunate that his wife Bagdagyul was not there. She would've given it to me.

Coming back, I gave Yagmur a colourful account of what had happened. He almost split laughing.

At noon we came to the mulberry-tree growing near Bilgir's yard.

Jakhan and Bostan had made a fire and put the *tunchas** on the fire.

Bostan shouted to us:

"If you want tea, gather some brushwood."

"If you're treating us to tea, you should get the brushwood yourself," said Yagmur.

Bostan took our *tunchas* off the fire without saying anything.

"Bostan, don't be angry, it was a joke," Yagmur pleaded.

"It was a stupid joke, unworthy of a *jigit*."

Jakhan took our *tunchas* and put them on the fire again.

Yagmur put his hand on my shoulder and suggested:

"Let's go get some brushwood."

Having gathered an armful Yagmur returned to the fire, while I kept on walking around and picking up some sticks afraid of approaching Jakhan.

"Are you looking for a treasure?" I suddenly heard Jakhan's voice. When I returned to the fire, Jakhan handed me a cup of strong tea without looking at me. I couldn't make a single gulp.

"What's wrong, Kuvanch?" asked Yagmur.

"Perhaps he's got a headache?" said Bostan and

Tuncha—a small copper pot. —*Tr.*

laughed. Then she took the *tuncha* with a broken handle, handed it to me and bid me bring some water. Before I made a few steps, I heard Bostan's derisive voice:

"Kuvanch, can't you take the second *tuncha* or are you afraid you'll strain yourself?"

I turned and saw Jakhan get up, take the *tuncha* and come toward me. I couldn't make myself wait for her but was unable to walk properly either, and so I limped like a hobbled horse. Jakhan caught up with me very quickly. My knees were giving way. We walked to the *aryk* in silence. When I stooped to scoop the water Jakhan asked me quickly:

"Did you write the letter?"

"Yyyes..." All went dark before my eyes and I almost fell into the *aryk*.

"Did you write the poetry yourself?"

"Myself."

"Why are you lying? The poem is Mollanepes' 'Gozel'.* You just replaced Gozel with Jakhan."

I didn't know what to answer. I never read Mollanepes.

"If you write another letter, I'll push you into the *aryk*!"

"I'll write it anyway."

"I'll tell Father, and he'll box your ears."

"Let him!"

"Why're you so bold?"

"Jakhan, let's be friends."

Jakhan laughed, grabbed the *tuncha* from my hands,

Mollanepes Kadyrberdy ogly (1810-1862)—a Turkmen poet and musician. —Ed.

filled it with water and walked away quickly, and I trudged after her. Suddenly she turned and said:

"What if I pour water over you?"

"Do!"

She bit her lip, then smiled:

"What if you catch a cold?"

When we reached the fire, Bostan and Yagmur were quietly talking about something and didn't notice us. Jakhan cleared her throat.

"Why'd you return so quickly?" asked Bostan and eyed us in annoyance.

"We can go if we are in the way."

"Never mind! Let's sing a song while the tea is coming to a boil," said Yagmur and sat on a thick branch. The girls sat next to him.

I climbed up to the highest branch. Bostan said smilingly:

"Even if you fall off the branch, you'll never reach the ground," and looked at Jakhan. But the latter pretended that she hadn't heard.

Bostan and Jakhan began to sing. The song floated over the old fences behind which our fathers and forefathers had lived, over the wide cotton fields. It seemed that nature was holding its breath to listen to the girls.

Meanwhile life in the village went its way.

Aunty Orazgyul, her son Allak and daughter-in-law Bagdagyul are our neighbours. Many of their window-panes are broken and old sweaters stop up the holes.

Aunty Orazgyul often scolds her son and daughter-in-law:

"Idlers, do-nothings. You're used to being served by others."

Aunty Orazgyul's voice can be heard all over the village. As soon as dawn breaks she begins to yell:

"Allak, Bagdagyul! Will you wake up? I milked the cow and made the tea."

After these words Bagdagyul usually opened her eyes, stretched sleepily and got up. Allak would go on sleeping. Then Aunty Orazgyul would begin to curse him:

"I wish you'd sleep forever." But, having said the words, she would be frightened and wail in fear: "O Allah, forgive me, I'm a sinner and I take my words back."

Bagdagyul would watch her mother-in-law unperturbed.

It was even more fun to watch the goings-on in their house in the summer, when Allak slept on the roof. He always lifted the ladder after he had climbed up. Scolding and cursing, Aunty Orazgyul would run around the house, but Allak was out of reach. She would finally lose her temper, start throwing stones at Allak. But she did not have enough strength and the stones did not reach the roof. Then Orazgyul would bring her daughter-in-law and force her to throw stones. But Bagdagyul's stones flew over the roof.

"Are you afraid of hitting your lazy husband?" asked Orazgyul angrily.

"And you're afraid of hitting your lazy son."

"I have one foot in the grave. I don't have enough strength."

"I've got too much strength. We need someone of average strength."

Aunty Orazgyul ran to our house and grabbed me by the hand.

"Come along, my boy."

"I'm late as it is. Kuvanch-aga asked me to come earlier today."

"Only two stones, my boy, only two."

"He'll never get up with only two stones!"

At first I was quite eager to throw stones at Allak. But soon it palled. I had to throw stones for at least half an hour to wake him. And unless a stone hit him really hard, he did not get up anyway.

One day Yagmur and I found a wasps' nest in the undergrowth. I wrapped it carefully in paper, so not one of the wasps could fly away, and waited impatiently for Aunty Orazgyul to call me to throw stones. It was not a long wait, she came running the next morning.

"Come along, my boy."

I held the paper package in my left hand and stones in my right hand. It was difficult to throw the stones because my left hand was occupied. Bagdagyul came out of the house yawning.

"When will this end?" she said. "Even snakes and scorpions do not touch a sleepy head."

"All right, I won't throw any more stones."

I made to go home, but Aunty Orazgyul stopped me:

"Well, did you wake him?"

"No, I didn't. Bagdagyul told me not to throw any more stones."

"If that lazy-bones were a real woman, Allak would

keep his nose to the grindstone. No, let's go and throw some more!"

I returned.

"Why're you holding that damned parcel?" Bagdagyul cried. "You've come here to throw stones, but you hold on to that parcel like a babe to its dummy. Give me that thing." Bagdagyul pulled the paper and I felt a bite in my palm.

I jerked my hand back. Half the paper remained in Bagdagyul's hands. The wasps flew in all directions buzzing.

Bagdagyul was the first to start running, followed by Aunty Orazgyul, screaming curses. Orazgyul flew like an arrow, not thinking where she was going and soon overtook Bagdagyul. The ends of her kerchief waved like flags. She ran waving her hands. I laughed, but at that point my left eyelid was tinged by pain. I also began to wave my hands to ward off the wasps. I felt bites on my ear and on my nose. I ran towards the *aryk* and dived into it. Allak stood up on the roof and shouted to me:

"Are you catching fish, or what?"

When I came home Mother cried out in horror:

"Whatever happened to you?"

I was in no hurry to explain what had happened.

"What happened to your eyes and your lips?" she wailed. "I'll show that Allak how to torment my only son," she grabbed an iron poker and ran to Orazgyul's house.

"Ma, the wasps bit me," I mumbled through swollen lips.

Mother didn't understand what I said but lingered

a moment, then rushed on again with agility such as only children are capable of.

"Mother, wait, it's wasps!" I shouted as loudly as I could.

"Wasps? Those damned wasps!" A rag immediately appeared in her hands God knows from where, she moistened it and began to apply it to the bitten places. A red rash appeared on my body. "We must get a red dress."

Mother borrowed a red dress from Jakhan.

"Go into the room and put on the dress," ordered Mother.

I entered the house and hugged the dress. It seemed to me that Jakhan was next to me.

"Did you put it on?" I heard Mother's voice from outside. "Sit still, it'll soon be over. I'm going to work."

My whole body burned, and Jakhan's folded dress lay on my lap. I brought it to my face and felt the familiar smell. My heart melted and I forgot about pain.

After that even Allak stopped sleeping on the roof. But he and Bagdagyul continued to be late for work and did not appear in the fields before midday.

Kuvanch decided to attend to Allak and Bagdagyul personally. One morning he came to their house and tried to wake them but all his attempts proved futile. Then he poured cold water on them. Allak and Bagdagyul screamed in fright.

On the same day Kuvanch suggested at the team-meeting to fine Allak and Bagdagyul for violating work discipline.

"Why are you persecuting us, you beardless pest?

What harm have we done you?" cried Bagdagyul.

"You work badly."

On the next day Allak told Kuvanch that he was leaving the team and the collective farm altogether.

"Where'll you work, Allak?"

"I'll drive the bread waggon in the district centre. I've been already taken on."

"You'll eat all the bread."

"That's none of your business."

Allak walked off.

"You won't be able to work anywhere," Kuvanch cried after him.

Getting ready to move, Allak and Bagdagyul decided to take along the firewood they had piled up near the Jepbi *aryk*. Before sunset they harnessed the donkey and set out for the wood. The road was all full of ruts. The reeds caught at the waggon shafts. The going was very difficult. On the way back the overloaded waggon got stuck. Bagdagyul began to whip the donkey furiously with a chain while the husband pushed from behind.

"Give it to him!" Allak shouted ever so often.

"The donkey is not like me, it's not afraid of your yells."

"Then I'll harness you instead of the donkey!"

"I told you to load less wood, it's better to make ten trips than get stuck."

"As if I could force you to make even two trips!"

"If you were a man, a woman wouldn't have to bother with firewood."

"Do you mean I'm not a man?"

"Oh, you are a man."

"Then shut your mouth!"

At this point the shaft broke.

In despair and anger Allak set fire to the reed bush. The flame flared up and spread to the waggon in an instant.

Frightened by the fire the donkey jerked the waggon free and galloped as fast as it could, dragging along the flaming waggon.

"Stop the donkey, stop it!" shouted Allak.

But it was too late.

The donkey flew ahead of the burning waggon along the road that divided the village into two parts. It burst into the shed with the burning wreckage.

When Yagmur and I reached the place, not only the shed but also Aunty Orazgyul's house was on fire. The entire village helped put it out. So did I. As I was leading the calf out of the burning shed, a burning beam caved in. Falling, it grazed my shoulder and side. The shirt on me caught fire. The calf and I shot out of the shed. People threw a felt mat on me. Nevertheless, I got burnt and was taken to hospital.

Mother, Kuvanch, Yagmur and Bostan visited me. But the visitor I awaited most eagerly was Jakhan. They told me that Aunty Orazgyul's house had burned down almost completely, but that the villagers had decided to help them build a new house.

"Aren't they moving?"

"No, they've changed their minds," said Kuvanch.

Having recounted all the news the visitors left. I was left alone with my bitter thoughts. I was thinking about Jakhan. Why hadn't she come? Why hadn't I burnt to death? The day dragged on agonisingly.

In the evening the nurse opened the door to my ward and said:

"Visitor for you, Kuvanch. No, don't move, you're not permitted to move!"

I didn't hear what she was saying. Jakhan stood in the doorway. I rose on my elbows. Tears of happiness welled up in my eyes.

Jakhan sat down on the edge of the bed in silence. I realised that if one of us said even a word we would both burst out crying.

Finally, Jakhan took herself in hand and said:

"Does it hurt?"

"No, it doesn't."

"Tomorrow I'll bring you some goose fat. It's good for burns."

"Don't worry, it'll be all right. I only fear that a light spot will be left on my side from the burn and they'll call me Spot, like a dog."

"Silly boy."

Jakhan bent down, kissed me on the cheek and quickly walked out of the ward.

I forgot everything in the world, my soul was so light and easy.

I lay there with eyes closed and smiled. I saw Jakhan in a red dress which was fluttering in the wind. There was so much I wanted to say to her, and not in simple words but in verse. And I must write those verses myself. Now I would be able. I would write them by all means!

Lev Salnikov

THE RING

Lev Salnikov was born in Moscow in 1946. He has a degree in engineering from the Moscow Polytechnic Institute, and worked in industry for several years after graduating, before taking up a post in a scientific-research institute. He is an excellent sportsman.

His first writing appeared in 1969. He has since published *First Trials*, a collection of short stories. *The Ring*, a short novel about boxers, was awarded the annual prize of the magazine *Smena*.

1

He was sitting in the changing-room alone, leaning against the back of the hard bench, dozing a bit, with his body relaxed and his eyes slightly closed. Pa Ashot wouldn't have approved if he'd seen him like that. Relaxing is fine, even necessary before you go into the ring, but dozing isn't. It takes away the body's "springiness".

But Pa Ashot wasn't around. He'd gone into the ring to get the feel of the audience. So Val had allowed himself this little digression... But people kept opening the door and peeping in. It was impossible to get any privacy.

"Never mind, it's better this way," he reassured himself. "I'd probably wind right down otherwise."

Val got up and went out into the corridor again. It had grown quite crowded out there. Coaches were passing through, seconds dashing about, relatives strolling around, friends of the contestants huddling in little bunches, talking happily, cheering continually.

"Mine might turn up too," Val thought, looking at the agitated faces. "Serge will come for sure, and probably drag someone else along with him as well."

Val didn't like the hangers-on, especially the regular fans. He tried hard to remain indifferent, but always felt a pleasant tingling running along his nerves—which, in a boxer, should remain particularly invulnerable.

He went back into the changing-room and closed the door behind him.

The smell of sweat was even stronger here: the sweet healthy sweat of hot muscles mingling with the rich odour of the vaseline which Val had smeared, like most boxers, in a thin layer across the parts of his face most in need of protection from cuts and bruises: his eyebrows, cheekbones, and the bridge of his nose.

There was still some time left, and he was free to use it as he wanted—at least in his thoughts. He chose to think about his opponent.

By and large he's a loudmouth. That's what our "adult class" boxers call him—adding with a smile that all their lot are like that, from the coach down. But I don't agree with this pulling people to pieces outside the ring. This morning our teams happened to be together at the weighing-in. The boys were stripping off, laughing at each other, then stepping on to the scales and, once they'd weighed themselves, going to get dressed again. Pa Ashot had said quietly:

"Their boys are all big talkers, but they still know how to fight."

He wagged his finger at us meaningfully.

At breakfast in the canteen, our light-heavyweight Alexei sat at my table. Two bruises were spreading under his eyes from the place where the bridge of his nose had been smashed in yesterday's fight. Nodding over to the table next to the juke-box, he said:

"Look over by the music machine. Do you see that chatterbox? He's your opponent for today. Take a good look at him."

I didn't answer, but I felt a sudden emptiness and fluttering in my stomach. I just can't look at my opponent before it's time. Meanwhile our light-heavyweight went rambling on:

"Pa Ashot, by the way, when he was a young man,

used to have a couple of drinks before every fight and then lay them all out all the same. Yours can really knock them back too. Don't worry about it, Val. You've got a nice pair of legs. They work well. Your left straight is very pretty, and your right comes at them like something out of the blue."

But I had already stopped listening to him. I was looking at "my man". He had cheerfully opened a long-necked bottle of wine, and was absorbing his friends in some entertaining story. The wine he poured into their glasses was transparent and slightly shot with gold against the background of the big sunny window. It wasn't the drink which amazed me— though it didn't figure in my idea of Sport—but his cheerful acceptance of everything life might offer, when the heavyweights and light-heavyweights—moving like fantastic robots with lilac, red and blue bruises under their eyes—were walking and sitting all around him; and the gloomy, unsuccessful losers were silently scrutinising the surrounding people. Winking at the waitress, my opponent was proposing a toast. I could overhear the words:

"If you don't knock one back in the Bar, you won't knock one out in the Ring."

He seems a bit temperamental, this "adult class" boxer who is my opponent today. He's only the third "adult" I've met in this competition, or actually in any competition I've taken part in so far. He is temperamental... I forced myself to go on watching him. Yes he is temperamental... In the ring and out of it. It was particularly obvious just now, as he was sitting at the table, that the main feature of his character was a lack of self-control. I distinctly recollected his last fight and the persistent doubt which had bothered me while I was watching it: there was something not quite right about him even though he out-boxed his opponent ... or rather, "out-slashed". But what was it? Was he temperamental from an excess of energy, or from worry? Take me for instance. When I'm on form, I'm always calm, even—so they tell me—a bit cold. Whereas when I'm worried, I mope around all over the place. Perhaps these things affect people differently. His fight was straight after mine yesterday. That's why my coach didn't take me to the changing-room as usual after my victory had been announced, but instead helped me to struggle into my track suit with my sweaty body, wound my neck with a towel to make me sweat more and so reduce my weight, and pushed me back into the audience.

"Watch very carefully! Tomorrow's winner will be clear today—now!"

I decided not to climb high in the stands, but got a place at the bottom of the steps of one of the gangways. The grown-up lad I was squatting beside smiled at me and, nodding towards the ring where the fight had already started, said knowingly:

"One of them's your opponent for tomorrow, isn't he?"

I nodded. He rubbed his hands, grinned, and said:

"So now we'll see what sort of a fish you've got for tomorrow. You really wiped the floor with today's."

"Oh yes," I thought, listening to him with one ear, but concentrating my attention on the ring, where a mutual "carve-up" had been going on since the very first minute. Oh yes... "wiped the floor" ... if it hadn't been for Pa Ashot...

But the lad went on:

"You know to tell you the truth, I didn't really go for you at first... Well, I said to myself, what kind of a boxer is he supposed to be? He backs away, hides, dodges, weaves in and out; but he doesn't land any punches—which is what boxing is all about after all. He just pokes a bit with his left... And I completely gave up on you at the end of the first round. That was the end I thought. That was curtains. But you were all right. I saw you get moving. And that did it. That turned the tables. That's how you should always do it. Get straight in there, straight in."

I could suddenly picture the fight I had just finished. After the bell announcing the first round, we had come together in the middle of the ring, and I had stretched out my gloves towards my opponent in the traditional greeting. But he pretended not to have understood my intention. He struck out sharply with his left and connected with my chin—not very strongly, but enough to make itself felt. My consciousness shifted for a moment. His face went completely black, like a negative. I flung myself forward, but the dimness in my eyes prevented me from finding my bearings. I would always run into a permanent barrage of stop blows, and at the end of the first round I suddenly found myself on the floor... Back on my feet again, I listened to the referee's counting in bewilderment, and when, after the count of "Eight!" and the command "Box!", my opponent rushed down on me, and having got me squeezed up in the corner, was obviously intent on "grinding me up"—though his coach was shouting to him not to "do the youth right in"—all my confusion suddenly evaporated and everything changed. I quickly regained my strength. Pa Ashot, in the interval between the rounds, had softly but impressively brought home to me (I could see his eyes, his heavy eyelids and moistened eyelashes very close to me) that I should never repeat this piece of negligence again, that I should re-start the fight as though from the very beginning, and follow the plan which we had worked out together beforehand. And that's just what I did do. I started the second round with a light left straight, and at the end of it, when he had grown noticeably groggy, knocked him out with a glancing left which caught him exactly on the point of the chin. And though there was no doubt that this punch had emerged purely by chance— "Jumped out by accident like all knock out blows," as Pa Ashot said later—it was already becoming my typical punch—again according to Pa Ashot. Pa said: "Don't think consciously about this punch. Put it right out of your mind. Then, subconsciously, it'll come back to you on its own."

I was roused from my recollections by a sharp nudge from my neighbour.

"Just look how your bloke threshes his arms. He'll be a hard nut for you to crack... Believe me, I know this kind. Just watch him knock the wind out of this lamp-post now."

By "lamp-post" he meant the tall red-haired bloke from the Burevestnik Club. I had seen him several times in the Ring, in various competitions for "adult class" boxers. He was very disconcerting. Everything he did was haphazard. His technique was crooked and his punches were scattered: a "snag" we would call him in boxing. Fighting with him gave you the permanent impression that he could launch a punch from behind the back, from under his leg or from any old place: that's how irregular he seemed. His punches were sticky and he himself seemed glutinous and impregnable. I've always been afraid of such opponents, and I was now very glad to see him losing.

Yet by and large the fight was uninteresting. It was violent too, as is usual with "adult class" boxers; the "youth class" know that well. Watching the "adult" boxing competitions, I'd noticed another thing which distinguishes them from "youth" fights. They are in some way merciless. I can't explain it; but I always feel it in my guts. I feel my stomach rising. And this time too, I was amazed by the power of the punches from both boxers, and, more especially, by the number of them which were let through on both sides.

"Look how they're feeding each other," my neighbour said quietly, but with apparent admiration and, shaking his head, gave me a meaningful glance, as much as to say: "Hold tight tomorrow, lad!"

And now this same man must be sitting in the audience, waiting for my entrance and thinking: "What kind of fish is this lad who was sitting next to me yesterday, apparently watching his opponent so calmly and indifferently. What has he got to offer against the tough, fine fencer who is coming out against him now. He's just a youth—maybe a talented one—but a youth nevertheless."

Yes. What indeed?

And Val felt how his stomach contracted without his wanting it to. He swallowed. His mouth had gone dry. He could feel the tension across his hollow cheeks and strained cheekbones.

2

He was due on after the fourth pair. Nothing unexpected should happen in these four fights—he knew all the boxers well. He was almost ready now. Only the gloves were left, and they had just been brought by a boy, one of the voluntary assistants in the judges' party and, as usual, the kind of weedy-looking kid he had once been himself—or at least a lot of people had considered him like that in the club to which his schoolmates had taken him. The boy gave Val the gloves, smiled ingratiatingly, and then silently walked over to one side where he could watch Val pressing them, stretching them, and trying them on without lacing them.

Val suddenly grinned at him. The boy's eyes lit up immediately with grateful delight and embarrassment in response and, blushing happily, he disappeared behind the door.

Val smiled to himself, as though he had suddenly discovered in this world narrowed down to the square of the Ring, something so simple, and at the same time so extraordinarily beautiful, that it made the coming fight seem suddenly trivial in comparison. This unforeseen discovery had put him into a cheerful and lighthearted frame of mind.

Dancing slightly on his light, springy feet, he went the length of the room and back, jumped on to a bench and, making its wide board bend beneath his weight by bouncing up and down on it, jumped back to the floor and did a handstand. Taking away first his right hand, then his left, he stood for a while on his right hand again, then a bit longer on the left, pleasantly savouring its strength with a feeling of cheerfulness and daring. Then, turning in the air, he sprang lightly on to both feet at once. Now he felt really good. This was probably, he thought, the real Joy of Sport—the Joy which is called Fair Play.

He looked into the neighbouring, coaches' compartment of the changing-room, then went up to Pa Ashot, waited for him to finish changing his shoes, sat down next to him, and put the gloves down between them on the wide bench.

The only thing which remained to be done was to put them on and lace them up, though in such a way that the hand would not feel it was in a glove: as Pa Ashot always said. Pa would lace them up for Val himself, without haste, chatting about one thing and another, little by little getting him into the mood of the fight, accurately, confidently and lovingly working at his pupil's hand...

"That's the lot," he said, puffing importantly and tucking the ends of the laces in under the cuffs, which were now tightly bound around Val's wrists. "Break them in a bit, knock them together, then do two rounds of shadow boxing, without straining, just to get yourself into a light sweat."

The gloves were new as always in competitions at

this level. They seemed so stiff that the youths called them "ironing boards".

Val wriggled his fingers, which were now packed tightly, knuckle to knuckle, under the special elastic bandage inside. He rolled one glove up and down the other for a while, pressing the leading bulges—that's the striking edges—one against the other. He hit the clenched left glove into the palm of the open right, then the clenched right into the open left. One! Two! Three! He folded his thumbs—which are the most vulnerable part of the hands in a bad punch—as comfortably as possible, then he dropped both arms downwards simultaneously, relaxing them completely. He lifted both arms back to shoulder level and shook them several times, getting rid of the remaining tension. Then he dropped them again, finally convincing himself that he was ready for the fight. There was no feeling in his hands or arms any more, just a sense that they were there: not as a part of his body, but already as something independent, with a life and capability for action of their own, reducing Val's role to that of an interested spectator.

He moved away from the centre of the corridor and did one or two rounds of shadow boxing, rested for a moment and then approached his coach, who was also standing in the corridor. He was sweating slightly, but his breathing was light and free.

Pa Ashot sat Val down in the wide arm-chair beside him, and covered his shoulders, back and arms with a big thick towel. They sat like that in silence for a couple of minutes. Then they stood up. Pa Ashot lifted the towel off again, wiped Val's face, neck, shoulders and arms, put the towel on the back of the arm-chair, and stepped to one side. Holding his hands out flat in front of him, palms upwards, and dancing in the way a boxer does when choosing the right position for a punch, he started moving forwards towards Val, explaining as he did so, what to do when the opponent started to attack. Then he repeated the exercise, this time making Val attack. Then he "twisted him" for a while, speeding it up as they closed in together. At last he broke the distance, and, panting hard, taking fire and getting Val into the same state by doing so, made him attack in his turn, with straight punches to the head from both fists. Having gradually built up the speed to the maximum, he finished this warm-up with his back to the wall, defending himself from Val's quick, light, sparring blows—One-two! Left-right!—showing him, in this way, just how and where he should finish the fight.

"That's it!" Pa Ashot breathed out sharply when he heard the sound of the bell coming from the Ring. "Just two rounds to go now. Walk around for a bit, then put a towel over you, and sit here with your eyes closed till I come. I'll go and see why they're making such a noise out there."

And with a worried expression, he hurriedly disappeared behind the door, leaving Val alone with his thoughts.

3

Val Kardin had ended up in the Stroitel Amateur Sports Association by chance. At first he used to go to the Locomotive Club—it was near his home in Komsomolskaya, the Moscow square with three railway stations. He'd got his Grade Three Boxing Certificate there, and had a sound training in outfighting with Alexandrov, the ex-Champion of the Navy: a clever, proud but unlucky man with light brown hair on a firm, bony skull, and brows which were scarred by long years of boxing. Alexandrov had no Coaching Diploma—he'd never stayed long enough in one place.

Alexandrov did not stay long in the Locomotive Club either. To his pupils, especially the ones close to him, he said:

"I'm giving up Sport. You stay here for a while. If I take up a job as a coach anywhere, I'll come and fetch you."

He never came back, and nobody knew where he'd disappeared to. For a long time Val would see Alexandrov's scarred brows in his dreams; and he would wake from these dreams like someone coming round from unconsciousness. Then all day he would think, with a heavy feeling of helplessness, about the coming evening's work in the unfamiliar sports hall.

"Ashot Petrovich just looks askance at us out of the corner of his eye. He pays practically no attention to us. So where's the proverbial impartiality of the coach. Three of us have already given up and left: the first to Dynamo where he has a friend; the second to Burevestnik; and the third flitted about from one place to another, didn't settle anywhere, and in the end grew bitter and gave up Sport altogether—either because of the difficult personality which Alexandrov had been developing but the other coaches would just laugh at, or for some other reason, perhaps, because new groups of boys don't always welcome you with open arms straight away. Out of all the boys I am the only one who is left here, and I'll leave here for somewhere else too. But where? The boys who were our friends at the Locomotive don't say hello to us at the competitions. They think of us as traitors. And I don't want to go to any other clubs—I don't feel at home in any of them. But I don't feel at home here in the Stroitel either. Whenever I have to go to a training session I feel such a strong sense of reluctance inside... It's as though I have to go behind enemy lines."

Once, at one of these unwelcome training sessions, when he was sparring with a pupil of Ashot Petrovich's who was physically strong but quite straightforward in technique, Val, who was winning round after round without particular effort, had let his mind go wandering back to the past... He remembered his coach Alexandrov, and how he had trained his straight left to be as reliable and accurate as it was being now, giving Val the means—from any position and as often and from as many directions as he wanted—to break through the defence of this close-cropped, round-headed, robust opponent with his strong fists and mighty arms. He remembered the small hall of the Locomotive Club in Komsomolskaya, and himself, thirteen years old, carrying his plimsolls under his arm, waiting for his fate to be decided. The coach, a tall, stooping man with broken brows which hung down over his eyes like two enormous sunshades, was looking down at him from above, deciding whether to take the boy or

389

not. "He's added a year on to his age of course. He isn't fourteen yet. That's why he's afraid to look up at me. Physically he's not so hot, but he's shy, and that's good. He'll work hard...

"Okay. Get changed and stand in line."

He had been accepted! He would prove that the coach was not mistaken! If they would only let him out into the ring, even with a Third-Grader...

And the coach did let him out into the ring that day, and gave him the chance to go two rounds with a Third-Grader...

A strong blow on the head had jerked him back to the present. His feet became immediately unsteady. He was being swung to the left, to the right, he felt himself being pulled down to the floor. He was still resisting, trying not to go down, when suddenly something started to drag him backwards. With an enormous effort he straightened his back, which seemed to have stopped obeying him. He had already lost control of his feet—it was as though they belonged to somebody else, and were leading him at an unsteady pace along the ropes...

Ashot Petrovich stopped the bout at once. He helped Val climb through the ropes and took him over to one side, giving him time to regain his breathing and consciousness. Looking at him guiltily, he said:

"You don't pay enough attention to defence... But you see, I've got so many of my own pupils. If you want, you can join us. Then we'll work hard. But you seem to be worth working with. Think it over."

Val stood for a long time under the cool jet of water in the shower-room. His feeling of nausea had already gone, but the mesh he kept seeing in front of his right eye would not go away, however hard he rubbed it or screwed it up...

He was the last person to leave the changing-room. As he was saying goodbye to Ashot Petrovich, without lifting his eyes from the floor, he gave him his consent.

4

His new coach, the former light-heavyweight champion of the Soviet Union, was an Armenian, big and cumbersome to look at, but still light on his feet, and with a rapid way of walking. His curly hair was jet-black, shiny ánd wiry; he had a stern Caucasian face and angry eyes. An engineer by profession, he worked in the Planning and Design Institute and gave up all his evenings and weekends to coaching. His mood was permanently gloomy and preoccupied, as though he were under the weight of a difficult and insoluble choice about the right direction he should take in life; or perhaps he used to get so tired that he just couldn't smile any more. Only on very rare occasions would his glance grow warmer: when one of his pupils placed a good punch, put up an excellent defence, or showed lightness and good tactical thinking in his positioning in the ring—because these were the things which mattered to him most.

"I want to make serious boxers out of you: true athletes, strong men," Ashot Petrovich used to say, standing in a corner of the ring, looking around the hushed boys. Starting flat and hollow, his voice, warmed by an inner heat, would grow more and more inspired with each word, enflaming the boys with enthusiasm:

"In the end, I want you to understand that Sport isn't a game, or an entertainment, or a recreation. Sport is the beginning of a responsible life for each of you."

At the end of each session, when the boys had finished sparring, or practising with the various pieces of equipment, and had taken their gloves off, unwound their bandages and were finishing the last circuit or doing warm-down exercises, Ashot Petrovich would sit down on a low bench by the edge of the ring, and start to talk about the necessity for sportsmanship—which was no less important, in his opinion, than the need for physical training.

"In the Ring, the audience can read your life like an open book. Just a couple of minutes and a dozen movements—examples of technique, punches—and the spectator can already see who he's got in front of him. He can see it! And that decides if he'll help you, or stop you winning... And so he should stop you, if you're not worth it. A sportsman doesn't go out onto the ring—or the stage, the mat, or whatever—so that the girls can clap their hands. He goes there to overcome his weak points and also to win a victory over the best in his chosen activity. Do you understand what that means? To win! That means growing as a human being, growing one level higher: so that Life can move forward."

5

Pa Ashot returned surprisingly soon. He came into the changing-room quickly, obviously worried, almost het up, apparently even confused.

Val jumped up to meet his coach. His stomach contracted; his feet were ceasing to obey him.

"Time for me to go on," said Val, dropping his voice to a whisper for some reason, as he tried to stop the towel falling from his shoulders... "It's already time..."

Ashot Petrovich stopped abruptly, and pulled himself together with a noticeable effort of will. He came up closer, bent down calmly, picked up the towel, shook it, and covered Val's back and shoulders with it again. Then he sat him down in the arm-chair once more.

"Why have you got up? Why have you left the corridor? It's a long way from the ring here. You can't hear anything. You could easily go off the boil."

"What's happened?" asked Val, sensing the state that Pa Ashot was in despite his trying to hide it.

"Sit still, sit still, nothing special... That young lad was a bit on the weak side anyway... His coach is a sensible bloke. He threw the towel in time."

Val realised who Pa Ashot was talking about: the youth from Trudoviye Reserve Club, who was the same age as Val, and only one weight class lower. This year—like Val—he had fought for the National Youth Team in the European Championship, and—also like Val—he had brought back a gold medal. That was why both of them had been allowed to take part in the National Championship of the Soviet Union. Now, suddenly, he'd been defeated—and resoundingly, as was clear from the referee's "stopped contest" decision... Of course, in such a situation, the towel doesn't necessarily mean a real "stopped contest"... Perhaps his coach wanted to be on the safe side... But still... That moment must have been the limit.

Val suddenly became aware of his coach's voice:

"I'm talking to you but you aren't listening! I'm talking to you but your aren't listening! How many times do I have to tell you?"

Close by, he saw his coach's face, watching him in alarm, not corresponding to the irritated voice.

"In the Ring nothing is trivial. Age doesn't count. There's only skill, intelligence and will. Well..." Pa Ashot put his arm round Val's shoulders, looked at him with unusually shining eyes, and said:

"Let's go now. Without hurrying..."

From the window-sill Pa Ashot took a round plastic jar. It contained the gum-shield—a protective rubber ring which is put over the upper teeth to guard the inner surface of the lips from cuts under the impact of blows and knocks. Then he threw a towel over his arm, and looked Val up and down again with attentive—but now almost cold—eyes. Letting Val go first, he set off behind him into the shadowy corridor.

It was almost empty. Before they had gone even a few steps, Serge jumped out to meet them from the steps of the nearest passageway leading to the stands.

"Your opponent is already in the ring. It's the second time they've announced a call for Kardin."

"Shut up," snarled Pa Ashot, and gave Serge such a

withering look that he recoiled against the wall. Pa Ashot stopped near the main boxers' entrance to the arena and stood still for a few seconds. Without looking back at Val, but feeling Val's almost audible breathing behind him, he resolutely parted the curtains with his free hand.

Val's attention was immediately absorbed by the blinding sugarcube whiteness of the ring, by the unbearably tense sense of expectation which was buzzing all around him in the stands.

He climbed on to the podium, ducked under the ropes and, taking his corner, cast a quick glance at the stand on the right. The boys were all there, looking tensely in his direction. They were sitting with their bodies forwards, pressing their hands down on their knees. And she was there too, in the same posture. He could even catch the expression in her face, which was drawn with strain and expectation—an expression which took form in his memory as one phrase: "It's impossible."

And immediately he answered the drift of her thoughts, which were silent, but to him very clear:

"Of course it's impossible... It's impossible to lose."

6

In the ring, the referee was already looking at Val's gloves, checking they were correctly laced, and examining his face for dangerous cuts, scratches or bruises, so that he could keep them under special surveillance, and stop the fight immediately if anything endangered the boxer's safety. When he'd finished the examination, the referee turned to the coach with the traditional question: "Is the boxer ready?" Having received confirmation from Pa Ashot, he went over to the opposite corner and Val's opponent. But Val had decided not to look over there... Glancing as quickly as possible to see if his opponent was ready, trying to define his mood, or seeking out signs of worry in his face—none of that was necessary now. The main thing was his own state.

He was rubbing the leather soles of his boxing-boots with rosin. "Rosin-powder increases the friction of leather on canvas"—he suddenly remembered Alexandrov's instructions to him when he started. It was the time he won his first fight in "the Open Ring". After that he'd won a second, then one more, then again and again... And each time, returning to his victorious corner, he had seen Alexandrov's eyes: amber and transparent under the sunshades of his broken eyebrows, looking straight at him, encouraging him, promising a far-reaching and reliable future.

"Rosin-powder increases the friction of leather on canvas."

When he'd finished, Val suddenly pushed the shallow plywood box beyond the ropes with his foot, so that it knocked against Ashot Petrovich's feet. Pa looked at Val attentively, but didn't say anything. He started to massage Val's neck, particularly the back of it. That's where tiredness begins—as Ashot Petrovich knew very well.

Not understanding the reason for Val's sudden change of mood, but sensing that he wouldn't let it be altered, Ashot Petrovich wanted somehow, in these very last minutes, to dampen down his dangerous excitement.

"Get your nose warm, and guard it best of all. You're not breathing properly."

Val shook his head, but lightly massaged his nose with his glove a bit all the same—especially at its most vulnerable point. (He'd been accidentally hit there by someone's head at a training session a year ago, and the cartilage of his nose had been split. Ironically, it had been done by a beginner Val was teaching how to enter an in-fighting and then come out of it with a punch. And that was just how he did come out—only he punched with his head instead of his glove. A "butting" boxers call it.)

"Get it properly warm," snapped Pa Ashot, following, with bewilderment, the movements of his pupil, who was trying to avoid his gaze.

Val shook first one foot then the other, then his shoulders and his whole perspiring body. He rotated his neck from left to right, and then from right to left. He drew in a few deep breaths, and asked his coach for the gum-shield.

Quickly, Pa Ashot took the rather huge, but very soft piece of red rubber from its place in the jar full of water, and skilfully crammed it into Val's mouth, tightly covering the upper teeth.

Taking it with his tongue and lips, Val sucked it in firmly against his gums. Immediately, from behind his back, came the commanding voice of the referee:

"Boxers into the centre."

His whole body turned towards the voice, and he

started to walk lightly towards the middle of the ring, sensing the springiness of his step with pleasure. His opponent was coming towards him, smiling. Val smiled back. Both stretched their gloves out simultaneously, exchanged a handshake and searched each other's eyes. His opponent's eyes were small, cheerful, and shining with reckless courage. Such an attitude in the ring was beyond Val's comprehension. Though no-one had ever called him scared, it was what he called himself sometimes. And now that he sensed that his opponent's attitude was not bravado, but a permanent feature of his character, Val felt envious. "All I've got is my wariness: in my eyes and my whole body. Nothing else."

The referee gave them both their final instructions in "Sportsmanlike Behaviour", promised to judge them both strictly, wished them both success, and, spreading his arms wide like white wings of happiness soaring above the ring (this last image came back to Val from those distant—as they now seemed—times when he could only dream about boxing), motioned them both to their corners.

"Boxers ready!" The referee's voice came loudly and distinctly in the ensuing silence. "Round One!"

Val just had time to reach his corner and catch Pa Ashot's last piece of advice: "In the first round work on his torso..." The abrupt, cracklingly metallic sound of the bell reverberated, and for Val everything disappeared. He turned sharply and started to walk towards his enemy who, moving towards him, already in a fighting stance and no longer smiling, was all the time adjusting his left shoulder, trying to hide his chin more comfortably behind its cast-iron roundness. This shoulder amazed Val—amazed him because it was perfectly formed. For the first time he could really see the difference between the muscles of a man and the muscles of a youth. There it was—this shoulder—moving down on him with visible power. Closer and closer. Though he had not yet touched his opponent, he could already feel the hidden strength in every tendon and bulge of the dense and enormous body: a strength which was easily capable of breaking him—almost as it might break a toy—if he made even the slightest mistake. Yet, to his surprise, he was not scared of this emotion. He gathered his strength together even more, making himself into one solid piece of young muscle, still fluid, still malleable, still (you could almost say) raw—but springy and elastic, loaded with a wonderful energy, and containing an inexpressible sense of freedom.

With the silence of the strained, tensed audience, holding its breath, hanging above you, the first moments of closing together with an opponent are terrifying to the point of delight for both body and spirit. The audience is here, and all around you. You feel it with every pore of your skin and in every movement; yet at the same time it doesn't exist for you. There is nothing and nobody but the eyes of your opponent and the part of his face which constantly appears and disappears behind the continual movement—forward, back; up, down; right, left—of the leather gloves. The other things he is doing—the footwork, body shifts, turns, feints, lunges and so on—you see those too: but with a different, almost internal way of seeing, which training sessions have made automatic. In each fight—however many there have been in your experience of the sport—you have to think through every moment. You must evaluate each instant immediately, with no time to make a rough copy. You are graded for your decisions instantly: on your head, your body, and the most vulnerable pain centres of your nervous system. And in accordance with these grades, you reorganise your entire programme for the fight.

The bell sounds, and you are tormented by doubts for the endlessly long minutes, which afterwards, looking back, seem so interminable, that you wonder how they were ever squeezed into the span of the tentative first round. The interval flashes by. Round Two. This one is many times longer than the first—incomparably longer. In the second round, the outline of the fight usually starts to take shape, and it is here that the final form of one boxer's victory over another becomes clear. Then the third and final round, which the media—though they are far from the truth—usually call "the decisive one", lasts for an eternity. The third round really shows what you are made of—down to the very last detail.

7

Val had not yet managed to take the measure of his opponent as he ought to have done, or to feel, with the peculiar instinct of a boxer, what—for him—was exactly the right distance. Interposing his glove in a stop blow, he felt the weight of his opponent's "hammer" shudder through his whole body. Everybody had warned him about it, including Pa Ashot. Yet despite this he placed his feet wrongly and was caught on a half hop, bending his left arm in front of him and failing to stretch it out to its full length in time. He came up roughly against the extended fist of his opponent.

Something happened which Val had not foreseen at all—or, more precisely, had always recognised as a possibility, especially when his nose-bone and the split cartilage beneath it had not yet healed. He had recognised it as a possibility, but usually, at the training sessions, during sparring bouts or during the heats (tough as they were) he had not paid much attention to it—though more recently he had started to fear instinctively for his weak nose, which was so vulnerable to punches. And now here, during the first minute of the first round of the semi-final, his opponent had hit his nose—and not only hit it—that happened in almost every training session—but hit it very badly. Blood started to pour from both nostrils.

At first Val did not understand anything except the sudden feeling of sharp pain in his nose, shooting through his head like an electric shock and striking orange-green spurts of tears from both his eyes simultaneously. He continued moving quickly round the ring, but the tears distorted his opponent's face, shoulders and gloves. The strong flow of blood prevented him from breathing. Val pulled away and without ceasing to circle his opponent began making feints, side-steps, half-steps, retreats—left, right and back—trying to regain his equilibrium. His nose had grown numb and swollen, but still he was managing to breathe through it, keeping his mouth tightly closed to prevent the gum-shield from falling out.

He started to breathe unevenly and with greater and greater difficulty, letting punches through without the strength to give them the attention they deserved. He had only one thought now: not to suffocate.

In the end he couldn't stand it any longer. He spat the gum-shield out of his mouth to clear a passage for the air. Immediately he heard the audience gasp out at a fever pitch of tension. Either they caught their breath in surprise at seeing the red rubber gum-shield fall out and bounce on the white canvas of the ring, or they were reacting to the punch which followed, catching Val on the head with a left hook. It wasn't Val who jumped to one side himself—it was more that he was thrown back by this driving punch towards the ropes. It wasn't a strong blow, but one of those which usually impress the audience. Pushing himself free from the rebounding ropes, he escaped his pursuer with a sliding step to the left, and breathing freely, glanced quickly into the stands. He saw her immediately... She was sitting slightly apart from the boys, with her face buried in her hands. Serge, turned towards her, was trying to persuade her of something. But suddenly she stood up, shaking her head, and, without taking her hands from her face, started to make her way through towards the exit.

It wasn't the fact that she was afraid or felt sorry for him that surprised him. No! He was amazed by the sense of his own doom which he could read in her posture, in the hands covering her face, and, most of all, in her running away from the stands. "She is sure I'm finished..." It didn't insult him, or anger him; it just changed him. He suddenly pictured himself as such a miserable nonentity, messed up with his own blood, and he at once grew reserved and locked inside himself, as he always did when Life was unjust. He became completely indifferent, both to himself and his surroundings. He concentrated all his attention on his opponent, who was now chasing round the ring behind him, almost at a trot, obviously trying to drive the bewildered youth into a corner and close in to finish him off. And each time he just failed by a second. The youth would slip out of the corner, managing to avoid the punch, ducking under it, making an evasive movement with his torso, or deflecting the next series of heavy rights to one side, or—using his weak but quick straight left—extinguishing an attack in its inception, only to receive the weight of his opponent's enormous body, heated by the sense of imminent victory within its grasp. Lightly pushing away from it without punching, Val would somehow appear again in the very centre of the ring.

8

Pa Ashot was outside the ropes, sitting on the stool which is placed there for the boxer to rest on during the intervals between rounds. He was holding a wet towel in one hand and a gum-shield jar full of fresh water in the other. On the other stool, beside him, there was an aluminium bowl with water and pieces of ice in it, and a white enamel jug. The doctor was there too, with ammonium chloride; he was standing, and his gaze moved backwards and forwards between the ring and the gloomy face of Pa Ashot. The coach was gradually growing calmer. There had been a moment when he considered throwing in the towel.

Yes, he had considered it. But now he was looking at Val again, and was probably repeating to himself: "Nothing is unimportant to a boxer during a fight. A boxer's head isn't just there to be hit and then wondered at: 'Look what it can take!' and so on. A boxer's head is there to think its way through the fight—to think!"

Ashot Petrovich had often said these words to the boys. Val had certainly heard them more than once. And now the coach could see that his words had not been in vain. Watching the fight, he returned in his memory to that very first day when such boys as Val, one ofter another, had stepped at different times across the threshold of the gym and found themselves face to face with him, the coach, who represented, for each of those teenagers, a fabulous dream. And, like many others in the same position, he had looked intently into each novice's face, and thought: "Why has he chosen boxing? Not tennis or swimming, fencing or wrestling, football or ice hockey—but boxing. Just boxing." Ashot Petrovich had long ago abandoned the idea of asking directly. He knew how stereotyped the answers could be: "I want to become strong so I'm not afraid of hooligans", "I want to defend the weak, to help people who've been picked on unjustly", and so on and so forth. He wanted to answer the question himself. He felt there was something more serious in it than the things he heard in the inconsistent answers of the boys. It's good to have strong, elastic, fast-reacting muscles of course—but that's not, in the end, the decisive thing in Sport. Otherwise living in this world would be easy. Serge, for example, that friend of Val Kardin's with untidy, shoulder-length hair, visits all the competitions. He gets more involved in them than Kardin himself. But he doesn't do any serious sport himself. Why? In fact it's the same with the rest of that crowd. Look at Stass for example. He's got such an athletic build, but he's still just a spectator. Why? Or Alexei, our light-heavyweight. Fortune's child. I remember how his father brought him along: twelve years old but already quite a well-developed youth—big, slender and bashful. "I beg you," said his father, looking up at his son, "make a man out of him." He didn't ask me to "make a person", but to "make a man".

Ashot Petrovich now compared *that* Alexei—the twelve-year-old who was so easily embarrassed, blushed at each question and never knew where to look—with today's Alexei Plisin—the good-looking, strapping, nineteen-year-old, who already had a man's body. He had a strong character, but more often than not he had shown signs of cruelty in the ring, and neglected the advice of both his companions and his coach.

Not long before these Competitions, during one of the training sessions, Ashot Petrovich had been coming into the changing-room a little bit later that usual, when he heard Plisin telling the boys—who were standing round him in a circle—about his scandalous victory at the National Junior Championship:

"...I didn't break the rules. I hit after the command 'Box!' It's not my fault he hadn't managed to lift his hands up to his chin. That's the way you have to establish yourself in 'The World of Sport' these days."

Aunty Polya, the cleaner, who happened to be wiping the floor, stopped moving her mop.

"My goodness me! But what'll happen to his head?"

Alexei laughed. He said: "Oh nothing. He'll waggle his ears a bit less." He demonstrated how his opponent used to "waggle his ears". Turning back to the boys, he burst into boisterous laughter.

"You shameless bully," said Aunty Polya, and started to move her mop along the floor, angrily catching at the boys' feet with it.

Ashot Petrovich took a decisive stride towards Plisin.

"What do you mean by behaving so disgracefully in front of an old lady? What do you mean by giving such a distorted version of a fight where you behaved like a lout?"

Completely unembarrassed, Alexei replied: "We aren't ordinary sportsmen. We're machines. We're programmed to be violent by our occupation. We're the gladiators of the twentieth century."

Ashot Petrovich was lost for words. Only Val Kardin objected:

"Gladiators were not free people. They were slaves, destined for violence by a slave-owning society. But we..."

"...act like a bunch of idiots," interrupted Aunty Polya, who was worrying herself about the fate of someone she had never met. "You're a lot of miserable parasites, that's what you are."

Ashot Petrovich looked around at the boys. Some were puzzled, some were embarrassed. Val had grown gloomy. Plisin was smiling. Hardly able to control himself, the coach said:

"Get out of here!"

Pa Ashot had sat on his own in the changing-room for a long time after that. He was comparing two of his best boxers in his mind. Look at Val Kardin. He is no less talented. He wins more victories. Yet his behaviour is absolutely the opposite. Val Kardin's sports career is on the way up. But you couldn't say the same of Alexei Plisin's. It wasn't for nothing that Val had once told Alexei: "The armour you put on is very pretty, but it's hollow." Kardin devotes most of his attention to his inner state; Plisin concentrates on the exterior. The philosophy of boxing doesn't concern the strength, or even the accuracy of a punch—though such factors are indispensable too of course. The philosophy of boxing, as of Sport in general, is in moral behaviour. For a boxer, that means both in the Ring, and out of it; for a football player, it's both in the field and off it; for all sportsmen, it means both in Sport and out of it, in Life in general, among people at large, and the way their behaviour enriches those people around them with beauty, power, and a striving towards the heights of physical and spiritual achievement. Sport isn't showing off, or a school for money-makers. Sport is hard work, and, to the ones that understand that, victory comes in the end. Victory, in general, is rarely gained accidentally.

Going out on the street, Ashot Petrovich saw the boys. They were standing near the sports billboard. Plisin was standing slightly apart. The boys were warily silent, trying to avoid his eyes.

When he saw the coach, Alexei came up to him and asked for his forgiveness. Pa Ashot shifted his fat briefcase from one hand to the other and started to walk towards the trolley-bus stop.

Real boxers are neither comedians nor killers. Real boxers are labourers for His Majesty Sport.

Ashot Petrovich didn't know what the boys had been talking about, but he knew that something had been said.

It's difficult to know where sportsman and coach reveal themselves most: in the Ring itself, or in the "outer Ring" of Life. Pa Ashot didn't think about it. For him the world was indivisible: it all came under the heading of Boxing. He tried to teach his pupils a similar view of the world.

A human being must always remain human. Even if circumstances raise him to the crest of success.

Breathing easily through his mouth now it was free of the gum-shield, Val was quickly recovering. He had broken away from his opponent and would not let him come any closer. Abrupt, sweeping punches came whistling past Val's bloody nose, like the flapping, dislocated sails of a windmill. These were hooks: apparently his mighty assailant's favourite punches.

A medium distance—the most convenient for exchanging punches—is usually characteristic of such "hard-hitters". In in-fighting, as in out-fighting, they feel less confident—because then it is skill which is most important. Meanwhile the opponent's hooks went wandering past Val Kardin's head: here very close to the chin, there touching the hair on his crown; here cutting the air beside his ear, there blocked by a raised glove. Left-right, left-right—like a clockwork machine. Only one thing had changed: the daring fire which had shone out at him during the opening seconds, had now vanished without trace from his opponent's sweat-covered eyes. There was now a desperate worry in them. Victory, which had seemed so close, was slipping from his grasp.

Val sensed this turning point, more with the instinct of a boxer than with his mind. Using a left arm feint and a sliding sidestep backwards and to the right, he broke the recently established medium distance, and moved beyond his opponent's reach. Rather uncouthly, he wiped his bleeding nose with his right forearm, remembering immediately afterwards how Pa Ashot had told him that this was not the right thing to do, and was against the rules of etiquette as well. Maintaining the advantage he had gained by keeping his distance, he began circling his opponent. As last he could recover and replenish his muscles with oxygen. It was wonderful. Feeling able to continue the fight! Returning to life!

By the end of the first round, Val, while retreating, had managed to deliver three straight rights to his opponent, who was still grunting with anticipation of a quick victory. Yet before the bell, Val let through a clean, light but sharp straight left to his chin, and would have found himself on the floor if the referee had not stopped the fight at exactly that instant to reprimand the opponent's second for giving advice. The sound of the bell found both boxers in the centre of the ring—at a considerable distance from each other.

Val went unsteadily over to his corner, still feeling the ringing sensation in his head: ticklingly sharp and—at the same time—burning. The floor of the ring was swaying beneath him, and he was making each step carefully, putting each foot down smoothly: first one and then the other; first one and then the other. He must have been doing it too smoothly, because at one moment, with an accidental movement of his eye, he caught Pa Ashot's gaze directed at him, and, through it, perceived his own state. He heard the buzzing of the stands more distinctly; they floated in a blur before his eyes. And he sensed—in this alarmed rumbling, and in the distorted faces—a danger to himself. He moved towards the gaze of Pa Ashot, as though towards a beacon.

No sooner had Val reached his corner, than Pa Ashot instantaneously placed the stool in front of him, quickly and silently sat him down on it, wiped his face with a cold, wet towel, then folded it into four, laid it across the back of his neck, and slipped a cold, damp sponge under his vest, just level with his heart. Pulling forward the thick elastic of the blood-spotted white satin shorts to free Val's stomach muscles for easier and deeper breathing, he started fanning him quickly and continuously with a wet towel, creating the effect of a strong ventilator, making a light whirlwind of air in front of Val's face.

The doctor came up too, in a business-like manner, and shoved a big cotton wool pad soaked in ammonium chloride under his nose. It cleared Val's head considerably. Then the doctor inserted another piece of cotton wool—soaked in something different as it seemed to Val, but probably the same—first in one nostril, then in the other. Then immediately he repeated the whole process from the very beginning. And only after that did he leave him alone.

Pa Ashot had stopped fanning him too. From time to time he applied an ice-filled towel to Val's temples, and spoke to him in an even voice—with a quietness which was almost tangible:

"The worst is over now, son. You mustn't let any more punches through. You've lost the first round very badly. Make sure you win the second and the third. By the end of this round, you were already starting to pick out his weak points. Now hit them. Not strongly, just suddenly and accurately. You've regained your breath—now make him lose his. And keep your distance. Don't, under any circumstances, go in close. And remember: no strength in your punches, just sharpness and quickness. That's all. Work without your gumshield. Be careful!"

The bell sounded. The referee shouted abruptly:

"Seconds out. Round Two. Box!"

Val could see how hastily his opponent stood up, and how fast—almost running—he crossed the centre of the ring and was already in Val's half. That was smart.

411

But it didn't worry Val just then. His natural ability to calculate the odds had started to work. He'd always had it: even before his first experience of boxing, even in scraps when he was a kid. There'd been very few of those—but the ones that there were, had always been serious. They had always been for important moral reasons. "Whether the cause was just or unjust"—that was always the deciding factor when Val was a child. As the years passed, his understanding of justice had become more complicated, grown over with reservations, corrections, digressions, explanations.

He hadn't a father—or rather, he had one, but he didn't live with them, and who or where he was, Val didn't know. His mother never said anything about it, although Val was sure she was in no way guilty—he knew her too well for that. When Val one day referred to his father as a "rat", however, his mother started to defend him, saying that you shouldn't talk like that about someone you don't really know. And Val withdrew into himself completely after that. He became wary of strangers, harder towards his friends, more considerate—but simultaneously colder—towards his mother. He had come to think of his everyday life as a kind of continuous out-fighting, and he thought more and more often about Alexandrov. A premonition that he would one day reappear was growing stronger.

And one day he did reappear, and came up to Val. It was at the heats in Leningrad, coinciding with a period of the most wonderful spring days. Val had won his final against Slava Yelshin, the holder of the Emile Gremo Cup.

Alexandrov had come up to Val while he was alone in the changing-room. Pa Ashot had just sent all the well-wishers packing and then gone out with Alexei Plisin into the corridor leading to the ring, preparing him for his crucial fight.

"Well done, Val."

"Thank you."

"Well, how are you?"

"All right."

"You've grown a lot... I'm glad... I remember..."

"Don't let's remember."

They had not succeeded in talking.

It's true that you shouldn't talk about someone you don't really know. But how hard it is to get to know someone. Even Pa Ashot hadn't become "Pa" straight away. How he used to look at them all at the beginning...

Probably the most complicated thing, and the hardest to understand, was his relationship with Zhanna. He hadn't invited her today. Serge swore blind that she had come on her own—though it was definitely his doing. She had come, all the same, but broken down when she saw the blood. It was rather weak of her...

Once again, Val saw only his opponent's eyes. They had none of that desperate anxiety he'd seen in them during the last seconds of the first round. The light in them now was predatory. It was flaring up, and it was very close. Val didn't hurry. He was waiting. He could wait, when he was sure of himself. At last, feeling the movement of air caused by the approaching glove of his opponent, he took a tentative—and therefore very light step, backwards and sideways simultaneously.

413

His opponent's straight punch passed through immediately, losing all its impetus in its combat with the air. During these instants Val managed to reach his opponent's chin with a left and right straights from the side. The audience immediately came to life. The sound reached Val's ears. But he switched off this dangerous drift of his attention straight away. He turned round quickly, and again made ready to meet his opponent who, after making a big circle around the ring, was once more rushing into the attack. And suddenly Val saw clearly that his opponent was confused.

Val Kardin pretended to make a punch at the head. He indicated the beginning of one. Then straightaway, bending low from the waist, he lunged forward with his left arm and whole body, abruptly connecting a straight left into the stomach, just above the waistband of the shorts, at the very edge of the permitted area. The punch was accurate, appreciable. Its echo resounded hollowly around the hall. Val could hear the applause. But it was too early to cheer. The audience was only showing its appreciation of the fact that the fight had not finished in the primitive and childish way it had seemed it was going to at first. It could still be interesting—if the "youth" could pull himself together.

10

"You don't by any chance do any boxing, do you?" she had asked suddenly.

He widened his eyes in surprise.

414

"Why do you ask such a question? Did I let it slip somehow while we were talking?"

"No. I'm sorry. It's just that you keep so completely quiet about it. That's how it seems to me."

He went red. He was immediately conscious, whenever she started to talk to him like that, that she was older than him. And it made him lose confidence.

"To be honest, it's your friend who told me."

She never referred to Serge by name, but simply as "your friend". Serge's attitude towards women was very light-hearted. "Listen Val," he would say. "Why do you bother about her so much. Invite her up to your luxury room in the hotel. All that arrogance will evaporate immediately."

But this girl's arrogance wasn't going to evaporate. In fact, one could hardly call it "arrogance". It was more a question of pride, bare and challenging: "That's how I am. I'm free. *I* choose you—you don't choose me." He didn't even consider why she repaid his attention.

Before the competitions, Pa Ashot had said: "Invite your girl if you want." He'd seen them on the lake when they were boating. Zhanna had been rowing, and Val had been sitting in the bows. Pa Ashot had joked: "You're handing over the reins, Val."

Val had not even thought of inviting her. He thought women brought bad luck in a fight, and that's what he told Pa Ashot. Pa Ashot had laughed, loudly as usual, and very endearingly, losing his breath like a child. Val started to explain: "You feel easier in the ring when there's no-one close to you in the audience—especially women. I don't understand how some of the

415

boys can invite their parents. My mother would die of fright."

Pa Ashot did not stop laughing. Val even began to feel offended. But the coach put his arm round his shoulders: "Invite your girl all the same. Don't be afraid of evil spirits. The forces of goodness and light will win in the end."

Val didn't like these words—"goodness and light". People use them when they start getting old. Ashot Petrovich wasn't that sort of person. Yet even coming from him, these words sounded unreal. However hard he tried, Val couldn't feel any life in them. Life is something quite ordinary. It's here—all around you. Without effort, without pressure—there's no victory.

After this conversation with Pa Ashot, Val had invited her.

While there was still some time left to go, they had gone out together on to the highest tier of the stands. The hall was high, voluminous, round, decorated with the flags of the different sports clubs, with pendants, slogans and banners. It was already almost full.

Val glanced at the floodlit ring. He felt a light shiver prickling the skin of his back, shoulders and neck. He was surprised. The sight of the ring had not hit him like that for a long while. It was as though he were a novice again, seeing it for the first time. From up here, from the height of the stands, it shone with a stunning whiteness beneath the enormous bank of floodlights. And at that moment Val forgot about the girl who was standing next to him. He felt suddenly terribly lonely, and that here and now the last strength was seeping away from every fibre of his body—which had been so strong, only a moment ago.

She touched his arm. He started.

"Roll your shirt-sleeves down," she said.

"There's no need," he answered, surprised at the sound of his own voice, which seemed to be coming from somebody else. She also grew quiet, but she didn't take her hand away from his arm. She was looking at him, and he saw that in her eyes, which were usually so attentive and mocking, there were now two shadows. "She is worried about me," he thought. And he suddenly wanted to say something nice.

"Zhanna," he said, "I don't know anything about you really. Tell me. Who are you?"

"Why should you want to know who I am, Val?" she said without looking away. "I'm a free woman. That's all. Isn't that enough."

11

The situation in the ring was changing considerably. The stands were humming. "The youth" was coming more and more into his own. Indeed, though his "adult" opponent with the "cast-iron" shoulders was continuing to attack in the same pressing but straightforward manner, the youth, delivering light, quick blows—now to the head, now to the stomach—was quickly catching up on points.

By the end of the round, the sluggishness of his opponent had become evident. He was moving around the ring dragging his feet—as Pa Ashot used to put it. The drawn-out length of his punches allowed Val to avoid them easily by bends, ducks, sidesteps and backsteps. He wasn't even afraid of taking them on his shoulder or glove, whereas, during the first round, any one of these punches would have made him shudder to the soles of his feet. It was becoming more and more apparent that his opponent was growing nervous because of his failures, and the unsuccessful attacks, which all fell through. They made him hurry too much to correct himself, pushing forwards without preparation, and more and more frequently he was running up against the stop blows of "the youth".

"He's all right actually, this youth," Val's neighbour from yesterday was saying in the stands. He'd been completely nonplussed at first. Now he started to shake his friend by the shoulder again—he'd brought him here especially to show him this excellent lad—maybe the next national champion. "Just look. He's coming back to life now. He's quick as lightning. See how he hangs on. That's what matters most. He won't lose, you'll see. I won't let him. He can't let me down."

And now, when it seemed that Val had triumphed over the impossible, both in himself and in the outside world, and was delivering one punch after another, he started to believe so much in his advantage, that, without realising it, he let his attention wander to the applause he was receiving from the audience. He was punished for it at once. He let through a strong punch on to the jaw: a left hook. It not only connected with his jaw, but also—partly—with his neck and ear. In other words inaccurately—"messily" as boxers call it. Val felt it ringing in his head. He hardly managed to stay on his feet. The referee did not count it as a "knock-down", but he didn't make any reprimand either. Without giving Val time to recover, his opponent rushed forward to consolidate his success— to finish him. Val heard his characteristic snarl again, and saw the predatory light sparkling in his eyes— impossible to forget.

No, Val would never forget that light in his opponent's small, sweat-covered eyes, any more than he would forget the whole fight, which was laid out in his memory to the last detail: the movements, turns, bends, ducks, feints, shifts of the centre of gravity, relaxation and instant re-tensing of muscles, abruptly caught breaths, and sharp short punches like sudden breathing out.

Val failed to move away by only half a step, seeking to keep the necessary distance. He omitted half a step—either back or to the side—just because of the attention he was paying to the applause which had broken through the sound-proof curtain of his inner concentration. But he reacted instinctively, bending slightly away from the punch, letting the glove go past his cheek. Immediately he felt the heavy lash of his opponent's arm falling on his shoulder. And at the same time the massive body leaned down on him with all its weight, pressing him against the ropes. Val was unable to wriggle out. He tried to get a couple of single punches through from this posture, inconvenient and dangerous as it was. His opponent was hanging on him, using his whole weight to try and push him against the ropes, all the time pummelling Val from below with one arm—on his sides and on his stomach. With the other arm bent at the elbow and shoved under Val's armpit, he was trying to reach for Val's jaw... "Trying" was not the right word; he was "struggling" to get through. And each time he would fail by the tiniest amount, and hit Val's ear or else the back of his head, because Val wasn't wasting any time either. For his part he was trying to squash the hand shoved under his armpit, at the same time hiding his jaw in his opponent's shoulder, trying to press himself up as tightly as possible against him, thus constraining his movements.

The referee was watching them carefully, moving quickly round the ring: now going away, now coming closer, now freezing near the kernel of the fight. In the ring the referee is the third and equal participant in the combat. Every part of him is involved: every movement of his shoulders and hands, face and eyes, every drop of sweat. So far he had not parted the adversaries. He was giving them the opportunity to work together in an in-fighting. From time to time, with sudden quick movements of his hands, he would help—first one, then the other—pulling out a glove which had been incorrectly squashed, or freeing an arm which had been pushed out too far. But the in-fighting was failing, because both boxers—the young one and his more experienced opponent, but particularly the latter—were noticeably tired, and therefore only "clinching" each other. The referee was on the verge of parting them. He raised his arm to shout "Break!" Just at that moment, Val Kardin did take an abrupt step—describing an arc backwards and to the side—and wrenched both his arms downwards at the same time. The opponent had missed his chance.

The momentum of Val's movement made his arms stretch out, lowering his fists and opening his chin. It gave Val just enough time to deliver two side punches on to the opened chin. Taking one more step backwards, he reached the centre of the ring. His opponent was left still turning in his direction, while Val, with another step backwards, twisted his entire torso to the left, and shifted to the side with a sliding half-step, taking up a convenient stance for an attack. Such a lucky combination of circumstances happens very rarely in a fight; and when it does, it should be exploited to the utmost.

Out of the corner of his eye, Val noticed that Pa Ashot had got up from his stool. This was a signal. Fifteen seconds were left to the end of the round.

The opponent had recovered. Feeling victory slipping through his fingers, he came forward with a straight left, clearly not considering whether this was the best thing to do when the "youth" was completely out of reach. And Val's eye picked out, in the tense figure of his opponent, that he had raised his left shoulder too high, that his right arm had gone down from his chin and pulled back, sticking the elbow out towards the side.

How hard comes the moment of victory!

"You should outwit your opponent in a fight, not just brawl"—the frequently repeated advice of Pa Ashot.

"Beat them all, and you'll be king"—the frequently repeated, unambiguous words of Stass, during gatherings in the yard-entrances in their street near the station.

"A knock-out must be really painful"—the frequently repeated lamentation of his mother.

"How can you avoid it in boxing..."—Val's frequently repeated answer.

"Sportsmanship is just one of your philosophical notions, Val"—the frequently repeated prattle of Alexei Plisin.

"Fair Play Is the Most Important Characteristic of Soviet Boxing"—the poster in the Physical Training Institute Val dreamed of entering.

And in this moment—frozen, as it seemed to Val—he completed the difficult distance between being a boy in the street near the railway station, and being a fighter in the National Ring.

The inexpressible sensation of complete control of one's body! To Val it seemed that he could see each element of his body's movement with a suddenly opening inner sight.

His torso started to unwind quickly, leaning the right shoulder backwards, pushing the left shoulder forwards and upwards—its strength growing more tangible as it rose. Following the left shoulder, lagging behind it at first, then with each instant—with each fraction of an instant—increasing its speed until it overtook it, the left arm started its movement, stretching like a bow-string, to compress at the last moment into a stone fist, and strike the chosen target squarely.

Val heard a muffled crack, then felt an extraordinary pressure in his glove at the point of its contact with the body of his opponent—and before he even had time to raise the fist back to his chin to resume his stance for the continuation of the fight, before he had time to take a step backwards or even to consider doing so, he saw how his opponent's body was crumpling into a hot palpitating ball, and how it—this "ball-opponent"—was sinking, with a wet and apathetic face, towards the floor.

A very long moment... Around him something was already happening... But Val could not understand... What was it?.. The referee pushed him away—Val could see his excited face, its crooked streams of sweat and bewildered eyes... Bewildered... Why bewildered?..

The referee's voice reached Val's ears at last: "Go to your corner! Go to your corner!" And then suddenly he realised what had happened. It was a knock-out. Still stunned, Val turned round. Stumbling over the feet of his prone opponent, he hurried to the corner, where his coach, Pa Ashot, also terribly excited, his eyes burning with an unfamiliar light, was signalling to him desperately.

Val stopped right in the corner, touching the ropes with his forearms. He heard how, behind his back, the referee had started the count:

"One... Two... Three... Four... Nine... Ten... Out!"

The referee dropped his arm abruptly, froze, and then, after a pause of several seconds, completely relaxed. Turning, he started to walk towards Val. There was no excitement on the referee's face any more. It was calm—even emotionless. Silently, sacredly, strictly he took hold of Val's arm just above the wrist near the neck of the glove, led him out into the middle of the ring and threw his arm up. At the same moment the announcer, sitting at the table with the panel of judges, read out—with a slight air of deliberate superciliousness, but still very clearly—Val Kardin's victory by a knock-out.

But Val did not feel the great happiness he had imagined he would while thinking about this before the fight, or even before these competitions. While the noise of the applause and the yelling of his friends was still ringing in his ears, he suddenly had the feeling that probably today—in this enormous, empty ring—the first crack would appear in his life: though he knew with his mind—which was still excited, but calm enough to control him—that it was silly to think in this way at such a dazzlingly bright moment. Yet what could he do about it, if that was how he felt?

"There's been a woman in my life—but it was probably just a passing phase. In any case, does a sportsman need a woman? Some of them probably do—but not me. I haven't got time for them. And Love, as Pa Ashot says, is like Sport: either you should give yourself to it completely—or what's the point of deceiving yourself and everybody else who pins their hopes on you—especially when people have so few hopes fulfilled in life anyway."

A heavy bank of floodlights was hanging above the ring, drenching it with light. There was too much light. From all over the stands, the powerful projectors were aiming at the ring. Crystals of rosin-powder sparkled under his feet, making the entire canvas glisten with its cold and sugary whiteness.

Val's opponent was already on his feet. Val went over to his corner. There was a final handshake. His opponent was smiling in confusion.

424

Val went back to his own corner. Pa Ashot quietly congratulated him in a business-like manner, then helped him to take off his gloves and unbandage his hands, wiped his face, neck and chest with a wet towel, parted the ropes and helped him climb through them, silently leading him towards the exit. The stands, particularly the one they were approaching, greeted them with rapturous applause. Many people had risen, and were now giving him a standing ovation, shouting that the boy was great, that he should do the same tomorrow in the Final.

Val suddenly saw Zhanna—and stopped. But Ashot Petrovich urged him forward: time to relax ... to relax...

She was standing at the bottom, almost right up against the barrier, applauding and smiling too, like the others. Yet her smile seemed to Val to be different from everybody else's, and different too from her usual, confident, slightly supercilious smile, and different again from the lost, weak, humiliated smile she had worn during the first round. It was a different smile now—deeply sad, and probably understanding too. He wanted very much to believe in that understanding, and he looked at Zhanna's smiling face without taking any notice of Pa Ashot's grumbling behind his back, and at her hands, whose violent clapping was sending him all her bitter happiness. A sudden wave of warm and heartfelt emotion filled him completely. He turned round. His coach, as though guessing his state, put his arm around his shoulders, catching the towel which was slipping from them. And suddenly Val and Pa Ashot both smiled. To a burst of applause from the part of the audience which was closest to them, they disappeared behind the soft curtains of the exit, away from the electrified hall.

12

As soon as the door had closed behind them in the changing-room, Pa Ashot became stern. He started telling Val off for his flippant behaviour in the ring. "Flippant behaviour" referred to the punch which Val had let through at the end of the second round, and which had almost knocked him down.

"From the very beginning, you did the whole round as we outlined it in the interval. You did it, as you can do the most important and serious fights now—and you should do them in this way. Just with that degree of skill... and more. All the fights. And not start strutting about at the first hint of success!"

Glancing at Alexei Plisin—whose entrance for the next fight was imminent and who was only waiting to have his gloves laced—Ashot Petrovich continued with constrained but deep passion:

"Show-offs! I don't train up show-offs who lose their heads for the sake of a few claps. I, Ashot Armen, raise sportsmen and fighters—thinking fighters..."

He turned abruptly back to Alexei Plisin, who was looking at the window with feigned indifference.

"...who think first and foremost of their comrades."

Alexei frowned, and got up from his arm-chair. He came up to Pa and stretched out his gloves. Pa Ashot started lacing them. He had calmed down, and soon took Alexei out into the corridor for the final warm-up.

Val was left alone in the changing-room. He was calm. He knew that the greater part of these angry words had not been for his benefit, but for Alexei's. Pa kept Plisin agitated before a fight on purpose—because Plisin was not Kardin. To summarise them: Kardin was thin-skinned; Plisin was thick-skinned. From now on Pa Ashot would not leave Plisin alone until his fight. He wouldn't come back here after the warm-up in the corridor, but would take him to the hall, and keep him there until they were called into the ring. Val would have burned out. There would have been very little left of him in the ring after that. Plisin on the other hand could keep chatting with his blonde admirers until the very minute when the fight began. Clinging to each other, whispering and sighing, these girls had been running here almost since daybreak. Plisin had fought in the Small Hall yesterday, at the same time as Val. Pa had gone to second Val, entrusting Plisin to the care of his assistant, one of the "adult class" boxers. Plisin had nearly lost, despite the fact that his opponent was quite weak. The boys had been telling everyone how he had run out of breath—he'd been in charge for the first two rounds then fizzled out during the third—he'd smoked so much with his blondes. When Pa gathered the whole team together and started talking to him, Alexei denied everything and said:

"But I haven't lost, have I? I haven't lost. And even if I had, the fate of the world doesn't depend on this one fight in the ring."

Ashot Petrovich's expression suddenly changed.

"And what if it did?" he said sternly. Plisin had no answer to this.

"What if it had been important?" Val thought with sudden surprise. More with his heart than with his mind, he suddenly realised the importance of his occupation. It wasn't so much that he didn't really value it, now that he'd been doing it for so many years. It was just that—like most of his peers and many older people too—he had come to think of it as a game.

Yet all games have their causes and their consequences. This was especially true of his game—which is openly called a fight. It's written down plainly in the protocol for the panel of judges: "The formula for a fight is three rounds of three minutes each". "Formula for a fight"—on the surface the meaning of the words is simple and straightforward: the number of rounds and their duration. That's all! Yet the inner meaning is much deeper. It's the essence of the whole distance you have covered: the essence which—during nine minutes of pure combat, face to face with your opponent in the ring—will show who you are and what you will become—not only to you yourself, but to everyone who is watching from the stands as well. That's the kind of game boxing is! Violent? Courageous? Dangerous? Subtle? That's just for the chatter and babble of the fans.

Of course Val Kardin had never thought of boxing as a game himself. It would sound too light-hearted beside names like Nikolai Korolyov, Yevgeny Ogurenkov, Konstantin Gradopopov, Algerdas Shotsikas, Gennady Shatkov. For them it had been work—hard, exhausting, painstaking work—but bringing them happiness in the end. It wasn't for nothing that Val, from his very first arrival in the gym, had noticed and remembered forever, that the coach used the word "work" more frequently than any other: to work individually; to work in pairs; to work with the equipment; to work with the punch-bag; to work with the rope; to work more intensively; to work with more concentration; to work ... to work... The word had entered his life immediately, as something inseparable from boxing, dissolving in the hot sweat of endless training sessions. Through it, to the admiration of Alexandrov, he had quickly started to learn something which the others had not yet glimpsed, and which was, for some of them who lacked talent, simply beyond their reach. But Alexandrov never connected boxing with the fate of the world, whereas Ashot Petrovich did.

The recollection of his first coach stung his memory with the unpleasant words "fair play". With time, the stinging had become less sharp. Yet it had never disappeared completely. And Val already knew that it would never disappear.

He got up, put on his track suit, and went towards the hall. The team badly needed Plisin's victory. And perhaps ... perhaps ... he would still see Alexandrov there...

Tenghiz Adygov

HOT JULY SUN

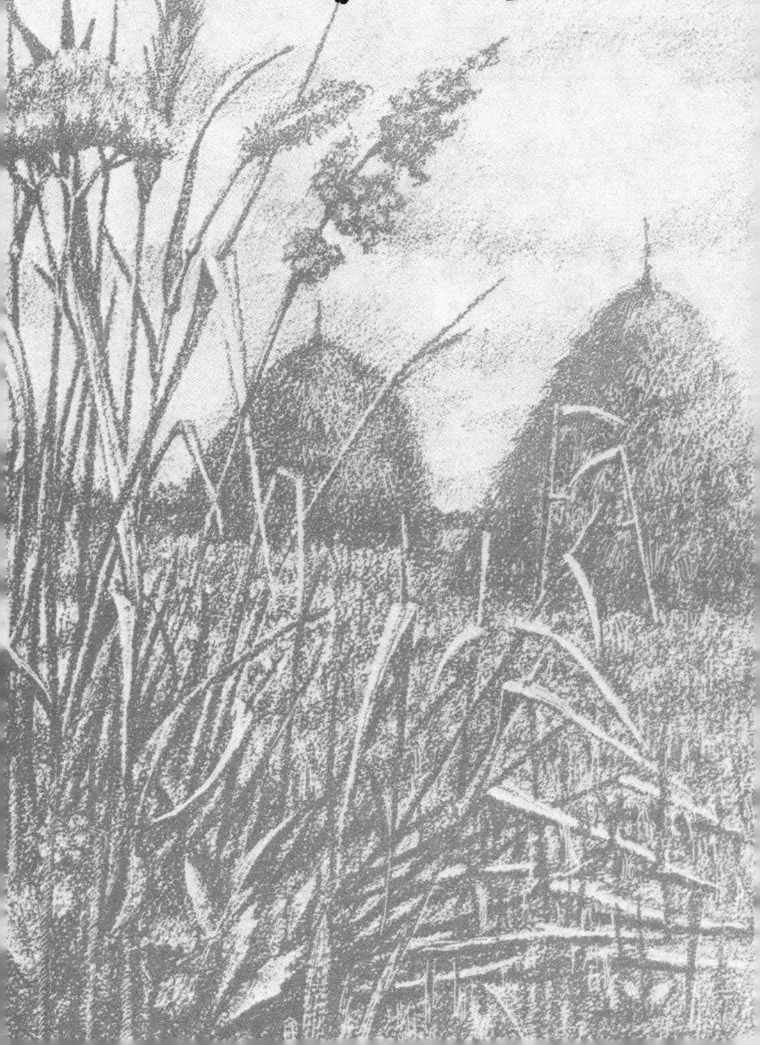

Tenghiz Adygov was born in 1945 in the small town of Zolskoye in the Kabardino-Balkarsky Autonomous Soviet Socialist Republic. He graduated from a teachers' training college and has worked as a teacher, a builder and a journalist. His first stories were published in 1969. In 1979, he graduated from the Gorky Literary Institute. He is the author of two books of stories in Kabardinian, which were put out by Elbrus Publishers. He is a member of the USSR Writers' Union.

Tenghiz Adygov's work depicts the life and everyday activities of the ordinary people of his republic, their concerns and the world as they see it. This young prose writer embellishes his stories by skilfully interweaving into them popular legends and traditions, drawing widely on the language and rhythms of folk-lore.

One sweep. Another. One, two, three... The thin blade of the scythe glinting in the sun cuts through the thick grass gleaming green and silvery-blue, and brings it down with a whirring sound. Like a clod of earth thrown to one side by the ploughshare, the hay falls into a thick heap.

My muscles do not feel anything any more, and my fingers seem to be grafted on to the scythe handle wrapped round with a ring of plaited grass so that my hands should not slip. My scythe and my body are as if welded together in a single, indivisible whole. Rather than the scythe being wielded by me, the scythe is in charge.

The sun is burning down mercilessly and because of the heat my head seems to be going round in circles. Sweat is pouring over my hot skin, as if I had just come out of a steam bath. The legs of my trousers, now soaked through with sweat, are sticking to my thighs and making the mowing ten times harder.

In front of me I see just one tiny piece of ground. Beyond that I see Lana, shapely and long-legged, wearing a thin short dress. I see the thick tresses of her hair cascading down on to her shoulders, and her sunburnt skin almost as black as olives. Lana is still out there ahead of me and I cannot catch her up however hard I try. The pole is not far. It is hammered into the ground at the end of the plot which Khamata, Lana's grandfather, measured off. He walked a hundred paces away from us and then stuck the pole into the ground. He did that without saying a word: he thought that if people had decided to lay on a spectacle they might as well get on with it. He himself was prepared to watch as long as they did not waste time over it. Khamata had not objected against Lana and me having a trial of strength. We had been working here since early morning. Lana had brought food along for us and a three-litre jug of sour milk. After drinking his fill the old man had given a nod in my direction, and Lana, looking askance, handed me the jug as if she had been handing it into thin air, as if there had not been anyone there.

"Here you are," she said, an ironic smile slightly twisting the corners of her mouth. "Expert mower."

She spoke as if this gentle irony had not been directed at me, nor the deliberate off-handedness implicit in her words, uttered casually, by chance, but at someone else, at some outsider. I sighed and took the jug out of her hands, trying as hard as I could to make it clear that her stinging remarks had made no impression on me: her arrows were too delicate and my armour too dependable... The thick sour milk was straight from the fridge. The succulent lumps in it burnt the inside of my mouth as if they were pieces of melting ice.

"A mower I am well and truly," I said, cutting her short and accepting the new title she had given me. For no particular reason I began to inspect my scythe and, pretending to notice something, I drew my thumb along the blade. "So as to form an opinion people have at least got to have some idea what they're up against. It's easy to judge for someone who had never picked up a scythe in her life..."

"So that's it!" chipped in Lana. "That's what you think about me, is it?!"

"Perhaps you have, I don't know. So as to move it from one place to another, you may have done at some stage..."

"Move it from one place to another!" called Lana mockingly, echoing my words. "You'll very soon find out. Grandad, give me your scythe," she called, scampering over to the old man.

Khamata did not answer.

"Grandad, do let me!"

Perhaps because he thought there would be no harm in letting Lana do a little mowing, or perhaps just for the sake of peace and quiet, Khamata gave in.

"Right away, right away!" called Lana, clapping her hands and taking up her position right beside me. "We'll see who can mow fastest! Grandad, measure a stretch off for us!"

Taking his time about it, Khamata complied with Lana's request and then settled down in the "heat-shelter" as he had called the awning made of poles and woven grass. At a signal from Lana he gave the sign for us to start.

Then we got down to it. Lana made a quick get-away. It was as if there had been a conspiracy between them as to the minute when the old man would tell us to start, and she had prepared herself for it in advance. I fumbled it. While I was working out how best to start mowing and settle into my stride Lana moved on several scythe strokes ahead of me. And here I am trying to catch her up with all my might. Only nothing is working out right. What if she manages to mow as far as the pole first? Then I am done for. I am already a figure of fun for the whole village. I had been demobbed later than expected, they had kept me on till July. My parents had gone almost crazy with worry. They had already started planning to send off someone to the unit where I was serving, but fortunately they did not get round to it in time. Other people used to assure them that I must have gone to visit a friend on the way home but that I would be back soon, since there was nowhere else for me to go. They were wailing and snivelling, and kept asking themselves: is our Tembulat still alive, and never gave the whole village a moment's rest, while I was serving my time all right.

The other lads of my age were coming back from their military service some as drivers, others as mechanics or motor engineers. As luck would have it I was singled out for the only cavalry regiment in the whole of the Soviet Union. When I came home of course all the neighbours, friends and relatives came running. Hugs, kisses, slaps on the back... Then, as we were sitting out in the garden, someone started up a conversation asking me to tell them what training I had been given. All my friends have learnt a trade in the army, I was told. One of them had been a tank-driver, and he had been given a tractor to drive and he had already managed to show what he was made of in the spring sowing. Another had been in a construction battalion and had learnt several trades: now he could work as a mason, plasterer, painter and fitter. He had set up a building gang in the collective farm and was putting up some granaries, and built to last too, what's more. What could I boast about? What had I done in the army?

"I was in the cavarly," I replied. "A groom then," commented one of the men. "What a pity our last mare, that lame one, the chairman sold last year to the slaughter-house, otherwise there'd be someone to look after her and you'd have a job..." People all around me started smirking. "I was filmed on horseback," I said. "Filmed?" The smirking got louder after that. It was not that they had doubts about what I had told them, they did not believe a word I was saying. If only they'd see me in a film on horseback, brandishing a sabre, or better still in close-up filling half the screen! The village hall would have collapsed outright. They would have shouted: "Look, look! It's our Tembulat, would you believe it!" Then the whole village would have been hailing me as a hero. All I had done though was appear as an extra, to "make up numbers" for the crowd scenes: as luck would have it I was always right in the thick of the crush and my face was not a conspicuous one at the best of times. Later, however hard I tried, I could never pick myself out. "Nothing wrong with the cinema, it's a fine occupation," one of them said, raising his eyebrows in a knowing way, as if he had been doing nothing else all his life other than making films. Then he added: "So you'll be opening a film studio down at the club-house?" He said all this in a completely serious voice and I failed to notice his sarcasm at first. "No," I replied, shaking my head, "it's a complicated business." Then they all burst out laughing. They went on to ask me what I wanted to do later on, and I told them my plans in all seriousness: "I'll stay around here for a bit and then I'll be off to town. What's there to do out here in the country?

437

There's no interesting work, it's boring and in the towns there are factories, technical schools, dancing, cafés." "Where are you off to?" another asked. "Aren't you planning to go and train as an actor? You'll have to toddle off to Moscow for that." After that I started to get angry. "I'll see," I said, "and then I'll decide. Perhaps I will set off there and go and be an actor." "No," they all insisted, "you tell us in advance exactly what you're going to do, then we can get fitted up with glasses, put them on and get a better look at you." Of course that set them all off laughing again: their guffaws were deafening. I wanted to think up some scathing answer, but then Khamata came to the rescue. "You, scoffers, why do you go on at the lad so? It's true, there is a cavalry regiment like that, it was specially set up to be used for the cinema. You ought to pay more attention to the newspapers. About the town and going off there, well, if that's what he wants and he doesn't feel happy back home..."

All this stupid fuss over me, and I had only been out of the army for a couple of days. What with the incident with Lana today on top of all the rest—their jibing would soon be the death of me. They would say that a slip of a girl managed to cut hay twice as fast as a cavalryman. No, whatever happened I just had to catch up with her and finish my strip first!

Sweep, another sweep and then again and again... I made a last desperate attempt to get my muscles under control. All at once a new wave of strength seemed to come to me and thrust me forward.

The distance between us was growing smaller and I was gradually gaining on Lana! Now, I could really see her—to one side of me and just a fraction in front. The beads of sweat on her sunburnt skin were like drops of water on a ripe plum. I could hear her breathing: rapid, jerky, forced. I sensed, or guessed that she was nearly at the end of her tether.

The pole was rapidly bearing down on us. One more push, just one more—and our scythes were even and they rang out as one as we cut into the grass.

Lana had got used to the idea that I was losing and she was reluctant to be overtaken. She made one last effort to pull away from me. She resorted to cunning and started making her strip only half as wide as mine. Yet even so I was beginning to get the better of her. The pole was very near now. As if she was in a frenzy, Lana began to make her sweeps quicker and quicker. Realising now that there was no way she was going to get back in the lead she pushed the pole while making it look like an accident so that it should fall on me but it fell behind me.

"Sto-op!" called Khamata. "That's it!"

It was hard to change gear by then and we both made a few more sweeps with our scythes.

"That's the end. I said stop!"

We stopped as one, hardly able to get our breath back or bring any words out. Khamata was sitting there in his "heat-shelter", craning his neck to watch us, and at the same time drinking from the jug.

"I did win, didn't I?" asked Lana.

Khamata did not say anything at first, as if he was out to tease Lana.

"Well, go on, Grandad!"

"I'll announce the result later. Now just sit down

quietly and give your arms and legs a rest."

I collapsed under the awning.

"Come on, Grandad! You always have to have your fun!"

Not knowing whether to take offense for real or just pretend, Lana began to walk round the "heat-shelter". One minute she stood up on tiptoe, then she threw her arms into the air only to let them flop down again; she would bend down, swinging her arms to and fro, as if shaking off her tiredness, and would then clutch hold of her shoulders, take a deep breath and let it out again through mischievously pouting lips. When she had got her breath, Lana came back to us, sat down close by, stretched out her legs in front of her, showing her round little knees that looked like upturned teacups.

Khamata put down the jug, brought out bread, cheese and some salted cucumbers, then wiped a broad knife on the hem of his loosely hanging soldier's tunic which I had given him complete with my sergeant's epaulettes. He placed a flat round smoked cheese up on end on the ground and holding it still with his hard, wrinkled fingers, began to cut off small pieces for us.

"After a good day's mowing like that you deserve a good meal," the old man muttered.

But was I feeling like food? Muttering something incomprehensible, I pointed to Lana to say that she should get on and eat. Lana was looking quiet and placid by this time: she was half-lying down with her elbows bent under her to prop her up. Her head was thrown back and her thick hair reached the ground;

her eyelids were half-shut and she was so tired she felt too lazy even to open her mouth.

"Lana, do you want some cheese? Or perhaps I should give you a cucumber?"

No answer.

"Come on, do eat something, otherwise Tembulat here will gobble down the lot."

Silence.

"Don't get upset about losing, after all Tembulat is a man."

"That's not right!" Lana flared up at once. "I won, I did!"

"No-o!" the old man's thin lips stretched into a smile. "Fair's fair!"

"No, Grandad, I won! Ask Tembulat, I'm right, aren't I?"

For the first time in two days Lana looked straight at me and I felt weak at the knees. Her enormous eyes with that elusive laughter lurking in their depths were studying me carefully and at the same time they were warning me: just you dare say "No"! Her long eyelashes fluttered up and down as if counting out the time allocated for my answer. There was something naive in her face, a note of helpless childish purity. Her cheeks at the edge of her mouth looked slightly puffed, as if she was sucking a fruit-drop; her generous lips were slightly parted just inviting someone to trace round them with the tip of a finger. A mere three years ago she had been just an ordinary-looking, clumsy girl with a face covered in large ginger freckles. How she had changed! I had not recognised her immediately when I had first seen her two days before. I had been standing in the middle of our garden when she had walked past. I thought to myself that she would be glad to see me, would come rushing over and start asking me all sorts of questions. After all our houses were right next to each other, and there was not even a fence between them. I had looked upon Lana as a little sister ever since my earliest childhood. Pretending that she had not noticed me, Lana had just walked past, graceful, nimble, beautiful. I wanted to shout something mocking after her but could not bring myself to: it was as if I had suddenly forgotten how to speak altogether.

Nevertheless in the evening she was brought in to see me by her mother. Both she and I felt awkward for some reason and greeted each other like strangers: she quickly stretched out her hand and then quickly wrested it from my grip. We bumped into each other twice the next day, and whenever I set eyes on her I felt strangely awkward.

"Tembulat, aren't I right?"

The repeated question—her impatience, the touch of anger in her voice and the light-hearted confidence that even if she was wrong three times over she would still not hear any objections—got the better of me.

"Yes, yes, you..."

The corners of her lips curled upwards, the sparkle in her eyes grew brighter and I lost my bearings completely. Surely she realised how embarrassed I felt. Perhaps she thought it was because of her that I had offered to come and help Khamata that morning? Perhaps though, it was because of her? I had been lying out in the garden in the hayrick, as I always liked sleeping out of doors in the summer. Khamata had started bustling about early sweeping the yard, and was about to whet his scythe, when he suddenly dropped the idea so as not to wake me.

"Get on, get on, Grandad, I'm not sleeping!" I shouted out.

"So you've woken up? I thought you'd have a good sleep, make the most of the chance." The old man walked over to me. "What's it like being home again after the barracks?"

"It's hard to get used to it."

"You'll manage." The old man began to sharpen the blade. "I'm getting ready to do some mowing."

"Can I come along too?" I heard myself ask, even before the idea had really taken root in my mind.

"Why not? Off we go, if you're in the mood, you can loosen up those old bones of yours."

I quickly made myself ready.

On our way out of the village we climbed up the hill, taking a diagonal path and leaving footprints behind us in the damp crisp grass. Every now and then, with a desperate flapping of wings, quails would take wing in fright and swoop off to one side of us. I walked behind the old man, knocking the large sparkling dewdrops to the ground with my army boots. As I walked along I breathed in the cool of morning in hungry gasps. Ten minutes later we were at the top of the hillock, and I looked round. Down below beyond the bend of the dazzlingly bright river lay my village Arasai, a typical Caucasian village. In places roofs of buildings showed through the thick branches of the trees. Our houses were in the centre: I caught sight of them and thought to myself for a moment, how Lana must look as she slept with her hair strewn over the white pillow... The rim of the sun was now peeping out from behind the crest of the mountains and its first rays set the dew-covered slope sparkling. The sun came up slowly until the enormous red globe hung over the horizon. A warm haze hovered above the earth which seemed to soak in the heat, stirring up feelings and thoughts that we were hardly aware of, filling me with a sense of something more significant than anything I had known before, something vitally important, a key to what life on earth was all about. Still unable to grasp properly the feelings that had suddenly welled up within me I looked down at the amazingly pure, remarkable world that I was beholding as if for the first time. I felt I was discovering it all over again as I picked out the places I knew. Above me the sky was stretched taut like a silk canvas and in its distant depths the songs of the larks blended in an endless happy tune. "My village," I thought to myself in an absent-minded kind of way. "Lana..." Khamata's words I did not catch at once, although I guessed the gist.

"You must have missed it all," came a distant voice floating towards me. "How long have you been away from home? Two years?" On the old man's face I could read sympathetic awareness of my present feelings, concern and worry.

"Two and a half," I whispered in reply, although they seemed to have vanished away to nothing—just as if my childhood, school-days, army service, as if my whole past had suddenly disappeared: it was as if I had only just appeared on the planet.

"Come on, or we'll get behind the others," said Khamata, touching me on the shoulder.

We moved on.

"What a year we've been having: rain one day, sun the next, the spring crops came up really thick and we're all hoping for a good harvest," went on Khamata admiringly. "We're bringing in the second haycrop this year, if Allah's willing, there'll be a third as well."

Khamata told me that they were having problems in the collective farm bringing in the harvest. Everyone that they could possibly find had been roped in. The old men had followed his example and each taken a patch of one and a half to two hectares on the slopes where all the hay had to be cut by hand.

I walked along in silence, listening to Khamata and thinking about other things of more immediate concern to me, trying to understand what was happening to me, for a start trying to find reasons for this sudden urge of mine to go off and start hay-making...

In the morning I had not come to any conclusion, but now I knew: it was because of Lana that I had felt the inexplicable urge to come into contact with her, at least indirectly, with Grandfather as a go-between. I had felt sure that she too would come along, sure with nothing but intuition to go on.

Lana should on no account guess what was happening to me though! So as not to give myself away, I turned to stare in another direction and leant up against the pole.

"You see, Tembulat agrees, and you said it wasn't me."

Lana by chance touched my shoulder as she leant forward to speak, and I felt as if I was on fire.

"As you like, it makes no difference to me." The old man for some reason gave me a long searching look. "As long as you two are ready to agree."

I hardly dared breathe, as I sat there motionless so as not to bump into Lana again and feel that hot skin brush against me, unexpectedly smooth like a poplar-leaf. Lana said nothing. The old man's gaze lighted first on me, then on her, as if he could no longer recognise us.

"Are you at least going to eat?"

Neither of us said anything.

"All right then. Since you don't want to eat, I'm going to go off and say my prayers. When I come back we'll eat together."

Khamata pulled his broad-rimmed white felt hat down over his eyes, rose with one quick jerk, and set off down to the river: he needed to splash his face with water before praying and wash his hands and feet. Tall and dignified, he set off without hurrying as if he was counting as he stepped over all the piles of hay that stretched in even rows right across the slope. Other old men could be seen coming up over the hills, also wearing white felt hats. They too were going down to the river for their ablutions: it was time for their mid-day prayer. It was almost as if Khamata had given them the signal to assemble.

It would take him ten minutes to get down there and as many to say his prayers and then there would be plenty of talking to the other old men—we would have nearly an hour alone! Lana's breaths were coming unevenly, her breasts rose and fell, and her mouth was open just wide enough for the tiny end of her tongue every now and then to lick her sun-parched lips.

We are sitting close to each other and a tiny move is all I have to make to touch her. Lana feels my gaze, lifts her head, and we look at each other. In her eyes there appears an expression I have not seen before, a gentle elusive look, like a ripple of warmth in the summer air, and then she lowers her eyelids as if she wants to hide from me an enormous secret. I turn away and, without seeing it, I look down at the steep slope, feeling somehow taken aback at the decision I have suddenly made, that the rest of my life shall be linked to my home village, to this native earth of mine and Lana... That morning, the hay-making, Khamata and Lana have resolved it shall be so.

Gennadi Nenashev

DOWN THE CHUISKY HIGHWAY

Gennadi Nenashev was born in 1944 in the Altai region in Western Siberia. After completing his secondary education he worked as a builder, a sailor on river steamers, a joiner and a journalist. He graduated from the journalism department of Far-Eastern University as an external student. He has now been living in Chukotka for twenty years in the town of Anadyr and working as a joiner in the building co-operative "Chukotkales".

Nenashev takes for his subjects the stern landscape of Chukotka, the selfless labour of its people working to win the natural resources of this distant Northern region. His collection of stories entitled *Joiners* won a prize in the Maxim Gorky All-Union Competition for the best first book by a young author.

Filat Snegiryov had decided what he wanted to be while still a young boy. Like all his playmates in that quiet suburb he dreamt of one thing, and one thing only—of becoming a lorry-driver. The nearest railway line was sixty miles from his home, he and the other lads had never seen a steam-engine, aeroplane, let alone a steamer. Motor vehicles were so rare in those parts that during the war of 1941-45 and the early post-war years to become a driver seemed even more wonderful than being selected as a cosmonaut would be nowadays. This meant that none of the local boys wanted to drive a goods train, conquer the skies or plough the seas—they were fanatical about motor-cars and nothing else.

Sometimes, after he had been swimming in the nearby river till he could hardly think straight, so tired he was, little Filat would lie down on the hot sand; screwing up his eyes in the bright sunlight he would mull over day-dreams about his future.

He would be cruising along at top speed, then nip into a little lane, do a nifty U-turn and bring his 15cwt-lorry to a smart halt right in front of his house. Slowly and with great swank, expected of drivers, he would come down from the cab: he would be wearing leather gloves right up to his elbows and a big heart-shaped patch, also made of leather, on the seat of his trousers and there would be a cigarette hanging out of his mouth, not one filled with any home-grown tobacco, but the real thing or even a genuine "Kazbek". He would stride over to the gate in his squeaking, soldier-style boots and all the neighbours would come running out: "Filat Andreevich, give us a hand!"

"Filat Andreevich, do us a good turn, there are just a few forkfuls of hay left in the village."

"Filat Andreevich, don't leave me in the lurch, I've been promised some planks!"

"Filat Andreevich, I'm almost out of firewood!"

"Filat Andreevich!"

He would listen to all their requests, swagger up and down and then start making out that it was no easy matter for him: "I'm pressed for time ... you must understand..." Yet he would help them all, nevertheless: he would be a proper neighbour, you could not let people down. Whatever anyone might say, wheels are wheels, he felt he had to help out... Before you could turn around the back of the lorry would be full ... and then off he would go, as if it were no trouble at all. He could manage 15 hundredweight at a time. As for the speed—he was doing no less than thirty miles an hour... That was the kind of giant lorry Filat was going to manoeuvre with! It warmed his heart just to indulge in daydreams of that sort; that adventure was soon followed in his memory by a picture of a very different kind.

This time a lorry was hurtling along the Chuisky Highway by the banks of the treacherous Katun River and Filat was at the wheel. His father was next to him with his foot on the accelerator but leaving the rest to his son. His eyes were sparkling mischievously from under his thick forelock that came nearly down to his eyebrows. He was smiling, egging on his son: "Well done, Filat! You'll make a fine driver. No doubt about it. Can't let the family down, can we!" Then he gave Filat a friendly pat on the knee and started singing:

Down the Chuisky Highway
There's a road—
All the drivers speed down it
With their load.
Snegiryov's the wildest
Of them all:
"I'll get there first!" Filat
Would always call.

In the real song the driver had been called Nikolai not Filat, but his father had always put the name Filat in, even when out with his friends. The song was about a wild old hand of a driver called Nikolai who fell in love with a girl called Raya. Raya worked on the lorries too and was not prepared to marry Nikolai until he had overtaken her in her Ford. The story came to a sad end when Nikolai crashed at high speed, carried away by the exciting chase.

Thinking back to his father brought Filat's happy day-dreams to an abrupt stop, because his father too had been killed in a crash on the Chike-Taman Pass a couple of years back. He had got as far as Berlin in the war only to be caught off his guard here, back home... Filat could still recall the sound of his father's lorry chugging desperately up the hill with a full load of timber, and the way the trailer swerved out to one side on the bend and at last how the lorry tumbled down into the ravine, hurled first to one side and then the other on the way down... His father's face had seemed fearless to the last as he gripped the wheel still singing.

At those memories Filat frowned sadly and he rubbed his damp eyes with his fists.

453

Filat was sure that his father had been singing right up to the last moment, for he had heard among other things, how his father had told Alim Trushkokov, a morose shell-shocked old soldier who lived near by: "I've bawled out that song, Alim, right through Germany! On Victory Day at the Reichstag as well! I didn't know how to put things into words so happy I was, so I sang! Happiness, happiness that came later when you've had time to think about things, but that day I was really excited, so I had to roar out about my Chuisky Highway and how it had taken me all the way to Berlin. You know, I felt better after that, I could breathe again. I felt so proud of all the lads, we'd made it all the way from the Altai Mountains, I'll never forget!

"Another time—it was in Poland—I was taking some shells down to the front line. All of a sudden I saw a Messerschmitt overhead. It started coming for me. I swerved to the side, luckily the ground was flat for miles around. So I began to make real figures: first to the right, then to the left, first I accelerate like mad and then take my foot right off the accelerator. The German's hurling bloody bombs at me, and firing a whole stream of bullets out of his machine-gun! It was beyond me why he took it into his head to chase after one miserable lorry like that. Earth was being thrown up all around me, smoke, whistling bullets and I was gripping that wheel as if I had some German by the throat and roaring: "Snegiryov's the wildest of them all!.." and not a bit afraid. That Kraut got so carried away chasing after me that he forgot all about our anti-aircraft boys and they brought him down with an almighty crash. I climbed down out of the cab and shook my fist at him: 'So you wouldn't leave me in peace, and look where it got you!'" (At that point in the story Father used to lift his arms right up into the air and brandish his fists to and fro). "Then I looked round at the lorry loaded with shells and thought for a moment what would have happened if all that lot had gone up in smoke! And then I laughed on the other side of my face..."

"Snegiryov! Let's play flicks, shall we?" called Yuri Ogryzkov, Filat's best friend.

Yuri had very hard fingers and when he flicked at his friends' foreheads after they had lost, they often ended up with bruised or swollen foreheads. Sometimes he would give someone such a whack that they would see stars, but Filat was still keen to try his luck. He would usually agree to game for a round or two. There was nothing complicated about the rules of the game: each player chose a vehicle registration number code such as AA or AB. Whoever saw their letter combination go by first had the right to flick the other in the forehead the same amount of times that matched up with the last number on the number plate.

"I don't feel like it today," replied Filat, out of sorts.

"Then let's be off home. I'm starving!"

Each one of them took a wheel rim and rolled it home using make-shift hooks made of thick wire. They bounced up and down on the road clinking as they went, and Filat, who had forgotten the sad memories of a little while before, pooped as loud as he could alarming the piglets napping in the dust at the side of the road.

...After seven years of secondary school Filat had gone straight round to the personnel office of the lorry depot and found himself a job as an apprentice mechanic. The very first day he got his brand-new work kit, hands and face into such a mess that hardly anyone could recognise him. His mother cooked a special supper to celebrate and could hardly take her anxious eyes off his rapturous face.

Filat soon had a good grasp of a mechanic's skills. Indeed few problems had been expected, since he had long since examined every part a lorry could possibly have and given it the once over, a hundred times if not more. There was only one thing—the crucial test—left for Filat, making a thorough study of the engine.

Filat completed his driver's course at a club run by the local civil defense organisation and he managed to spend another year working at the lorry depot before he was called up for his military service.

His first drive along the Chuisky Highway on his own... That was something Filat would never forget. In his last moments he was still bound to remember the thrilling pride, enough to make his heart burst, the rapturous excitement and God knows what other feelings with which he drove out on to the asphalt road after climbing the Maimin Hill.

It had not been a sunny or a rainy day—just an ordinary grey one. Filat was aglow within though, so that everything wore a bright and festive look, as far as he was concerned.

There was a song in his heart echoed by the wheels, and the poplars and birch-trees that he passed seemed to greet him with their light-hearted rustle as he drove across mile after mile of the road that meekly stretched out before him: every leaf seemed to wave to him in greeting, so did the seething rapids of the Katun River and the mountains ahead seemed to make way for him. Make merry Filat Snegiryov! From now on you're our willing prisoner. Wherever you might be later on, your heart will belong to us. We're your home, your eternal love. We'll teach you to understand beauty, to set store by male friendship, here out on the highway you shall meet your one-and-only, then after an accident you'll understand what carelessness can lead to. It's dangerous to get on too familiar terms with this Highway.

Just look how steep this climb in the road is! Have all parts of the lorry been checked out properly? On this particular part of the road where there's no room for two lorries to pass unless one moves over into a passing place, up so high where not a single tree grows, above the deep ravine where Chuya River seethes and foams held in by the rocks, don't look back to wonder at the untamed waters: your head will start to spin and that will be the end. When the road is like a flat grey arrow, Filat, that's the time to sing. Sing the song your father used to rock you to sleep with in your hammock cradle. Ahead lie many years of demanding work: driving through piles of earth and snow, bleeding scratches, rough nails on frost-bitten hands... But today was a memorable day—his birth as a driver. Filat was singing his favourite song and the hills all around him sent back the echo. No, he would never be able to forget his very first haul!

After his three years' doing his military service in the Far East of the country Filat came home. He climbed into a new ZIL, tried out what it could do and the top speed it could manage. This was some lorry!

> The mighty new green Ford
> Chased by ZIL
> Flying like speedy arrows
> Down the hill...

He remembered some more words of the song and light of heart now he thought to himself: "I can just imagine those old crocks flying along like arrows!" He felt a soft spot for the Nikolai of the song, thinking: "If you'd had a lorry like mine you'd have caught up with your Raya on the very first mile..."

Filat had long since grown used to the routine of getting up at the crack of dawn, starting up his lorry, setting off on the next trip marked up in his log-book.

On this particular morning though he felt just as elated all over as he did on his first haul. The day before, he had brought his very own Lyuba from the maternity home, where she had just given birth to their first child. A son! Filat had seen him the day after the birth, but what kind of an impression could you get through a window? But now he had carried into his own home the tiny blanket bundle with Nikolai or Kolya for short (he had chosen that name so that it would fit in with the song properly), unwrapped the covers with his calloused, work-worn hands and, with a broad sheepish smile studied the pink scrap, vaguely reminiscent of a human being. He had cried out happily: "The spitting image of his grandad! He'll be a driver! Ace driver on the Chuisky Highway—Nikolai Filatovich Snegiryov!"

He had then planted Lyuba on his lap, given her a hug, with his astonished gaze still glued to his son. The ten-day-old "ace" started kicking out on his blanket, thrusting his legs to and fro, with a high demanding squeak.

"Just look at that, the nappy's wet! This won't do, our driver's radiator's sprung a leak!" exclaimed Filat in peals of happy laughter.

When he had delivered his load in Kosh-Agach Filat set off back to his own town with his empty ZIL. Each milestone was a happy reminder that home was getting nearer. The familiar road which he knew like the back of his hand did not stop him thinking about less everyday things and he tried hard to come to grips with the mystery of man's birth. "Just imagine," he mused, giving himself a happy slap on the thigh. "There was nothing there, nothing and then suddenly just for the asking—head, nose, legs... Why? How? He's breathing, moving, his hands have got not six, not three fingers but five like all the rest of us and with tiny nails—all as it should be! There's no stopping Nature! Then if you take death: someone's there one minute and vanishes the next. His thoughts, ideas and the man himself all disappeared into thin air. The stars used to shine for him and the sun rise in the mornings ... and then nothing but dark emptiness. You can't even be sure it's dark... What's it all mean?"

459

Today was too happy an occasion to go thinking thoughts like that.

On the outskirts of Ongudai a man stepped out into the road and on seeing the lorry, when Filat was still a good distance away, he began to wave him down, with both his arms, frantically and imploringly. "He's not from these parts," realised Filat straight away. "Folks round here don't try and persuade you to take them like that. They talk you into it."

There was a big bulging briefcase at the stranger's feet, his short, wide-sleeved raincoat was unfastened. His sporty little cap was perched casually on one side of his head as if someone had thrown it to land on his head. His open raincoat was flapping in the wind and he looked less like a person than a scarecrow who had got fed up with standing in an allotment and had come out to the highway instead.

Filat was not allowed to take passengers, but he could not bring himself simply to drive past someone standing there all on his own at the deserted roadside, waving pathetically. His good mood got the better of Filat, and he did not want to disappoint anyone. He stopped the lorry.

The man walked away from his briefcase and came running up to the cab: "Would you take me with you to Gorny please... I'm desperate for a lift!"

"In you get!" said Filat giving in cheerfully.

The man hurried back for his briefcase, and then clawed at the door trying in vain to press in the knob of the handle.

"Thank you," he said, heaving a sigh of relief when Filat helped him up into the seat next to him. "You

see, my colleagues left on a bus and I turned up too
late."

"We'll be driving past a militiaman on point duty in a
minute, so bend down when we get there," warned Filat
as he set off again. When he drew level with the militiaman leaning on his motor-bike in a lazy sort of way, he
bared his teeth in a forced smile and gave him a wave.

The militiaman answered with a friendly nod:
"Have a good trip!"

"We're all right, you can sit up again!" said Filat
to his doubled up passenger.

"I had to wait at least two hours for a lift," complained the stranger, sitting up straight again. "I'm
lucky that it's not raining, otherwise you might as well
just lie down and die in this part of the world."

"The people here are very friendly, they wouldn't
let you come to a sticky end," commented Filat by
way of conversation. "You go into any house and they
let you spend the night, get warm and have something
to eat. Where are you from? From Moscow I'd reckon?"

"That's right."

"Have you come out here for work or a holiday?"

"I'm here with an expedition."

As Filat drove along he peered at the long-nosed
profile of his passenger, only glancing at the road
every now and then. This frivolity on the part of his
driver obviously made the passenger highly uneasy:
his answers were only reluctant ones and at the bends
he turned visibly pale clutching on to the handrail
above the glove compartment.

"So you're a geologist, are you?" said Filat to keep
the chat going.

"No, a linguist."

"What d'you mean by that?"

"I study language. I've been collecting folk-tales in these parts."

"Now I get you! You've been collecting fairy-stories," said Filat with greater interest now as he lit up a cigarette, managing to steer with his elbows, "this place is a regular mine of stories out here, you'll have a job listening to them all. You ought to get together with Zhenya Laptev on the petrol tanker, he can't say anything without throwing in a joke or a story for good measure. As soon as he opens his mouth at the depot, half of the lads have clustered round him. There's no stopping him once he gets them laughing! They can hardly stand up straight. They'll be rolling around, killing themselves. He's a real master in his way."

"This road's a hell of a bone-shaker," observed the linguist with a nervous laugh, giving no ear to what Filat was saying. "A famous route they call it, and there's no asphalt in sight."

"There's not meant to be any on these bends," explained Filat defending it loyally. "In the bad weather, especially when you're coming downhill, you just slide off asphalt like a fly off a window-pane." To himself he thought: "What a scarecrow! Just my luck to pick up a moaner..."

By this time the lorry was climbing up to the Siminsky Pass.

When they got up to the very top Filat turned off the engine. From here he liked to look down the mountain valley, to admire the endless blue of the sky above it and watch how the grey foam of mist

462

gently wove its way, caressing the green trees of the taiga as it made its way slowly up to the tops of the mountains that lay far below where they stood. It was only from a vantage point such as theirs that you could understand why the Altai was often called the Blue Mountains.

"My ears are popping," complained Filat's passenger, shaking his head, but Filat did not bother to reply.

He climbed down from the cab, stretched his aching limbs so hard that he made his bones crack, turned his cramped neck this way and that, took a good look all around him and lit up a cigarette.

In the distance Filat caught sight of another lorry moving towards them: he could tell from the dilapidated front that it was Yuri Ogryzkov with his timber lorry. Ten days previously Yuri had popped in to visit his father-in-law in Cherga, had "a drop too much" and then overturned before he was hardly out of the village. He had got off lightly: a squashed bonnet and right wing not to mention two front teeth in exchange for no more than a "severe reprimand".

"Cheers, mate!" called Yuri, his gap-toothed mouth stretched in a broad grin as he drew up door to door with Filat. "How's your son?"

"Growing," answered a proud Filat. "He can't half yell already!"

"Now you've started her off, you'll have to catch up with us. My Nyurka's going to have her fourth soon. Soon we won't have a home but a drivers' pull-up. There's no stopping her. What can I do about it? I have to satisfy the growing demand, as the depot boss keeps telling us!"

"Have you sorted everything out with the garage manager?" asked Filat.

"And how! That was a right old hoo-ha!" said Yuri as he burst out laughing. He slapped his own cheek and his mischievous eyes rolled upwards as he spoke. 'I'm not letting you anywhere near another lorry!' he shouted, and he said the same to the chief mechanic about me. Then the mechanic really tore the other fellow apart and said, 'You'll have to go out on the timber run then instead of him!' The boss came to look at my lorry and saw that everything was up to scratch, after I'd done my repair job. He shook his fist right under my nose and said he wasn't going to give me any more chances. I've had a reprimand stamped into my labour card," Yuri added sadly. "Bye for now, see you this evening. A bit further down the road's really ploughed up, be careful, don't come adrift—keep to the side nearest the drop," he warned and then sped on his way.

"There's a fellow for you!" Filat thought out loud. "Whether it's work or play, there's no stopping him. If he gets into a fight all hell breaks loose. He used to sleep under Nyurka's window for a whole year, before she finally gave in."

The passenger gave a tactful cough but did not say a word.

Once over the pass Filat came out on to a flat stretch of road and got up speed. His good mood that had evaporated for some reason was now coming back. Perhaps it was because of the chance meeting with his friend or the chance to get up a good speed again or thinking happily about his son; whatever it was, all of a sudden it gave him the urge to start up his favourite song. He could not get the tune out of his head and in the end it forced its way out.

In a fairly tuneful voice he began:

> *Down the Chuisky Highway*
> *There's a road—*
> *All the drivers speed down it*
> *With their load.*
> *Snegiryov's the wildest*
> *Of them all.*
> *"I'll get there first!" Kolya*
> *Would always call.*

They crossed the Ust-Siminsky bridge and after that the road followed the river. The sheer banks and the pale blue glint of the foaming waters transformed this remarkable landscape. It was early autumn. The trees and various grasses were starting to try on their bright garb—still timid and hesitant. Singing as he drove, Filat remembered how long ago on just such a sunny and colourful autumn day he had been driving along in the cab of his father's lorry: after loosening the collar of his old sweater with a calloused hand as if it had been suffocating him, the father said in an unusually stern, solemn voice: "Look Filat! All that's our homeland. Mine and yours. The Chuisky Highway is our pride and joy. Without it the Altai Mountains would be like the North without the Northern Lights..."

> *He loved her like a sister,*
> *This green three-tonner.*

sang Filat with happy gusto filling the landscape with the tune familiar since early childhood that he held so dear. It always seemed to meet the occasion whatever his mood of the moment might be.

Carried away by the song, he forgot about the underlying hostility he felt for his passenger: he wanted to say to him, "My son's called Kolya, too, you know, and his name's Snegiryov. He's eleven days old today and he's going to be a driver too, for sure." Yet he decided not to hurry and to make more of an impression by throwing out that important piece of information at the learned passenger in passing so to speak.

"Is your expedition collecting songs too?" inquired Filat in a vague sort of way.

"Yes, of course."

"The song about the Highway must have been the first one you recorded, wasn't it?" asked Filat, quite sure the answer would be Yes.

"No, we didn't record that one."

"Why?" asked Filat in surprise and then thought to himself: "There wouldn't have been any point, of course, because everyone knows it already."

"It's trash," remarked the linguist in an off-hand fashion. He hesitated for a moment and then added in a bored tone: "Abracadabra".

The last word sounded just as if someone had drawn the end of stick along the top of a fence.

"What?" Filat asked trying to make out the word, made wary by its unfamiliar bouncing sound.

"Nonsense, to put it briefly," explained the language expert.

Filat was prepared to believe anything, but to say that his song was nonsense! That was going too far... The Highway would not be the same without it. It was like a sister to him that song, part and parcel of him!

"What makes you call it nonsense?" he said in as controlled a voice as he could muster, still hoping that he was being teased.

The passenger, who did not, however, appear to be in any mood for jokes turned to Filat.

"Tell me now, what's out there?" he asked tapping at the windscreen in front of him with a long thin finger.

"What d'you mean 'what is it?' It's a road!"

"Precisely—it's a road! And what's a highway? That's a road as well. But you go on singing 'Down the Chuisky Highway there's a road.' You end up singing there's a road down the road. It's absurd. It's tautology." He turned away after that, obviously regarding the matter as closed.

"Hm-mm," muttered Filat in bewilderment. "How could it have come to this? We've always sung it and it went with a real swing and then that pen-pusher went and rubbed my song in the dirt. Polite but heartless." It was that cold, thick-skinned politeness that Filat found harder than anything else to stomach. To himself he made all sorts of objections to his passenger, but whichever way he tried to twist things round he turned out to be right after all: that blasted road going down the Highway! It made it look as if the man who had made up the song had been taking them all for a ride. His father, all the drivers, even his little Kolya? It sounded now as if he was not driving down the one and only Chuisky Highway, but just another road like hundreds or even thousands of others all over the country—ordinary roads with nothing special about them. The Altai Mountains did not seem so blue any more or the Katun so beautiful, just another river. Ordinary mountains, ordinary roads, ordinary taiga, which made him, Filat, just another driver, no longer the conqueror of steep and perilous passes. Just another... just another... just another... Suddenly the whole world began to look grey, faded and dull to Filat. He looked unblinkingly at the road and felt as if he had been robbed of all his riches at one fell swoop.

He had felt like this once before long ago in his childhood during the war. His mother had sent him to the shop to buy bread when he was only eight because she was ill. When it was his turn at last in the queue he had exchanged his bread ration slips for a loaf and had then walked home feeling happy and very grown-up. He had not even bitten the end off the loaf, even though he was sorely tempted. He had just licked the crust smelling of delicious rye, removing a tiny 'wart' from the end which might have broken off and got lost anyway...

In a small patch of waste ground on his way home a man had drawn even with Filat. He had given Filat a friendly pat on the head, said something funny, asked what his name was and then suddenly ... grabbed at the loaf. Filat could not move from the shock and gradually he was overwhelmed by horror at what had happened... By the time he was able to move, shout or cry again the man had vanished into thin air. Filat ran up and down the streets tear-stained and barefoot until it was nearly dark, his hands still clutched to his front where a few hours before there had been that soft, warm bread. It took him even longer to find a name for what the man had done... He never really did find the right word.

Nowadays there were plenty of songs just as there was plenty of bread, but the one about the Highway had been not just another song for Filat, just as that loaf grabbed from a child by an adult had been more than just "bread".

Filat drew over to the right hand edge of the road and braked with a sudden jerk: the lorry gave a lurch and then stopped.

"Out you get!" said Filat looking angrily at the passenger who had long since forgotten the short lecture he had delivered on the subject of the song.

"What d'you mean out? There's still..."

"Shift yourself, I said!!" yelled Filat.

"What's up? What's the matter?" mumbled the linguist quite unaware of what was happening.

Filat picked up his briefcase from the floor of the lorry and hurled it through the open window onto the side of the road.

"How dare you?!" shouted the passenger in alarm, clambering clumsily out of the cab. "All my findings are in there!"

"You know what you can do with those findings of yours! You go and make off down the road, while I'll take the Highway."

Filat went a few kilometres further, but feeling his hands shaking unpleasantly he stopped. He walked down to the river where there stood a bas-relief monument to the writer Vyacheslav Shishkov* right by the Katun in a small well-tended clearing. The better part of the clearing had been filled up with fresh piles of gravel.

Filat sat down by the water's edge on a tree-stump. The little waves were lapping gently on the pebbles by the bank, and Filat, sitting there, tried to listen to the river, but the river was not singing for him today...

"What's the matter with me, to hell with it all!" he said angrily to himself all of a sudden. "That linguist chap was right. The Chuisky Highway is not what it used to be, not the same lorries and not the same people... I suppose we need a different song ... a new one!"

As he walked back through the clearing Filat kicked viciously at a large stone.

"What a mess they've made here ... those eggheads!"

He climbed back into the cab and started up in second gear.

*V. Ya. Shishkov (1873-1945)—Soviet Russian writer well known for his historical novel *Ugryum River* about Siberia. —Ed.

Nadezhda Petrunina

THE DISPLACED HEART

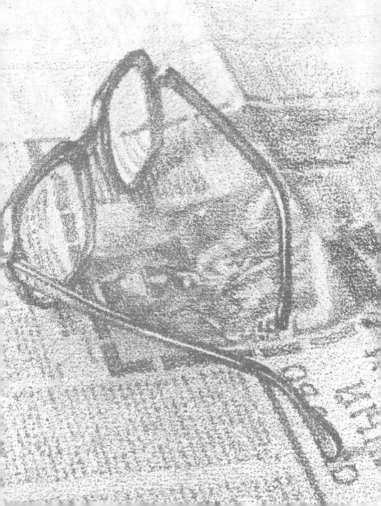

Nadezhda Petrunina was born in Ryazan. She graduated from the teachers' training college in that city. She has worked as a nursery school teacher and subsequently as a journalist in newspapers for young readers. She has written a book of stories entitled *All Is Sweetness and Light*, which was brought out by the Moscow Molodaya Gvardiya Publishers.

Nadezhda Petrunina's writings are concerned with the life and people in Soviet villages. Many of her stories treat the relationships between those in charge of the farms and the young people working under their guidance.

Anya was standing by the counter and could hardly bring herself to look at the door. It was nearly dinner-time. "They're going to turn up any minute... How should I smile at them?" she wondered.

They came into the shop—her brother Vassily and his family: a wife and two girls—and all at once the customers stopped talking among themselves and turned to look at the newcomers.

Vassily was a tall stout man with a round face like Anya's, only it was a different colour, red not white. He looked anxiously from his wife to his sister, then at his children, and smiled sheepishly, hoping not to offend anyone. His wife, a thin woman who looked as if she was all sinew, hissed quietly through her teeth at her daughters how they should behave. The strange words she could not understand put Anya on her guard. She could not help feeling that this starched German lady was muttering something unkind about her. Only the girls looked really happy. The elder, Cora, pushed her long hair back behind her shoulders with a movement that already betrayed the confidence of a grown woman, and gave a coquettish smile. Little Annette, aged ten, leant over the counter to hug her aunt: Anya felt the warm plump cheek against her hand.

Her brother Vassily had arrived the day before with his family from Out There. For a visit. That morning Anya's husband Nikolai had taken them round the town to show them the sights.

Nikolai had brought them here not to buy socks or mittens but for an outing... The smart clothes and neat appearance of the whole family seemed like a masquerade to Anya. After all mummers always used to put on a show of good cheer with the help of bright clothes and grease-paint...

There was only one thing Anya felt sure about: it was there, where Vassily, her brother, had come from, that the people were taking cover, the people from whom she and her mother had had to run away abandoning their house... The people to whom killing was an everyday occupation just as selling stockings was for her...

When it was announced over the wireless that war had broken out her mother had slumped down on a bench and then called out: "Anya, run and fetch your father quickly, best foot first!"

Anya turned round in the covered porch, almost stumbling over her own feet, ran outside and rushed off. Two houses further down the street she tripped in a small ditch and caught a piece of broken bottle in the sole of her foot. The unexpected fright, the jagged wound full of dirt that was oozing blood, and the burning pain—all that merged together in a painful memory called war. That was how she remembered it...

They had been living in a small town. She had been fifteen at the time, and Vassily a year younger. Her mother and father had been young but she had not realised it at the time.

Her mother had started packing her father's things together. Anya could not remember what she had packed, but she could remember the long crease that ran across the middle of her mother's forehead and also the way her father scolded, saying: "Why on earth are you packing so much?"

Her father had given everyone special instructions as he left: he had told her mother "not to wail", had promised Anya to be back within two months and had called upon Vassily to be the mainstay and defender of the family. The local medical orderly had on the other hand kept saying something very different about Vassily: "What kind of a mainstay is he... It's a very rare disorder—*ectopia cordis*!'" The medical orderly loved to use grand words but he could give an explanation in plain Russian as well: "Vassily's heart is a whole three centimetres out of the true! He was born with that handicap! And why—God alone knows!'"

According to the old wives' tales it was at the dead of night that all-knowing God was most likely to steal away the sick and in the dark Anya often used to worry for hours on end that Vassily might die. She even used to get out of bed sometimes and go and make sure he was still breathing. Her mother used to get angry with her but she herself used to go over to the sleeping child to keep watch, even more often than little Anya.

Sometimes Mother used to say: "Anya, don't be angry when Vassily gets bigger helpings. He's got to pull through. He's got a displaced heart after all and no-one knows how things are going to turn out... Remember how the orderly said back in the spring that even the doctors in the town don't really know what the matter is and what to do about it."

Anya herself used to make sure Vassily always got the best share of the availabe food. People with

475

normal hearts were very hungry in those days, let alone anyone with a displaced one.

Their foodstocks soon dwindled and they were not getting any news of their father. Sometimes the children would not see their mother for several days and nights on end when she was away working in the granary.

Anya used to take charge of the cooking. She would fry potato cakes; in the beginning they used to consist of potato and later they had to make do with potato peelings. People who came to live in their village as evacuees taught her to make coffee out of acorns. They managed. The only thing that they worried about was how their father was getting on, they wanted him back so much...

When they ran out of firewood the children used to go up to Bald Head Hill to gather kindling. Never again afterwards did Anya ever see such a bare wood without a single spare twig. The old forester used to chase everyone who went up there, threatening them with the courts, and he meant what he said. Anya used to shiver at the thought but she went along all the same. You could not keep the stove burning on wishful thinking or with the help of the Holy Ghost.

On one occasion she had gone up there with Vassily. They had taken a saw so as to be able to reach more twigs. The trunks of the trees were like hard ice and the slightest noise rang out for all to hear. The forester was lame and he squinted, but his hearing was excellent. He heard them and started to give chase. He may have been lame, but he still managed to catch up with them and to seize hold of their saw.

When they came running home Anya's teeth were chattering so loudly that they could be heard all over the house; she wanted to clench her teeth shut but it was impossible. She was sobbing and her teeth were chattering from the cold, and from the feeling that she had been unfairly treated.

Vassily had lain down on the trunk, clutched the left side of his chest with his thin fingers, blue with cold, and whispered: "My heart's going to slip out, my heart's going to slip!"

Anya, thinking to herself in horror that with fingers as skinny as that he might not be able to keep his slippery heart in place behind his ribs, ran over to him and pressed down on his chest with both her broad little palms.

In the evening the forester came hobbling up to bring back the saw. Mother pushed a plate of potato cakes over to him. He did not eat any, just cursed the Gerries so wildly that it was enough to make the dead turn in their graves...

When the fighting came uncomfortably near to their town Anya's mother tried to put off going till the very last minute. "Breaking up the family nest—that's the last thing I'll ever do. Father said we were to wait for him here." Yet they could not stay on and just wait for the Gerries! Suddenly they noticed Vassily was missing—he seemed to have disappeared into thin air. Then a woman shouted as she ran past their house that the lads were "giving a hand to the wounded". Vassily was there along with the others. They would catch up with the rest.

With heavy hearts and in a hectic rush they set off,

abandoning their house, but Vassily never did catch them up... Later Anya was to hear how the village women whispered to each other: "Those boys, you see, must have had it."

Vassily had not caught up with them, yet the notification about their father's death did catch up.

They came back home a year later.

While she was clearing out the attic, Anya's mother had found a photograph of the whole family together, when the children were just six and five. Vassily had been given a right old scolding over that photograph for he had poked out everyone's eyes with an awl. ("Why do those goggles have to stare at me like that?!") Now Mother enjoyed sitting and gazing at that photograph for a long time at a stretch.

Anya then began to work as a waitress in the local tearoom. It was there that she had attracted the attention of Fyodor—a shy lieutenant. He was not like the local lads from roundabout, although he had been born and bred on a farm.

He had a thin face, and enormous pale eyes. Instead of proposing he thrust a piece of paper into Anya's hands with the address of his garrison that he was now being sent to serve in, and asked: "Will you come?"

"I'll come," she answered although the prospect was frightening: the Far East of the country might as well have been on the other side of the moon, and then there would be no-one to look after Mother.

"Off you go, since he's asking for you. Nowadays husbands don't grow on trees," Anya's mother reminded her.

Fyodor was waiting for her when she got there: he

had hung up a curtain to make his room look more inviting. In his small quarters there was a narrow couch, a rickety table, a chair and crates to take the place of a further two chairs.

Anya spread out a counterpane with lace edging on the couch and spread out a little rug on the floor next to it. Then they laid the table, called in Fyodor's friends, and the wedding was duly celebrated.

In the spring they had a son—Vladimir or Vova for short. Fyodor was supposed to be coming to fetch her with a car that one of his commanding officers had promised to let him have for the occasion. Anya was surprised when instead of her husband she was met by his friend.

She asked where Fyodor was, but the friend kept talking about baby Vova, saying what a bonny boy he was. Then she asked again about Fyodor, but the friend held out his hands to take the baby and Anya noticed that his hands were trembling. Mechanically she placed the baby in his arms but the word "frontier" kept hurtling through her mind and she let out a tortured cry...

Anya returned home with Vova, a tiny baby.

Her mother had aged very dramatically. Often she would sit down on the settee, plant the palms of her hands on her knees and begin to sway mechanically from side to side, staring in front of her with dull eyes.

One warm day Anya had left Vova lying on a blanket in the front garden, while she ran back into the house for his little cotton scarf.

Her mother was sitting on the settee, swaying to

and fro. She was wearing a warm head-scarf and a jersey. Anya was going to tell her that it was hot outside and called out to her. Her mother did not hear. Then Vova began to squawk loudly out in the garden.

Her mother started and rushed to the door in a shaky old person's trot, rather than a run. Suddenly she stopped and began to sink to the floor. Anya ran up and thrust her strong arms under her mother's armpits but could not lift her to her feet. Her body seemed made of lead. Anya took fright and called out—then her mother came to her senses and after that it was easy to lift her up.

Unsteady on her feet, Mother walked over to the settee, stretched herself out on it face downwards, and stayed there till night fell. In the night she wanted to get up but could not manage it. A month later they buried her.

Life seemed quite empty for Anya after that. Yet she still had to get up early in the mornings, go to work in the shop and go to the neighbour's house afterwards to fetch Vova.

Anya could still remember perfectly clearly how Nikolai had first walked over to her counter. He had been tall and thin, with a funny face: he had a long nose and eyes set very close to it. He said that he worked in a factory and bought some shaving lotion.

One day he had bought a child's drum and come over to see Anya home after work. He waited while Anya went into her neighbour's to fetch Vova. He came into Anya's sad house without being invited. He gave the drum to Vova and said: "Here you are, little rogue, here's a drum!" He noticed that the leg of the kitchen-table was rickety, found the necessary tools himself and mended it. For a week he came on regular visits and then he moved in. Life gradually began to follow a steady pattern: Vova could now grow up with a father and they were turning into a real family.

Nikolai used to work as a mechanic. He always handed over the whole of his pay-packet to Anya, without leaving even the tiniest of secret treasures for himself. When he needed something Anya used to buy it. He was respected by the fellow-workers at his factory. As he grew older they began to address him as Nikolai Dmitrich. If his photo was not to be seen up on the factory's Board of Honour it was only because it was being changed for a new, more recent one. He was well thought of.

Right from the start Nikolai had taken on Vova as his own. It was often difficult for the teacher to persuade childrens' real parents to go along to parents' meetings but Nikolai always came along with half an hour to spare. He used to ask detailed questions about Vova when he talked to the teachers before the meetings and afterwards.

Vova was praised and known as the pride of the school. He was rewarded with a gold medal for his outstanding success in his studies when he completed school. Everyone had expected him to become a scientist but he ended up by going off to train as a naval officer. He was tall and handsome, looking the part of a naval officer right from the start.

Then Nikolai and Anya moved into a new house. Nikolai walked round the new house with its empty echoing rooms, tapping at the walls and sometimes even leaning against them as hard as he could as if he was trying out how tough they were. "Well, what about it? Are you pleased? Have they made you happy?" he asked. Anya just smiled.

Nikolai loved reading newspapers. After spreading them out on the table so that they covered it completely, he would sit down and put on his square-framed glasses. Behind the lenses his eyes grew blurred and looked enormous, rather like a calf's. Anya would shake her head and smile broadly.

In the eveinings they watched TV. Whenever Nikolai saw a ship, no matter whether it was a passenger liner or a naval vessel, he would call out: "Look, Anya, there goes our Vova out to sea!"

One day he called Anya in from the kitchen, and when she saw a ship on the screen she burst out crying.

"What's up? What is it, Anya?" asked Nikolai in alarm. He made her sit down and fussed round her like a mother-hen over its chick.

"Sailors, if they drown, are never going to have a grave, Nikolai."

He stood up straight again and took a step backwards in astonishment, exclaiming: "What's got into you? Are you off your rocker?"

Then he came over serious and concerned again, and Anya explained: "It's not just that... You see, our Vassily was just like a sailor—he's got no grave... We know where Papa's buried but there's no trace of Vassily..."

She covered her face with her hands held stiff like

two planks, and began to sway from side to side in her anguish. Nikolai's strong hand stroked her head.

During the night Anya woke with a start and in the dark she discovered that Nikolai was not there next to her.

He was out in the kitchen by the window, rubbing his left arm with his right hand, shivering as he did so. Anya quickly went up to him, pressed close up against him as if she wanted to be part of him, so that the pain of his cramp could pass through into her... When the pain had died down she said: "Nikolai, you know, Vassily can't have been killed in the war. He should not have been fighting at all, not just because of his age. After all they had discovered he had a rare disease, if you remember, a displaced heart."

Nikolai slowly stroked her hair with his large hand and said in a quiet voice: "All our hearts have been pushed out of the true by war..."

In the middle of winter Anya received an unexpected telephone call and was asked to come to the District Executive Committee.

In the spacious office a brown-eyed man told her to sit down, addressing her as Anna Ivanovna and telling her not to worry. That was what first made her feel something must be wrong. A familiar shiver went down her spine: poor Fyodor's friend had just as confusedly asked her not to worry that day in the maternity home.

Anya plucked up her courage and said: "Tell me please straight out why you've called me here. I can face up to it. What I can't bear is not knowing."

The man got up and said in a calm voice: "Anna Ivanovna, your brother Vassily has been found. He is in West Germany. He's asking for an invitation from you. He wants to come and see you with his family."

Something must have happened to her face at that stage because the man came running up with a glass of water, began to make a fuss, and for some reason encourage her to cry. Yet crying was not what she wanted to do...

Not long afterwards she received a letter on thin crisp paper. It began with the words: "My dear sister Anya!"

The letter shook in her hand and then fluttered to the floor accompanied in her mind by deafening noise and the whine of sirens...

Vassily wrote that he was working as a motor-mechanic, that there was far more to tell her than he could put in just a letter, that his wife was called Helga, that he was very sorry to know about Mamma and Papa, that his daughters were mischievous little things and the younger one was covered with freckles.

"Well, so that's it," said Anya, straightening out the letter on her knees with her fist. "There we are... Let him come. On his own, that is, by himself. There's no open house for the others! They won't find a welcome here! No."

She lay down on the bed, with her face to the wall. She heard Nikolai come back from work. He looked into the room, thought that his wife must be sleeping, and began to rustle up the supper on his own. When it was ready, he called Anya.

She came into the kitchen and sat down.

"What's bitten you? Your whole face has gone blue! Are you ill?" he asked, leaning right across the table to take a close look at her.

Anya brought out the letter, which she had folded in four from behind the mirror; she straightened it out, making the paper crackle as she did so, and laid it on the table in front of her husband. The unfamiliar envelope with watermarks on it surprised him, she noticed that quite clearly.

Carefully and for some reason using only two of his work-hardened, clumsy fingers, Nikolai brought out the piece of paper. He read the first line, looked over at his wife quite incredulously and then bent over the letter, unable to believe his weak, and evidently bewildered, eyes. He read it through another three or four times. Then he stuck the letter back into the envelope. He gave a sigh and said: "So that's it."

That night Nikolai had another severe attack of cramp in his arm which had been frost-bitten while he had been fighting near Stalingrad. When Anya came out into the kitchen to sympathise, he drew her close to him and said: "Don't worry! Write to them and say: 'Come!' Let them come and see us in the summer! We'll get a piglet in one of the villages and call over all the folks! We won't feed them on bread like theirs, that tastes of kerosene!"

Anya laid her head on his shoulder and began to cry.

They stood by Anya's counter and every one was looking at them. It was obvious that they had come from abroad and felt awkward and out of place.

Anya remembered her brother Vassily as tall and

thin, and could not imagine how he had turned into this strong-looking red-faced man with bald patches over each temple gleaming with sweat.

They went back to Anya's house by bus. Vassily was looking out of the window, hungrily taking everything in. That hunger for his home was the first thing that had cheered Anya in the two days since they had arrived.

Helga sat very erect and glanced out of the window every now and then for politeness's sake. Cora was leaning back on her seat in a very casual kind of way. Only little Annette with her curls and her freckles was a sight for sore eyes. Anya thought she noticed the scent of fresh milk hovering about her little niece. Her warm head was leaning up against the bend of Anya's elbow. Suddenly the little girl sat up with a start and began to pull at her aunt's sleeve.

"What is it, Freckles?" asked Anya and all at once she realised without needing any words—it was ice-cream.

The booth where they were selling it was by the roadside. Someone had bought her some vanilla ice-cream there the day before and she had remembered, amazing!

Anya called to the driver to stop and got out of the bus with her niece. Little Annette ran at once over to the booth and began to explain to the ice-cream seller what she wanted, using sign language.

When Anya caught up a little while later, the woman nodded in greet to her and said in a sympathetic voice: "What a tragedy..."

The ice-cream seller's own troubles suddenly melted

away to nothing when confronted by the tragedy of a mother whose child was dumb.

Anya went back to the bus looking so miserable that Nikolai shook his finger in warning at the girls and joking said: "Now, my little dummies, you better learn to talk our way just as quick as you can or you'll be the death of your poor aunt!"

Vassily was only too happy to translate and he was the first to laugh out loud at the joke. Helga smiled, baring her large teeth. Anya gave the little curly head next to her a warm cuddle and thought to herself:

"He hasn't even taught them to ask for bread in Russian. They just rattle on in that horrible language."

Back home the tables were piled high with food. Crowds of relatives, close and distant ones, were bustling about the flat, getting things ready.

"It's like a regular wedding!" called Aunty Groonya, one of the neighbours, already with one foot in the grave, but somehow very like a small child in her excitement.

"We might as well make this a proper party," called Nikolai, rubbing his hands happily.

They all sat down, with Vassily next to Anya, in the place of honour. On the other side of her were Aunty Groonya and Nikolai. The first toast was drunk: "To this happy reunion!"

Vassily turned to Anya and started telling her what had been happening to him. He lived in a four-room flat. He had shelves full of books at home, including plenty of Russian classics and these meant a great deal to him. She wanted to know about the children? Well, Cora was at college now. Her empty-headed friends would finish up breaking the phone, so many calls they made her. He was against letting his daughters have a free hand with it. He was all for firm rules for behaviour. Moral decline was the scourge of modern times. He was not going to allow them to do whatever they pleased. He...

Anya looked at her brother. Good-naturedness beamed out of every pore, and somehow he seemed almost too obliging in the attentive way he addressed anyone who spoke to him, as if he was ready to jump up and carry out any of the guests' whims that might come into their heads.

"And you, Anya," Vassily went on, "haven't put on weight at all! No way! What's the word, when your stomach's right out here?"

She could not grasp his meaning at first.

"You know, right out here! What's the word? Fat! That's what I'm looking for! You aren't fat not a bit!"

"She looked even better six months ago!" commented Nikolai with a note of reproach in his voice.

Aunty Groonya started fidgeting and shaking her wrinkled fist in Helga's direction, muttering: "Your wife's a bad sort... A bad sort... It needn't worry Anya though. She's got a fine husband!"

Vassily gave another beaming smile, knitting his eyebrows as if to say: we'll forgive the old dear for being tactless, she didn't really mean it. Nikolai did not like that sugary smile of his. He put his elbows down on the table with a bang and said huskily: "Well then, Vassily, everything's shaping up for you in that new country of yours, is it? How's the good life? You're not short of cash, I hope?"

Vassily laughed embarrassedly, but straightaway put his hand in his trouser pocket for his wallet.

"I asked you if you had plenty of cash. So you have! Well, off you go to the market then and buy a goose. Then you can fill his brains with twaddle, *his*, not mine!"

Vassily realised what Nikolai was getting at. He passed the palm of his hand over first one and then the other bald streaks, and said: "I know what you're on about, Nikolai. I don't want you to think... Don't imagine that I... There was no other way to survive. I didn't do anyone any harm, no-one at all. It was a question of survival. There was no other way..."

Nikolai leant over towards him, a hank of long straight hair slipping down over his eyes that had an angry glint in them now as he said: "Oh, yes, of course! You had to! Surely! What about my mates though? Sasha Khomut! Petya from the farm! There was no need for them to survive! That wasn't important! They were better off dead!.. After those five days and five nights when we were out in the snow round Stalingrad, with no hope of a rest..."

Nikolai suddenly caught sight of Anya, sitting proud and straight, as if she was at a wake, her face deathly white. He shook his head, banged his fist down on the table and shouted: "Where's a harmonica! Quick, over here!"

He started up with a wild song that soon had the guests up and dancing. He played on and on and needed no encouraging.

Helga and Cora were smiling cautiously, Vassily was wheezing away, while Freckles spun round among the dancers, squealing with delight and trying to catch the rhythm of the tap-dance.

When the floor-boards began to cave from the thudding feet Vassily leant over to Nikolai and whispered: "We might be turned out!"

In response to that Nikolai bellowed: "Give us Stepan!"* in such a loud voice that all the near-by residents must have heard him.

Then at the top of their voices everyone began to sing. There was a happy yet shattering power behind that singing. The red faces of the guests came over sterner now and everyone present assumed a solemn expression.

Helga's eyes nearly popped out of her head, she was so taken aback by it all, and Vassily thought to himself with irritation that his wife's face had never worn an expression like the one which all the singers had at that moment. What he did not realise though was that his too had never had this look about it.

Nikolai rounded off the final chord and then called out: "The singing's over!"

A curly blonde-haired youngster came running over to him. With an unmistakable wink in Vassily's direction he started singing a bitter little song about the Gerries, squatting down and kicking out his feet as he did so.

Suddenly Nikolai came over all tense, hurled his fist down on the table and shouted out hoarsely: "Belt up! Don't start telling your grandfather how to suck eggs! If it's necessary, I'll say what has to be said!

*i.e. the well-known song about the folk-hero Stepan Razin.

I'll say it all, but you belt up! Hold your tongue! You don't know what lying out in the snow for four days on the trot is like! Belt up! "

He took the bottle and brought it over to where Vassily's glass stood. Vassily covered it with his left hand and patted his chest with his right, pointing out: "It's my heart."

Then suddenly Anya found her maternal instincts getting the upper hand, and she asked in worried tones: "How is it nowadays? If only Mamma could have lived to see you! If only she could have known!"

Vassily got up, knocking the table to one side as he did so, and walked out quickly into the corridor. Moving the chairs aside as quickly as she could and knocking into their corners in her haste, Anya ran after her brother.

Vassily was standing out in the kitchen, his forehead pressed up against the window-pane. Without turning round he said: "I didn't betray anyone, Anya, not a soul."

Anya put her arm round his shoulders from behind. He had a broad, strong wall of a back. As she patted it Anya suddenly could hear again quite clearly the words of the medical orderly from their home town saying that Vassily would never be the family's mainstay...

After the meal they sat down on the settee and Helga began showing them her family photographs. There was Helga standing by her father's garage which would one day be hers, baring her teeth in a triumphant smile, then came little Annette lying naked as a baby on a blanket, then Helga at the wheel of their car,

Cora in her school uniform, Vassily repairing a car, and then... Anya gave a start... There was Helga as a young girl wearing a Hitler Youth uniform, the high collar tightly buttoned at the neck. Prodding the photo with one of her long red nails, Helga quickly muttered something in German.

Stumbling over his words in his haste to translate, Vassily explained: "They were forced to join. They were given no choice. She's older than I am, don't forget. She was forced to. She was only an ordinary telephone operator."

Anya nodded mechanically and she clutched at the collar of her lace blouse, she felt short of breath, she wanted to tear the button off.

The whole of the next week Anya was the busy hostess: she prepared meat in aspic, beetroot soup. She fried large pieces of meat big enough to drown any plate. Tasks like that which did not leave her a moment to sit down were just what she wanted. They did not leave her any time to think.

They all travelled to Moscow to see Vassily off, using the bus to get there. When they were standing on the platform waiting for the train to leave, little Annette nestled up to Anya. Helga muttered something to her in a sharp voice.

"The wife's asking if she wants to stay behind?" translated Vassily.

Annette moved her head from her aunt's elbow with a quick jerk and, swallowing in surprise, answered loud and clear: "*Ja, ja!*"

"So you do, do you?!" asked Vassily with a forced

smile of an adult, who, while pretending to agree, is planning the very next moment to quash a child's whim with such irrefutable arguments as: "What about Mamma and Papa? And what about your dear old Frantz?" ("Her favourite teddy-bear," he explained to his sister.)

Freckles began talking so quickly that Anya lost the thread and only made out the word "Nikolai".

Vassily declared in the voice of a condescending radio announcer: "Oh, so Frantz is now going to be called Nikolai!"

Nikolai picked up Annette and threw her up into the air.

Vassily gave his sister a hug and then quietly let go... Then he quickly hugged her again and kissed her hard on both cheeks, saying in a subdued voice: "So Mamma said you should pray for my soul, did she?.."

He nodded and was gone...

By the end of the summer Anya began to pine and grow thin. Nikolai also noticed that she began talking to herself. She would walk down the street doing so, loudly enough for passers-by to turn round and stare at her. Nikolai decided to take her to the doctor.

Anya sat in the clean consulting room, in its cold whiteness, and looked over at the young doctor in an absent-minded kind of way. He spoke quietly, glancing anxiously over at her every now and then, hurriedly agreeing with everything she said and Anya thought to herself after that, that she really must be ill.

The doctor passed a small shiny metal hammer under her nose, told her to raise her arms, touch her nose, bend her leg at the knee—and she meekly complied with all his instuctions.

When the two of them sat down on the couch covered with cold plastic, she looked out of the window and said: "How can someone live with a displaced heart?"

The doctor thought she had been talking to him and got up, gasping in bewilderment, as he began to explain that her heart was all right. He added that she was a little tired and ought to take things easy, that everything would soon be far better than before, that there was nothing really to worry about and she must believe that...

Anya was not listening. Swaying gently to and fro as she spoke, she whispered: "When it's not in the right place.. With a heart like that..."

The next day she was admitted to hospital.

After losing consciousness she tossed from side to side on her hospital bed, pulling at the collar of her night-dress even though the neck-opening was a wide one. She kept on pulling as if she was trying to tear away from her throat something that was tightly stuck to it.

Seven years have passed since Anya died.

All those years Nikolai went on receiving letters in neat crisp envelopes and he still receives them to this day. Vassily keeps asking him to go and pay them a visit. Nikolai makes no move to do so.

Each year Vova comes home to see how his father is getting on.

One evening when it was already dark, father and

son were having supper in the kitchen. The father talked of his suffering: "That's how it all turned out! She never chatted away for the sake of it. She bottled everything up inside! Doctors always say that's the worst thing to do! Life's always easier for the empty-headed ones: they babble on and don't keep anything to themselves. All that worry was more than her heart could bear."

"You mustn't torture yourself, Papa," begged Vova quietly.

"It has nothing to do with me!" snorted Nikolai angrily, pulling at the collar of his shirt. "The enemy did not get to her! But Vassily did! He finished her off! He was the death of *my* Anya! The enemy didn't do it, he did!"

"What about little Annette with the freckles? How's she getting on?" asked Vova.

"That's a very different story!" cried Nikolai. "I wanted to tell you about her. She's run away from home. She just upped and left, that's what they write. They can't find her. I feel sorry for her. Sometimes I wake at night and imagine all sorts of horrible things that might be happening to her. Then I say to myself: life can't be up to much out there if children just leave their homes like that!"

Lyubov Yunina

REDECORATING THE HOUSE

Lyubov Yunina was born in the village of Pochinki in the Penza Region. She graduated from the Law Institute and the Higher Party School affiliated to the Central Committee of the Communist Party of the Soviet Union.

Her scetches, articles, and stories have appeared in national publications. In her stories, although the settings may be of an everyday kind, she treats interesting moral issues.

Anastasia had planned to redecorate the flat from top to bottom. They would have to do it because, strictly speaking, the flat had not been properly redecorated for thirty years, ever since her grandmother, after getting hold of some old painter, who had learnt his trade ages ago, decorated the flat in the "moiré" style that had been popular at that time. He had been quite a craftsman, that painter, and the walls of the flat had really looked like shot silk, with all the colours rippling from shade to shade. Yet, as the years passed, the paint had started cracking and peeling, and no-one felt up to imitating the original effect.

Of course, it had been given a face-lift from time to time: the ceilings had been given a new coat of whitewash, blue tiles had been stuck on the kitchen walls, and in the corridor plastic wall-covering with an imitation-wood effect had been put. Most of the work had been amateurish efforts on the part of Anastasia's mother, Nadezhda Petrovna. Yet no-one had ever got round to doing up the whole flat. There had not been enough money or time or someone had been ill.

Anastasia's grandfather Pyotr Petrovich had been allocated that flat in 1934 or '35 after Nadezhda, his daughter, was born. At first, there had been plenty of room in it but then the family grew far larger: Lidia and Leonid had been born, and Pyotr Petrovich's elder sister left her native village to come and help look after the children. Anastasia herself could only remember the flat with herself, her mother and her grandparents in it.

Her grandfather's sister had been killed in the war, Aunt Lidia had got married and left to live in the town of Tyumen in Siberia, and Uncle Leonid, the youngest of the three, had trained as a naval officer after leaving school and lived in Vladivostok ever since. Anastasia could hardly remember what her uncle looked like: all she knew was what his voice sounded like on the telephone.

A year ago, Anastasia's mother had died prematurely from a heart attack before she had even reached her fiftieth birthday. It had been such a terrible shock that, if Sasha had not been there to see her through it, Anastasia did not know how she would have coped with it. Sasha had been a tower of strength at the time.

Now Anastasia had passed her twenty-fifth birthday. She worked as a designer in a well-established research institute where promotion prospects were good and where she enjoyed the work; she loved her Sasha and felt content with her lot. She was just starting out on adult life and, when someone is starting out on a project like that, the urge is to do everything differently, in one's own style.

Anastasia was even a little surprised by her new independence and really enjoyed it: here she was now with a job of her own, a flat of her own and a brand-new husband. So Sasha's proposal that they do up the flat from top to bottom had seemed perfectly natural to her.

The two of them went to visit various friends who had recently done up their flats, listened to all their advice and had then drawn up their own plan of action.

One evening at supper Sasha had asked:

"What shall we do about the furniture? Replace it all?"

"We shall have to think."

Anastasia was carefully putting some jam in a dish. The independence she had only so recently acquired obliged her to sound serious and capable.

"We don't have to replace it all. Perhaps we could just throw out the old pieces. Then the place would seem more spacious."

"No," objected Anastasia, "we'll have to replace some. The armchair and the desk at least."

"And all that rubbish in the top cupboard will have to be thrown out, quite ruthlessly. There probably isn't a single thing worth keeping up there."

"You're probably right," agreed Anastasia. "I used to say to Mamma so often: 'Why do we need all that?' She would say she'd do it later on when she retired and had time to sort it all out..." A shake came into Anastasia's voice.

"Come on, don't get upset," Sasha covered Anastasia's hand with his own, stroking it gently. "Come now..."

"Poor Mamma! She thought she would live to a ripe old age and used to ponder saying, 'When I'll be sixty', or 'When I'll be as old as the hills'."

"Things always work out like that. I had a great-uncle who was sure he would live to be ninety-nine. D'you remember how I told you our ancestors used to make a habit of living a long time... Well at sixty-eight that uncle became a widower and decided to marry again. He chose a woman twenty years younger than he was. He proposed and she accepted him, believe it or not!"

"What happened then?"

"He died, of course, just a week before the wedding."

"Why 'of course'?" asked Anastasia in surprise, sensing a hint of disrespect in relation to her mother on her husband's part.

"It's funny to think about love at that age!"

"Mamma used to say that Grandmother and Grandfather used to love each other very much... We don't really know the first thing about our ancestors and the lives they led, do we?"

"What would be the point?" said Sasha without the slightest hesitation. "If there were some Decembrists among them or if we were the descendants of Pugachyov* that would be different. After all our ancestors were very ordinary people. They had their problems, and we've got ours."

"I don't think there is such a thing as an ordinary person. Everyone of us is special. Perhaps it isn't funny after all that your great-uncle wanted to marry a young woman."

"I wish that was all we had to worry about!" laughed Sasha.

Anastasia smiled as well. He was right, really, what was the point of worrying about people long since dead and buried, when they had so many of their own problems to see to.

When the wallpaper had been chosen and purchased at last and they had got hold of some incredibly attractive lino for the kitchen Anastasia took a few days' unpaid leave from work so as to sort out the top

*Emelyan Pugachyov—leader of the Peasant War (1773-1775) in Russia.—Ed.

cupboard and the other cupboards, to get rid of things that were no longer needed, so as to be fully prepared for the redecorating work.

They decided to keep the wall units that Anastasia's mother had bought only a few years back, the settee, the bed the grandparents had used and the bookshelves because they were still acceptable by present-day standards and looked good. The old armchairs, the old-fashioned forties-style three-door wardrobe and the chest of drawers, Grandfather's desk, and Grandmother's secretaire (that had also seen better days but unfortunately could not be regarded as an antique by any stretch of the imagination) they would take down to the second-hand shop.

"What if they refuse to take them?" asked Anastasia in worried tones. "What then?"

"Then we'll give them away to someone who has a summer cottage. Anything will do out in the country."

"None of our friends have got a summer cottage though."

"Then we'll just have to dump it with the rubbish." Sasha was particularly unrelenting when it came to the question of furniture: for him these old pieces were not linked with any memories or habits of a lifetime. He just saw them as ugly objects which clashed with the interior of the flat as he envisaged it.

Anastasia experienced a few misgivings, not so much because of memories but more out of rational considerations. She was prepared to sell things or just give them away but to throw them out with the rubbish, that she could not bring herself to do.

"They still have a function, Sasha," she said feeling

rather put out. "People made them. If we throw them out with the rubbish they'll be burnt. It isn't right somehow..."

Sasha stood by Grandfather's desk, slapped the palm of his hand down on the faded felt top and said:

"What on earth do we want this shabby desk for? Just look how ugly it is."

"Of course it's ugly, although Mamma used to say that Grandfather was very fond of that desk."

"He was just used to having it around," objected Sasha, quite sure that he was right.

"I think so too."

* * *

That desk had been bought by Anastasia Ivanovna, Anastasia's grandmother, all by herself, as a present for her husband in honour of his thirtieth birthday. They had only just moved into the flat, a flat all of their own which was such a miracle in those days! All that then stood in the empty echoing rooms was a round dining-table, four chairs, a nickel-plated iron bed, and last but not least a cot. There was nothing else in the Cherkassovs' new flat, for the time being. Their clothes were hanging up on nails, behind a muslin curtain and their underclothes were piled on chairs. Strictly speaking the first thing that should have been purchased was a wardrobe, but Anastasia Ivanovna wanted so much to give her husband a treat and, what was more, her husband knew that she was saving up for a wardrobe. The plans for buying the desk, on the

504

other hand, she was keeping a secret from him. It was difficult to keep a secret from her husband, because so far she had not had any from him. Yet Anastasia Ivanovna's urge to give her husband a big surprise had got the better of her.

She had been admiring the desk for some time and if she needed to go in the same direction as the furniture shop she always made a point of popping in to feast her eyes on it. She had already selected a place for it in the room by the window but at an appropriate angle so that the sun would not get in her husband's eyes. The year that she lived with her secret had been a very special one somehow: one of rejoicing in anticipation of the pleasure she would get from giving her beloved Pyotr the desk and also one of trepidation because she was keeping something back from her husband and telling him a small, albeit well-intentioned, lie.

She had thought of everything. On her husband's birthday she asked for time off from work so as to get back early. Anastasia Ivanovna was working in the registration department of the housing committee and at the same time attending night-school to complete her secondary education. She set off with the janitors Fyodor Sergeevich and Vasya whom she had asked in advance to carry the desk home for her. On reaching the shop the three of them carefully surveyed all the desks and chose just what was required. Then they went down the street, the men carrying the desk and Anastasia Ivanovna tripping along beside them, her flushed face wearing a happy smile. No-one could have been happier than she that day!

The desk was brought into the flat, placed by the window and Anastasia Ivanovna shook the janitors' hands and then made them a bow of gratitude:

"Thank you so much lads, I'll make it up to you. If there's anything your wives need to have made in the clothes line, just bring it along and I'll get sewing!"

The janitors left after that, clattering down the stairs in their boots and Anastasia Ivanovna brought out from another secret hiding place (where on earth could hiding places have been in that empty flat?) a thin piece of metal, on which a locksmith she knew had engraved the words: *"To my ·beloved husband Pyotr on his thirtieth birthday from Anastasia. May you enjoy working at it! 30:XII: 35."* She then nailed the plaque to the corner of the desk at the edge, where there was no felt.

Later, the plaque had come off and been lost, but how impressive it had looked at first!

Anastasia Ivanovna wiped down the wood with a soft cloth, and the green felt with a damp one. She was quite carried away by now imagining to herself. "What we ought to have here is a lamp with a proper shade," she mused with a sigh. Then she lined the drawers with fresh newspapers. At last she gave another sigh, but this time a happy one: "My, how nice it looks here!"

In the evening when Pyotr Petrovich came home and caught sight of the desk he clutched his head in amazement and cried:

"Oh, what a spendthrift, you are, love!" Then he picked her up, swung her round and gave her a kiss. "You're a sweet thing, you really are ... but why should

I be spoilt like this and treated like some big shot?"

"You are graduating soon, Pyotr," Anastasia Ivanovna replied, "how can you manage without a desk? It is quite a smart one though, isn't it?"

They then took it in turns to sit down at the desk and confirmed that it was comfortable as well. Pyotr Petrovich was to spend many hours at that desk, write endless articles at it and read countless books. He found it pleasant to work at and his children after him. Nadezhda, his daughter, had written her thesis at it later.

The very next day after the purchase, the three of them decided to go and have a photograph taken of the whole family. For a long time that photograph had stood in a frame on Pyotr Petrovich's desk. Side by side were a young, curly-headed and laughing Anastasia Ivanovna at twenty-five (the same age as her granddaughter now), then Pyotr Petrovich looking rather sheepish despite his smile, in his new shirt, and, in the middle, with her arms round her parents' shoulders, Nadezhda holding the key of the flat in her hand. She had been making a fuss and protesting about the photograph and so they had given her the key by way of a toy to play with. Nadya had come out frowning in the photograph, giving the photographer a sideways look. The photo had always been referred to after that in the family as "the photo with the key." Then it had got lost somewhere amongst the family papers, and Anastasia had probably never seen it and even if she had she would not have known the story that went behind with it.

* * *

Before the furniture they no longer needed could
be discarded, the things that had been stored in them
needed sorting out. By the evening Anastasia had
finished with the wardrobe and, when Sasha returned
from work, she sorted through the desk. In the two
top drawers there were papers that belonged to Anastasia herself: some old chits, identity cards, forgotten
diplomas. None of them was really important but
somehow it seemed a pity to throw them out. For that
reason what was already her "archives" Anastasia
packed away into an old leather document-case of her
grandfather's which he had brought home years before
after a work assignment in England. After the zip had
come adrift Grandfather had sewn it together with
very tough thread. Letters had been kept in it before,
Anastasia remembered, but now the document-case
was quite empty.

Everything else which might some day come in
useful she transferred to a large envelope. In the
other drawers her mother's papers had been stored.
Anastasia for some reason had never found the time
before to go through them and now she started out on
the task without any particular enthusiasm. She found
it boring to be sitting in this room without Sasha.
After pulling out the drawer she took it into the sitting-room, staggering under its weight as she went.
Then she put it on the floor and sat down next to it
leaning her back up against an armchair.

"Why are you sitting on the floor?" asked Sasha in
worried tones.

"It's more comfortable," was Anastasia's short reply and she looked up at her husband with a smile. He was half-lying on the settee, smoking a pipe, as he himself admitted—just to impress—so that the sweet smell of Golden Fleece tobacco filled the room. A tune by some pop group rippled softly in the room. Sasha loved that music and the tape-recorder in their flat was only turned off when he was not at home or asleep.

The stereo hi-fi system which they had acquired had cost a hell of a lot of money, an incredible amount, but Anastasia had wanted very much to make Sasha's dream of a stereo system like that come true. Of course, when they had first had the idea they had had no money. They had just not started earning yet. They earned what from Anastasia's point of view was chicken-feed: she brought home a hundred and thirty roubles a month and Sasha a hundred and forty. Their friends who earned about the same still managed to buy whatever they pleased and managed to keep their heads above water.

A stereo system was something which, according to Sasha, they just had to have. It was an essential part of modern living. His parents had given him five hundred roubles towards it and Anastasia had asked her mother for another five hundred. Her mother had handed over the money with a very disapproving look on her face. Even now Anastasia could not forget that look: she had been terribly hurt by it at the time but had not let it show.

It was not that Nadezhda Petrovna had begrudged her the money. It just disappointed her to think that her daughter could ask for and then spend her mother's hard-earned savings on a mere whim, to keep up with the latest fashion. Her whole life long she had tried to borrow as little as possible from her parents, not because she was proud but because she had a very keen sense of fairness.

The stereo system which Sasha had really wanted had cost two and a half thousand but that was something they could only dream about, so they decided to opt for a cheaper one.

"We'll work things out later," Sasha had said.

He had a great weakness for that phrase: "We'll work things out later." Sasha was one of those people for whom everything always seems to turn out right, of its own accord, so to speak. Something always seemed to lead him to make the right decision. As a result, he did not like pondering over anything for a long time and would say instead, "We'll work things out later," and in the end everything always did seem to work itself out.

They had not bought the stereo system that time, for Nadezhda Petrovna had died and almost all the money had gone on the funeral expenses.

When the initial blow of Anastasia's loss was over and everything seemed to have fallen back into place again— life went on regardless—Anastasia began to think to herself and wonder where they could get the money for the stereo system from. They decided they would sell Nadezhda Petrovna's fur coat which had been an expensive one. It had brought in just the sum they needed.

"You'll get cold on the floor, let me bring you a cushion," said Sasha.

"Don't worry, everything's fine... I've bought some shrimps, perhaps you'd go down and get some beer?"

"I'll be back in a flash," exclaimed Sasha. "No trouble at all!"

He jumped to his feet, carefully emptied his pipe in the brass Indian ash-tray while Anastasia admired her handsome husband: there was no denying how handsome her Sasha was.

He called back to her from the hall:

"Don't worry if I'm a long time, there may be a queue."

"Why don't you jump it?" suggested Anastasia.

"You know I can't bring myself to do that."

Anastasia laughed and said:

"That's why I love you, my Sasha!"

He left and Anastasia again lent over the drawer which contained the letters to her mother from her sister Lidia. Despite the gap of five years between them which had shrunk to almost nothing as the years went by, the two sisters had been very fond of each other. Although they had lived apart for many years they kept up a regular correspondence. Anastasia had felt that it was very old-fashioned to write such long letters. Time was in such short supply anyway. Yet once a week and sometimes twice her mother would sit down of an evening at Grandfather's desk and write away till midnight by the light of the table-lamp. In the morning she would entrust the thick envelope to Anastasia and ask her to post it. Anastasia was a very methodical person, it was a trait she had inherited from her grandfather. He mother, despite being very thorough and business-like over small things, was often absent-minded, and a letter might languish at the bottom of her bag for a week.

Anastasia turned over the envelopes wondering what she ought to do with them. She felt embarrassed about actually reading them and anyway did not expect they would be interesting. Should she throw them out, or perhaps send them back to Aunt Lidia? Yet what if such a reminder of her mother should come as a bitter blow to her aunt? Catching herself thinking that, Anastasia felt her face turn hot: she felt ashamed as if she had betrayed someone. How could such a thought have occurred to her: so as to stop suffering you have to forget first...

"I shall send them to Aunt Lidia," decided Anastasia, putting the letters together in a neat pile. One of them had lost its envelope and Anastasia began to read it: Nadya dear, what made you think I'd be hurt by that? You're a funny one, you really are! Of course let the little spoon stay where it is, in your house—in *our* house. I asked you for it because my children are interested in the history of our family and they take pride in the lives of our parents: they feel sad that we have no family heirlooms in our home here... I'm glad to see this because I want them to understand us and the lives we led. I remember that little spoon as very battered and can just imagine what it must look like now! The children have hung Papa's gold watch that you sent us up on the wall. It's amazing to think what enormous pocket-watches they used to wear in those days..."

* * *

After his military service Pyort Petrovich had graduated from the Workers' Faculty,* worked in a factory and had then been allocated a room. It had only
been seven square metres, but it had been a room of
his own. It was there that he brought home his young
wife Anastasia. She had come to the city from the village to find work as a servant. She had met Pyotr
by chance, it had been love at first sight and that love
remained intact until her dying day.

One morning soon after, probably the third of their
married life together, Pyotr Petrovich announced:

"I've got my wages. Here you are, housewife. Let's
go out and buy something together, shall we?"

Blushing, Anastasia had taken the money (she was
not used to dealing with money she had not earned
herself) and said shyly:

"We need some crockery..."

"So we do," said Pyotr Petrovich as he kissed his
wife on her dimpled rosy cheek, unable to resist the
temptation. "Off we go!"

Anastasia looked at herself in their piece of mirror.
They did not have a whole one in those days. That was
in 1928.

Feeling rather special they walked along the street:
curly-headed Anastasia Ivanovna, small and very slim,
and Pyotr Petrovich, tall and rather stolid, wearing a

*Educational establishments, first set up in 1919 as special depart-
ments in existing colleges to enable workers without secondary education to prepare for higher education. By 1941 they had all been assimi-
lated into the general educational system—*Tr.*

pale blue sports shirt and canvas shoes. Anastasia Ivanovna had been wearing a dark blue sateen skirt and a white blouse. Yet everything she was wearing had been beautifully starched and ironed. She had always been terribly particular about her appearance, Grandmother Anastasia.

They bustled about among the other customers in the shop for a long time, moving from one counter to another. Anastasia Petrovna first looked at frying-pans, then saucepans and cups, scrutinising them carefully and moving her lips as she made calculations. Then at last she had announced resolutely:

"Let's buy this teaspoon, Pyotr."

"Teaspoon?" he inquired in astonishment. "You said it was crockery that we needed."

"We need teaspoons to eat with as well?" she said craftily. After that Pyotr Petrovich could not think up any other objection.

For a long time after that they used to refer to the new spoon as "crockery". When he sat down to drink his tea, Pyotr Petrovich used to say: "Give me the crockery please, I need to stir my tea."

Then Anastasia Ivanovna would pass him the little spoon. Nadezhda and Lidia remembered that joke, but their little brother Leonid was unlikely to be able to.

Then came the war and evacuation and the spoon was mislaid: afterwards it turned up unexpectedly though, and Anastasia Ivanovna used to tell the story to her daughters, and Nadezhda after that always made a point of using that little spoon and none other. It began to be known as Nadya's spoon. By that time a

514

more expensive cupro-nickel cutlery set appeared in the house with which the little spoon looked quite out of place, yet Nadya still used it all the same.

* * *

Anastasia cried as she read her aunt's letter and she cried about her mother whom her sister had been so attached to. What about her, Anastasia? Had she not loved her mother in the same way? Suddenly she remembered that disapproving look on her mother's face when she had laid the five hundred roubles down on the table.

Anastasia was unable to explain to Sasha the reason for her tears, and not because she did not want to. She simply knew that he would not understand her tears, that they were something strictly personal, which even her beloved Sasha could never hope to grasp.

"Well, what is it, little one?" Sasha asked as he squatted down near his wife and stroked her head covered with curls just like her grandmother's. "Come along, curly-top," he murmured, "calm down: what's been worrying you so much? Let's throw the whole lot out. What's the point of worrying about other people's pasts and getting upset over them?"

"No!" cried Anastasia and sprung free from the touch of his soft warm hands. "You just don't understand anything."

She ran away into the kitchen and began to rummage everywhere in search of the small spoon, as if it might have told her about its history and why it was so important to Grandfather, Grandmother, Aunt Lidia and even Aunt Lidia's children. Yet she found nothing: the little spoon had vanished. "Perhaps Mamma did send it to Aunt Lidia after all?" thought Anastasia and rushed back into the room. She took a quick look at the date of her aunt's letter and then dropped the letter in astonishment. The white page fluttered and then landed by her feet. Her mother had received the letter only a matter of hours before her death. "It was in the evening," Anastasia recalled, "and Mamma died at dawn. It was twenty to six on the clock."

"Would you like me to cook the shrimps?" asked Sasha, who, although he had no idea what was the matter with his wife, was anxious to calm her down at all costs. "Just tell me how much salt I need to put into the saucepan."

Anastasia looked at her husband and felt a little ashamed: after all it was not as if he could help it, what concern was her family history of his?

"I'm sorry," she said quietly. "Take the white saucepan and two level teaspoons of salf will do... Sasha," she said hesitating, "do you remember what my grandmother's name was?"

"Grandmother?" Sasha asked in a rather surprised tone and then paused for a moment as he tried to think back. He had never even seen his wife's grandmother. "But of course, how stupid of me!" he cried, tapping his forehead with the palm of his hand. "Anastasia! It was in honour of her that they gave you the name Anastasia!"

His wife gave a grateful nod and asked:

516

"Have you put the beer in the fridge?"

"Of course I did, straightaway..."

"All right then, you go and boil up the shrimps and I'll do a bit more tidying up." Anastasia gave a sigh and sat down again on the floor. She wanted to read Aunt Lidia's letters because that somehow had brought her mother back much nearer all of a sudden and now there was some kind of link, albeit a rather vague one between her, Grandmother, her mother and Grandfather. That letter from Aunt Lidia had made something turn over in her inside. How little Anastasia knew about the people who had come before her! Nevertheless, she still could not bring herself to read the letters for the time being and she packed them away in a large bootbox.

In another drawer Anastasia found some notes that had been sent to her mother when she had been in the maternity home. She scanned through them but there was little of interest. In a match-box lay a lock of her hair from the day when her hair had been cut for the first time, a fair curl as soft as a feather! In another twist of paper Anastasia's first tooth had been preserved. "Heavens, how tiny it is," she thought to herself and called out to her husband: "Sasha, come here! Look, here's my first tooth and my hair!"

"How fair you were!" he said in surprise. "And it's not curly. You must have been crimping it in secret all this time!"

"Naturally!" she laughed. "Strictly in secret."

"I could never understand why people collect and keep all that kind of nonsense. First tooth! First leggings, first shoes, first school exercise book. My mother collected all that kind of stuff, too. Whatever do they do it for? You've grown up, and that hair isn't really yours anymore. So help me God, I just don't understand!" And with that Sasha went back into the kitchen.

"Really, what is the point of it all?" Anastasia asked herself. "In fact, it isn't of any use to anyone." All the same she did not really plan to throw anything out at all: on the contrary she collected everything up again and wrapped it in an old cloth.

At the very bottom of the drawer there lay a small box, of the kind in which half a dozen silver spoons would usually be sold.

"Sasha!" she called out to her husband. "We're rich, we've got some silver."

"Just a moment!" he called back. "I've just got to the crucial moment with these shrimps."

Anastasia opened the box. Inside lay a solitary silver spoon, very small, the kind which would be used for salt or for drinking the very strongest coffee out of a tiny cup. Next to it was that very spoon which Aunt Lidia had written about in her letter, a very old battered spoon, with a pattern you could hardly see any more. Why had Mamma kept it side by side with the little silver spoon that Anastasia had never seen before? Why had she held it so dear? Anastasia had no idea.

* * *

When her daughter had got married Nadezhda Petrovna had decided to make her a present of a ring.

She too had been given a ring by her mother when she had married: it had been a simple one with one small aquamarine. Now that people had started to live more prosperously, a better ring ought to be chosen for the occasion.

She wanted to choose something out of the ordinary for her Anastasia, something like a grey pearl, or a real white topaz and she set off to the best jeweller's. It was there that she picked out the beautiful ring with the tiny dark blue sapphire which all Anastasia's girlfriends still envied.

Nadezhda Petrovna had asked the shop-assistant to show her the ring, she had tried it on and looked at it happily. Then she asked: "How much is it?" The price of course had been horrifying. It had meant one and a half months' salary but there were no two ways about it, her daughter was getting married for the first and, she hoped, the last time. Her Anastasia and Sasha seemed madly in love with each other.

The savings-bank was not far away, so the whole transaction was soon complete.

When the assistant was wrapping up the velvet-lined box with the ring in fine tissue paper, however, Nadezhda Petrovna had suddenly noticed a small silver spoon in the window.

"How gorgeous!" she cried. "May I have a look?"

She held the spoon in her hand for a moment, surprised in view of its miniature size at how heavy it was. Nadezhda Petrovna suddenly remembered how she had been feeding little Anastasia with her milk pudding, when unexpectedly she had heard a tiny knocking noise in the child's mouth.

"Come now! Show me what's in there!" she had asked, happily anticipating the exciting discovery. She looked inside and saw a tiny tooth showing white against the pink gums. "Mamma!" she shouted, "Mamma! The baby's cutting a tooth!"

Anastasia Ivanovna came running up—she was not even fifty at that time with nothing of the old woman about her and hardly any grey showing in her hair. She did, however, always refer to herself as a grandmother wherever she went and took a great deal of pride in this first grandchild.

"A tooth, a tooth!" she shouted. "What a pity that the spoon isn't a silver one. It's very important that the knock against the first tooth should be with a silver spoon. Why didn't we think of it in time?"

For a moment the little spoon had brought back to Nadezhda Petrovna the whole of that happy day, all the fuss and excitement over that first tooth and without another moment's hesitation, she had bought the silver spoon ready for her grandchild's first tooth.

"When Anastasia has her baby, then the spoon will be ready," Nadezhda Petrovna thought to herself. As she made her way home she for some strange reason felt more excited about the little silver spoon than the ring, although she had no idea when she would have the chance to give it to her daughter's child. Sensibly enough at the time, she had not said anything to Anastasia, deciding that the silver spoon would be her little secret.

* * *

"Well then, where's your family silver?" asked Sasha who had dealt with the critical situation in the kitchen and was now standing in front of Anastasia.

She lifted the spoon to her eye-level and said: "Look what I found among Mamma's things!"

"That's all? Not much of a find! Well, show it to me... That's nothing. Well, why don't we get you a ring made out of that silver spoon? It's a pity, it wouldn't be enough for a bracelet. There's bound to be enough for two rings though. Half would make a ring for you and we'd pay for the work with the rest. Silver's quite a price nowadays."

"Why not," said Anastasia. "What good is one spoon to us after all, and such a small one into the bargain."

* * *

Anastasia had sorted out nearly everything in the flat now. She had thrown out the old cracked china, a whole bundle of old clothes, gloves, shoes, yellow bundles of old newspapers and magazines. All that she still had left to do was sort out the large case and the box tied round with a string, which she had brought down from the top cupboard.

Anastasia did not even know what was in the case, or rather she knew that it was old bits and pieces, as her mother used to say, but as far as she could remember she had never actually looked inside it herself.

On the very top wrapped in a sheet lay Grandmother's dress for special occasions. Anastasia recognised it straightaway: it was a very pretty dress made of black velvet with satin lapels, embroidered with tiny beads. Anastasia remembered how Grandmother used to put on that dress when she went to the theatre or to visit friends and that she had also had a muff made of black-fox fur. Thinking back, it seemed to her that there had existed a very funny photograph that Grandfather had taken. Grandmother had been wearing that dress complete with a special hair-do and she had been wearing a muff and high-heeled patent-leather shoes on her feet. She had been standing in the middle of the room and to one side of her were slippers with pompons on them. Grandmother had forgotten to put them away, and Grandfather of course had not noticed them.

Anastasia took out the dress, shook it and tried it up against herself. It was a pretty dress but too small for her. Grandmother had been petite, while Anastasia was a real bean-pole... "What shall I do with it?" Anastasia wondered. "And why did Mamma keep it?"

Among the other things in the case was Grandfather's best suit complete with his medal ribbons and a few old photograph-albums: Grandfather had been a great enthusiast in his youth and had photographed whatever he could lay his hands on. Anastasia leafed through them but the faces and the landscapes did not mean anything to her. There was also a box full of postcards, some paper patterns, cut-glass bottles for perfume with broken tops and other such nonsense. "I'll throw all this lot out," decided Anastasia.

At the bottom there lay something else wrapped in an old baby's blanket. Anastasia unwrapped it and found a large celluloid doll with eyes that opened and shut and hair curled up in a roll at the nape of her neck. The hair was also celluloid but there was a hole and many cracks in the doll's head. "What on earth did Mamma go and hang on to this for?" thought Anastasia to herself in astonishment. "Really! Whatever next!"

* * *

Not long before the war Pyotr Petrovich had been sent on an assignment to Sweden, and, although the trip had not been a long one, Anastasia Ivanovna had still grown very miserable. She loved welcoming him home in the evenings, telling him about the children— there were three of them by then, and Pyotr Petrovich's sister had come to live with them, too. Talking to her, however, could not in any way make up for the intimate evening conversations she might have been having with her husband.

Anastasia Ivanovna did not go to meet her husband as she did not really have any idea when he would arrive. Pyotr Petrovich turned up late in the evening when almost everyone was already asleep, carrying a suitcase and a long cardboard box. The box was wrapped in pretty coloured paper, and Anastasia Ivanovna hoped that it might contain a nice dress for her.

She went to see to the supper while Pyotr Petrovich had a bath to freshen up after the journey and soon emerged with wet, neatly parted hair.

"Come and sit down, sit down and have supper, Pyotr," said Anastasia Ivanovna, moving the plates nearer to where he had sat down, while she herself kept eyeing the box.

"Don't look now," said Pyotr Petrovich with a laugh, "I haven't brought you a dress, don't be angry with me. I'm no good at buying dresses. D'you remember what happened with those shoes?"

Anastasia Ivanovna giggled, wrinkling her pretty little snub nose. How could she forget!

In their first year of marriage for his wife's birthday Pyotr Petrovich had decided to give her a pair of shoes as a present. He had gone to the shop by himself, chose the first pair of shoes he liked and could afford: they turned out to be some five sizes bigger than Anastasia Ivanovna took, for she had extremely small feet.

"I've brought a doll home for the girls," announced Pyotr Petrovich at last.

"A doll?" sighed Anastasia Ivanovna in disappointment. "What kind of doll for heaven's sake?"

Anastasia Ivanovna took another sideways glance at the box and decided that her husband must be joking. He got up from the table, however, carefully undid the ribbon, which Anastasia Ivanovna put into the pocket of her apron, commenting:

"Nadya will be able to use it for her plaits."

When Pyotr Petrovich lifted up the lid and undid the silky soft paper before finally bringing out the beautifully dressed doll just as big as Lidia, then aged two and a half, Anastasia Ivanovna sat down quite flabbergasted, gasping:

"But it's beautiful, Pyotr! Let me hold her. It's

524

like a real baby! The eyes look straight at you! And the dress, just look at the dress! Well I never!"

"D'you like it?"

"How could I help but like it? I just can't believe it's only a doll. It's so real. No, I can't let the girls have this, they'll break it. She'll sit on the settee."

"Come now, Anastasia, it's only a toy."

"No, no, I mean it! Who's ever been allowed to play with something like this? Don't you try it on, you're always trying to spoil them." Anastasia Ivanovna, despite her gentle manner, always stuck firmly to her principles.

The doll used to sit on the settee right up until the war, filling all Nadya's and Lidia's friends with envy. Sometimes on special occasions they were allowed to play with her very carefully.

When the war broke out in 1941 and they were evacuated, Anastasia Ivanovna did not leave the doll in Moscow but took her with them. During the journey a disaster occurred—the fragile celluloid cracked. Yet for Anastasia Ivanovna the doll still remained a model of all that was beautiful and she could not bring herself to throw the doll out. She kept the doll while evacuated and then when they returned to Moscow she brought it home. For a time the doll sat on the settee again in a strange bonnet which Anastasia Ivanovna had sewn for her, so as to cover up the cracks, but in the end she wrapped it up in the baby's blanket and put it out of the way in the top cupboard. Her daughter Nadezhda could not bring herself to part with the doll either and she had left it in the suitcase with the other things that her parents had cherished.

* * *

Anastasia spread out a flannel blanket on the floor and collected together in it the photograph-albums, the doll, the old postcards, a collection of scraps of material, a piece of oil-cloth preserved for no apparent reason, some tiny marble elephants, some men's skiing mittens made of once-white deer skin, ski-boots stiff with age. She wondered for a long time about what she should do with the dress and the suit belonging to her grandparents. In the end, after taking off the medal ribbons, she put them in the general pile with the rest of the things, tied up the bundle and dragged it out to the rubbish dump. Then Anastasia settled down to sorting out the box. It proved to be full of papers. There was everything in it that Anastasia Ivanovna and Pyotr Petrovich had decided needed keeping throughout their lives: everything that they held dear had been kept in this large box. Papers, letters, notebooks—they were all tidily folded away. Probably Nadezhda had seen to that in her day and probably she had not even read through them all.

Anastasia did not feel like reading all the contents either, she just leafed through the pile, glancing here and there at the tidy bundles of yellow papers tied up with a string. There were letters there dating back to the thirties. "Heavens, nearly half a century, how time flies!" thought Anastasia to herself. "This lot all needs burning." She wondered how it ought to be done for the best. In the old days people used to burn unimportant letters in stoves or with candles. "I could buy some candles," she thought to herself automatically, "but it would take a whole week to get rid of them that way."

Suddenly she came across a small red patent-leather bag: it was very old and had almost turned white at the seams. Anastasia could not remember the bag, probably she had not seen it before. There was an envelope inside it, on which was written in Grandmother's old-fashioned handwriting: *"To be given to Pyotr Petrovich after my death."*

She opened the envelope carefully and found inside two pieces of paper, one of which was quite old and tattered: Anastasia unfolded that one first and recognised her grandfather's handwriting.

"Darling Anastasia! I am leaving on an assignment, and have to admit that it is a dangerous one. If I don't come back, do everything you can to bring up the children so that they turn into people like you. I love you and your love is the greatest happiness that I have known in life.

Your Pyotr

May 19, 1942."

* * *

When the war began Anastasia Ivanovna was evacuated with the children to Perm in the Urals, where Pyotr Petrovich had some distant relatives. In the beginning they helped her to settle in. She worked from morning to night and the children of course had to be left very much to their own devices. That was not the most terrible thing though. Reports from the front were alarming. Yet as soon as the Nazis had been pushed back from Moscow she began to try as hard as she could to get home.

Pyotr Petrovich was not taken on in the army despite all his efforts: he was left to work in Moscow and his work was really important in the interests of the country and ultimate victory. He used to write letters regularly, every ten days, short ones, like war bulletins. There was no time for long ones. After all, what was there to write when the most important things of all, that were of vital concern to everybody in those desperate times, were in the newspapers and being broadcast on the wireless. Most important of all were the bulletins issued by the Soviet Information Bureau.

In the letter dated May 25, 1942, which Anastasia Ivanovna received at the end of the month her husband informed her that he was well, working and missing her. The usual things. In actual fact, that letter had been written a week earlier like those that followed and which Anastasia Ivanovna subsequently received: they had been posted in a Moscow letter-box by one of Pyotr Petrovich's colleagues in accordance with his specific instructions. Pyotr Petrovich himself at the time was miles away overseas. He had flown abroad on a diplomatic mission on a TB-7 heavy bomber, across the front line and over Nazi Germany at night. His destination had been first Great Britain and then the United States. It was cold in the plane and the pilots' arctic uniforms that had been issued to the passengers in Moscow—fur flying boots and suits — proved inadequate to keep them warm. The Foreign Minister was jotting things down in a notebook as they travelled, by the light of a small torch, while the others snatched what sleep they could.

Like his comrades Pyotr Petrovich felt no fear, although he knew that the plane might be discovered. Of course he wanted to live, he was still young, only thirty-seven, but there was a war on and here on the plane, he and his comrades and even the Minister were all soldiers on that occasion. During that flight Pyotr Petrovich was not thinking about the possibility of his being killed, he was eager to carry out the important mission that had been assigned to him and his comrades; he wanted to return home, to see his wife, his children and to live to see Victory. The great Battle for Stalingrad had not yet taken place, the Germans were only advancing towards the banks of the Volga, the tank battle at Kursk had not yet taken place, the T-34 tanks were only being assembled in Siberia and had not yet gone into action: so much was still to come and the Nazis believed that they were about to achieve victory any moment... But Russia knew she would win.

Pyotr Petrovich sometimes thought about what would happen if he did not return. He felt sorry for his Anastasia, who despite her strong character and staunch common sense would not find it easy to bring up three children to face the world. In a country that was in the throes of an unprecedented war every day added to the total of widows and orphans, all of whom faced hard times and a bitter future. He felt sorry for all of them, yet there was no-one on this earth quite like his Anastasia...

On June 12th, 1942, Anastasia Ivanovna read a communique in the paper about a visit made to London and Washington by the Minister of Foreign Affairs and the ratification of treaties and agreements between Britain, the U.S.A. and the Soviet Union on mutual assistance. On reading it, she thought to herself, like many others, that now Hitler would be easier to defeat with three countries joining forces against him, but she did not in any way imagine that there might be a link between that event and her own life.

Everything was true in that report except for one detail: on June 12th the TB-7 heavy bomber was still on its way to home base. Nor did it mention that the Minister had already returned home. But, if the treaties had been ratified it might mean that the delegation had already returned home. That little "bluff" was used for the Germans' benefit, just in case they had got wind of that journey that had been shrouded in the utmost secrecy. The Germans swallowed the bait, dropped their alert and on June 13th the plane landed at the Moscow aerodrome.

That same day Pyotr Petrovich himself was able to post a letter he had just written, informing his wife as usual that he was in good health, working hard and missing her.

When it came to the note, the farewell note that he had written to his wife and put away in her favourite little red bag, it was not so much that he forgot about it as that he had been unable to get back to his flat to destroy it as he had planned. Like many other people at that time he ate and slept at his office; in the end of course he did forget about it, after all in those days many people were having to work up to twenty hours a day.

At the end of '42 Anastasia Ivanovna came back to Moscow with the children and found the letter. She did not say anything to her husband about the letter, but preserved it as her most treasured possession.

* * *

Anastasia placed the note on her lap with tears pouring down her cheeks, she felt so moved by those simple words of love. What could have been happening, for she knew that her Grandfather had not gone to the front. Oh, yes, she remembered now, that he had told them something about flying over enemy territory during the war. She looked at the date again: May 19, 1942. She went over to the bookshelves, took down an encyclopaedia and a history of the Great Patriotic War 1941-45 and began to hunt for clues as to what had been happening then in May 1942. What fatal danger could have been threatening her Grandfather—the tall, thin old man who had not looked the part of the hero at all? She remembered him dressed in a knitted waistcoat that he would never part with, always close-shaven and wearing thick-lensed glasses. In his old age he had had very poor eyesight.

Ah!.. There it was!.. Anastasia quickly read about the events of nearly forty years before. So that was it!

Why though had Grandmother kept the note in an envelope on which was written: *"To be given to Pyotr Petrovich after my death."* Anastasia quickly brought out the second piece of paper. It was written in Grandmother's handwriting:

"Dearest Pyotr! I have kept your letter all my life.

You and I have spent a very happy life together and we were able to bear all our sorrows because our love kept us going. We have done so much together on this earth: worked together to our hearts' content, brought up fine children, and helped look after our grandchildren. I know that it will be hard for you without me, but don't forget that I'm always with you. You put the finishing touches to the things I didn't complete. I'll still be with you, for as long as there's at least one person left who remembers me. Live a long time so as to bring happiness to the children, and never forget the great love that we had for each other."

There was no signature or date at the bottom of the letter.

* * *

When Anastasia Ivanovna had discovered what illness she had, her first reaction was one of blind panic. She had discovered it because of a piece of carelessness on a doctor's part, but not a single muscle in her face had moved. When she came out of the clinic her stone-like expression did not give anything away. Afterwards she could not remember how she made her way back to the flat which had been empty at the time, how she had collapsed on her bed, still fully-dressed and cried her heart out. It would be wrong to say that at the time she had only been crying out of pity for her husband and her children. She had been crying out of pity for herself, too, because she wanted to live, she was so happy and far from old. "Why, why does it have to be me?" she whispered in the silence. Then suddenly she stopped crying and pulled herself together. She got up and washed and then sat down at the kitchen-table and began to think. First of all she decided not to tell Pyotr Petrovich, but then she was filled with shame. A lie? But that would mean she had no faith in his love for her surely? On the other hand, why should she make him suffer, when it was her illness after all? She went to the wardrobe and brought out the little red bag. She took out the note which her husband had written way back in '42—she always used to read it through at difficult moments, although she knew it by heart—and then put it back slowly, still wondering what she should do. She had still not decided what to do when the telephone rang and took her by surprise. Pyotr Petrovich asked:

"Well, what did the doctor say?"

"The doctor?" she paused for a moment. "Oh yes, the doctor..." And then she came out with it straight: "Things don't look good."

"What did he say?"

"I only caught a quick glance at the test results, well you know the biopsy they did..."

"Well, what about it?" asked Pyotr Petrovich in worried tones. "I don't think we should jump to conclusions, I'll pop in there quickly and find out what's what."

"Fine," agreed Anastasia Ivanovna obediently. A faint spark of hope made her feel better.

An hour later Pyotr Petrovich rushed home carrying an armful of flowers and a special cake. He kissed her on both cheeks and swung her round.

"It was a mistake, nothing but a mistake. The doctor told me all about it and I've seen the test results. It's a mistake!"Although he was all happy and excited, Anastasia Ivanovna still could not really bring herself to believe him.

She had to agree to an operation nevertheless, although Pyotr Petrovich and the children put on brave faces and lied as hard as they could that everything was all right.

She had said to Pyotr Petrovich in the end: "Come on, Pyotr, let's face up to the truth."

"I don't want to," he said.

"Whether you want to or not, we've got to. I know everything that's happening to me, but I'm going to fight. I'm not going to give in that easily. I'll put up a fight," she repeated.

Not for one year, or even two but for nearly ten years Anastasia Ivanovna was to live on after that operation and she grew so used to her illness that she almost stopped thinking about it. Of course, there were times when she felt bad and even had to go back into hospital, when she had to have radio-therapy and would then return home feeling weak and worn out, but she always kept her spirits up. She had written her letter to Pyotr Petrovich not long before her death, when she realised that this time she was not going to be able to pull through.

* * *

Anastasia began reading first her Grandfather's letter, then her Grandmother's. She could not remember her Grandmother in good health. For as long as

...e could remember Grandmother had always felt ...eak and tired but tried to hide the fact from other ...eople. *"I'll still be with you, for as long as there's ...t least one person left who remembers me,"* she ...ad once more. Suddenly she jumped up, as if struck ...y lightning and rushed out of the house. She ran ...hrough the dark backyard to the rubbish dump, ...magining to herself with horror that someone might ...ave undone the bundle of old belongings that she had ...hrown out, torn up the photograph-albums, scattered ...he postcards to the winds and finished off the cracked ...loll... "Perhaps, I'll be in time," she thought to her-...elf, hope against hope.

The bundle was lying where she had left it. A grey ...at was walking round it sniffing. Anastasia snatched ...up the bundle and brought it back home.

She then discovered that she had left her key in-...side the flat and so, after putting the bundle down by ...the door, she sat down next to it and leant her back up ...against the wall. It was close on seven and Sasha was ...due to come back any moment.

Anastasia could not explain why she had brought ...the things back and why she needed them. It was ...more than likely that she would put them back in the ...top cupboard and they would lie there till all the ...people to whom they meant something were dead. ...She sat there thinking back, remembering. Her re-...latives' past experiences, their lives suddenly seemed ...to be inextricably bound up with the present, with her, ...Anastasia, and with her existence on this planet.

There was a whirr in the lift-shaft, and then the door ...opened. Sasha came out and looked at his wife huddled up by the wall in surprise. He guessed what must hav happened and asked with a smile:

"So you shut yourself out?"

Anastasia gave a nod, lifted up the bundle an dragged it into the flat.

"Have you sorted everything out?" Sasha asked a he took off his good-quality leather jacket, hung i carefully on a hanger and changed his shoes, while Anastasia stood there in the hall without saying any thing. She was still holding the bundle in her hands

"What's come over you?" Sasha asked. Then he took the bundle from her, dropped it down on the floor, turned her face round to his and kissed her. She let her face lean limply against his shoulder. "Are you tired?" he asked next and then informed her: "I've arranged for a valuer to come up tomorrow from the second-hand store and have a look at the furniture. If the worst comes to the worst, the Filkins are ready to take some of it off our hands. Haven't I been busy?!"

Anastasia nodded, giving him a smile, and then unexpectedly she came out with:

"How little we know about ourselves."

"What are you on about now?" queried Sasha in astonishment.

She did not reply but walked on into the sitting-room. When he looked in a little later, Anastasia was sitting at the writing-desk piled high with old letters on yellowing paper, with her curly head bent over them, reading...

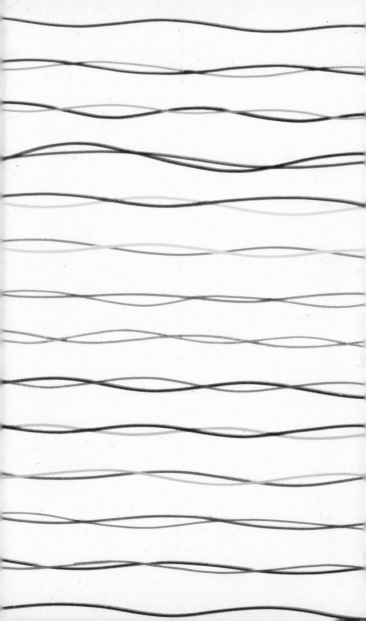